M000012718

The Landlooker

A novel by William F. Steuber, Jr.

Prairie Classics No. 1

PRAIRIE OAK PRESS

Madison, Wisconsin

Second edition, second printing, 1997
Copyright ©1957 by William F. Steuber, Jr.
Copyright renewed in 1985

Prairie Oak Press edition copyright ©1991

Prairie Oak Press
821 Prospect Place
Madison, Wisconsin 53703

Cover design by Jane Tenenbaum, Tenenbaum Design, Madison, Wisconsin

Printed in the United States of America by BookCrafters, Chelsea, Michigan.

Library of Congress Cataloging-in-Publication Data
Steuber, William F., 1904–
    The landlooker/William F. Steuber, Jr.—2nd ed.
      p.   cm.—(Prairie classics; no. 1)
    Summary: Fifteen-year-old Emil finds both adventure and tragedy in the rough-and-tumble Wisconsin wilderness when he goes there to sell harness in 1871.
    ISBN 1–879483–04–1 (pbk.): $12.95
    [1. Frontier and pioneer life—Wisconsin—Fiction. 2. Wisconsin—Fiction. 3. Adventure and adventurers—Fiction.] I. Title. II. Series.
    [PS3569.T436L36   1991]
    813'.54—dc20
    [Fic]   91–32880
                                   CIP
                                   AC

This edition is dedicated to the many who wanted THE LANDLOOKER, *even advertising for it, during the long years it was out of print.*

With my sincere thanks to Prairie Oak Press for bringing it out now.

William F. Steuber, Jr.
Madison, Wisconsin
July 12, 1991

Introduction

The difficult art of historical fiction is particularly strong in Wisconsin because the land is so evocative and the mythology rests so close to the surface. Our tellers-of-legend return to us fragments of our pertinent past. These special people whose roots run deep are so necessary to our lives because the Earth and our true place on it decrees their imagination and their being. Only with this particular vision do we become creatures who exist within a circular flow of life.

William Steuber was born in the Sauk Prairie community, which has also given us August Derleth and Mark Schorer, two other Wisconsin writers who have re-created the old days of our country. That these three were born in this place is truly a synchronistic occurence. Is there something especially powerful here to have made this happen? The Wisconsin River passes through this land and it is the center of our region as well as the carrier of dreams and shadows. Steuber and the others must have spent their childhoods soaking up everything as it flowed past their doors.

The Landlooker, published originally in 1957, won for Mr. Steuber the commendation of *The Friends of American Writers.* "Tho loaded with precisely rendered data," wrote reviewer and novelist Warren Beck, "the book escapes that cumbersomeness and eddying which generally afflict regional historical fiction. The hero's always acute responses under varied experience provide a firm dramatic thread and a focus of human interest."

Steuber details for us the story of fifteen-year-old Emil Rohland of Chicago, as he travels around 1871 Wisconsin, selling horse harness to the inhabitants. As in all true life-quests, Emil's existence grows ever more intense the deeper he travels the countryside. He passes through Milwaukee, through the Chippewa and Kickapoo valleys, through the Wisconsin Dells and finally north again to Green Bay and the wisdom brought about by living through the Peshtigo fire. He vividly describes death he encounters in his travels as well as renewed life.

Old Man Rohland one day tells his son: "From every man you meet, from the land, from the times, from what you see that makes you think, from what men have built or found out or neglected ahead of you, you also are inheritor."

There is a fine internal balance in *The Landlooker,* between the self and the environment, probably because the experiences, in one way or another, are so close to all of us. This is called *living the story,* as Bill Steuber has expressed it. He writes, through Emil Rohland, that "Sometimes a thing is so wonderful and comes so sudden you just sit there without moving anything inside or outside because you can't. The whole outside shuts off to keep you from blowing up or dying or something, I don't know what."

So it is to "sit beneath the Great Tree," the sort of experience not to be qualified. Here is a hope that you also will *live the story* and you also will be helped in a quest to become your own *landlooker.* This is within the wonderful power of Bill Steuber's novel.

Jim Stephens
July 1991

1

I'M Emil Rohland. That's a proud name, the last part of it, anyhow, and I guess you know why if you ever hitched up a horse anywhere near Chicago. The Rohland harness is absolutely the best you can get. I don't exactly make them, but Pa and my brothers and all the harness makers they can hire do, and I'm part of the factory just like they are.

Chicago wouldn't be half the place it is without the Rohland harness. You take a drayman working a load of marble up Water Street toward Michigan Avenue and think of the mess he'd be in if a tug would break in all that rush and tangle. Well, with a Rohland harness, it won't. Or the horsecars, they've used our harness for years. The Chicago fire department depends on us. We've got some pretty fancy jobs in the stable houses for the mansions on the lake shore too, and maybe you never thought of it, but the war could have come out a lot different if the artillery and quartermaster corps of the Union Army hadn't had contracts for Rohland harness. Ask President Grant. And if he's forgot, look up Jefferson Davis.

In Pa's factory, every one of his boys is a foreman.

That's why our harness is so good, because a Rohland is in charge of every step from buying the leather to cleaning up behind the customers. There's nine of us, and every time a young Rohland gets to be twelve he comes into the firm and everybody else moves up one notch. That's all right except that I'm fifteen years old and stuck at the end of the line. Pa never let fifteen years go by before without adding another Rohland. Makes me wonder, sometimes, if I kind of discouraged him. Pa's awful proud of quality in whatever he makes.

I'm the outside man. Most of our big accounts like the breweries and the coal companies and the meat packers and the lumber yards and the livery stables have their own saddlers. They buy from us wholesale and do their own fitting, but little concerns with only two or three teams bring them in to get outfitted. There's so much of that we have to keep a big courtyard with stalls all around for changing. Well, you know a horse. Geldings, mares, stallions, new-broke colts, they're all alike. Touch new leather to them and first thing, they let loose on it. It doesn't make the slightest difference, a high-stepping carriage team from the Palmer House or a dignified pair of blacks for a hearse are just as careless as a rag picker's swayback.

People will go to all kinds of trouble to housebreak a dog, and what have they got when they're done? But does anybody take the trouble to beat some system or pound a little regularity into a horse where it could really amount to something? I'm foreman of a broom, a shovel and a wheelbarrow. I can tell from the size of my pile how good a day we've had and lots quicker than the bookkeeper.

We've got so much business Pa has to write to the Old Country every couple of months begging more harness makers to come over from Prussia. That's where he came from. Trouble is, though, they can't come any more. Bismarck won't let them go on account of his war with France. Pa praises Bismarck all over the place. He figures the reason the French are losing is because Bismarck's harness makers are better. A Prussian who's moved out is the most intense kind there is, anybody knows that, but it disappoints Pa that a man he admires so has to be so stingy with the five or six more men we could use over here.

Our factory is a big and sprawly place shaped like a horseshoe around my courtyard. Inside the buildings it's cozy and homey, especially after a raw January day when the horses steam and the manure pile steams, but you can't, and your fingers get blue and your nose runs. I was plenty glad to see ten o'clock come and lock up the gates and blow out my lantern.

Saturday nights we don't just lock up and go home like other businesses do. Pa holds a meeting. Only us Rohlands. Anybody can talk about anything he wants, but that's only to get started. It doesn't matter what we begin with, it always leads up to some place where our business fits in and then we hash over what it means to the harness trade. Like Casper and Jacob. They were at Chickamauga, and all kinds of places, and rode thousands of miles in the cavalry, and talked to real slaves and blew up bridges, but every time one of them tells about it on a Saturday night Pa works him around to how the different harness they saw stood up. I don't know how many times I've got all hot and trembly hearing what happened at Lookout Mountain and the Palisades and a dozen other places where men were brave, but it always peters off into Pa's getting them to remember what strap busted and where it busted when this or that supply wagon stuck in the mud.

Just the same, the Saturday nights are special. Most all the factory is dark, it's warm and quiet, and the rich tanned leather all around and the oil-dressed harness that is done mix up the finest sort of exciting smell. It's a manly businesslike smell that makes you think of a million places where harnesses go, and what they do, and what they mean.

How could this be such a bustling, booming time, if it wasn't for harness? How could a doctor get to the place where a baby was coming? How could the wheat get to the railroads? How could a city grow like Chicago does? How could a dead man get to a cemetery? You just can't do anything nowadays without its depending on a harness. Even the girls know that. They'll go every time for a man with a leather smell. A lot of good that does me though, I smell horsey all right, but it sure isn't leather.

This Saturday, the one when the important things began, we were sitting around the stove. It sent out little flickers of light. But the kerosene lamp in the wall bracket behind Pa burned clear and steady and made Pa's underwear gleam around the edges, like light behind always does. I knew it was smudgy in front from leaning over things all day, but the stove light wasn't bright enough to tell dirt from shadow. Pa never wears a shirt, winter or summer, just his underwear, a clean white set every morning because he's rich now. It's his way of showing who's boss. It works too, because it's the only patch of white anywhere in the plant and a customer coming in can spot him the length of the factory. A leather cutter we had from New York tried leaving his shirt off once. Pa fired him on the spot.

There was a calendar right there on the wall and I don't think anybody was doubting it, but Pa always starts out with what you know and goes on from there. "January 1871, now it is," he said, "and in a modern, scientific age we're living. Fast, things are changing, like railroads opening up new country and Bismarck ready to take Paris, and land as far west as Iowa bringing up to ten dollars an acre. Nowadays a miller or even a sawmill can set up business without hunting a stream or building a dam, steam engines so fast are improving."

Pa talked like usual, but he didn't look quite right. "Thirty years I lived, and never I saw water make power

in any other way except it runs downhill. Any water anywhere is power today if a boiler and a fire you have. Why,
I see even for running grain threshers now, steam engines
they advertise. Am I against that because it takes away
from horses their work? No. For everybody, and for our
business it is best when horses are used to carry people and
goods, not harnessed to go around and around in a horse-
mill the same little circle.''

Pa was working up to something, we all could sense it.
Most Saturday nights he looks like a kindly old apostle
right out of the Bible; that is, if you'd forget the robes they
always wore and could catch one in his underwear. Flickers
out of the stove lights would play onto his white beard and
shine back fatherly from his eyes. The lamp behind caught
the fringes around his bushy head and tried ever so hard,
but tonight the apostle effect was missing, like I noticed
before and couldn't pin down. While I was puzzling, a
knot in the stove must have flared up extra high, and then
I saw it. Part of Pa's beard was gone, enough gone to give
him sort of a kitty-corner look. You wanted to walk up
and adjust something, like when a powerful team comes
along and one of them has a twisted collar.

''What happened?'' I whispered to brother Karl.

''Experimenting on a machine with a row of awls coming down and a row coming up with the leather between,
operated with a foot treadle and a flywheel,'' Karl said,
his hand up to his face, partly to whisper behind, mostly
to pet his big black mustache. ''Heard a yell and there he
was, chin stitched tight to a breeching strap by his own
beard. Had to snip him loose, he was so snarled and tangled. Looks kind of rakish, don't he?''

''So much going on,'' Pa was saying, ''makes more people move around more and makes more people to this country want to come. Chicago growing and prospering right
under your eyes you are seeing. Well, all over the country
is going on the same thing. Emil, too close to the stove you

13

are. Makes you smell too strong. Move away a little.''

I moved. I should have thought of it myself, but a fellow forgets when there's good talk about what's going on in the world. Pa kept right on. "More people, more going on, more business, more things bought and sold and hauled. What does that tell us to do?''

I saw my chance to do something right and show I was listening so I spoke up quick before anyone else could beat me to it. "To make more harness, Pa, and make it better than anyone else.''

Pa stretched up about a foot and a half and pointed his bias beard straight at me. "Already we make better harness than anybody else, anywhere. Always we have. Emil,'' Pa said real slow and careful, "this you remember. Any time you take the first idea that into your head pops up, only trouble you get. The mind is like a pile of horse manure. Corn to grow it can make, or even oak trees, but out of it what comes first? Toadstools. Only to make harness would put us in the poorhouse. Selling harness, that is the important thing.''

"We sell all we can make,'' Gottlieb spoke up. He's the oldest, in charge of fancy buggy and dress-up jobs that cost the most. "You said yourself you wanted more harness makers.''

"We sell nothing,'' Pa said. "People come and buy. We should have an agent out.''

I didn't want to open my mouth and get criticized all over again. When you're the youngest, whatever you say is wrong just because you are. But if Pa wanted an agent that would be a new department he'd have to have a Rohland for and I was the only one he could spare. An agent! Could I ever go places and see things then. Over to the McCormick factory and watch them build reapers, along the docks where the boats unload the piny-smelling fresh lumber, over to the *Tribune* where they print thirty thousand papers every day and sell them all, at the mill where

14

they take rags and make paper, to the machine shops where they make those powerful steam engines Pa always talks about. They need harness wherever there's excitement. By golly, Pa had a wonderful clever idea.

Adolph, he's next to Gottlieb and bald and keeps his hat on all the time and hates to be seen anywhere, was against it. "Agents are for sewing machines and things where you can show people what they'll do. Everybody knows what a harness is for. Wherever there's a horse there already is a harness, it stands to reason. How can we tell when it's worn out so we can be there at the right time with a new one? We don't know when they need us, but they know where we are and that's the best way."

"It's not for you, Adolph," Pa said. "The fastest stitcher in Chicago you are, and shorthanded like I am, right where you are I need you."

"It don't make sense. Here we're shorthanded," Casper said, "and can't make harness fast enough for our orders and you talk about an agent."

"Ach," Pa grunted and scowled at us, "as bad as a wife with no sons, sons with no ideas are. Casper, and you too, Jacob, in the war four years. Out of it six, and still from it you got no ideas."

"Pa, what are you talking about?"

"Government harness. Rohland harness. On war contract, all that teamster harness, every set made from perfect leather, the strongest linen stitching, the most skilled workmen I could get. Now something I tell you. Thousands of sets we made the last two years never touched a horse. Well, in a warehouse I heard of it stored and bid it back dirt cheap. Now we'll *sell* harness!"

"How much of it is there?"

"Two thousand double sets," Pa said, and let it sink in.

"Better shut down the factory," Gottlieb mumbled behind his beard that's getting to look a lot like Pa's. "Put each of us on a wagon and we'll go up and down the streets

15

like fish peddlers. Two thousand sets! It'll take a year to get rid of them, I don't care how big Chicago is.''

"Not Chicago, Gottlieb. These are for our expansion. To grow, to take the name of Rohland and make it famous for good harness where the country is new, where men are taming the wild places, and pioneer industries starting. At the rail heads, at the new clearings, in the growing villages, where what a man works with must be made strong, must last and give him no trouble.''

Karl and August looked at him a long time, then started talking low together pulling their mustaches. Chris sat with his head in his hands, toeing a couple sticks of wood on the other side of the stove. Rudolph, he's the handsome one next to me with seven years between us, sat quiet with a puzzled grin breaking through his brown silky beard he'd trained just about the way he wanted it, but maybe not quite because he does a lot of examining every time he gets a chance at a mirror.

"Now," Pa said, "who will we send and where will we send him? Off the end of some railroad it will be. Pick up a wagon and drive long hard days, talk harness everywhere with everyone you see. Uncomfortable, and out in the weather and maybe days on end there will be when everything goes wrong. You may be gone a year, it is no test until all the seasons you run through, but once it's done and you come back and tell me, we'll know more about the harness market than any other harness firm in the country will know. Some money maybe you'll make too, cheap we can sell this work harness. Who now has ideas where to head for?''

Everybody thought and thought without saying anything. I did too. I thought about the Union Pacific, and the Rocky Mountains and buffalo hunting and chasing Indians across the prairies like I been reading about. Out where the wild horses are and catching them; you put a team of those snorting kicking devils on a wagon, well, it would take a Rohland harness to hold them.

16

"Out on the plains toward the mountains," I said.

"No good," Pa said. "Not settled enough. People too far apart, and in their pockets nothing, when you find them. No boy's game is this. Emil, you keep quiet."

A youngest son nowadays hasn't got much to look forward to. When Pa was fifteen he'd already crossed the ocean. Gottlieb and the next two had their own benches when they were my age. Casper and Jacob by fifteen had been big enough to lie about their ages and join the cavalry. Rudolph wasn't any older when Pa took him all the way to Springfield on that trip to be sure that the livery teams for Lincoln's funeral would have their new harness on time. Pa, with all his management and reputation is pretty careless, it seems to me, to let a Rohland go to waste on the manure pile. I didn't say anything, but it made me mad.

When you're mad and you daresn't argue you think. When you think maybe you don't hear so good, anyhow I didn't pay much attention while they talked and talked who needed the most harnesses where. Southern Illinois and Kentucky in the coalfields, over in Ohio with all her factories, down South with the cotton and sugar plantations, what's the difference how magic any far-off place sounds when all you'll ever see is the hind end of a Chicago horse winking at you?

I don't remember how they got to Wisconsin. The Germans there, I guess, and little farms. Something about lumber, too, and no time to waste because January and the snow is the height of the season.

And who did Pa pick? I paid real attention when he got around to that. Not Gottlieb or any of them who really know how to build a harness, nor Casper or Jacob who'd been through the pulling and hauling of four years of the toughest grinds harness could ever be asked to take. Not me, when I was the only one Pa could spare. Rudolph, that's who he picked.

Why? Just because he's good-looking and talks to people easy, and because he's built powerful and loves to

17

show off. Maybe that's all right. Maybe strangers don't care how careful we choose the leather or how sure we are about the strength of the linen we stitch with. I don't know. All I know is they never get the awe in their faces fingering the harness that they do watching Rudolph throw it on a team.

Anybody can take their own horse in its own stall and throw on the harness it is used to, but Rudolph works all day on horses who've never seen him before and in a place that's strange to them, and for him they'll stand. He says a word or two, pats a hand here and there, and from then on they'll let out the extra breath they've been holding like a person does too when he's scared and don't know what's coming next. After that they're quiet, and trustful, and won't even ripple a wither. Then he'll take both harnesses in his arms, walk in front of the team to let them smell them and touch their noses to them, stand to the side and throw on one harness and then the other in two quick motions of his shoulders and arms. It's beautiful to see and it takes strength and knowing what you're doing. I wish I could do it, but I'm skinny and awkward to boot. But that isn't selling harness, it's just showing off. How the dickens can Pa ever know what I can do if he never gives me a chance? I felt I'd be stuck to my wheelbarrow for good without any hope.

"It's good," Pa said. "Rudolph to Wisconsin. As soon as we can get ready. Now we'll pray."

Pa got down on one knee and turned his barrel-sized bottom toward us and we all turned and kneeled too. It worked out I got next to the stove again and my head pretty close in to the heat, but what really burned me up was the way Pa had forgot I was ever around. Why does everybody hold it against a person so just because there's no whiskers on his chin?

Pa thanked God for the skill in fingers that could pull a tight stitch, for the forests that give the bark to the tanners, for the grass that cows eat to give them tough hides, for the sun and rain that fall on flax fields to make sturdy fibers, for the mines and mills that fashion honest buckles and rivets and snaps and swivels. He praised the divine providence that put horses on this earth, and traced them step by step back to Genesis to show God he knew what he was talking about. He asked special blessings for teamsters, farmers, draymen, stagecoach drivers, the transfer people and every hand that held a rein. He prophesied a great and wonderful future with practically everybody owning their own team, and men with buggy whips in their hands clucking this country straight into prosperity.

He asked the Lord to look with favor on this new venture born tonight, and explained to Him that this was missionarying, and an extra special quality at that, because good harness keeps religion going strong just like it keeps everything else on the go too. Pa ended a little more modest than he usually is. He never mentioned the Rohland brand once, figuring, I suppose, that God would be fair in keeping His own books straight.

Everybody straightened out and the meeting was over. Pa hauled out a whisky bottle and explained how sharp the outside was and a little fortification was what we all needed. We always have one every time we end a meeting and Pa always uses it to adjust the weather for us. He took a big pull, and passed it on to Gottlieb. From there on it worked down in the order he raised us. It always takes a pint to go around, but I never finish it. I give it back to Pa and he takes the last swallow in honor of the son he says he's still got inside him. "Emil, the team bring round," Pa said, poking down the fire.

Out walking alone in the dark through the courtyard I felt tired and heavy. That meeting wasn't anything more than just what Pa wanted. We can talk and argue all we please, but where does it lead to? Whatever decision Pa wants and that's all. We never vote or anything. We're

19

just that much oats Pa shovels into whatever bag he wants. He's another Bismarck, that's what he is. I wish he was a Lincoln instead. I thought about that a little, but I might just as well have been wondering how to change the temperature over Illinois.

By the time I harnessed and hitched the team and drove out the courtyard and around in front they'd bundled up and checked all the stoves, tried the doors and blew out the light and Pa had locked the big front door. We had a five-seated sleigh painted bright, and bells on the glistening black harness. The team was lively after all day in the stall and a full manger and I'd have loved to drive home gliding quiet over the snow behind those sassy steppers and jingling bells, but Pa took the reins and butted me over. Sure, I can shovel all day behind those blacks and keep their oat bins up and water them and curry them and harness and hitch them, but when the Rohland team trots tail high on the Chicago streets who always has the fun? Pa.

We pulled up the lap robes. Pa sat there in his black hat and black overcoat with the beaver collar, his spreading beard taking the place of a shirt and muffler both, and clucked the horses. The fire-house crew that rides with the chief hasn't anything for style when us Rohlands ride home. Only thing to make it perfect would be if I could drive once.

"I been thinking," Pa bellowed out and the steam from his breath blew back over all my brothers, "so much to learn and find out on that Wisconsin trip Rudolph is going to take. The younger the man, the more what he learns is going to be worth in the long run. More important than cutting or stitching or riveting it might be. Emil is going along with Rudolph."

2

Sometimes a thing is just too important to say anything. Sometimes a thing is so big it scares you. Sometimes a thing is so wonderful and comes so sudden you just sit there without moving anything inside or outside because you can't. The whole outside shuts off to keep you from blowing up or dying or something, I don't know what. No more scraping a shovel across the cobblestones. No more squidgy stinky shoes. From now on I look down at a horse's rump instead of up to it. Places. People. Go. See. Drive in the dawn. Whip through the rain. Never the same road twice. Wisconsin. Strong harness, good harness, tough harness, honest harness. Rohland harness.

"You say nothing, Emil?"

I didn't blame Pa for being puzzled. He had taken me off the manure pile and I couldn't even say thanks. A new job no Rohland ever tried before, all I had to do was just go along and watch, and learn things, and have fun, and I couldn't even tell him I liked it. A chance to help make a reputation for Rohland harness where they'd never gone before and Pa trusting me to help. What kind of words can you dig up that are any good at a time like that?

"You said everything yourself, Pa. Makes me think."

"Good," Pa said and rein-slapped the blacks into an extra spurt. Fresh and sharp-shod like they were they kicked up sparks whenever they hit a cobblestone sticking out bare. Behind us, from the other seats, there was a little talk back and forth with Rudolph about what the trip would be like, but not very much on account of the cold and their being Saturday-night tired, and hungry and maybe pretty jealous of Rudolph and me. I couldn't blame them. All those things kill talk every time. Nothing stopped Pa though, he was really wound up and following him stirred me up like stepping along behind a brass band.

Some of the teams and sleighs we met were important people coming home from visits, but their outfits weren't a bit better than ours. There weren't many people out so late, but those that were knew Pa, or made out they did, and bowed to us. The mayor wouldn't have had to lift his hat more often than Pa.

"Now you take steam," Pa rumbled and slowed the team down as we passed the pumping station so he could point with the whip. "Something big, steam is. No windmill. No waterfall. No horses going around and around. Power that can be built any place you need it. Power that can be put on wheels and go anywhere. The railroads are only a start. Steamboats are only a start. Machine shops are only a start. You'll see the day when tiny steam engines will run ladies' sewing machines and their men's grindstones. You'll see the day when steam engines will pull stumps out on the farms and special ones in the kitchens so that a steam cooker will take the place of a stove. There'll be machines for stitching leather and putting rivets in by power and running a whole harness factory from a boiler room in one corner."

I never thought of it before, but Pa's excitement made the future as definite as the blacks in front. I could see the wonderful times ahead just as clear as anything.

22

"And steam engines to do the plowing and little steam engines tucked away under the frames to make buggies go by themselves," I said.

Pa laughed so hard he scared the horses into a gallop and he had to pull like everything or we'd have had a runaway. "You can't blame them for trying to kill you for talking like that," he said, "a world that wouldn't need horses! Our whole civilization depends on the horse and until the end of time that will not change. Steam will never replace the horse. Its job is the work that horses cannot or should not do. As a harness agent you'll see plenty of horses used in all forms of treadmill. Forget them, don't waste your time. Already old-fashioned, steam has made them. The harness market we want is in those places where the horse cannot be replaced, on the land and over the road."

I guess Pa forgot that Rudolph was the one he should have been talking to, but I didn't mind. There's nothing to build up a person like trusting him with something that has to be done far ahead and far away.

"Now," Pa asked, "what is the first thing you and Rudolph will do as soon as you get off the train?"

That stumped me for a minute and scared me, it seemed so close, like I was there already, and lonesome too. "Why, go to the livery stable, I suppose, and rent a horse and wagon."

"Horse and wagon." Pa spit. "Always that is what everybody says. Horse and *harness* and wagon they really mean. Our own fault it is. Like the horsemen and wagonmakers do, us harness makers should brag and talk and advertise. That is your job, you and Rudolph from now on—to make people talk and think harness. Horse and wagon! Without us, good for nothing. But you are right. A horse and wagon is all you rent from the livery stable. The harness will be Rohland, from the stock you carry along."

23

Pa went on, grumbling and complaining about the reputations Percherons and Clydesdales and Belgians and Morgans have and not one word in all history about the harness that made their power usable. It hurt him that the Conestoga wagon gets all the credit for the West and not one old settler ever mentions the harness that got him there.

He raised hell with the poets too, never putting harnesses in literature, particularly Oliver Wendell Holmes and his yarn about a carriage that lasted a hundred years. What a wonderful place to put a word in about the harness, to show what it'll stand when you make it good and take care of it, but it was missed and there went a poem just ordinary when it could have been great.

Pa spent the whole trip home praising progress. When we went past the gas works that was pretty great too, cooking up coal, pushing the gas from it through pipes and right into houses so that you don't have to carry a lamp from room to room, or clean chimneys or mess around with kerosene. We got it at home and it's pretty nice. Pa says they even make stoves to try to get people to cook with it, and it's too damn expensive, but he's going to put one in anyhow and Ma will just have to get over being scared. Besides, she won't have to go near it if she doesn't want to, that's what the help is for. I never saw one, but the way Pa describes it the stuff burns on top of the stove instead of inside it and when you need to bake, you just set an oven on top of the fire and go ahead. I don't think it will ever amount to anything, because half the fun of a kitchen is sitting around the stove smelling if it's good oak or maple that's burning. Kindling you can't trust. We got a load once that, come to find out, was split-up stall flooring from a brewery stable they took down. Talk about wood with memories for a fire to cook out. Every horse that ever stunk it up came back and repeated in our kitchen.

"Trouble with Momma," Pa said, "in her ways she's set. If a thing is new, it is wrong. If I was like that, I'd still be a one-man harness shop and over the shop we'd live instead of on Michigan Avenue.''

The farther away we get from the factory, the faster the sleigh empties. Karl first, because he's the last one married and hasn't saved enough to live anywhere except in two rooms over a saloon, then Casper and Jacob who have little houses aside each other, then one by one the others getting into a better neighborhood each time and finally Gottlieb, who is right on Michigan Avenue, but not on the lake side like Pa's place. After Gottlieb gets out there's only Pa and Rudolph and me. The nearer home we get the less Pa says. I've noticed that every trip. He never said why, and I'm not going to ask. I get to thinking things I don't want anybody butting in on and I suppose he's just the same. I know if I was old and had got rich by working hard and had nine sons and had come to Chicago in a wagon when it was nothing but a shanty town, I'd get pleased with myself and thoughtful too driving down the best street in town toward my brand-new house with ten bedrooms and a stone front all paid for by harness.

Maybe though, Pa was thinking of Ma and how uncomfortable a new house can be when it goes to a woman's head. We got fireplaces, but nobody dare light them. They might smoke up the wallpaper. We got chairs you daresn't sit in and books you can't open, and dishes to hang on the wall too fancy to eat from. It worries her when we walk on the new carpet. Going around it scuffs the varnish. We haven't had potato pancakes a year now, ever since we moved in. They spit grease and smoke. Nor friedcakes either, or codfish or boiled cabbage. The smell lights on the lace curtains and hangs there. Ma's got a maid and can boss her around all she wants, which should be fun, but it just adds another person to put wear on a house and bring on its age. Ma's lost twenty pounds and Pa's lost limburger cheese and beefsteak and all his pipes. It doesn't bother me one way or the other, it's just a change in where I am who gives the orders. Either one is mighty particular.

25

Pa handed me the lines again when we stopped at the side porch with the roof out over the drive to keep company from getting wet. He and Rudolph went in. I drove into the carriage house, unhitched, stalled the horses, filled their mangers and bedded them down. Ma won't let me in in my horse clothes. I keep clean ones hanging neat in the harness room off the oat bin to change into, and another pair of shoes. By the time I'm ready to go in, I've used up considerable time no matter how I hurry.

Soon as I opened the back door it smelled good enough to start my belly growling and my throat to swallowing. Roast meat, and spicy. Pork maybe, brown on the outside, juicy inside. Done to the minute, white all through inside the crust, and tasty with the fat baked out and lying hot in the bottom of the pan waiting to go into the gravy. It was the liveliest smell since we moved in.

Nobody had sat down yet. Pa had a white shirt on. Ma won't let him eat in his underwear because the maid might talk. They gossip something awful.

"So ashamed I could die, I am," Ma was saying.

"Always we put horse manure around the basement," Pa roared. "You never complained before. Since Thanksgiving it has been there, and now in January, with snow on it, you want it taken off. Well, I will not."

"Yes, you will." Ma is tiny and white-haired now, the kind of lady people offer to help cross a street. She needs help about as much as a hornet does. "At the old place where everybody did it, that might have been all right. Last November I didn't know any better. Today I see, in the whole neighborhood we are the only ones. Off now quick you take it."

"Look," Pa said, going to the window and parting the curtains to let the moonlight reflect in. "That is Lake Michigan. That is north. Except for the Illinois Central trestle, for three hundred miles comes the winter wind at us."

"I do not care. That stuff you get away."

26

"To be reasonable I ask you now, Momma. In the cellar your potatoes will freeze. Cold as a doghouse we will get."

"More wood we can buy. On Michigan Avenue! Right here with the Armours and the Ogdens and the Leiters yet. Do you see them have manure around their houses piled?"

"To hell, dammit, what anybody else does on Michigan Avenue. Anybody that knows anything knows in horse manure there is heat all winter. Protection I want. In a barn you think I want to live?"

"That is just what you do. A barn you make of this beautiful place."

"All our pipes will freeze, you take it away. Dammit, Momma, here there is even more need for it than at the old place where we had a well and a privy. Those things you bring inside the house is all the more reason protection you got to have around the walls. Maybe inside the house you have the say, but on the outside I am boss. The horse manure we keep."

Once Pa gets started on a thing, he keeps coming and coming from all directions like ants centering in on something they've found. He explained all the way into the dining room and around the table and while he sat and we sat how his father in the Old Country always banked up for winter, and he did the same for himself the years he'd been in this country. Every house he ever wintered in depended on manure for protection, and he'd always done it that way, and a good thing that works fine should be left alone.

Sarah, she's the maid, brought in the meat platter piled high and set it in its place in front of Pa. She was nineteen and pretty and tried ever so hard to do things right, because she came out of the country to take her first job in Chicago.

"Sarah," Pa said, "your folks pack horse manure all around the foundation for winter, don't they?"

Sarah looked scared at Ma, and admitted they did.

"See," Pa said.

"Nothing that proves," Ma said.

27

Pa forked into the meat. He dug through the whole platterful inspecting it instead of taking any.

"Spareribs," he said, "but what you do to them?"

"They're baked."

"Girl," Pa said to Sarah, "baking is for meat cuts that have a body to them. Spareribs are for boiling. With sauerkraut." Pa said it sorrowful, like he was talking about an old friend he'd lost track of years ago.

"It is a new recipe," Ma said.

"Always something new," Pa said. "Ach, for the good old ways we used to eat."

Sarah took it as criticizing her cooking. Little drops of nervousness came out on her temples and lip. She lost her steadiness with the dishes. She spilled coffee on the table-cloth filling Pa's cup. That started her crying. She ran back to the kitchen.

"Now," Ma said, "a fine trouble you make. Maybe you want she should pack up and go back to Wisconsin?"

"Wisconsin?" Pa said. "That girl you get back in here. I talk to her."

"Talk, talk, talk. The same way you hurt, now you think you can make all right. What you know of her Wisconsin?"

"I'll handle it," Rudolph said and then he went to the kitchen.

Pa told Ma Wisconsin was where Rudolph and I were going, for maybe as much as a year. Anything we could find out about it we'd need, and a lot more too. Ma wasn't interested in Wisconsin. She said it was a terrible thing to take her two last boys away from her and especially me because I was so young and the cruel world would spoil me and she'd never forgive herself. She went through the war again and how she suffered worrying night and day about Casper and Jacob and now it was the same thing all over with Rudolph and me, only worse because she was older and just knew something terrible would happen this time. Pa said hell this wasn't no war, and she said that was just

28

why it was so terrible, our going when we didn't have to. She said it was a long ways off and that made it dangerous. Pa said it wasn't, all it was was selling harness. She said it was too dangerous and if harnesses were so innocent how come he had lost so much of his beard right here in town even. Pa said never mind and dug into his baked spareribs.

I don't know what Rudolph did, it seemed he wasn't gone two or three minutes, anyhow they came out of the kitchen together, Sarah all calm and steady again. She had started to quit all right, the sassy little cap Ma makes her wear was a little sideways like she'd started to take it off and then maybe Rudolph had changed her mind. Her eyes were prettier than ever, cry-washed a little and stopped before any redness started. Honest to goodness, Rudolph had soothed the nervous jitteryness right out of her just as quick and sure as he does it with a horse. Ma and Pa had funny looks. I've seen that same look a dozen times in the courtyard when customers watch Rudolph get co-operation they never dreamed was there.

After she was sure Pa wasn't going to criticize again, Sarah wanted to talk about Wisconsin just as much as he wanted to hear. Pa had her sit right at the table with us just as if she was company. Sarah told about the little town she came from, way up north. Its name is Peshtigo. There's lumber camps there and a factory too, and seventeen hundred people; why we've got wards a lot bigger than that. The factory is what surprised us, she said it was the largest place in the world for making kegs and pails and barrels and tubs or anything put together with staves.

"Put Peshtigo down," Pa said. "That ought to be a first-rate place for harness. Where else you been?"

Sarah told how she had to go through Milwaukee to get here. That reminded Pa of beer, and when he said beer she told about the good wages she'd made a year or two ago picking hops in Sauk County. Worked out of a place called Kilbourn.

"Go there too," Pa told Rudolph. "There's big

money in hops. Wherever money comes quick and fast people spend good too.''

Every time Sarah mentioned a new name Ma flinched a little more, like it was another Shiloh or Mechanicsville or Wilderness. Pa was disgusted. Rudolph and I tried to comfort her, but we couldn't get very far unless we'd call the trip off and who'd do that? It finally got to bothering her so bad she had to leave and go to her bedroom. Poor Ma, I wished I could have satisfied her that there wasn't any more harm in our going to Wisconsin than there was in Sarah coming to Chicago.

We had the nicest talk, us men and Sarah. We learned a lot because Sarah was smart and had gone to high school and graduated and even would have gone to the University of Wisconsin, but they don't let women in. Pa said that was sensible and the way it should be or first thing you know they'd all want to vote too like that Susan Anthony woman.

We'd have talked all night, but there were dishes to do and Sarah had to get at them. Before she left Pa asked for the scissors and took them with him to get Ma to trim the notch out of his beard. Rudolph and I went into the kitchen. Sarah had helped us, and to be fair about it, we pitched into the dishes with her. The gas jet just gleamed in her hair, brown and sleek like a curried chestnut. She made the whole kitchen gay. That's the nice thing about a big fancy house, the kitchen is way off to one end and we could laugh and cut up as long as we wanted without shushing or anything like you have to in a little place when your folks are gone to bed. After a while I got too sleepy to keep up and left them and went to my room. I dropped off stretching and imagining what Wisconsin must be like.

It must have been three or four hours later, far enough along anyhow to be in that space when you've had a good rest, but not enough to get up, a terrible yelping and groaning woke me, horrible moans and howling like a dog whipped in a fight right under the window. It wasn't a dog or anything important. I recognized just as soon as it woke

30

me that it was only Rudolph in one of his nightmares. I had to get him awake quick, he suffers so until somebody shakes him out of it. He gets them every once in a while. That's why my room is just across the hall from his so I can get in there and stop him before the houses up the street think there's a murder.

I got in there right quick, yelling his name to wake him up. I struck a match. Sarah was standing just in her night-gown aside his bed, scared half to death. I don't blame her, a nightmare is a terrible thing to hear, especially when you're not used to it. Rudolph in bed was scared like he always is after one. This had been a bad one all right, I never saw the bedclothes so churned up. A nightmare takes the strongest kind of energy fighting off the locomotives or coffin worms or whatever horror thing the dream specializes in. The whole room smelled downright sweaty.

"Gee, Sarah," I said, "how'd you get here so fast? I'm right across the hall and usually I get here the first yap he makes."

Sarah put the back of her hand across her mouth. Above it I could see her eyes pick up the glisten of my match shimmering and flickering in the wetness they were making. All of a sudden I knew. My match went out.

My stomach and the rest of my insides took a plop down and settled there in a rock, leaving a lonely empty space where they'd been. A wonderful girl like Sarah, and smart as a whip, letting Rudolph make trash out of her. Another match flared up over the bed. Rudolph reached out and lit his lamp. He sat up in bed. "She sure did get here fast, didn't she, Emil? Those spareribs, I guess. But you can both go now. I'm all right. Sorry you had to find me like this, Sarah."

Sarah gave him a funny look, and me a scared begging one, and ran out and back down the hall. She made it so fast it seemed maybe she could have got there while I was waking up.

I was puzzled. Not at Rudolph, that old tomcat has been

31

sneaking out and staying all night ever since we moved into this big house where the folks can't hear all the doors, and besides I've heard him brag. I've heard him say there wasn't a girl anywhere he couldn't have once he went after her. He wouldn't hold back any if he saw a chance to fast-talk a clean little country girl into something she'd be sorry for.

Back in my bed I tossed around and churned things up wondering and trying to figure it out. If Sarah had just got there ahead of me, she couldn't help but know what I'd think seeing her there. She couldn't explain, that would be admitting knowing about something that girls are supposed to act as if they never heard about. If she was in there all the time, the only possible thing they could do would be to act as if she hadn't been.

No matter how hard I figured I couldn't be sure one way or the other. One time it looked one way and next it looked the other. Sarah knows, of course, what she did or what she didn't, that part of it is settled, but she must be plenty upset either way too, wondering what I was thinking. The only thing I knew for sure was that, out of the three of us, Rudolph was the one who wouldn't lose any sleep for thinking.

Toward morning I dropped off. I got one of those nightmares myself. Nobody came in to get me out of it.

3

Monday Pa was mad because he had to come around to roust me out. "Five o'clock already, and other folks hustling off to work with a Rohland still in bed. A whole city is bustling, and you *Faulenzer* still in the nest yet. Is this how you sell harness? Maybe I make a mistake you take advantage of?"

He told me to put my good clothes on, because the arrangements we had to make would take us around town all day. Good clothes on a Monday—that's something no Rohland of Pa's has ever been invited to do and Pa doesn't go around that way himself very often either.

I rolled out in a hurry, but it was too late to keep me from being last at the table. It didn't make any difference. By the time I sat down Pa had picked up the sound of a whistle faint in the distance and his mind had gone off to meet it. "Hush," he said with his hand up. Sarah couldn't even set the buckwheat cakes down, she had to freeze holding them aside Rudolph's ear. It gave me a good chance to study both of them. She used the same time to study me. It didn't settle anything for either of us.

Whistles get listened to in our house. Every one is a close

33

friend of Pa's drifting in to say Good Morning. "That is new," Pa said proud and pleased. "Another factory for Chicago. A big one too. A man does not buy a deep, distance-biting whistle like that to put on a seven horsepower boiler. It would take all the steam he could raise."

A train came tooting along on the Illinois Central trestle out in Lake Michigan and when that was done the whistle had quit. Sarah set down the plate.

"If that was a factory, they bought the whistle from the *William B. Ogden*. She's a steam barge with five, maybe six hookers of lumber in tow, probably straight from Peshtigo Harbor. I've watched her load time after time and you can't fool me on her whistle. Seems like a message from home to hear her again." Sarah set her jaw, like she had something inside to firm up and what she had said was more for that than for its own sense.

I expected Pa to blow up, getting contradicted on something he'd taken a liking to, and by a hired girl at that, but darned if he didn't enjoy it.

"Loyalty," Pa said, smiling at her. "A good thing, keeping your Peshtigo always in the front of your mind. But that whistle was a Chicago whistle, and if you would think, you would know. It is January, girl, and in the harbor is only ice."

Sarah blushed. Maybe it was Pa correcting her, maybe it was she and me looking so hard at each other for the things that couldn't be asked, you never quite know exactly what goes on when a girl blushes. Pa reached around and patted her and told her it was all right, just leave the thinking to the men, they're used to it and can handle it. She never said another thing all breakfast. Ma just sighed and stirred her coffee. Rudolph concentrated on his eating. There was an awful lot of silence around for a while that Pa had made.

"That is a weakness in the harness business," Pa said. "No whistles. Forty-two men I got in my factory, and you can stand in the street in front and never hear when we start or quit. A factory with no voice, it is not right. Armour calls his butchers to work with steam left over from scalding hogs. Any little blind-and-sash plant can toot out the hour. When McCormick loads a car of mowers on the North Western they can screech out a duet, one tone from his boiler room, the other from their locomotive. Even a vacant-lot circus has a steam calliope. I tell you steam is the voice to boss a job nowadays. High pitch here, low one there, all Chicago is one big pipe organ playing the music of manufacture. And where in the tune is the Rohland works? Silent. The best harness factory in Chicago, ach, in the whole Middle West, and the only way we can whistle is our lips to pucker. It makes me mad, what all steam can do and no way for us to use it. Here we sew and stitch by hand and any woman living in a log cabin, without a floor yet, can have a sewing machine. One of these days I write the Singer people if they cannot work up a design that will stitch strap leather. With steam running a line shaft and the Singer belted to the line shaft, all it needs is to make the needles heavy enough for leather and the driving machinery heavy enough to handle the needles. By Judas Priest then we turn out harness so fast everybody can have Rohland harness and our whistle toots proud too.''

By that time Pa's buckwheat cakes and his sausages were so cold the grease had stiffened, but he'd got himself so warmed up he never noticed.

First place Pa took Rudolph and me was a big disappointment. We went back to the factory. Pa never so much as took his hat off, but marched straight past everybody to Gottlieb's bench. ''Show me now those three sets of carriage harness with the silver monograms I ask for special.''

''All done,'' Gottlieb said.

''That I expect,'' Pa said. ''Right *now*, I have to have them.''

Pa went over all six harnesses sharp-eyed from bit to

rein end. He passed every inch through his thumb and forefinger, he squinted at the monogrammed rosettes and rubbed his sleeve over them to bring out the last sunbeam caught in the polished silver. He looked for thread ends to the stitching and couldn't find any. Strong and supple the leather glistened and came to life under its rich blacking. I'd like to see the carriage teams snappy enough to match harness like that. "It is good," Pa said. "These I give away."

Gottlieb sucked in his breath and clamped his mouth so hard it set up a pulsing in the part of his beard that springs from his jaws. Days and days of painstaking to make them perfect only to have them given away, I don't blame him for thumping behind his beard.

It was too much for Rudolph too. "Pa," he said, "what's the sense of sending us way off to Wisconsin to sell harness and you stay home to give them away? That doesn't fit."

"I know what I do," Pa bristled. "To give away sometimes is necessary before you can sell. Is the reason sometimes, why there is anything *to* sell. It is not taking your work, Gottlieb, and in the dirt tramping it. An honor, I mean it. A man buys our good harness and something he does not like, he has right to expect we stand back and fix it. Give a present to a man you take away even his chance to complain. Something wrong with the present would be worse than no present. From Rohland it is perfect, Gottlieb makes no other kind. Emil, put them in the sleigh. Come, Rudolph, now we deliver."

Pa wouldn't explain anything, and worst of all behind all that beard you couldn't see much of his face to read it. Ma had trimmed the damage so that he lost a little length and looked younger, but all of the dense thickness was still there. His mouth was hid like a mousehole under last year's grass. His eyes were out in the open, but they didn't tell anything, because they switched expression every few minutes. For a while they'd crinkle up happy and sure of

36

himself like the day we moved onto Michigan Avenue, then they would stiffen into a fierce hardness and after a while soften into the crinkles again. You could get more reliability out of a weather almanac than trying to figure him out.

"Something's bothering you, Pa," Rudolph guessed.

"Politics," Pa said, but I don't think that was it any more than his saying Judas Priest is thinking about religion. It couldn't be, because Pa is Republican and they've got things cinched around here and always will have.

Even when we stopped at a fancy livery stable I'd never been to before it didn't tell us anything. Pa asked if the Colonel's team was there and the man said it was. "A set of harness for the Colonel," Pa said. "Tell him it's from Rohland, exactly what I promised him. And mind you, for the Colonel it is for, so keep your hands off of it in your own trade."

The man fingered the harness like it was jewelry. "Yes sir, the Colonel told me he was expecting a new set." His gnarled old hands caressed the leather. "Must have cost him plenty."

Pa grunted and flipped the reins.

"That takes care of the Colonel," Pa said. "Next is the Congressman."

"And who are you," Rudolph asked, "Santa Claus? How do you pick your good little boys?"

"The presents? Look Rudolph, and you too, Emil. To buy back that war harness I have to deal with the Government. The Government is hard to get to. So I find somebody here, somebody there, who knows somebody else until it gets so far away that the warehouse full of harness here is in Washington just a row of figures on a page in a ledger nobody remembers. With no war, the harness is no good to the United States, they even forget they pay warehouse rent, so I remind the Colonel. He reminds the War Department. Maybe he gets a promotion besides my present."

37

I thought a congressman would be important and powerful enough to live in a big stone house near the lake or on the north side, but the house we went to was more ordinary than our old place. It was between the stockyards and the lake, far enough from both so that he couldn't smell one or see the other.

"Don't suppose we'll see him either, with Congress in session," Rudolph said, disappointing me too. I never saw a congressman.

"Ach," Pa said, stopping the horses in front of the house, "it is wonderful times we have now. Sleeping cars and fast trains and passes. Every time Congress recesses from Friday to Tuesday he can be home for church and Monday business, and be back to vote the next roll call. Steam. Even speeds up Congress, that steam."

The Congressman was round and shiny and glistening, all smiles and manners. Clean-shaved and ruddy like the wind had been at him, he didn't have the worn-out look the pictures of statesmen always show. If I'd meet him on the street, I'd think maybe he owned a meat market and made sausages instead of laws. Pa showed him the harness at the sleigh. He said Pa shouldn't have done it and then asked Rudolph to drive back to the barn to hang them up. Pa and me he invited in.

He had a quiet side room the family kept out of. Pa asked how President Grant was.

"Well sir"—the Congressman folded his hands over his stomach—"fine, just fine. Had a word with him just Thursday. One of the best presidents ever to grace the White House. A man of the people. Hits the country's problems like he hit the enemy, eye on the object, and trust in the men under him. A good policy, and your harness bid couldn't be more timely. Glad to help you. In a way you helped me too. I aired the whole concept on the floor and, of course, it's printed in the *Congressional Globe*."

Pa gulped. "My bid?"

38

"No, no, man, the concept, not the details. War is a thing of the past. Differences from now on, nations will settle by arbitration, not battlefields. We've set up a Geneva Conference, the United States, England, Italy, Brazil, Switzerland. The *Alabama* claims, the Canadian fisheries, the Northwest boundary, all are to be settled peaceably. The border dispute, for example, will be heard by the Emperor of Germany and his decisions will be absolute, final, conclusive."

Pa's eyes got as big as a bull's. "The German Emperor? A conference he sits in because I bid Government harness?"

"Not exactly, those things were in the making before your bid, but a statesman's job is to fit many circumstances together to read the trends for the good of the country and the interest of his constituents. With these proofs for peace the United States Army is reduced now to thirty thousand, and if it weren't for the damn Indians we wouldn't need that many. Like you pointed out, war is wasteful and there's no need to carry on that waste when there is no war. And so my contribution is to get the Army warehouses empty, to return the usable goods to the channels of industry. By the way, have you got the papers? Called my friends in the War Department a day before I left Washington and they said they'd been sent."

"Came Saturday," Pa said. "Appreciate all you've done for me."

"Not at all, not at all. You get the harness, I get the credit. We both help the country. That harness out to the farmers will raise production; in the warehouse its storage takes tax money. Been nice to work with you on this, Mr. Rohland."

Out in the sleigh again I couldn't help looking at Pa with a lot of admiration, working with people who know the President and the Emperor of Germany. That's big stuff. Pa never said anything, but I guess it kind of went to his head too, anyways, he drove right to the end of a dead-end street without noticing he went down there or came back.

The last place was way out toward Calumet Lake, a dismal dreary stretch, flat and treeless with forlorn shacks sitting around the edges of deep diggings where they scratch out clay to bake into bricks. A wind-swept big old shed with everything on the bias was the factory where they press them, and row after row of mud-plastered kilns where they bake them stood charcoal-streaked and the snow was melted into muddy circles all around. A pretty big industry, Pa said, but I wouldn't want to live so bare and bleak for anything. It was discouraging just to drive through. I don't suppose it ever could have been a pretty place even before men and business and families came, but now what little nature it started with was completely kicked around. It sure spoils the looks of things when people open big rough pits any old place and slap sheds together and haul in fuel and pitch out ashes to keep a plant going.

We tied the team to a crooked hitching post in front of a big two-story saloon near by. Pa said we'd better all go in, it had been a long cold drive a nip would fix up. I was glad to get inside to get away from that miserable-looking landscape, but why we came there in the first place I couldn't figure out a reason for. I asked Pa. He said he was trying to figure it out himself and not to bother him.

The saloon was just as dead inside as outside and then again it wasn't. They had paintings of girls standing around wherever there was room to lean them, big pictures as big as the girls themselves would be. They were all naked. Pa never paid any attention, he asked for the owner of the place. Rudolph and I looked at the pictures. You didn't have to imagine anything and yet they made you imagine for all there was in you. After a little I see Rudolph put his hands in his pockets. It was a good idea, the only way I know to make a fellow look relaxed when he isn't. By and by I saw they had names lettered on each picture, Nancy, Collette, Sue and like that, big as their feet, but printing was the last thing I found. I suppose their names are important, but what does that matter, you can find out simple things like that about anybody, clothes or not. What interests me is what you can't ordinarily see.

"You know something," I said to Rudolph, "I think this is a whorehouse."

"You don't say," he said. "Didn't know you knew. Which one you like? Just whisper her name in the barkeep's ear. Lucky kid. Most of us discover these things a different way, not with our Pa and a brother along. Notice how Pa disappeared on us? Doesn't have to pick, knew what he wanted right away."

That made me mad. The smirk on Rudolph's face made me madder yet. I was so mad I was yelling. "Why the hell didn't you come here Saturday night instead of—well, you know what I mean."

"Sarah?" He let his eyes brighten and his tongue sweep his closed mouth. I wanted to paste him one, saying that name in here.

My insides hurt again, him telling me so plain what he'd done to Sarah. But had he really? If it would give him a chance to impress anybody, Rudolph would brag he'd slept with the Governor's daughter without bothering to find out if the Governor even had a daughter. I still didn't know for sure one way or the other. "Aw, Pa didn't come here for that."

"OK, bright boy, you tell me then why he came here."

"To deliver harness, you know that, but somehow I get the idea he doesn't like it to bring a set here."

"What's the matter? Think Pa is particular who uses our goods? Think it should bother him to have whores pulled around town with Rohland harness? You got a lot to learn. Girls are business just like renting horses or sell-

41

ing herring. Lot of money changes hands over them. Surprises me though that Pa is connected with it.''

I felt ashamed, and mighty curious all at once. A place like this is wrong, we learned it in Bible study, but they don't go into particulars. I was itching to ask where the girls were, and where the trade all came from and if they had to take just anybody whether they liked them or not and what they did with the babies and a million other things, but Pa came back before I got those kind of questions out and then it was too late.

Pa and another man came out of a door behind the bar, both of them growling and spitting like hot horseshoes getting dipped in water. Pa's eyes could have set kindling afire, his whiskers curled smoke, his cheeks and forehead were iron, tonged out of a blacksmith's forge. That kind of mad you only see when there's trouble in the harness business, serious trouble.

A thunderstorm in clothes walked aside Pa, but they had to spread apart a good bit so much arm waving went on. The man with Pa was big as a hod carrier in Sunday clothes, purple face, black overhanging eyebrows, waxed mustache, bulky lips. I couldn't take my eyes off him any more than I could disregard a churning sky. He even had the lightning to go along with it, gold flashed in his teeth as he swore, flashed from his cuff links when he crushed a fist on the bar, glistened from a stick pin, zipped across his belly along the loops of a monster gold watch chain.

''In hell I'll see you first,'' Pa roared and kicked a hole in Collette.

''Next time you come to me to begin with,'' the man hissed.

''Next time!'' Pa spit. ''You should live so long. Come on, boys.''

We drove off with the last set still in the sleigh. ''His monograms come off,'' Pa said, ''and with soap and water

42

a brand new harness gets scrubbed, then I sell it second-hand. Man dirt is the worst kind.''

Rudolph caught my eye, scared with a begging look not to let on how he'd bragged about the girls. I wouldn't have anyhow. It would have been just the trigger for Pa to skin us both for practice in case he'd ever run across that man again.

Pa was so hot he left his overcoat wide open and trampled all over the lap robe instead of pulling it up. He cracked the whip off the ears of the blacks and we made such speed out of there I expected any second they'd break into a gallop. Curiosity ate me up, but I swallowed it. Pretty soon the horses would settle back into a jog and then they'd walk and Pa would talk. This time, though, you'd think they were two-milers with the grandstand roaring. We were back into a respectable section of town before Pa could let the lines slack a little. He buttoned up his overcoat and pulled up the robe. He slapped his mittens together like a couple of rifle shots, but the blacks never even noticed. They were run out.

I thought I was going to hear all about the whorehouse and how that was the trouble, but it wasn't. Pa's fight was just politics. The odd thing about it was that it was between Republicans which was new to me because I thought being one made anybody right. The way Pa told it, I gather the politics business is more complicated than the harness business. When you mix the two the devil himself can't figure it out. Pa explained how the Colonel fixed it up with the Army for his bid, and to show he appreciated it Pa had the special harness made up. That kind of deal was fine with the Congressman too and they were the ones who put it across. But then this fellow heard about it and sent word to Pa and Pa had a free set made up for him. A party boss, he is, owns all kinds of saloons and whorehouses and controls all the votes and says who can run for office and who can't. He says he elected the Congressman, and anybody wants to deal with the Government they got to see him first.

"To hell with your harness, he tells me, my price is a thousand dollars. I should give him a thousand dollars when right here in my pocket is the warehouse release? Thief, he gets nothing."

"But, Pa," Rudolph said, "he'll get back at you, he'll hire a bum to set fire to your hay or something. Maybe the thousand dollars would be cheaper to pay."

Pa lit into Rudolph then, but I think he jolted Pa just the same. There's fires all over all the time and darn little answer how they start. We stopped at a boardinghouse for dinner, but I noticed Pa didn't eat very much.

After dinner we started out slow for the river. Pa said he wanted to look over what he'd bought. We met less and less teams. The street got emptier and emptier until there were only six or eight old ruts through the snow and nothing moved but us. You wouldn't think it was in Chicago at all except for the buildings and sheds built one aside the other, long two and three-story stretches without a window just like big storage boxes set in rows. Once in a while a platform with kids' tracks across it, maybe left there from a hide-and-seek game last week, it was a forlorn, forgotten place. All the buildings were cold, the snow on the roofs showed that and no chimneys or stovepipes poked up. Big barn doors on tracks at the platforms had painted numbers and rusty padlocks. Pa said a railroad siding ran along here from platform to platform, but if there was there hadn't been an engine through all winter. The only sign in three blocks that maybe there might be life around was one platform with a path to it and up and over it to the door. Not a shoveled path, a ragged, lonesome, tramped path. That's where Pa stopped. Our bright sleigh looked out of place and when I threw the blankets over the blacks they drooped a little. Maybe a dray team wouldn't have cared, but our blacks are sensitive.

44

The door wasn't padlocked like the rest, it was bolted from behind, proving somebody was inside. I expected it would take a lot of banging and pounding, but we'd scarcely started before you could hear the bar bump loose and lift and the door squeal on its rusty rollers. The man behind was the same as a hundred Ma used to hand a plate to out the back door before we moved to Michigan Avenue. Twitchy eyes, twitchy hands, a coat he'd found, whiskers without a pattern, the only difference he was sober, not sober between hangovers, but sober from not drinking. You could tell by the clear eyes between their darting, the smooth nose with a good color to it.

"This Government property?" Pa asked.

"You tell me your business before I tell mine."

"Fair enough," Pa said. "I've got a Government order here."

"Let's see it."

"Not until I know you got a right to see it," Pa said. "For all I know you could be a tramp broke in here to sleep."

"A tramp." The man bristled. "All through the Army of the Potomac, related to a Senator, appointed custodian, six years here in protection service. Would a tramp wear this?" He opened his overcoat to a badge flopping loose on the breast of his jacket. You could see it was his, and belonged there, because as it flopped it uncovered a bright spot its own shape where the jacket hadn't faded.

"Don't blame you for being careful," Pa said. "You got a lot of responsibility here. Here's my order."

"War Department seal. Hmm. Signed by the Secretary. Letter of identification signed by Colonel Jasper. Yes sir, Mr. Rohland." His eyes flicked us over like a squirrel exploring a new tree. His hands made a zig-zag run along his clothes. They couldn't really fix anything except to give him the comfort of a try. "Where these harnesses going?"

"Wisconsin," Rudolph said.

45

"Wisconsin?" His hands spread out wide from the bottom of his sleeves like trying to get away from something sticky.

"What's wrong with Wisconsin?" Rudolph poked his beard out, defending for all he was worth. I'd have done the same thing if I could have thought of a way how. Once you decide to go somewhere it makes you mad to hear the place criticized.

"Well, I never been there and ain't never going." He said it with his tongue exploring the hole an upper tooth used to be in. Made him look like he had secret information he might tell, and he might not, but he'd be mighty interested to have us try for it.

Pa gave me a backhand pinch warning me to be quiet and interrupted Rudolph before either of us could let on to the fellow that he had made us curious. "Let's see that harness."

It was three buildings away. First we had to go deep in the dark building we were in for the watchman to get his keys. He had a cubbyhole partitioned off the back wall with a window looking out over the river and a stovepipe tinned through one of the lights and a table. It was neat in there too, and warm, and rows and rows of books in shelves against two walls. While he hunted out his keys Pa stood in front of his books. I guess they were powerful respectful books because Pa held his hands crossed behind his back and wouldn't touch them with anything but his eyes as he leaned forward.

On the way to the other warehouse, this one only had canvasses in it, stacks and stacks of folded tents and wagon covers, the watchman grumbled about the Senator. His second cousin was married to the Senator's nephew, and out of the hundreds and hundreds of appointments the old fool could pass out this was what a faithful veteran, a loyal Republican and a member of his family had to put up with.

46

What he should have had, he said, was Postmaster of Chicago.

"A man with ambition, I like," Pa told him.

The warehouse we went to I didn't see any harness. Stacks and stacks of good solid boxes, like carpenter tool-chests, rose solid from floor to rafters.

"We open one," Pa said.

We had to climb up the pile and hand one down from the top. Inside were two harnesses, two collars, two bridles, a whip, and a brush and curry comb. Pa ran the leather through his hands, looked whether the mice got into the collars. " 'S good," he said. "Made good, stays good."

"Why is it in boxes?" I asked. "Hinged cover and iron-bound when all you need is a peg in the barn?"

"Guess you weren't working at the factory yet when we made these and don't remember the boxes," Rudolph answered. "No barns for an army at war. No harness pegs in a horse tent. If there's time at all to free the horses, the harness goes back in this box, always with the wagon, so that wagon and harness are never separated."

"Let's see," the watchman figured. "Two thousand of these boxes you bought. We shipped some to General Custer last year, if I remember right we got about three hundred thirty in a carload. That'll take six carloads. You'll need a loading crew. Now it just so happens I . . . "

Pa's eyes snapped. "These are Rohland harness with Rohlands selling them. For six seven years they lay here. A dray comes here to get them, not a railroad train. Every strap, every buckle we check in our factory, *then* we load on a train. When a Rohland sells, first he must know it is good."

"Well, it's your harness. You're taking a lot of extra trouble and going to extra expense you don't need. Anything goes in Wisconsin."

"What you mean, anything goes in Wisconsin?"

47

His tongue petted the tooth hole again. His eyes slowed their flitting down to examine us closer and rested them first on Pa, then on Rudolph and then me to see how much curiosity he had planted, and then back to Pa.

"You act like Wisconsin was somebody's daughter laying in the bushes with the boys and itching to describe it," Pa said. "Go ahead, tell what is bad up there."

"Maybe you'd better find out for yourself."

Whatever he had he sure was stretching to make it last. I suppose they get that way with nobody to talk to for a month at a time, maybe, and plan out ways to keep the next who come from going away too fast.

Pa slammed the box shut. "This afternoon a drayman I'll send. Have him put on all he can hold."

"Wisconsin. Where legislators shoot each other right in the Assembly. Where two Governors try to sit in the chair at the same time, where railroaders bribe off every state official right down through all the legislators. Up there the railroads get farmers to mortgage their land to buy shares of stock, then manipulate the stock down to hell and poor widows and orphans in New York who bought the mortgages starve because the legislature passes laws saying the farmers don't need to pay interest or principal. Thieves buy a forty and log off a township. River logger gangs fight sawmill gangs, and somebody builds a dam for a gristmill on a river they want, they both swoop down and tear it out. Graft and cheating and violence, that's Wisconsin. And some poor railroad-swindled farmer off in a valley, you think he'll buy your harness? Between the chinch bugs, depreciated bank notes, and freight rates that eat up the whole wheat crop, who you expect to sell your harness to? He's busy chopping out a yoke and splicing old rope to hitch up his oxen."

Pa sat down on the harness box. "Paper is patient. It does not judge what somebody writes on it. What you been reading anyhow?"

48

"It's history, you can check me, and keeping up with the daily papers. It's going on all over, but Wisconsin is especially bad. I just thought you ought to know, that's all. It'll be better someday, but it takes time."

Rudolph laughed. "You got a lot of time, sitting here with your books and your thinking. I'll bet you got it all worked out."

The watchman's eyes stopped roving and settled to bore deep into Rudolph. When he stopped them those eyes were regular gimlets. "It's rotten crookedness makes everything wrong. Soon as we wipe that out we'll get somewhere. I been studying a book that the whole world ought to have. It doesn't say anything about Wisconsin, but it explains exactly what's going on there. Tells how, too, we can do away with it. The Communists in Paris are following the book because they're starting to take over while Bismarck is pounding on the outside. Wisconsin is ready for the book, you ought to sell that instead of harness. What they need up there is something for their minds and hearts, not their horses."

"My boys sell harness, not Bibles."

"This isn't a Bible, but someday it will be. You could help make it so."

Rudolph's eyes caught a little of the fire. "A good, fast-selling book wouldn't be too bad to have along at that," he mused. "We'll cover a lot of ground and everybody won't need a harness, that's sure. A book might go pretty good at that. What's the name of it?"

"It's a part of a set that isn't even done yet, only the first volume is out. It'll change the world if he never writes another sentence. Karl Marx is the writer and the name of the book is *Das Kapital*."

"Ach, a *Deutsche Buch*," Pa said. "They write the best. Makes me feel good all over to hear how fine Germans make out whatever they do. But my boys will be harness agents, not peddlers. And Wisconsin must not be all bad,

49

Germans are there. Germans in trouble fix themselves. With Rohland harness and Germans, where can we go better than Wisconsin?"

Pa had us load up the box we had been looking at to take back to the factory so he could examine it close and think and make plans. "That watchman," I said, "think he knows what he was talking about?"

"He reads," Pa said. "Hard books, not easy ones. That kind you cannot read without thinking. Any man who thinks, I give credit to. Lots of things he says make me think too. What you think?"

"Well," I said, "seems to me if his reading and studying did him any good he'd have got himself a decent job. Tied down in that lonesome hole I'd think he'd get a little crazy and seems to me he has."

"To read takes time," Pa said, "time you have to take from something else. To have reading time and have pay for it too comes not often. But it is a difference it makes, to read to pass time or to hunt time to read."

"That's easy," Rudolph said, "he grumbled about his job, you heard him, so his reading is to kill time."

"So?" Pa asked. "Maybe you judge too quick. Strange things he reads. Always what is wrong. Always plans for better times. A whole system is wrong, he says. What happens to him is only example."

I was all mixed up. "If the fellow wants to read, why should the job that lets him be something to complain about?"

"I don't understand it too good myself," Pa said, "but it is something big his ideas are. What he said about Wisconsin, I never knew. But Wisconsin again, he used, I think, only for example. The world is wrong, we got to admit, and out of garrets and poor places and colleges comes the brains that maybe do something better. Yes, maybe from a warehouse. A man buys books when he needs clothes is to be watched. I maybe get *Das Kapital*. Some

50

day I get machines for making harness, maybe I get time to read.''

''Pa, you talk like a whirlwind, first one way, then the other.'' Rudolph chuckled. ''The kind of reading that counts, you just said it yourself, is when you make it the important business, not something you pick up after everything else is done. Anyhow, all he's talking about, it seems to me, is criticizing the rich like any poor man does. That's what capital is, isn't it, people with money?''

''Yah sure,'' Pa said. ''It is in the Bible even, the camel and the needle's eye, so the man and his book, they talk about the right things.''

''I'll bet Bismarck thinks a lot of that book,'' I said, ''helping him take Paris from the inside. Must be an awful powerful book if it can take over a city before an army can.''

''A powerful book,'' Pa said, ''sometimes is stronger than an army. What made all the North hate slavery so? *Uncle Tom's Cabin.* Such a book must be *Das Kapital.*''

We drove along a while thinking about it. After a while Pa started growling low and rumbling around in German. He worked up to swearing and switched back and forth across the Atlantic sorting through both languages for strength. What he took apart most was himself, and the way Pa is built that takes real blasting powder. ''Because it helps Bismarck, fool, I think it is good. Paris rioters, not for Bismarck, but against their Government. That watchman, a revolutionist! Selling anarchist books! It isn't Wisconsin he's against, it's Government.''

''You sure switch around this morning, Pa,'' Rudolph said. ''Two minutes ago you were smiling and nodding 'yah, yah' at the guy's reasoning. Seems you set him up pretty high there for a while.''

''Right and good everybody wants. Seventy years, I see many kinds, many ways people try. To find right, first must be knowledge of wrong. With wrong pointed out, is

51

call for change. What change to make, aha. Harness I know, right and good is not so easy. A German book by a German writer, I listen. I run away from German Revolution. Damn fool, to think I listen to such talk and not know what it is.''

Seems to me Pa gets awful riled up sometimes about little things that can't amount to anything.

4

Back at the factory the brick walls and tight doors and iron gates looked mighty solid. Anybody send a firebug here to do his damage, the fellow couldn't hurt a thing from the outside. Bells in the steeples bonged five o'clock, whistles *wheen*-ed to help. A coach dog in the courtyard who'd come along with a customer howled in the same tune. The yardmen began to light their lanterns. Pa reset his lips a couple of times and the leverage worked his beard like a pump handle. He had the harness box sent in to his bench.

I saw a new kid trundling the wheelbarrow and went over to boss him around a little. He was older than me, and heavier and could have knocked me over as easy as dumping his load, but he wouldn't dare no matter how mad I'd make him. I made him follow me around with a broom and a shovel for a good ten minutes. I couldn't find enough for him to empty it once. He was a hard one to pin down anything to boss him on and grinned friendly no matter how hard I tried. It got to be more fun just talking to him.

I asked him if he'd ever been to a whorehouse and he said sure. Then I asked him if he'd been today and he said no, so I had him there and told about the one I'd been to. When he got nosy about the upstairs I changed the subject and gave him notice he was all done if he ever let anyone in that wasn't a customer, and if he ever let any bum sleep in the hay we'd hang the both of them and bury them in the manure pile, because fire was the worst thing could ever happen. I hope I made him think enough so he'll remember.

I don't know whether Pa figured if they couldn't get in the factory they might try to burn down the Government warehouse, anyhow next morning he hired every dray he could get hold of to go get his boxes. Lucky thing we're shy of harness makers. By crowding the benches of those we have and taking the space where we haven't any and piling up to the roof he figured we could get all the boxes in and still have an aisle down the middle to sort and inspect and repair and repack them.

Pa pulled Casper and Jacob off their orders and moved them in the aisle because they were the best for this job having worked with Army harness all through the war besides making work harness ever since. He put Rudolph in with them so he'd know the answers to all the questions when he'd sell them.

Pa had a different job for me. The first dozen we opened he had me load up the empty boxes on a flat sleigh, along with the whips and curry combs and brushes.

"Now," he said, "you drive over to South Water Street and sell these things for the best you can get. I will see what kind of an agent you will make."

I didn't know if I liked that or not, especially when I saw it was our old work team instead of the blacks. "But, Pa, the boxes we'll need again for shipping."

"For shipping I buy gunny sacks and get three times as many in a carload. I save once on the freight and once again for whatever you get. Off now and see what you can do."

I think it was mostly to keep me busy because South

Water Street isn't exactly noted for the best prices goods will bring. And in the cold and snow how many people can you get to stand around stomping their feet while you explain what you've got and why they should buy it? All the way over there I didn't feel so good. This was just like my old job, picking up the rubbish and hauling it away, only now I couldn't just wheel it over to a pile, I had to bring money home for it. Who can you sell old boxes to? Who would there be needing a horse brush or a curry comb or a whip that didn't already have one? Worst of all, if I couldn't sell these maybe Pa would think I couldn't sell harnesses either and keep me home from Wisconsin. It's a mean trick to test a person on something altogether different from the job you promise him.

I found a space in between a Jew selling buffalo robes from his sleigh and an awkward lanky guy in a Union overcoat who needed a haircut peddling bedbug powder. The bedbug man had a Negro with a banjo along to help him. I was between considerable action with the Jew hollering how prime his robes were and slapping full-armed around his chest to keep warm, and the Negro strumming and singing and jigging like sixty to keep from chattering his teeth loose. I bet he was pretty happy being a free man without an overseer.

Quite a lot of people were out. A drayman stopped to finger a buffalo robe. He and the Jew bid and asked and insulted each other with a couple dollars' difference between them, but they worked and worked at it until the drayman swore it was the worst cheating he'd ever taken and the Jew complained that for that price the buffalo even should be ashamed and they settled. The drayman slung his robe over his shoulder and started out for his rig, past me and past the old soldier and his helper.

"Man, you bought yourself a fine robe. Maybe it's clean and maybe it isn't. How'd the missus like it if you picked up a couple dozen families of free boarders along with it?"

The drayman stopped. He held the robe away from his clothes and looked at it, a little scared what might be down in between the hairs or under the flannel backing.

"Tell you what I'll do. These boxes are a quarter apiece, the best bedbug killer on the market, a few sprinkles of powder on a paper and they'll even die in the house across the street, it's that powerful. You're a hard bargainer, I been watching you, so I'll give in right away to save you the trouble, a dime for a box."

"Aw," the drayman said, "this robe is as cold as Hudson Bay, a bedbug in here would be frozen stiffer'n a fish, and we haven't any bugs at home." Just the same he dug out a dime for the powder. The Negro twanged a chord and grinned a big white happiness. Nobody gave a hoot for the stuff on my wagon.

The Negro played and sang "Oh! Susanna" so good you could feel spring coming and the warm breezes drifting around. More and more people stopped to enjoy it, standing off a little and then working closer. It's a wonderful thing how music can warm you up. When I took my eyes away for a second and glanced along my load, there was a man looking and thinking at my boxes instead of watching the Negro. He was a big man kind of sunk together with the starch all out of him. He lifted his face and I saw he was Irish, blue eyes and red hair and white eyebrows and all. The Jew on one side of me, the Negro on the other, an Irishman coming toward me, my own pa once a Prussian, it just goes to show what a magnet Chicago is to pull people from all over. I couldn't tell what the old soldier was but the U.S. on his collar sort of answered. The Irishman stood at the sleigh box. He looked up at me. On a face made for laughing and joking all the fun was washed away and trouble had eaten in.

"These boxes, can I look at one?"

I got one down and showed him. "Strong and solid, full inch lumber, hinged and hasped. Make a good carpenter

56

chest, or for anything valuable you want to keep tight and sound.''

''It'll have to do,'' he said. ''Comes so fast and so often I've no money left for another coffin.''

''Coffin?'' My hair pushed up against my cap.

''My last little girl,'' he said. ''Five years old. Two days ago I buried her sister and a week ago my little boy. Diphtheria. What you have to have for one of these boxes?''

The music had stopped. All of a sudden there wasn't anybody close by, just the Jew and the Negro and the bedbug man watching us and listening. I wanted to make a sale the worst way with those two experts looking on, but I couldn't. ''You pick out the best one you can find,'' I said. I wanted like everything to say something, to talk a little just for help, but my brain felt all scummed over. A little girl with nothing to lie in until Judgment Day but an old harness box, it was awful. He lifted a lid and looked careful in one of the boxes. He closed it. He lifted it up to his shoulder. His eyes and mine locked for a long silent look and then he walked away. The box hung ever so heavy slanting downward behind him.

The Jew came over, opened a box or two, and looked over my whips and stuff. He beckoned the bedbug man over, bringing the Negro.

''You gotta yell and act lively, kid, make a show out of it.'' The bedbug man grinned. ''Bucko, hit it.''

The Negro jumped up on the top row of my boxes, made his old banjo sound like it had a thousand strings and tapped his feet so fast the boxes rattled. In between dances the bedbug man hollered and joked to get people to stop to see my boxes and truck. The Jew circulated in the crowd we drew. Almost in no time I got a dollar apiece for two boxes a bricklayer wanted and the Jew had sold three sets of whips and stuff for a dollar a set. A candy boy with a railroad bought a box to use for a supply chest. It kept on

57

like that and kept on until all I had left were two boxes. The Jew and the bedbug man each said they'd like one, but when I wanted to give them theirs they wouldn't stand for it, and paid their dollars just like anybody else.

"Why'd you do all that for me?" I asked.

"Had to forget that poor fellow walking away with the first one." The bedbug man examined the frayed edges of the sleeves on his old army coat.

"Three girls I got," the Jew said deep down from somewhere under his beard. "Today they laugh and play. You understand?"

I didn't want to talk about the coffin so when I put a dollar of my own in to pay for it so I wouldn't have anything to explain, I had twenty-four dollars to spread out in front of Pa. "The boxes bring a dollar apiece and the other stuff seems to go in sets for a dollar too," I told him.

Pa took the money. He counted it and put it in the cash box in the office and told the bookkeeper just as if it was a customer paying for a harness. He didn't say whether I'd got a good or a poor price. In a way I was curious whether he was pleased or not, but I didn't want to bring it up for fear he'd ask for details. Worse yet, what he'd expect would be for the next load to go just as good.

That night at home after Pa was full and comfortable he pushed back his chair and stroked his beard. "Momma, you play the organ, maybe?"

Ma pumped slow and played her fingers ever so soft across the keys in the beautiful lullaby I can remember ever since I was a baby. It was so pretty it hurt. Ma couldn't know it, or anybody else, but to me it was for a tiny little Irish girl sleeping somewhere tonight in one of Pa's harness boxes. I kind of wished her father knew.

"Ach, Momma, play something livelier next," Pa said, "a march or something to celebrate a good day. Couple hundred sets of harness today we inspected and repacked and only three bits and two hame buckles rusted a little.

58

New ones we put in. Rudolph, a good agent you are getting. For the junk Emil gets just as much as for the harness I bid.''

''You bought that whole warehouse full for twenty-four dollars? The Government must be crazy.''

''Not twenty-four, Emil, four thousand I pay. But that is only two dollars a box, just what you brought home. A few cents I expect, but never did I think I get my cost back on just the extras. Good boy, Emil. Nine sons and every one is a happiness and a pride. Come, Momma, now the march so the feet can feel so good as the heart.''

I didn't feel as good about myself as Pa did. A fine agent I am. One box I got rid of and that I gave away. If it wasn't for the Jew and the Negro and the bedbug man, I'd have had to bring the whole load back. Credit is wonderful when you earn it, but when you get it for what somebody else did it takes all the starch out of it. It got to be pretty uncomfortable around Pa and the crinkles around his eyes as he looked at me. I edged and eased out of there and without thinking much where I was going I landed in the kitchen alone with Sarah.

I guess she expected Rudolph. She smiled nice enough, but it was only politeness rather than much interest. That was all right with me because interest, I just discovered, is sometimes exactly what you don't want.

''Why don't you stay where the music is?'' she asked. ''Such nice organ playing, sweep and power and rhythm, that's man music I'd think you'd want to be near.''

''Man music? Now that you say so, I notice you can sort of divide it into two kinds. Never thought of it that way before.''

''Everything divides into two kinds, and you tell how much it amounts to by whether a man labels it or a woman.''

''How d'you mean?''

''That's just what I mean. How old are you, fifteen? Full

59

grown practically, and haven't noticed that? No, you haven't. How could you? Have you ever heard of a brave woman?"

"Why, all kinds of them. Standing off Indians in log cabins and, and Barbara Frietchie who wouldn't take down the flag while the whole Confederate Army marched by."

"She was brave? Because she faced blood and pain and maybe risked her life? Once, in all her lifetime, men saw her face those things, and that gives her a reputation? Emil, the bravest day Barbara Frietchie ever faced she was alone, and thirteen, and found blood in her underpants."

"Wha-what you talking about?"

"What women never talk about. You think your pa is something wonderful special, don't you? Your ma is just somebody to run the house and darn your clothes, and see that what goes into your mouth tastes good. How often do you think about the nine times her belly ripped open while she yelled and panted and died and hung on?"

I didn't know what to say. People never mention such things and I told Sarah so.

"Of course they don't. You men can't stand it. Makes your wars and business and inventions and big talk a lot of puppy yelping. A woman can't run a business because she doesn't think. She can't run trains or steamboats because she's too delicate and most times that's the answer we get when we want a team."

"Gosh, Sarah, you're mad or something. Here now, I'll help you with the dishes. I don't know what you're talking about."

"Of course you don't. You never will. Look, Emil, have you ever, when you're all alone and thinking, wished you were a girl?"

"Gosh, no. Why would I do a crazy thing like that?"

"Not even when you're stuck with a mean, dirty, hard job out in the cold? When you're tired and discouraged and you feel everyone has forgotten you and nobody any-where cares a whoop whether you're dead or alive or even been born, don't you ever wonder, then, if it might not have been better to be a girl?''

I thought of the stinky miserable days on the manure pile when it looked like I'd be there for the rest of my life. I thought of tomorrow and another load for South Water Street and nobody to help me like I had today and Pa ex-pecting the same results, but by golly I never wished I was a girl. I wouldn't want that kind of a cure no matter how tough tomorrow looks, and I told Sarah so.

''All right then,'' she snapped, ''how do you suppose a girl likes it? It's so terribly one-sided, starts the day a baby is born. If it's a boy, there's enthusiasm and plan-ning. If it's a girl, they try to hide their disappointment. Boys are freedom, adventure, contest. Girls get the drudg-ery, the restrictions, the boredom things. To get them to thinking life is pleasant they primp their hair and put rib-bons and bright things on them, but no little girl is fooled. She grows up spending many a night crying herself to sleep wishing she'd been born a boy. I get so mad being a prisoner I'd like to smash these dishes over somebody's head.''

They were Ma's best tea-leaf gold pattern, thick enough to kill a man before they'd break, but they were in danger just in the dishpan, Sarah dabbed the dishrag so furious. ''What's the matter?'' I asked. ''Don't you like it here with us?''

''You aren't even listening,'' she said. ''Ahead of you is anything you want, politics, a business, fooling around with interesting new things, never the same tomorrow as it is today. It don't matter your pa is rich. It's because you're a man you can do the fun things. But what does a girl get? Baking and sewing and washing and cooking, single or married, in Peshtigo or Chicago, in a mansion or under the stars in a covered wagon. It's the same dreary things over and over for a woman until she dies. If there's meals to make and laundry to hang out in eternity, I suppose we'll get that too.''

I got disgusted and left the kitchen. It'd be a funny world she wanted, girls putting things together in factories, women doctors and lawyers and coach drivers, maybe preachers and reporters for the newspapers and lady bookkeepers. Men have a hard enough time of it finding work the way it is.

Next morning when we went to the factory and I saw all the boxes ready for South Water Street, they scared me. The Jew and the bedbug man would have their own troubles. I couldn't expect any more help from them and without them, well, I just feel like a fool standing in the street and yelling. Pa had our teamster bring around the sleigh and the work team.

''Emil, today you go again with me,'' Pa said. ''Enoch—'' that was our teamster—''you go to South Water Street every day starting today with a load of this. A dollar for a box, a dollar for a set of the other stuff it will bring, that's the price Emil got yesterday. See that you do as good.''

Enoch grinned, thinking, I suppose, that he'd caught a snap. I ducked out of there and went way to the other end of the factory to talk to Gottlieb before Enoch would think to start asking me questions.

Gottlieb squinted down a piece of strap he was making into a martingale. It had come to him cut a little crooked along one edge. He picked up his leather knife and free-handed sliced off a sliver, hair thin at the end, about a sixteenth of an inch in the middle, and hair thin again on the other end a foot and a half away. You couldn't stretch a thread any straighter than he'd made the strap edge. ''You get along good with Rudolph?'' he asked. ''Be a long time together in Wisconsin, you two alone.''

''You don't need to worry about me,'' I said. ''I won't make him any trouble.''

Gottlieb examined the cutting, dropped it into his scrap box, and wet it down with a squirt of tobacco juice. "Here we are nine Rohlands and Pa. In Wisconsin will be only two and no Pa. Maybe it makes no difference, maybe a big difference, but this you should know. Rudolph is no Pa to count on."

It took Pa a trip through the whole building to find me later on when he was ready to go. I was ready to take a piece of his temper.

Instead, it struck him right. "Aha, like a good agent should, you study at the best bench in the factory." His eyes were shining with pride. "Gottlieb, you give him good advice, yah? Emil, you listen good, I hope?"

This was sure a different day from yesterday the way things were going. Enoch away with the delivery sleigh and the work team, and the passenger sleigh and the blacks for us, the blacks prancing and nervous and eager, but they could let it out. I had to hold mine in, a man can't skitter around to show his excitement like you can when you're a kid.

It isn't very often I've been alone with Pa and the blacks. I would have been satisfied just to enjoy that much of it, but Pa was handing out all kinds of important extra things. "You drive," he said.

I took over the driver's seat. Pa untied the team and by the time he climbed up, the sleigh was on the go. Our blacks got real spirit, you spend most of your energy holding them in. You use your voice a lot more for *easy there,* and *whoa now;* giddyapping all the time and rump-slapping with the lines, that's for plugs.

"Better you should drive today," Pa said, "so you get experience with a fast, nervous team. You handle my blacks, you can handle anything. From a livery stable most always you get slowpokes and nags even a woman can drive, but sometimes you have to ask for the most spirited team in the place. Depends on who you're going to see.

63

Out calling on the farmers, where you'll sell one set of harness at a time, take a whole wagonload along and a slow team, it's not good to drive a better team than the farmer owns. Calling on a logging boss where maybe he needs forty sets all at once, you hire the snappiest team the livery has, and a light rig, and take along just one harness for a sample. The farmer, he has to see the full load to know you are in business, it is the size of your stock that impresses him. The boss of many crews, like the logger, or a railroad contractor or even a circus where they buy big, maybe even prunes by the barrel, a sample is all they ever work from and pay after the rest comes and lives up to the sample.''

Learning to handle the blacks and learning to handle a business both together at the same time was a little rough, but the only part Pa could judge now was how I was doing with the blacks, and so I concentrated on them.

''Where we going?''

''To the depot,'' Pa said.

Depot, that always was an exciting word, but hearing it now meant we'd be really getting started instead of just talking about going. I felt as quivery and skittish as the blacks do when they're let out of their stalls just a prancing to go. ''Which depot, Pa? There's fourteen different ones.''

''The North Western. That's the only railroad in Chicago that runs to Wisconsin. Be better if there were two, then I could get them bidding against each other to knock the freight rate down to rock bottom. One alone it is harder, but I try.''

Pa's tackled a lot of tough things, but taking on a railroad in an argument sounded a little too ambitious. After all, the Rohland plant isn't that big. ''For our few harnesses?'' I asked.

''Three carloads,'' Pa said. ''Except the Government in the war nobody ever has a shipment that big just harness. Into Chicago they got all the trade they can handle;

lumber, grain, stock; but out of it is mostly all manufactured goods, not so bulky. Lots of empty cars have to go back. Three carloads maybe they listen to me.''

Near the North Western depot it was busier than circus day, drays and horsecars, and cutters and sleds and carry-alls, and hotel carriages all milling around and the drivers shouting. The blacks got harder and harder to manage, but I held them without Pa ever touching a rein. We had to drive around three times before I could find a hitching space. We had to get one, a team like ours has to be tied to something solid. They don't make iron blocks you carry along heavy enough for our blacks, each of them could drag an anvil.

Depot crowds are different, somehow. Going and coming is a special kind of celebration with more variety to it than anything else, and besides that there's the bigness and excitement of the gear. Big high-wheeled passenger engines with painted yellow wheels and bright red trim on the cabs, headlights that have seen Omaha and buffalos, black boiler jackets with the brass banding and bell shined up so the sun just flashes back, steam hissing out and clouding up white, the impatient *chirr-chirr-chirr* of power that hates to rest, the tangy bite in your nose of the wood smoke mixed with steam. You wonder how wood that makes a fire, and water that should put it out, can make all that power. Inventions put the oddest things together.

You could see the engineer sitting high up there king of the world leaning on one elbow on the cab sill and his other hand up and out of sight on the bell rope and way up front the bell rocking lazy, the clapper just touching the rim each time, but ringing out ever so clear telling everybody to bustle whether they were going or not.

People were dressed up and people were slops. High hats and slouch hats, velvet overcoats and old Union blue, kids and dogs and feeble old grandmas and immigrants with tickets tied to their buttonholes, bundles tied with rope, canvas telescopes stretched so full the two parts were an inch from meeting, it sure was a beehive of a place. Golly, the money the North Western takes in. What we were seeing was only passengers, the freight has its own depot.

Once you buy a ticket there's no taking it back which is a sensible way to run a railroad. A ticket is a ticket, the same as a circus or a raffle. Those trains run on schedule, if you can't go they still have to. They live up to their part of the contract, and they hold you to yours. They're pretty decent about it though, you can sell your ticket just like they sell theirs. There were two guys on the platform, their hats stuck full of tickets, and others in their hands, selling Milwaukee and Madison and Dubuque and Rockford or any place you want on the North Western lots cheaper than the regular price. Their doing that didn't make sense to me, nobody would buy a ticket to more than one place at a time and nobody would buy tickets to lose money on them so I figured they couldn't be anything but counterfeit tickets and asked Pa why the North Western didn't run them off their platform.

"The tickets are good," Pa said. "Scalpers, those fellows are and it is a regular business. You buy a ticket and then cannot go, these fellows will buy it. Hardly anything you get, but it is better than losing all you paid. They make a good profit and still save money for whoever buys their tickets. The railroad doesn't care, they got their money the first time."

"Pa, that sounds just like your deal with the Government harness. Are you a scalper?"

Pa blazed up so hot I expected the ice on the platform to soften up and trickle away. He scorched me up and down, in German, at that. A family of immigrants near by understood the whole thing. The old ones brightened up and enjoyed it, but it scared their kids. I guess they hoped that America wouldn't allow Prussian stuff like that, but listening to Pa smashed their hopes. My cheeks burned from the blistering, and then again to have those strangers take it all in, but worst of all it risked all the ground that I'd gained with Pa after South Water Street.

Pa blew off enough pressure so that he could operate in English again. "Honest solid business to scalping you compare? A fly-by-night you think I am? Ach, Emil, is too fast maybe I try you out?"

Pa's temper is pretty much like shavings rather than timber. The littlest sort of spark will flare it up furious, but he burns out fast without a bit of danger to the solid old beams and posts he's made from. After his flash he organized his arguments to point out and prove in calm statements how his deal was altogether different from ticket scalping. He'd already settled it, the first time over was good enough for me. To Pa, though, that was only the splash coat that had to be followed with careful brush strokes that give a thing its finish.

Trouble was, his arguments wouldn't brush out and cover to suit him. Things he wanted to show were different, were the same. The tickets weren't used, but they were second-hand just the same. So is the harness. With harness we're going to help people save money and maybe help to build up trade—you can say the same thing for the tickets. Pa backed out of one idea after the other. Pretty soon a tiny little crinkle started around each eye and spread out fast. Pa looked at me. Then he laughed until his beard bounced like a mattress with kids jumping on it.

"Maybe at first I do not see it, but by Judas Priest, Emil, you are a smart one. Scalpers then we are, but only between me and you we let on. Not little scalpers, Emil, big ones we are and scalping we do only to find out how Rohland harness can grow in business."

Behind Pa, posted up on the depot wall, was a big sign with $100,000 over the top and another one with $80,000 printed out big. I wouldn't have traded the way I stood

67

with Pa for both of them together right then. Just the same, though, I read all the details because it was bigger money than we've ever talked about. They were lotteries, the big one out of the Public Library at Omaha and the $80,000 one by the Milwaukee Music Society. You could get the tickets for two dollars apiece. It seemed to me that would be about as good scalping as you'd ever run across and when I pointed it out to Pa he agreed. He wouldn't buy a ticket, though, or let me because he took a contrary idea to the print. "Scalping, yes," he said, "but it is in the two dollars, not the hundred thousand." Sometimes I don't think he reads English as good as he claims.

We never went into the passenger depot at all; it was the freight depot down the tracks a piece where we'd do business.

"Now you get an idea what prosperity is," Pa said as we got into the turmoil at the sprawling platform sticking out like a shelf all around the monster big barn of a building. "This is only one railroad, and it only goes north and northwest, but look at the activity and this is only the miscellaneous goods. Brick and lumber and heavy implements and hides and grain and all the stuff where it takes a carload or a trainload to move it never even stops here. Those outfits have their own sidings or load up out in the yards."

Drays by the dozens were bringing and taking, strings of boxcars stood and jerked and stood along the platform, some of them emptying, some filling, squads of noisy men wheeled and rolled stuff in and out. You could smell steam and smoke and horses and turpentine and rats and wood and fish and beer, sometimes separate, sometimes all jumbled up. My ears enjoyed it as much as anything, heavy hogsheads rumbling, thumping cartwheels over the platform planks, engines short tooting, car doors sliding, foremen swearing orders, it was hard to believe such stuff went on all the time and wasn't a special show just because you were there. That's the way Pa took it, though, as we walked around the tangle of stuff piled on the platform. More drays going and coming than he'd seen the last time he was here meant times were getting even better and Chicago was growing faster than when his eyes had measured before. Kinds of goods he hadn't noticed before, or a label to some new town told how fast new rails were stretching out. Talk about Indians reading signs, they'd have to scratch some to come up to Pa smelling out the health of the harness business.

Something else was bothering me. "Pa," I asked, "the more stuff a railroad can pack in a boxcar, I mean isn't it a waste when they don't use all the space?"

"Yah, sure. That's why I repack the Government harness out of the boxes and into gunny sacks. I save three carloads."

"Well then, why is everything, almost, in barrels and kegs and hogsheads, the crackers and sugar and dishes and stuff? A boxcar is square, barrels are round and leave a lot of empty spaces. If they used boxes, they'd fit tight. Look at all the platform space barrels take because they're only one high, boxes would pile three or four on top of each other."

"Huh," Pa said. "You think. Is good. But to think is no good stopping halfway. A box is lift and grunt. To put in a box what you get in a barrel takes four men to carry it. A barrel one man can roll. Space is cheaper than wages."

I don't know why I should have argued against barrels, in a backhand way they'd helped me pretty substantial on South Water Street. With barrels used for practically everything, a good box is pretty hard to come by. I see now that's why they brought such a good price.

The man we were after was the freight agent. We found him in a hot little cubbyhole of an office swarming with foremen coming in and out with waybills, a telegraph clicking mysteries, clerks copying lists and looking up distances, and a dealer yelling about his dining room chairs shipped out of Sheboygan ten days ago. Of all the wonderful work a railroad man has a chance at and then be stuck in a hole like that. Maybe he wrecked a train once and they stuck him here for punishment. Pa couldn't get anywhere with him. He had a rate for harness and that was it if you shipped one set or a trainload.

"I get my rate," Pa vowed walking back to where we'd tied the blacks.

We drove over to the Board of Trade building. "I know a man got an office in here is a director of the North Western."

It was the funniest office, no business going on or anything. The fellow sat there in his Sunday clothes in sort of a living room with curtains on the windows and a Brussels carpet on the floor and all the time in the world to talk. After the handshaking and Pa said I was Emil and the man was Mr. Collins and he asked Pa how the rest of his boys were he walked over to a cupboard and brought out a decanter and whisky glasses. Pa asked what was new on the North Western.

Mr. Collins put his elbows on his table and his fingers together in front of his chin. " 'Seventy-one will be a big year for us. We're spanning a lot more of Wisconsin. We're into Madison now, with a trestle right across Lake Monona where we cross the Milwaukee road out in the lake. I don't think there's another crossing like it in the world. Grading will get to Baraboo by fall and it's heavy quartzite, hard as granite through the Baraboo Bluffs at Devils Lake. Opening a quarry there, the stuff is beautiful red building stone and fine for paving blocks. Then the Escanaba and Lake Superior, the Peninsular Road we bought in 'sixty-four, we're connecting with it from our present terminal in Green Bay, up through Marinette and Menominee. Rich timber country north of Green Bay, we'll cream the lumber and wood products coming out of the area by ship now. We can offer year-round service. Yes sir, it'll be

70

a big year. That North Western stock I helped you get, I hope you're still holding it?"

Pa tossed off a whisky and beamed. Mr. Collins tossed his down and beamed. Mine felt pretty good too, but I think they were tasting an extra flavor. Pa sent out a feeler. "Build up business that brings you more shipping, make an area produce more, that's what the North Western wants to do?"

"Absolutely."

"Good," Pa said. "Maybe I got something to help."

I never heard anything like it. Pa gave a sermon on harness, building it up to be the most important thing on a farm or in a city. If there weren't decent ones, there wouldn't be anything for the North Western or any other railroad to haul except passengers and darned if he didn't lay out our whole plan as if it was the North Western he wanted to help. The only thing they had to do was make him a special rate because the Government harness was an experiment the North Western should have faith in too.

Mr. Collins nodded and smiled.

"We got a problem, though," Pa said. "We got to get them out where you haven't even got a survey yet. Part of the places I got to use the Milwaukee and St. Paul line."

"That's easy," Mr. Collins said. "Mr. Mitchell, our president, is also their president, and we have directors on both railroads. Just a minute."

He tinkled a tiny school bell on his table and a butler sort of a fellow popped out of a door and Mr. Collins introduced him as his secretary.

"Emory, have my operator reach Mr. Mitchell on the telegraph."

We had another whisky and Mr. Emory came back. "Our operator has reached his operator, sir."

Mr. Collins beckoned us through a door and into a little room where he had a private telegraph set and his own operator to run it for him. Pa told me he could get word

71

out to or in from any place in the country just like any other telegraph station because the price of wheat was his business and any news that might affect it he had to know as soon as it happened.

Mr. Collins put Pa's proposition into telegram words which is a bossy jerky sort of talk like you're out of breath. The operator clicked it off. We went back to the other office where he and Pa lit up cigars Mr. Collins keeps around for waiting out answers.

After a while the operator brought in a paper he'd written out with the message that came back. Mr. Collins read it out loud. " 'You arrange both roads will honor AM.' The A M doesn't mean time of day, that's Mr. Mitchell. Used to mix me up at first."

Mr. Collins got out some maps, but Pa didn't want any set destinations. Rudolph and I would have to adjust them as we went along depending how much we could get rid of at a time at any one place. Mr. Collins said that'd make it pretty tough to figure where we'd want cars and when and for how long. Pa said they did it in the war, they should be able to handle it a lot easier now. They seesawed back and forth until Pa got him to agree they'd haul the two thousand sets of harness from Chicago, a carload at a time anywhere in Wisconsin either line had tracks and if we couldn't sell out in one place they'd move the leftover to the next place we'd pick. He gave us until the first of November to wind it up and set the price at nine hundred dollars.

I watched Pa to see how fast such an awful price would purple him up. All along I'd been figuring Pa was shaping and fitting Mr. Collins and the North Western the way he wanted them as easy as he patterns a crupper strap. But nine hundred dollars, that turned it full around.

"Is good," Pa said. "You make out the papers."

Back behind the blacks I tried to puzzle out what kind of a bargain that was, costing a quarter as much to ship the

72

harness as Pa paid for it in the first place. They weren't selling it for us, all they had to do was move it. They weren't even going to load and unload it, Pa'd have those expenses on top of it. Pa was humming *"Die Wacht am Rhine"* which isn't exactly a modest tune. It sounded a lot like Mr. Collins' whisky had put a mellow picture to some pretty sharp terms. I took my eyes off the blacks a second to figure out Pa's thinking. He caught me at it.

"Cheap or expensive you shouldn't judge, Emil, just by the money. For the lottery tickets two dollars is expensive. To shuttle three boxcars all over Wisconsin the better part of a year, nine hundred is dirt cheap. The boxcar will be your warehouse wherever you go, it saves you a lot of trouble and draying charges. All that shipping and storage comes to less than fifty cents a set, a quarter a harness. The only way I lose is if Rudolph and you would be good-for-nothing agents."

I did a quick addition. Pretty near five thousand dollars Pa had already tied up taking a chance on Rudolph and me, and the only return he was sure of was twenty-four dollars from two peddlers on South Water Street he never even heard of. You can sweat just as hot out in a sleigh in the January wind as you can in July, I discovered.

We pulled up to a jewelry store and Pa had me tie the horses to the iron darky in front. Inside Pa bought a railroad watch, heavy and trim as a doorknob, and a gold chain so that the watch and its key would never be more than a vest apart. "For you," he said, hanging it across my chest. "Working so close with the railroads like you will be, and having schedules to watch, you should carry your own time."

A solid beautiful living thing it was, beating away like it represented Pa's heart. I couldn't let it hide away in my pocket alone, I kept one hand on it all the way home. Pretty soon it picked up the warmth of my body to remind me that that too came from Pa.

73

5

THINGS went along pretty fast. Every day for a week Enoch easy got rid of his load for South Water Street, bringing back twenty-four dollars every time and not taking a day for it either, like I did, but getting back once or twice in three hours. Pa'd never let him go more than one load a day for fear it would flood the market and beat down the price. "No use being our own competition," Pa said.

By the middle of the week Pa had picked up the railroad contract from Mr. Collins and by Friday morning he had word our first boxcar was waiting on one of the sidings in the North Western yard. Pa held Enoch off his South Water Street run and had him load up bagged harness along with the hired draymen. All I saw was the start of the loading. Pa sent me off alone with the blacks to locate the boxcar and guide Enoch and the draymen to it when they'd get there with the first loads.

Pa's blacks all to myself, if that would have happened two weeks before I'd have been so excited I'd probably have sawed their mouths sore, but now it was just one little part of something big we were all putting together. I don't think Pa ever gave it a thought that I'd never had them out alone before, which was a lot nicer way of getting them than after a quarter of an hour of do's and don'ts. Maybe Pa took a long time to discover I'm a man now, but once he did he went all the way. There isn't anybody drives his blacks.

Pa handed me the boxcar number Mr. Collins had given him, Number AX9006, and told me to find it somewhere in the North Western yard and to stay there to guide Enoch and the drays coming with the harness. The blacks handled ever so nice, spirited but responsive to the easiest guiding of the lines or the quietest direction of my voice. I got to the North Western yards as fast as Pa could have and I didn't make them breathe hard either.

The freight yard sprawled over blocks and blocks, strings of boxcars all over the place, some moving, some standing still, trains coming in and going out, men waving their arms, engines bumping, it sure was a lively place. Paths for drays ran all over, between the different tracks and crossing them. There weren't anywhere near enough paths to get where all the drays had to go, you could see that by the sleigh tracks taking off every which way.

I saw a lot of boxcars and every one had a number, but they were all mixed up and out of order so bad I had no idea which way to go for mine. The blacks got a little prancy being so near to so much moving and brakes squeaking and bells ringing and whistles tooting and steam snorting. They never were too comfortable near trains, and I don't suppose Pa ever had them where the trains came by as close and as often as meeting another rig. I had to hold a pretty tight rein.

There wasn't any AX9006 anywhere. Past a monster big woodpile with a crew of men pitching oak into the tenders of two engines at a time, past the water tank and the spout spilling over a tender and splashing on the ice built up on the ground, it made the blacks ever so nervous. At a narrow place a passenger pulling out thundered on one side and a stock train rumbled and swayed on the other side, the pigs squealing. The blacks broke into a scary run racing the passenger. I pulled with white knuckles and held them back enough so that the passenger could gain. As soon as the last car pulled ahead of us the blacks cut across the wind behind it and took out cross-lots. We hit a track. The sleigh bounced. Before I came down we were bumping across another, heading for a man at a switch. He yelled as we tore over it. That put the blacks into a gallop.

I was as scared to be where we were as they were. I was scared of them, a runaway is a terrible thing, even on a street where it's straight and level. I was scared of what Pa'd do, our best team, and his fancy sleigh. We tore across another track between a string of cars and another boxcar coming toward them. They bumped behind us, I heard the linkage crash and the brakeman holler, but I still had the lines. I'd started sitting, I don't know which bump threw me up so that I landed standing. I pulled for all I was worth, but most of the time I was bouncing in the air with nothing to brace against. The blacks turned a little and the tracks turned a little so that we weren't crossing them any more, but flying alongside. My feet stayed down. I could pull a little harder. Ahead the tracks were pulling together and boxcars were standing on both of them, the space getting narrower and narrower until way ahead they looked like they were almost touching. That would squeeze in the blacks until they'd have to stop, but first it would pinch the sleigh tight and they'd crash loose. I didn't know which part I'd stay with, it would be ruin either way.

We clattered down the narrow lane. I pulled with all the strength I had and prayed and whimpered inside while

I tried to put calmness and force into the whoas I yelled. It seemed they were tiring just a little but it was too late. Another hundred feet would wedge us tight even at a walk.

It wasn't my pulling, my strength was all gone. Any other team would have run as far as they could, but those blacks, I'll swear, saw that squeeze as clear as I did. They broke their gallop, they trotted a few paces, they walked a few more and stopped. There wasn't six inches left to either side of them.

I jumped off and squeezed up front to their heads to hold them. Their ears stayed back. They were breathing hard and their eyes were frightened wild, but they stood. Flinching and quivering, not knowing where to go or what to do, they stood and waited. I was shaking worse than they were.

Their ears came back straight. The wildness left their eyes. I wanted to pound the hell out of them to remind them who was boss and teach them a lesson. One of them laid his head across my shoulder, honest to goodness like he was sorry and begging my pardon. Pretty soon the other one did the same. I patted their cheeks and rubbed their noses and told them it was all right because that was just the way I felt. It was kind of a turned-around business, they were calming me down.

I talked a little more to them and held them by the bits to back them out. I never felt closer to a team. I knew right then that they and I understood each other and would depend one on the other whatever we'd get into. When you get right down to it you can get just as solid a promise out of a team, and have to give one just as good, as you'd expect from the right kind of a person. I never noticed before how much Pa's blacks are just like him.

A brakeman and a switchman came running up the tracks. Behind them were more railroad men until there were six or eight puffing around us. They all looked scared, and then surprised everything wasn't all smashed up, and

77

then mad because it wasn't. They tried to grab hold to help me back out, but I wouldn't let anybody touch anything.

"What the hell you doing all over the yard? You want to get killed?"

"Let me alone," I said, "and cut out your yelling. It's hard enough to keep the team calm."

I eased the team back and back a dickens of a distance until there was room to turn the sleigh around.

"This isn't any short cut, kid. It's railroad property, and you got no business here. Gimme the lines, I'll drive you out of here and back on the street." He was a big fellow. His hand on the arm rest to climb into the sleigh wasn't anything but a lump and a little finger.

"I got business here. Car AX9006, that's what I'm looking for and I can handle this team. I've got to find it. There's a procession of drays on the way to load that boxcar and I've got to show them where."

A couple of the others felt of their faces to help puzzle about me. They didn't have much for hands either, one had an arm that stopped at the wrist and another lacked a thumb and forefinger. I looked at the rest and saw a bandaged hand. Mittens and hands in their pockets kept me from seeing in what shape the rest were except one kid a little older than me. His hands were as good as anybody's.

"The way to find your car, kid, is to ask the yardmaster. But I'm a foreman. Who's the car for?"

"Rohland. Rohland harness."

"Where's it going?"

"Wisconsin, but we haven't decided where yet."

"Oh, that one. Special order right down the line from the president himself. Yeh, I know where that one is, up at the north end, on the far east siding. I'll drive you up there, kid." He grabbed for the lines.

"You show me," I said, "I'll drive."

78

"Guess you can all right, kid, pulling down your runaway like you did."

The blacks trotted along as nice as you please, jingling the harness and heads up. They took in everything around them. They let a locomotive go by without the slightest nervousness. I don't think anything could scare them from now on.

Way up at the far end he found our boxcar. I was disappointed. For nine hundred dollars they could have let us have a new one, or at least one with some paint left on it. And way up the north end like that, we'd have a good start toward Wisconsin by dray. It wasn't even empty, the foreman had to kick out a hobo who'd been attracted by all the straw left over from a load of face brick that had been shipped in. I was disgusted.

Just in time I got there, too. Way back at the far end of the yards I saw our work team, and three four drays following Enoch. He could recognize my rig as easy as I could see him and in a little they were there. My team whinnied. Enoch's team whinnied back. Our blacks had never recognized another team before, they were high noses and never spoke, not even to the Palmer House teams. They were so exclusive they wouldn't even fart when you'd turn them out for exercise. They turned oats into motion, not wind like the plugs do. They never even saw our work team before, that's the way they'd always make out even loose in the yard together and now they were whinnying back and forth like any other stable mates. I knew what it was. You just can't get as scared as they'd been without telling someone and the old work team answering back were like big brothers bringing the world back solid again. That scared me worse than anything. Pa never found fault the way his blacks were. If their spirit was gone, it would sure bring out plenty of his, and all aimed at me.

I told Enoch this was the car. He and the draymen cleaned out the straw and started loading in the bags of harness. I stood around worrying about the blacks and how to avoid Pa's finding out. It didn't exactly make comfortable thinking.

Enoch and the draymen loaded and talked. Every time Enoch came to the door for another armload he'd stop talking and look at me. Inside again he'd brag pretty loud how much work he did around the Rohland plant. Then he'd rest awhile inside to tell how important he was and how we couldn't get along without him and then complain how some people had it pretty easy, being the boss's son and never knowing what work and worry was.

After a time the foreman who had found our car for me came up and said they had to switch out another from behind us on the siding so ours would have to switch too. We'd have to stop loading for a little.

The foreman took off a mitten and pulled up his jacket to get at his watch. He had to go so high for it he could have got there quicker by going down from his neck, he was so long-legged and short-waisted. He didn't have much of a hand to hold it in, just the thumb and first finger making a pair of pinchers to squeeze the case open. I asked him what time he had. When he told me I pulled my watch out and mine was right on time with his. He got friendly as anything to find mine agree so exact with his and to see another railroad watch where he didn't expect it. I wanted to ask what happened to his hand, and to so many of the others, but while I was working up to it the switch engine came backing toward us whistling a couple of signal toots and carrying two brakemen, one of them arm-signaling from the ladder rungs bolted at the corner of the tender.

"Better not talk to the engineer or let any of your help," he told me, holding his good hand over his mustache and if I'd have been him I'd have covered it too. All he had was a curtain of hair hanging straight down from his upper lip over his mouth. Made him look awful mild for a railroad man.

I didn't have any idea of talking with the engineer, they sit up so high and get out of range so fast you can't do more than wave anyhow, but being told not to made me want to so I asked him why not.

"Lost his run, crack passenger to Omaha. Dozed a little and ran through an open switch and made kindling out of two baggage cars. Drunker'n hell this morning and owly. Let him alone, just our signals and he'll spot his cars closer than you can spit, but anything to make him madder yet, it wouldn't take much, and he's liable to ... well, I don't know what, but I'd hate to see a good man like him demoted any further."

I don't blame the engineer for being mad. His switch engine was bumped and bent and black, not shiny-polished black, but dirt-and-soot black, an old plug horse of an engine not going anywhere except back and forth.

"Should have seen his own engine," the foreman said, "heard tell he'd got seventy-two miles an hour out of it on some of those Iowa prairie straightaways. Bought his own bell for it, and sent off twelve silver dollars to melt in the brass when they cast it to give it a sweet tone. And the pictures he had painted on the cab and tender, buffalos in color a charging, and the shine he laid on the brass banding every minute he'd have free, a man get an engine like that taken from him ain't nobody to cross."

I was pretty curious to see that engineer, but I missed out. It was only the fireman on my side. The engine bumped our car and closed off any chance to duck through to see the other side of the cab. The young fellow, one of those who had come a running to me and the blacks, swung down from the tender to connect our car. There was a link in the tender coupler and another in the car coupler, which made one too many and they jammed together so tight he didn't have room to get either one out. The foreman saw

81

the fix and signaled the engine to pull ahead a little for slack. I never thought of it before, you never do until you see a thing for yourself, but a train holds together just by making a chain of it, the same in railroading as it is in draying, with pins to hold the connecting link. The engine pulled ahead a little and the young fellow pulled one of the pins and threw the extra link up on the beam across the end of the boxcar. As the engine moved back he held up the link connected to the engine to feed it into the slot in the boxcar coupling.

Instead of the engine feeling its way back slow and easy, it slammed in pretty hard, and instead of the two couplers swallowing the link and clanking against each other, all I heard was a mushy thump and a scream. A high-pitched scream that chopped off sudden. A salty taste flashed in my mouth, my armpits ran, and I felt wet all over. Silence now was a part of the shriek, the steam sizzling out of the engine saying *shhhh, shhhh*. The *thump thump* as the foreman ran the few steps to the boy seemed to take a year. He yelled the engine ahead. The boy lifted part of a hand. Red spurts shot from it, made an arch in the air, spattered the snow.

His gray-white face fought itself into a numbed smile. "Guess—they'll know—now—for sure—I'm a brakeman." His eyes sort of crossed and he fell in a heap.

In no time there were a dozen of us around him, railroadmen and draymen and Enoch. The foreman wouldn't let anybody touch him. He whipped out a blue handkerchief and tied a tourniquet, his thumb and finger pinchers flying as good, maybe quicker and more skillful than his other hand. He rubbed snow on the boy's face to bring him to. Somebody got the engineer's bottle and made the boy take a couple big slugs for the pain. After that they took up a collection and got nine dollars and asked for the fastest rig. The foreman and I took him to a doctor with the blacks, and then home to give the nine dollars to his mother.

By the time we got back the car was loaded and the foreman padlocked it and said I'd better tell him in a hurry where we wanted to ship it because a yard is for loading and unloading and taking trains apart and putting them together and not for storage. So I said all right, send it to Milwaukee.

Back at the factory I looked up Pa to tell him where I sent the car. He'd favored Milwaukee I remembered when Sarah mentioned it, and it wasn't too far and lines run out from there to wherever the tracks go in Wisconsin, but I was a little scared maybe he wanted to give the order himself. I didn't need to worry. Pa was tempering up at a stranger and was too busy to spread out over me.

"Internal Revenue? Cigars or whisky I do not make, and on harness there is no tax. Nothing, I pay you."

"That's right, Mr. Rohland. You've paid nothing. That's why I thought I'd better have a talk with you. How about the income tax?"

"Income tax? What is income tax?"

"Come now, Mr. Rohland, you're an industrialist, don't act like a confused immigrant. There's been a tax on income ever since the war. You know about that just as well as I do. The railroads pay it, the packers pay it, all manufacturers, and anybody that earns over two thousand dollars. There's no exception for harness makers."

"I cheat nobody. What I promise I pay. What I am billed fair, I pay. Many kinds of taxes I pay, but I get no bill for income tax. For four years there is war, and six years no war, why you come to me now?"

"Information comes to me. I'd like to see your books."

"My books? What right you got to see my books? Information, hah. So! Maybe that whoremeister out toward Calumet sends you. No? Maybe a thousand dollars you want and tell me it's for the Government? Out of here you get the hell, you blackmailer."

Pa grabbed one of the army whips. The fellow left so fast it put Pa in a roaring good mood. "Income tax! Soon as he said that, a faker I knew he was. I pay my income tax, the United States is good to me. Lots of places don't, that's what he was counting on. A clumsy tax it is, and no way to check on it, so I led him on to give me a clue who sent him. Gives me an idea. Whorehouses and blackmail and money from bribes, don't tell me a man in those things wouldn't cheat on his taxes too. Maybe the real Internal Revenue can throw a scare into that party boss.'' Pa laughed until his eyes overflowed, and he had to wipe his nose. The blast he bugled into his handkerchief, well, it was a good thing he was inside or they'd have opened a drawbridge or two and then wondered where the boat was.

"Our car is all loaded, Pa, and pulling out for Milwaukee.''

"Good. Then tomorrow morning you and Rudolph start out. Sit down, Emil. So many things yet you should know.''

There were things he should know too. South Water Street for instance, hiding the truth on what kind of an agent I was, and the blacks maybe spoiled. A poor kid losing half a hand and a stranger at that, before our first harnesses moved out of the yard, it makes a person think how much gets all upset when you plan big changes. Pa sat there solid as a weather-shined old boulder, his hands folded comfortable and snug around the bottom of his belly. Mr. Collins and his steep charges, the party boss and his try for blackmail and probably somebody waiting around for a chance to set fire to the place, if he could shove all that to one side just to talk, I guess I could listen instead of reporting more worries.

"High time the harness business gets a move on,'' Pa said. "We are so behind the times we stink. When I was fifteen, like you now, we did most things the same as in the Bible six thousand years ago. Plant by hand, cut with a sickle, thresh with a flail, haul in a cart. You did business as far as you could drive a horse and that was your limit.

84

You needed a new tool, you pounded it out on an anvil or sawed and planed it by hand. To get word from a near to a far place, it took somebody to carry it by horse or by boat. The speed of the messenger was the speed of the message. Everything is so different in the few years since I first sat at my bench. Yah, everything but the harness business. But that I change. Like McCormick brings change, like Morse and Stephenson, and Whitney, so will the name of Rohland.''

Pa unfolded his hands and stood up. He wasn't an old boulder letting the grass grow all around any more, he'd been in a kiln and changed to lime and had plenty of heat to give off. ''In every little town is a harness maker, in every city they're as common as saloons. Farming takes more teams, railroads make more draying, everything takes more harness, but nobody thinks how to make it faster and cheaper. Busy harness makers many you will see, rich harness makers you will not find. Why? Because a harness maker must be craftsman, manufacturer and merchant all at once and there should be profit for all three parts, but he charges only for the craftsmanship. Even so, you and Rudolph can sell cheaper. While you sell he worries. While you sell I figure out how to make harness by machine and make it fast and so cheap it costs no more than I paid for the Government harness.''

By that time Pa was stomping all around the place waving his arms to take in Vermont and California. ''Then comes our harness so quick and so much every harness maker can be a Rohland agent, and make a bigger profit selling ours than making his own. How you get along I must know all the time. Ach, what a wonderful time we live in! All in one day we can get word back and forth wherever you go. It is the telegraph we must use.''

''Gosh, Pa,'' I said, ''Rudolph should be around too when you talk like that.''

''To his tailor he is, speeding him up on his suit. I talk

to you together, maybe you both think the other one should remember."

We were plenty busy that night packing our stuff into telescopes and valises. Pa gave us a lot more business ideas than I can remember and Ma went altogether too strong on mufflers and socks and mittens. Pa gave us each a twenty-dollar bill for expenses and told us the better we lived the better work we could do, but we shouldn't take advantage of him. That ought to last, he thought, until we could take our expenses out of our sales.

Sarah helped us, but she went around awful quiet which was different for her. Time and again when Rudolph had his head down worrying the way a coat or a shirt was folded, the corner of my eye would catch her looking sober at the back of his head. By and by she came with a tin and held it out to him.

"Box of fudge I had a little time to make. If you've got space for it somewhere, it might be nice to chew on up in your room when there's nothing else to do in an evening. I'll pack a lunch tomorrow morning, this is extra and will keep."

"Aha," Pa said, "a girl giving a present should smile. You sad my boys go away?"

"I just envy them, that's all," Sarah said.

"Homesick a little? All this Wisconsin talk?"

"No, I'm not homesick."

"So?" Pa said looking at Sarah and then at Rudolph. "Now it comes to me, lately Rudolph stays home evenings." He got the kindliest expression and took Sarah's hand to hold between both his big ones. She pulled it away all embarrassed and looked to Rudolph. Rudolph turned his back to ask me whether I'd packed the hairbrush. Pa looked at him kind of funny for a minute. Rudolph closed his last valise. The fudge tin sat on the table. I picked it up and tucked it in with my things. Good fudge you can always use.

86

I expected Sarah to run crying to the kitchen again. She didn't. She didn't blush either like other times when what she did embarrassed her. She looked all around, straight at each of us and especially at Rudolph and he was like somebody she'd never laid eyes on before. Right there with all of us, Sarah was alone, alone like a statue on a lawn, alone like a person in a painting where the eyes look way beyond you.

6

M_A gave us breakfast. We never saw Sarah at
all. Ma said she was flying around packing the lunch for us
to eat on the train and there was a lot of racket from the
kitchen, but anybody could tell the noise was from feelings
slamming around, not food. You take a man feels mean,
he repairs it with good solid swearing and gets someplace.
Women, mostly, don't understand what tools to use. When
they need to swear they go at it as out of place as when they
try to do carpentering with a shoe heel. Dishpans and
knives to drop, and cupboards to slam and stove lids to
rattle make an awful poor substitute when all Sarah
needed to do to express herself was stick her head through
the door and yell, ''To hell with you, Rudolph Rohland.''
But she didn't.

After breakfast we went upstairs to dress for the trip.
When Rudolph came down he was the handsomest you ever
saw, his beard parted into two smart points at the bottom,
two more under his lips and his mustache matching them,
his new suit buttoned only once high on his chest and
spreading open to show an expensive splashy vest, his
pants ever so rumply and rich and none of those creases

like the ready-to-wear suits because his were tailor-made and flowed down narrow over his new shoes with the cloth straps snugged under his insteps so the trouser legs wouldn't climb when he sat down. When he lifted his silk hat and put it up on top and slipped into his new black overcoat, he looked ready to buy a bank or give a town a post office just as a favor.

Pa's eyes were all endorsement and maybe a little moist, like this was what he had in mind all those years making money and a reputation stitching leather sitting around in his undershirt.

Pa drove us to the depot and didn't talk like I expected he would, but mostly sat and thought. It made him look ever so tired and old not to be storming about anything or explaining harness or talking big plans. Pa just ordinary and Rudolph gathering all the glances, well, it almost seemed like a sign was ready to go up that says under new management. The blacks didn't seem so full of oats either. A whistle blew eight o'clock, and near by too, and they didn't pitch, nor Pa say anything. I was homesick already. I wished I was going along with Pa instead of with Rudolph.

At the depot, instead of going to the ticket window or to the scalpers, Pa dug out his wallet and unfolded it and took out two papers for each of us. They were passes, one of them good for anywhere in Wisconsin any time on the North Western and the other on the Milwaukee and St. Paul. Pa had two left. "These I use maybe sometime to catch up with you and look for myself."

Passes on the railroad! Ride anywhere free, as much as we wanted to, they were stamped right across the face, *Not to be taken up*. And Pa with his own set to come to us any time he wanted to, I felt wonderful better.

The excitement of the depot livened Pa up too, a dozen last-minute ideas to be said came tumbling out too fast for anybody to remember, but I did catch one. We got less

89

than a dollar and a half in each harness, burlap bags and transportation and everything, not counting the boxes and truck Enoch gets rid of. Harness makers charge fifteen to twenty-five dollars a single harness, depending on how much competition they make each other, and they charge extra for the collars which we plan to throw in free. Why, if everything goes extra good we can bring home up to eighty thousand dollars or we can be so miserable at it Pa will lose the five thousand dollars he's already spent. That's a lot of responsibility. One minute it makes you feel like a boiler fired up with your hand on the lever and the next you're without a middle like an oats sack splitting open. A person just isn't built with room enough inside to handle flip-flops as wild as that.

Pa dug in his breast pocket again. He came out with two wonderful rich, leather-covered notebooks and gave one to each of us. "These you keep separate. What's important every day, you write inside. When I come sometime, I don't tell you when, I ask for your journals."

Rudolph and I climbed into a car with the crowd and found a seat. The train jerked and started. I looked out of the window and saw Pa. He waved. The glass must have been ripply or something, it seemed to shrink him down. My eyes held to him as long as my window kept him in sight and then the angle hid him behind the window frame, flashed him once through the next window and then broke us apart. The engine whistled. Maybe the North Western does that regular, I don't know, but Pa thinks of everything and could have had it arranged for good luck. I let out a breath I'd kept overlong and looked around the car.

It was two-thirds full and everybody was adjusting and shifting and settling for comfort. A man across the aisle had brought in a good-sized jawful of tobacco and his cheeks were filling up with juice so fast he began to look bloated. He weaved his head like a bear in a cage, looking and hoping for a spittoon somewhere, but there wasn't any. I suppose they'd slosh too much in a train. His pressure got higher and higher and crowded his eyeballs. They looked like they'd either have to pop out or go under, but just in time he spied the stove all hot and inviting eight feet ahead of him. He didn't have time to get up and open the fire door, he let go from where he was in one brown climbing streak. The point of the streak hit the stove before the back end of it left his mouth, he was that full. I see now why they use round-bellied stoves and keep them so hot. It took the whole charge as snug as a sandbox and cooked itself off dry in one big sizzle. There were others nodded grateful to see what could be done and edged up within a range they could handle to make use of it. That made some of the women who'd chosen toasty seats a little worried. One by one they moved back from the mist and men took their places. Rudolph moved back there too, kind of risky for his new clothes he said on the quiet to me. Good clothes—what are they good for when they drive you away from fun? I stayed. That old stove sizzled and steamed and smelled rich and pretty soon a trainman had to fire it up again, they worked it so hard.

Wherever there's tobacco juice there's wonderful talk. It seems to oil up a man's throat. On a train with the *clickety clack* underneath taking everybody in the same direction it's news just to find out who a man is and what he does and where he's going and why he has to be somewhere else. The man who had spit so far came from a place called Oshkosh and he wrote a newspaper. He didn't come to Chicago for news, that comes over the telegraph, he had to buy paper and it was awful high.

A little bit of a man with a voice too deep for his size asked why he didn't grind up wood and make his own. The editor laughed and asked him where he got a crazy idea like that.

"Use the fibers like the wasps do."

"Wasps?"

"Sure, paper wasps. I'm a bee man. We've got bees bred for extra high production; well, a little experimenting and study with wasps to get them to lay it flat, and then build up big colonies of them and they'd turn out your paper like my bees turn out honey."

A preacher chimed in then because the industry of insects has a moral to it and where we make a bad mistake is copying the industry and forgetting the morals. That wasn't new, you hear how faithful ants and bees are every fourth Sunday or so, and like any other time an old idea comes up with nothing to say about it one way or the other, it just punches a hole in the talk. Preachers like to do that. They have plans for those holes. He sneaked in the Fourth Commandment and ripped the North Western apart for running trains on Sunday and all the other big railroads too and said they were an abomination over the land.

"Abomination is right," a farmer out of Elkhorn agreed, "and worse than their Sunday running is their poisoning the air. Before the railroads we used to get forty-bushel wheat, now my best acre won't do better than twenty. And all that whistling—it's vibrations, that's what it is—and it'll scab apples and make heifers drop their calves. Why do most dogs howl when the whistle comes over the hills? Because it pierces their ears, that's why, and if it hurts a tough old dog that proves the harm in it. Next time something goes wrong you can't explain you just think back if you didn't smell a train or hear a whistle beforehand."

"There's plenty wrong with the railroads that hurts more directly. I see it two places. First, because I'm an auctioneer and second, I'm in the Legislature—Assemblyman, Waukesha County—and that's the monopoly they have." He'd just moved up and stood in the aisle considering the empty seat Rudolph had left. "We got to put some sort of control on the rates they charge. Lad, what's your business?"

"Harness," I said. "Three carloads we're taking into Wisconsin, and you're right about freight rates. What would you say should be a fair price for hauling our harness?"

He never said. The conductor came through just then asking for tickets. I got my pass out and figured having one would rate me pretty high and get people to wondering who I was, but the preacher had one and the assemblyman had one, and so did the editor. The conductor didn't even look at me—he just punched it, to keep his punch from getting rusty, I suppose.

Seems almost everybody had passes and if they didn't they seldom had tickets either, but paid in cash which the conductor tucked into his coat pocket hanging open like a satchel. I don't mean he kept the money, he couldn't because his whole suit belonged to the North Western, it said so all over on it. I suppose they got special places in the depots where he gets on and off and where he undresses and can't get at his own clothes until the money in their suit tallies out.

After the conductor was out of sight a trainboy came through with candy and books and cigars and stuff. He did pretty well, especially on cigars around the stove and got real friendly with us. Then he dropped his voice and widened his eyes and whispered if we'd noticed there were whores aboard.

"Where?" the auctioneer asked.

"You see that snappy-dressed feller with his beard and mustache in six points in the middle of the car?" It was Rudolph he pointed out.

"Well, he's a big Chicago leather man on his way to buy out three four tanneries in Milwaukee, and those three he's sitting with, they're the whores. I can spot them anywhere."

"Aw," I said, "how can you tell?"

"Because they can smell money and shine up to a man

93

that's got it, that's how. Look at it stick out all over on that fellow, the expensive way he takes care of his face and his beard, the bearing of him, the clothes on him. Besides, I got literature tells all about whores with pictures showing what they do. I ain't supposed to have this and if they caught me I'd get put off, but if you've got half a dollar I'll let you have a set. Promise, though, you won't open the package until you're off the train. I got a mother to support.''

I wanted a set but I didn't like to buy it with all those fine people watching. The auctioneer said he knew about packages like that and waved him off.

''What would there be in such a package?'' the preacher asked the auctioneer. ''I mean, well, that is to what nature, ah, detail, so to speak?''

The trainboy stood there, waiting for the talk to do his advertising for him.

''Well, Reverend,'' the editor said, ''the type of detail depends on where they come from. Some are downright vile, and the worse they are the better they sell. There's pretty strong taste for that stuff around the livery stables, in the saloons, with the hired men on the farms, in the lumber camps, around the mills. Hell—I beg your pardon, Reverend, it slipped out unintentional—but you might say that almost any man has an urge for that stuff.''

The preacher put his hands together to make steeples of his fingers the way they always do when they turn the talk to religion. He didn't get too good a fit, we were jiggling so, and he had to adjust two or three times. ''The depths one has to descend for sermon material. Gentlemen, I have a flock to protect from these fleshpots, this carnal lust, and I'd better know what I'm talking about. Boy, give me one of those packets.''

''Like I said, you can't open it on the train.''

''That's all right, boy, I'll approach this with prayer and meditation in the secrecy of my study.''

94

The editor put his fingers together too, but I guess he felt funny at it and took them down right away. "Never had an editorial come so ready made," he said and dug down for his fifty cents.

Well, I'll never get a chance to hear that sermon or read the editorial in the Oshkosh paper so I hauled out fifty cents too. And as for the whores it isn't very often they're pointed out to you for sure, so one by one the men left the stove to go swaying down the aisle past them for a closer look.

I did too, only I didn't have to look and walk by and be satisfied. With Rudolph right there with them I used him for a chance to stop and study them close. Two were young and pretty, the other was past all that and probably not in business any more. I hear it ages them awful fast. After I stopped I wished I hadn't. I didn't know what to say or how to talk. Just because a trainboy says so, it came to me, doesn't make a person one thing or another—they lie like everything. Rudolph friendly with them didn't settle anything either, his taste is pretty wide. They could have been two daughters and their mother, or they could have been whores like the trainboy said. You don't talk to one like the other, I know that much, and if they were whores I didn't know how to start. I just stood there getting red, feeling like a fool.

Rudolph helped me out. "Here's my man now," he said, "and a finer fellow I've never had. I take him along wherever I go, can't get along without him. Emil, these ladies missed breakfast hurrying to make the train. We'll stop at Kenosha in a minute. I want you to go out and get some sandwiches."

I wasn't going to waste money buying food when we had a boxful and would get into Milwaukee before dinnertime anyhow, so when we got to Kenosha I just fooled around the platform a little and when I came in again I picked up the lunch Sarah made for us and carried it back.

Rudolph complimented himself over and over again on how good I was on taking care of every little comfort while he traveled, and said how hard it is to get digestible food when you're on the go and it didn't matter if it was Nebraska or Albany, I could always scout out a lunch he'd be proud to have a cabinet member munch with him, and where did I find such chicken, but never mind, don't answer, it was an art I just naturally had that could locate wonderful eating even if it was nothing but a wood-and-water stop, now help yourself, girls, there's nourishment here, and while you eat we'll work out an answer to your problems.

Those women had appetites to match anything Sarah could have had in mind while she sliced and spread and arranged pretty. Sarah had packed food enough for a Sunday-school picnic, but it seemed awful mean and sneaky to use her work for Rudolph to spread around as a kind of bait for other women, and maybe whores at that.

"Let's see now, you got a problem trying to establish yourself in Milwaukee," he said. "Emil, you crowd in and sit here too. These ladies have a business and business is something you should know more about. I always say one profession learns from another. We're leather and practical, and you ladies, well, yours boils down to attractiveness—yes, it's actually usable beauty you sell—but the principles behind us are exactly the same." That sounded like whore talk to me.

The old one had a hand up to her chin kind of biting her forefinger, and forgetting the sandwich in her other hand. The others were chewing thoughtful, their eyes big on Rudolph. I guess mine were just as big, him pointing out that harness and whores were alike.

"Location, that's the first thing. They have to be going by to come in, so set up where there's lots of traffic. Milwaukee is German, but that doesn't matter too much. If you don't speak it you can pick up a local girl for those who'd feel better dickering in their native tongue. Next is superior service and an air of elegance—it'll get you known quicker than anything and that again goes back to location. A shabby neighborhood will bring shabby trade and prices you can't live on. Aim for the best, I say, life is too short for anything else."

They nodded slow yeses to Rudolph and faster more sure ones to each other. Rudolph folded his hands across his vest like he was forty years old and so wonderful wise he had to sit back and rest just from the weight of it.

Pretty soon the trainboy came through again. When he saw me, and who I was with, his eyes poked out and the advertising he was giving a box of candy sort of hiccoughed and stopped. I had him figuring maybe I knew a lot more than I let on, which is always a good position to hold over a person. I built on a little. I looked straight at the black-haired, prettiest one and asked her whether business in the forenoon amounted to anything.

"It never has." Her voice could have threaded needles. "We use it to get ready for the trade and for studying new styles."

You could have tossed an apple into the trainboy's mouth, he'd have never noticed a little thing like that. He stood there froze and staring, and then I got uncomfortable too at what I'd started. Every trade has its own business words same as the harness business has, and any minute she might screech out theirs the same way men talk around a livery stable and get us all maybe put off the train. I passed the lunchbox again to keep them busy chewing. That lunch just danced around, and it wasn't all train rocking either. I was shaky too.

The conductor came through again just then. He put his hand on the trainboy's shoulder to get by and that unhypnotized him a little. It got him started, anyhow, hollering down the aisle once more, only it was candy he waved and cigars he described. The conductor stopped

97

and braced his hand on the back of the seat to talk to Rudolph. He asked him if there was anything he or the ladies needed to make the trip more pleasant. He gave Rudolph his own newspaper. He got out his watch and explained the reason we were seven minutes late and hoped Rudolph wouldn't be inconvenienced. I got out my watch, figuring his recognizing it as a railroad watch would include me in the conversation too, but it didn't do any good. He wasn't mistaking me for any North Western stockholder.

"Interesting thing coming up here in Racine. Damned if a doctor hasn't gone and mounted himself a boiler on a carriage bed and belted the flywheel to a carriage wheel and chugs around town on his own steam buggy."

That kind of talk would interest anybody. I was all eyes on the conductor which he liked, I could see it, only it was Rudolph's attention he wanted most.

"Just an oddity," Rudolph said. "I see men like that all over, never grow up. Build ships inside of bottles or maybe construct the Tower of Pisa on a tabletop gluing fifty thousand toothpicks together. What's he trying to do, invent the locomotive all over again?"

"Well, I don't say it's practical, but it's worth looking at." He clamped his mouth flat tight. He wore his mustache straight out and low on his lip, and it was coarse and yellow. It made him look like he'd fallen against a strawpile and came out with a mouthful. A man looks like that you expect what he says will be straw too, and I guess that's what Rudolph took it to be.

"You say a doctor would fool around foolish like that? What's the matter, doesn't he have any practice?"

"Dr. Carhart? I don't know, that isn't the point. But if you and the ladies want to see his rig, he tests it on the street every day about this time. Keep looking. This is Racine now."

I went to another seat I could have alone and where there was an empty opposite so I could watch both sides. I didn't

98

really expect to see anything, most things you hear about are gone by the time you get there or weren't anything except exaggeration in the first place, but you always hunt for them anyhow.

I had good luck. I saw the steam buggy and not just a flash of it either. As we stopped for wood or something our car was square across a street and coming toward us across the packed snow a sort of a wagon came jiggling and lurching without any horses. It steamed like a hog-scalding barrel. Kids and dogs raced around it. People stood on the plank sidewalks watching it. Horses shied. Everybody in the car crowded the windows. The doctor running it sat there stiff and proud and bundled-up and bouncing. He turned the thing right in front of us all by itself, without a turntable or tracks or anything. Near enough to show its details, it was trim and graceful and put together real shipshape. It was wonderful.

After we left Racine I got to thinking how Pa would like to see that steam buggy, it was just the sort of progress he believed in. Come to think of it, that night on the way home after he decided I was going along to Wisconsin and he was preaching steam and prophesying, it was me who predicted they'd make buggies run that way and Pa laughed at me. I'd never seen anything like that or heard about it and yet I predicted it.

I predicted it and somebody up and did it within a month, just like I said they would, only a lot sooner. It was a wonderful feeling, one minute to be somebody just ordinary and plain and then discover that the things you think about can really be done. I guess I've got a better head than I figured myself. Pa could see it, it comes to me now that's why all of a sudden he decided I'd better go along. Good old Pa, he knows the kind of stuff he put into me better than anybody. Sure, he laughed at me, but it was a proud laugh and a confident one, the kind that comes out when you expect something good and get more than you expect.

99

I felt wonderful good. All my worry how I'd do for Pa selling Rohland harness up and dissolved like breath on a mirror. I'd discovered something extra fine and to save it I got out the journal from Pa and my pencil to put it down, but the harder I tried the blanker the paper stayed. I couldn't write what I'd discovered any more than I could cork up moonbeams. That bothered me for quite a spell and then I thought why should it matter. In the journal I could lose it any time, but up in my head where it started I've always got it.

By and by Rudolph came back humming and sat down with me. We were alone and still not quite all by ourselves because every little while somebody would turn and bounce their eyes on him. There wasn't anybody in the car built like him or dressed like him or barbered so fine. It was a kind of confidence just to be sitting next to him.

"Emil," he said, "we're going to do extra well with our sales, I can feel it. It's going to be dead easy. All it takes is finding the right people and talking the right way, and we'll make good money. I can't wait to get to Milwaukee."

After that we just sat back and relaxed, enjoying everything. There isn't anything tastes better than being sure of yourself.

When we pulled into Milwaukee and I was getting our baggage together which made quite a load, Rudolph said he'd promised those women I'd help with theirs too. They had three big cardboard boxes besides their traveling bags. All I got of theirs were the boxes which wasn't as bad as you might think. They were bulky and clumsy, but so light there wasn't anything to them. If that isn't just like their kind, I was thinking, traveling with empty boxes, anything to get attention. Everybody in the train knowing what those women were and Rudolph lending me out as baggageman to them, that was a fine way to come new into a city where you expect to do thousands of dollars of respectable business. I didn't get any first impression of Milwaukee, I had boxes in front of my face. The old one

100

guided me over the platform and through the crowd and out to a sleigh and for thanks she invited Rudolph to come see them as soon as they located.

Rudolph looked around. The fanciest rig there said *Plankington House* so that's what we took. We tipped our hats good-by to the ladies, and I lugged our gear over to the hotel sleigh and we climbed in. "All that trouble with those boxes of theirs," I grumbled. "They were empty."

Rudolph laughed. "If one would have popped open, you'd have seen how empty it was. You'd have had to chase the breeze running forty dollars' worth of feathers down, one at a time."

"Feathers? What's feathers got to do with their business?"

"Kid, what's the matter with you? They can't get along without feathers any more than we can make harness without leather, you know that."

I figured and figured, and thought back all I'd ever heard, and then tried to imagine what kind of tricks whores could use feathers for in their trade. I didn't get anywhere. Then I thought of the packet. I was off the train so I could open it. It was cards, like a deck, but only about half as many. Pictures of girls all right, but they had all their clothes on and weren't doing anything wrong. I was stung for fifty cents. That poor preacher will have a time of it looking for sin for a sermon when he opens his. The editor is better off, those guys don't have to follow the Bible or anything else. They see sin wherever they have a mind to and write it up so interesting and put big-sounding names to it and get people all riled up to take sides on things they'd never worry about until it comes out in print. He'll probably ripsnort better on those cards than if they'd been what the trainboy advertised they were. Just the same I was out fifty cents and still didn't know what whores did with feathers. I leaned over on the quiet and asked Rudolph outright.

"Whores? Feathers? Damned if I know."

101

"What'd you say so for, then?"

"When?"

"When I carried their boxes and you said they were feathers."

"Them? You think those women are whores? Good gosh, Emil, if they knew what you were thinking they'd be so embarrassed it would drive them behind veils for the rest of their lives. They're milliners! On a buying trip to Chicago and planning to set up their own hat shop. You dumb kid, don't you know anything?"

"The way everybody was talking I thought they were ..."

"Quit talking about something you don't know anything about," he whispered with grit in it, "or you'll have everybody on this transfer looking at us. Don't you ever call a woman a whore unless she is one, and if you don't know, for God's sake act as if she isn't. You'll never find out anyhow until you're alone with her, no matter what people say."

At the Plankington House, which was a pretty elegant place, Rudolph marched up to the desk ahead of me and said he wanted a nice room with a little one connecting for his man to sleep. That's just what we got too, a big bedroom fixed up fancy as a parlor, with tables and three different kinds of chairs and a prism gas chandelier, which cost a dollar and a half a day without any meals. Off to a side was a cubbyhole for me with a cot and a jet that burned bare. That was fifty cents, but they probably lost money, because the gas had to go all day to take the place of windows. It didn't look fair to me and I said so. I also told Rudolph I didn't like that stuff about him calling me his man and making me rustle all the baggage.

He sat down and explained it. It wasn't for himself at all he had to do those things, but for Rohland harness. We weren't any two-bit outfit, we were the biggest harness manufacturers in the whole Midwest, which was a hell of a big place, and we had a position to maintain and dignity to

102

support. He was the dignity because he was older and in charge. I was the support because Pa chose him first and only thought of it to send me along for help after he picked him. We were going to talk to some pretty big people here in Milwaukee, Mr. Plankington who owned this hotel, which was only a plaything, his real business was butchering hogs and he had to use harness by the dozens to haul the meat around. Mr. Schlitz, for another, and Mr. Blatz and Mr. Best and Mr. Miller and Mr. Gettleman, all those fellows he had to see to get them to switch their beer-wagon harness to Rohland.

"To deal with big operators I naturally have to look and act big," he told me. "They won't bother with anything less because that's all they're used to. When I go to see them, I've got to look just so, and have a driver, and somebody to stand back of my elbow to hold my overcoat and hat and gloves, and whisk the snow off my shoes. All those things are your job and the better you handle it, the more our harness will impress them."

Rudolph was right. If we want them to be sure Rohland harness is the best, we have to show how successful it has made us. His taking all the talking and selling, which is the hard part, was a relief to me. I told him I wouldn't object.

"Fine," he said. "Now unpack and hang up my clothes while I do some planning and thinking."

He lay down on the bed and thought awful hard and then said we'd better go down for dinner. Afterwards we came back up again and I finished unpacking while he planned some more.

"Maybe we'd better get out and see our people," I said.

"On Saturday afternoon? Worst time in the world. If they've had a good week, they'll be satisfied with their old harness. If they've had a poor one, they'll be mean to talk to and say no because that's what they've been hearing all week themselves. Monday morning is the time. Then business is full of new plans and open for ideas. I've got to be ready then and sharp as a tack, so let me think."

103

I puttered around for a while, but that got to bothering his looking at the ceiling. He told me to stay in my room. I watched my gas jet, which was the only thing to look at, so long I think I know what it is that drives moths crazy. When I couldn't stand it any longer, I sneaked back. Rudolph had thought himself to sleep and wasn't using his window so I looked out of that for a while and watched the smoke drift up from a thousand chimneys as far as I could see. A city is a lazy-looking place from on top. Once you leave ground level there isn't much going on. I suppose that's why they mostly build houses with the bedrooms upstairs.

After a little Rudolph woke up and said he had it all worked out. There should be thirty places at least, in Milwaukee, that could use a dozen sets apiece and give or take a few either way there was our carload sold out and we'd better start deciding where we should telegraph Pa to send the next carload.

"Speaking of Pa," I said, "makes me think of home and when I think of home I wish you'd tell me something straight out. You and Sarah, that night."

He kind of thought back and liked it and then put his hands behind his head and laid on them. "Sure, anything you want to know about girls and things—that's what an older brother is for. There isn't anything more fun than an exciting girl, but there isn't anything more trouble than one either. It's just like stopping to pet a cute little puppy, next thing you know it's all tangled up with you and hurt when you can't take it along for good. You got to talk sharp to cut it off. Well, that's the way it was with Sarah. It was fun larking around with her, but then she wanted to get serious. There isn't any woman going to tie me down for a long time, and when one does she's going to have background and money and bring me power, or it's no deal. Servant girls can be mighty jolly to play with, but nix on the wedding bells."

104

"Then that night when she was in your bedroom, I mean you really did ..."

"Of course, but that was the last time. After that, well I cut her off."

"The last time? There were times before that? Sarah did it with you more than the once anybody might experiment just to find out what it's like?"

"Oh, maybe six or seven times, I forget."

"Six or seven times? That, why, that makes her a whore, plain and simple. Sarah the nicest, smartest girl Ma ever had! A whore, and you made her so. How can you sleep nights with such a thing on you?"

"Emil, you're always talking about whores and it's just a joke because every time you open your mouth it shows how much you don't know. Sarah isn't one and never will be. A girl isn't one unless she takes pay or lets anyone have her. Sarah has spunk and character, she's just as good a girl as any you'll ever see singing in the choir, or teaching little kids in school. Her affair with me won't make her free and easy, it'll work just the opposite to protect her. From now on there won't be a man can touch her no matter how smooth he is. You come right down to it, instead of ruining her like you might think, I've saved her, that's what, and she can be thankful."

"What kind of inside-out talk is that, anyhow, saving a person from going to hell by taking her there yourself? You've done something bad and mean no matter how you try to explain it."

"Oh, come now, do a little thinking yourself. You know it's a fact a person gets mumps on both sides, they can never get it again. They're immune from then on, you know that. Or vaccination, where they scratch a sort of smallpox into you so that you don't get smallpox. Well, Sarah has been vaccinated now, you might say."

Even if the words did fit together to make sort of a sense to excuse what Rudolph wants to do anyhow, the argument

105

was wrong, I could see that. "You aren't interested in what happens to Sarah one way or the other no matter how you reason it," I said. "Getting what you can, as handy as you can, that's all I hear in what you're saying."

Rudolph laughed. "Emil, you're old enough for me to talk plain, and the subject interests you because you've been hinting around it, all curiosity and funny ideas."

He got up on one elbow. "I'd like to put you straight on this business about girls. First of all, though, let's see how much of a man you really are yourself, otherwise I'm just wasting time and you'd never understand anyhow. Now then, tell me this. Suppose you get to be forty years old. What do you think you want for yourself then? How do you think you'll be living? What'll be behind you that you'll take most pride in?"

Those were questions to jolt a person. He got right inside where I don't take anybody and called off the things I been wondering about when I wake up nights. "Well," I said, "I don't know if that's any business of yours or not and you'll probably laugh at me, but I don't care. First, I want to be rich. I don't mean rich and people hate me, or rich from how much Pa leaves, but rich by myself at something people will say I deserved. I want people to like me a hundred miles farther away than I'll ever get. I want my name on a factory, or on something everybody uses, or maybe a county or a mountain, or in a history book, anything like that before it gets on a tombstone. I want to own a horse that can run faster than any other horse in the world."

"Quite a speech. You wouldn't have in mind running for Congress too?"

"If I wanted it, I'd go after that too, if you have to know."

"Okay, okay. You *are* ready for girls, no doubt about it. Now you listen to me, brother Emil. There's not a thing you said you wanted but has fight and contest to it. You

106

won't get a single one of them unless you get rough, unless you can stand it to know that in order for you to win, somebody else has to be smashed down and crawl away beaten. That's a man's world whether it's on a battlefield, or in the markets, or in a courtroom, or on a race track. Whenever you win it strengthens you to win again, but any of the things we've talked about so far can seem like empty barrels compared to the big and powerful and alive feeling you get when you call out every power that's in you to win a girl and she submits."

"That's a contest too? I thought it was love. Unless you mean with a whore."

"There you go again. Get whores out of your head and keep them out. What contest is there in paying the rate and getting open-stock merchandise? That isn't winning anything. That's for a willy-nilly who hasn't the knack to hunt up the property he wants and the spunk to go after it. Winning women on your own is the test of the man who can be successful. You point out any man you can name that people look up to, or is powerful or famous, and you investigate you'll find he's busier between the sheets than Brigham Young. Strong in one thing it's just natural he'll be strong in another."

Rudolph had me whirling. I've heard plenty of talk about girls, and done considerable myself, but any time such dealings with them are mentioned officially it's pointed out as a sin. What they say in church and what Rudolph recommended spread pretty far apart. I called his attention to the difference.

"Sure, it's sin," he said. "That's what's fun about it. Sin is for the strong."

I'd heard about dozens of different ways to test how strong a person is, but I never heard of measuring it with sin. Come to think of it, what Rudolph said was so, you can see it all around. Rich men greedy over more money, like Mr. Collins and what he charged Pa just to rent his boxcars, that's a good example of a powerful man using tricks to get more powerful. Like Rudolph said, somebody always gets hurt. Using the same kind of trick on Sarah made me so mad I got to breathing short.

"It's a dirty trick," I said, "to use love to hurt with. It's double dirty against somebody as nice as Sarah."

"They're all nice. You're shocked because it happened to be Sarah and you happen to know Sarah. Good gosh, Emil, that's how you have to start with any girl, be around where she is, get her a little used to you, say nice things back and forth, use a pet name on her, work up to little secrets together, snatch a kiss to see what her climate is like, and if it's warm give her some close-quarter hugging and squeezing. Then you promise her anything she happens to mention or whatever comes in your head and she's yours. The trick is in the promising, you got to use your imagination there and it's a small cost compared to what you get for it. You want a horse, it takes the cold cash, or for a suit of clothes the day comes when the bill is due, but a promise to a girl can always be paid off by adding a new promise. When it gets to the point you want a change, point out she was mistaken about the promises and she'll go to pieces or get mad and then you're free again. It works every time."

"What kind of talk is that from a Rohland? You didn't learn that from Pa, to even *think* promises you don't intend to keep. Why, I've seen a little girl come to Pa to beg a strap from the trimming box for a dog leash, and he said yah sure, only there wasn't any when he came to look and he said a promise was a promise and cut her one out of his best rein stock."

"Love and business work from different rules."

"Love. The kind you use is the same as a rooster calling the hens and lying about what he's found and *bang* he gives it to the first one that comes within jumping range."

108

"Guess I'd better quit. I see I made a mistake. You are too young at that."

"I am not. Go ahead and talk. I'm learning more than I expected."

He gave me a funny look, and got off his elbow and rolled his legs over the edge of the bed and sat up and stretched and yawned. It exercised him all the way from his shoes on up. He stretched all his buttonholes. He opened his mouth so big his jaws cracked and his eyes watered. He roared like a pipe organ winding up the Doxology. It was a regular hundred-and-eighty-proof of a yawn, and after he got it all in he had to comfort his whiskers and settle them back where they belonged with the back of his hand.

"Love," he said. "It helps and it hinders. It's what you work for so that she gets it and you don't. Where's that candy of mine you picked up last night?"

We ate some and it sure was good at a time like that when dinner has dissolved away and supper hasn't been scheduled yet and things down inside are growling around. I wondered how Sarah would feel if she knew the kind of talk we were eating her candy with.

7

AFTER supper we went out to look at Milwau-
kee. It was just as busy as Chicago, as near as I could tell.
Come to think of it I never been out Saturday nights to
speak of in Chicago either, that's our busiest day and it
runs late and after that Pa holds our meeting and by the
time that's over everything else has locked up too. It was
pretty nice to walk along just to watch other people work.
Seemed it was a mighty good chance to drop in almost
anywhere and ask how they were fixed for harness, but
Rudolph said nothing doing, that was for Monday, tonight
was for looking around getting used to the place. Even
when we got in front of a wood carver and peeked in the
window past his cigar Indians in the lamplight, and saw
him sandpapering a white horse like some in the business
use for advertising harness, Rudolph wouldn't let me go
in to talk. That fellow could have told us what the competition would be like, which is a good thing to know.
"Yeah," Rudolph said, "and tip off every harness maker
in town to make us trouble. He's got to protect them or
who'd buy his wooden horses?"

We came to a stairway to a hall upstairs and outside of

it there were signs advertising the Battle of Gettysburg going on up there for a quarter apiece. I felt I'd like to see something I'd heard so much about. That's just what Rudolph said too, so we went in.

Up front was a picture frame bigger than a barn door. Gas lights were behind the frame shining on big red and black letters reading THE BATTLE OF GETTYSBURG.

"Is that all it's going to be," I asked, "just a painting back there?"

"It's a panorama," Rudolph said, "like it says outside."

"What's a panorama?"

"It's a painting, but you forget that, it's so unusual. It's so big you have to look at it a little piece at a time. They roll it behind the frame, from one big spool on one side to another spool on the other side, and you watch it as it goes by. I hear tell some of them are hundreds of yards long and take half, three-quarters of an hour to roll by slow enough to show you everything."

Under the frame and in front, a half dozen drummers and flute and bugle players in Union blue were just sitting down. We had to take chairs about halfway back, it was filling up so, but we could see fine, the picture frame was so big. Velvet curtains from the ceiling down to the floor blocked off all the rest of the front. When the hall filled up, which didn't take long, they turned the gas jets, out where we were, real low and left those up at the picture frame nice and bright. A spanking crisp captain in uniform came out and bowed. He only had one arm. His empty sleeve was pinned back just so. It made your throat hurt as you sat there clapping which we could do without even thinking and he'd never be able to again as long as he lived.

He started off telling how Gettysburg was the biggest battle there ever was, where General Lee started from and what he had in mind, and how Meade was situated and how,

111

when those two monster armies slammed into each other, it busted the Civil War slick and clean in two and he was there to take us right through it again. "Let the battle be joined," he said. My heart started to pound in my ears, he made it such a real thing. Maybe it was lucky I wasn't around there when it really happened, because I'd have yelled and run, I just know it. Rudolph pulled on a cigar. He was just as calm as if the show wasn't going to be anything more than sitting through church. Pa sure got different results every time he made another Rohland.

Somebody in the band blew a bugle call, clear and sweet, but muffled like it came from far away. The lettering rolled off to one side. A rim of pretty hills rolled out behind the picture frame with clouds above just as real and then showed a valley and in it was a Union regiment. The drums started to roll a marching beat. The captain said it was the Second Wisconsin, which lost more men killed in battle than any other regiment in the whole war. Everybody cheered, and then the picture wound them out of sight and showed houses and stores which he explained was the village of Gettysburg. Right while we were watching that with the trains unloading more troops there was a *boo-oo-m* made to sound like it came from a long ways off and then the picture rolled to show a warehouse that had been hit and bricks were falling while they clattered the drums to show what it sounded like. One scene rolled into another to show how busy and mixed up a battle gets and how it runs out of hand all over the landscape and pretty soon you didn't notice the band any more at all, it was the battle you were hearing. You could even crane your neck and see around the picture frame a little for a last look at details before they rolled out of sight and on ahead a little to what was coming next.

Between battle sounds the captain explained how the fight was going and exactly who was in it at each place. He led us up Cemetery Ridge, and showed us the sharp-

112

shooters in the Devil's Den and how Culp's Hill stood off charge after charge. It showed the spring too, and how it was neutral ground where our boys laughed and joked with the Rebs while everybody filled their canteens like friends and then went back to good places to kill each other. The cavalry was in it and the artillery and the smoke. Sweating, lathering horses on supply wagons hauled up battle gear through orchards and wheat fields. The captain hollered out orders and it was all as real as anything except one place where a harness showed up wrong. The painter had the wheel horses pitching and blowing, which was all right, but they were hitched to a cannon carriage and he didn't show any breeching straps. You have to have breeching straps for a team to lean back against to handle the load when they back up and you can't tell me they can maneuver a cannon where they want it without backing.

You saw flags waving and gray hats peeking over stone fences with rifle barrels pointed square at you and some of them flashing angry orange. All that mixed-up detail the captain straightened out for us. He must have been everywhere all at once to know it so good, but how he had stomach to go through it all again just for us gave a pretty good idea of the iron he was built from. Casper and Jacob were brave too, but mostly they wouldn't talk about their battles unless Pa ordered them to.

It built up more gory all the time and came to a place he called the climax of Pickett's Charge at the fence corner. Rebels were all over, jumping straight toward you, fighting our artillery with their bayonettes, and fire and blood splashing every which way. One of them right out in front wasn't any older than I am and there he was, dying, and lunging his rifle and bayonet ahead the last time with his belly ripped open and his guts spilling out and all for nothing because the Rebels couldn't hold where they'd got to and lost the battle. It was mighty close, though, closer than

113

I had any idea up to now, and it took all the captain's wind and the noise of the fifes and bugles and drums to wind it up. The last glimpse of the corner of the rail fence where it happened rolled out of sight and letters rolled into the picture frame which read THE END.

The captain bowed and wiped his forehead. It was dead quiet, but he raised up his head for more silence and said for a fitting close he'd be happy for us to accompany him back to a later scene. The picture moved on behind its frame and it was a new graveyard with row after row in every direction you looked, all little round-topped white stones. It rolled on and on the same thing and he told how many had died at Gettysburg. Then the corner of a draped platform showed, and then the whole platform and there stood Abraham Lincoln, tall and sad and looking down. The picture stopped rolling. It was so quiet you didn't want to breathe. The captain started giving Lincoln's Gettysburg Address, and you heard it as if it was brand-new and coming slow and painful straight out of Lincoln for the first time.

His voice drifted away on "perish from the earth." A big ache tightened up my throat. Swallowing didn't help. On top of the ache, which was bad enough, a bugle played that slow sweet call an army mourns with. You wanted to die too.

It finished. The sounds had ended and were gone. Lincoln was still standing there like he'd been listening too, and then a curtain swished shut and there wasn't anything more to look at. Funny how ideas and words can be put down and kept and can be used over and over again, but the saying of them, how Lincoln himself made them sound, is gone forever. A sound hasn't any life to it at all, right while it's being made it's gone and no matter how important it is there's no way to store it. Maybe it's a good thing, who'd want to come into a house and have the walls echo out what everybody had said in there yesterday?

114

There wouldn't be any time for the things that have to be said today.

Later on we dropped in on a place called a Palm Garden. It wasn't really a garden, because gardens are outside where you can't sit around in winter, but it looked like one anyhow, with palms all around and growing out of big pots and their big leaves sticking out so that you had to walk around them as if they were bushes. Little tables were all over. People were drinking beer, whole families of them, kids and everybody and singing songs and eating sandwiches. It was a gay place with pretty girls bringing the beer, which was the only thing anybody had to pay for. The sandwiches were free, you just went up to a big table where they had ham and cheese and rye bread and mustard and sausages and made your own. They had a band there too, and it was all German, the songs everybody was singing. People were the friendliest you ever saw. The table next to us had a bent-backed man with a medium-big face, but it wasn't big enough to fill out the wrinkles in it. He had wrinkles crossing his wrinkles and up on his forehead it looked like cross-stitching. His wife was with him. There weren't any wrinkles on her, she was filled out like a Clydesdale. "You sit over here with us," he ordered. "With beer and singing it goes better not to be strangers."

Both those things are big helps to friendliness. It was top-rate beer and we were good and thirsty. A battle like that dries you out, you don't realize how much until the first touch of a cool drink wets so comfortable at the back of your throat. And those songs in German, why, it was just like a lively evening when Pa and Ma get lonesome and invite back Gottlieb and his wife, and all the rest of our families, and all their kids are there, and it makes a big crowd. We sang love songs and fighting songs and catchy little melodies your feet tap the time to while your tongue mixes up the sounds you're supposed to be singing with the laughing in your lungs, the words are so funny.

We sang homesick songs too, about mountains and beautiful villages people had to leave and would never see again. We sipped and sang and nibbled and sang and talked and sang and joked with the girls that brought the beer and it was the nicest time ever.

We joked with the Schmidts too, that was the name of the people who had us sit with them. Everything was fun to those people. The man even said he envied our name. That made me puff up because I figured he had probably got hold of some of our harness somehow and had experience with quality, but when I asked he just laughed and said he wasn't familiar with the brand. What he meant, he said, was that Rohland sets a person apart better than Schmidt does. A Schmidt meets a Schmidt, and it happens two three times a day, there were probably five in there right then and no relation, they always lose time straightening out who's who. Why, they can't even hold a family reunion like ordinary people, because it drives the committee crazy untangling which Schmidts are pedigreed and which ones should have gone to another park on another day. "That's why too," he said, "a Schmidt doesn't bother much to write a poem, or invent anything or run for President, because nobody could ever be sure which one it was and who wants to go to all that trouble and not nail down the credit?

"A Schmidt dies, for instance," he went on, "and people drop in confident with sympathy, like as not the corpse laid out is somebody altogether different from who they had in mind. It gets discouraging not to be sure of yourself even after you're dead."

"So," Mrs. Schmidt said, "we sing and drink beer." I don't think it worried her much, though, one way or the other.

Between times when he wasn't fooling around kidding and the singing let up long enough for serious talk he told us he had charge of the lard in a packing plant and his

116

spare time in helping run Milwaukee. He was on the fire commission and now that Milwaukee was planning a brand-new water system to pipe Lake Michigan through the streets their only problem in fire fighting would be to get there quick enough. Working in lard the way he did all day makes a person pretty jittery about fire. He said he had in mind newer, faster equipment all around.

Rudolph asked how many horses they had. I saw what he was getting at. New equipment also means new harness. Our first chance at a sale and a big one too. But fire harness is a special kind that opens up different because it has to drop down over the whole horse all at once, bridle and everything, and tightens instant, you don't fool around with ordinary buckles and snaps. Our army harness wouldn't do the trick. It wouldn't do any good either to say Pa could make it, which he does for all of Chicago, but short-handed like he was, he couldn't take on any out-of-town customers without hurting his Chicago trade. I don't know, business can get you dizzy quicker than beer. A carload of harness to get rid of, and a factory behind it making more and the first thing we ran into, neither one was right. I looked over at Rudolph and he had wrinkled up almost as bad as Mr. Schmidt. We didn't dare even mention harness.

Mr. Schmidt didn't notice, he'd taken the notion that lard is an interesting thing we'd come special to Milwaukee to hear about. We didn't ask him, and I don't recall we led him on one bit. He just dropped lard into the conversation careless like and let it spread and ring out like its habit is when it gets warm. First thing we knew we were listening to the different kinds of trouble the lard business gets into. When a person explains trouble you just can't help but listen, there isn't anything catchier. Like lamps, for example, they daresn't use them because if kerosene would get into a kettle by accident it would taint the whole batch. They have to practically give it away to anybody

117

they can find who's working up a batch of soap. Worse than kerosene, he said, is a boar hog. They bring their own taint and not just their own fat, they'll spoil all the lard theirs gets mixed with. Makes it smell like a hard-used chamber pot does when it gets rinsed with boiling water.

That wasn't nice talk around Mrs. Schmidt right there with us, but he had started it and made me curious. A boar pig can be pretty easy spotted, it seemed to me. I asked him why they didn't inspect what they butchered a little better.

"It's the damn lying farmers," he said. "The trouble isn't with a boar that's been left alone, we can always weed him out. But they use him for a boar for a season and then decommission him to a barrow and fatten him up and run him in with a batch that always were barrows, practically, and then we're in trouble. The flavor he's spread around his system while he was active stays right there, and lays quiet while we cut him up. Can't tell a thing, but as soon as a little heat starts his fat melting, whew! By that time he's mixed up with everything else and it's too late to sort him out."

"Well," Rudolph said, "I should think you could save yourself all that trouble pretty easy. While you have the hogs hanging, just after they've been butchered and before you cut them up, snip a little fat off each one, and keep the samples separate, and fry them out and when you get a stinker, go back to the hog it came from and sort it out and there you are."

That sounded sensible to me. Of course I don't know the lard business and neither does Rudolph. We just wanted to help. I guess Mr. Schmidt was awful proud and touchy. He changed the subject right quick to complain about his boss, who, he said, was a foolish man too and always wanted to try new ideas that interfered with Mr. Schmidt's work. "You know what he's playing around with now? Ice."

118

He looked at us and smiled like it should be a joke to us too. He waited a minute for us to see how funny that was, but we didn't and then he had to explain. "Noticed how pork keeps fresh in winter and spoils sudden in summer, which everybody knows, and how there's enough finicky people, especially in a big city, to make it pay to cut ice in winter and store it to sell in summer. That's all right, an icebox in a house is handy for those who don't have a cellar, but Mr. Cudahy, he's the touched one I'm talking about, thinks that everything except scalding and rendering should be kept cool. Wants to put up a big building as one huge icebox and has talked *his* boss, who is Mr. Plankington, into hiring an architect to plan it."

Mr. Schmidt ordered more beer and used his for complaining instead of singing. We couldn't sing either, we had to listen, but Mrs. Schmidt, I guess, knew everything that was coming. She sang. Loud too, which made Mr. Schmidt lean over intimate for fear there'd be parts we might miss. It wasn't just the ice that hurt him, it was because in summer his lard department was the most important in the whole plant. Hams they can make in summer because they're cured and so is the bacon. Mess pork, which is all the rest of the hog with meat on it, they could only sell in cold weather because it didn't keep. In warm weather they had to render it all which made Mr. Schmidt the man who kept the place running from May into October. He rendered in winter too, of course, but summer, that was the time he could really produce and taking his importance away from him like that was a dirty damn trick. Why, that Cudahy was so hot on ice he was even fooling around, he'd heard, with the people who make boxcars to get them to make boxcar iceboxes to ship meat in. To show how foolish the whole idea was, he mentioned it would take five or six trainloads of ice just to cool the building and they were shipping it in now on flat cars as fast as the men on some lake west of there were cutting it.

119

Rudolph asked quick where that lake was. That would take hauling, and hauling takes harness. A whole new business springing up, bulky and heavy ice that melts and they have to go back for more and more. That was just the kind of new use for harness Pa told us to hunt for. All of a sudden my beer glass was empty. So was Rudolph's. Mr. Schmidt had no idea what lake it was or where we could find it. He said any lake had ice on it, and to hell with all of them.

First thing Monday morning Rudolph had me trim his beard. He didn't need it, he'd just had it done the day before we left home, but he'd brought a special shears along and made me work on him. I didn't want to, he orders and criticizes and scolds so it makes me nervous. I worked real careful and just snipped air to satisfy him, but when he checked it in the mirror he said I'd ruined him and went down to the hotel barber who charged him ten cents and sprinkled a little perfume on him to calm him down. Near as I could tell all he did was snip air too. He charged for it, which makes a difference.

We found a livery stable near by and hired their best rig and drove to the North Western yards to locate our boxcar and load on a set for a sample. Rudolph likes to drive just as well as I do. It hurt him to miss the fun of finding out what a new team has in it. A person who has to be careful of his appearance and always be dignified and be waited on would look pretty silly driving his own help around. I felt a little sorry for him sitting there envying me, but dog-gone it, he picked the part of the work he wanted and it isn't my fault that the pleasant jobs and the easy ones were what was left.

He had me drive out to the biggest brewery, which was quite a place. It had to be, because just about everybody in Milwaukee goes through beer the way we and the Schmidts did Saturday night. It puts a strain on all the breweries to keep the supply up. When we stopped in front of the office we argued a little which was proper, to leave the harness in the rig and invite Mr. Best out to look at it, or if I should walk a little behind Rudolph carrying it handy so he could see it right away. One way was polite and the other was practical. We didn't have any clue which was most important. Different people have different preferences. "We'll just go in alone," Rudolph decided. "That way we can bring him out, or you can run out and bring it in, whichever he likes."

Neither way was any good. They had a man in there hired special just to find out your business and keep you out of theirs. He wouldn't even tell Mr. Best we had come. Harnesses, he said, came under the barn boss and he recommended we go see him. He ran his eyes all up and down Rudolph, and spread his nose just a little, you almost didn't notice it, and gave us our directions.

Their barn was around the block and in back. It was near as big as the brewery. The boss was talking with the blacksmith and you couldn't tell who was who, they were both such giants in work clothes.

The boss took a quick look at our harness and said, "Nope." He didn't ask price or look at the stitching or finger the buckles. The only thing he inspected was Rudolph, which he did quick-like and walked back into the barn. Rudolph followed him. I followed Rudolph.

"What's the matter with our harness?" Rudolph asked.

"Nothing," he said. "It just isn't Best."

"It's as good as any you can get," I said.

"That may be, boy," he said, "but the decoration is in the wrong place. I like it on the leather, not on the man selling it."

I thought Rudolph would get mad, insulted like that, but instead he laughed hearty. "Look," he said, "I thought I'd have to deal with Mr. Best and I dressed accordingly. If I came to his office in barn clothes, that would be just as wrong as these are here. Like you say, I'm selling harness,

121

not clothes, and by God, I'll clean your stables dressed the way I am if it takes that to convince you I believe in my harness.''

The barn boss looked startled and then he laughed hearty too, and then we all felt easy. He friendlied up awful nice and showed us his harness room. He was pretty proud of it, and explained how most of them were out because everybody is low on beer Monday morning. There were one or two hanging there, though, for him to show us what he meant. They were all special jobs again, like fire harness, only these were special in a different way with wide plates across the breast and over the shoulders and around the hips and especially fancy along the hames to hold tooled metal shined up sparkling.

''In Milwaukee,'' he said, ''we don't just deliver beer barrels, we make a parade out of it. We want people to stop and look when Best goes by. Why don't you try Blatz? I think they buy plain harness and hang their decoration on it later, that's the way it looks to me.''

We tried Blatz. Their man liked our harness and said it was twenty dollars a set less than he'd been paying, but he shook his head and said he didn't dare touch it. Rudolph braced himself for another lecture on clothes, I could see him tighten up, and asked, ''Why not?''

''Because we want to sell our beer, that's why. Word get around that we buy out-of-town harness, no harness maker, and Milwaukee has hundreds of them, will ever taste Blatz again. We're Milwaukee and we have to trade Milwaukee. Try a little brewery where they don't have to watch themselves so careful.''

We tried a little brewery. It went along good too, all the way until they decided to see how our harness looked on a horse. It wouldn't come together. It wasn't supposed to, not on such an elephant of a horse they brought around. ''That's not fair,'' I said.

''What's not fair?''

122

"That horse. There isn't any horse that big."

"Take that pony harness and get the hell out of here," the man roared. We were pretty anxious to leave, ourselves.

It wasn't pony harness, I knew that, or mule harness either, it was standard size work-horse harness just like we said it was. It was made for strong tough war horses, and those horses and that harness were plenty big enough to win that war. Brewery horses! Like fat ladies from a side show, nice to gape at, but who'd want them in a kitchen? The whole beer business was the same pattern—roly-poly barrels, big bulgy drivers, horses like houses—it was disgusting. We didn't call on any more breweries.

"Drive me back to the hotel," Rudolph said. "I got to think."

I let him off. I headed back toward the livery stable. When I got there I figured why should I turn the team in and pay for a whole day when most of it was still left. I drove on. I had to think too. I can't think like Rudolph can, lying quiet with shoes off and eyes shut. I got to be moving and looking to get fodder for thinking. I can't read it off the back of my eyelids, when I try that I just go to sleep. Driving a team, though, that's different. When I drive in a new place everything makes me think. I saw all kinds of things and enjoyed myself and thought about what I saw, but after a while the fun sort of dropped out of it.

See here, it came to me, Pa didn't send me up to Milwaukee for sight-seeing. I looked at my watch. It was two o'clock. Pretty near a whole Monday gone and for all I'd done that carload of harness could have stayed locked up another five years in the warehouse. I thought how big a carload was and how many harnesses it held which was an awful scary big quantity. Who could there be that could use them all? A harness maker in just about every block. I'd counted eleven since dinner, they'd know every time a colt was broke and have spies in all the carriage factories

123

to report where every sleigh and wagon went. What we had to find was a brand-new business coming up fast and get to them before the competition. Like that ice cutting Mr. Schmidt mentioned, if he could only remember what lake they were using. I inquired a little at the hotel Sunday figuring we could easy locate it on the landscape, but the map the clerk showed me kind of floored me. He said Wisconsin had more than six thousand lakes, and every time the surveyors up north bring more notes in, the count goes up. I tried to pin it down, Mr. Schmidt said it was west of Milwaukee, but there are dozens just in that direction.

I had to look for something new. That isn't easy any time. You just try it when you're new too in a city that's new to you. For that you have to have help so I tied the team in front of a saloon to go in and ask.

In the dim in there I drank a beer to take up a little time. You start asking questions in a hurry everybody freezes. "Nice town you got here," I said.

"It ain't exactly mine," the barkeeper said. "Those who do own it would rather you called it a city. Where you from?"

I told him Chicago. He said he'd been there and two of the six customers said so had they, and then all of us examined our beer wondering what we could say next. The barkeeper wiped the bar. I suppose that's why they call them barkeepers, they're always keeping their bars wiped.

"Hired a livery team and rig and been out since early this morning," I said, "just looking around." That made them all turn to glance out the door to see if it was so. When they turned back they looked me over with more interest which was what I was after. You can always count on a good team, they'll always do that for you.

"Looking special for something?"

"Well, yes. Whatever's new, I'd like to see, mostly. Things that never been done before, those are always exciting."

124

"Been down on River Street to see the girls? That's excitement."

"Naw, you heard the kid say something that's never been done before."

"Be new to him, I'll betcha."

They tried genuine to be a help to me, but like it so often is when somebody else tries to scratch where you itch, it wasn't too satisfactory. Somebody said I should go see the new opera house they were building, because it was going to have a thousand seats. They mentioned the new courthouse which wasn't even started yet and the new mansion Mr. Mitchell, the railroad millionaire, just moved into. I'd like to have seen that, like as not to help pay off the mortgage was where the nine hundred dollars Mr. Collins charged Pa for our boxcar went, but looking where money went isn't the way to replace it.

"Don't you have any brand-new business here, something just starting they don't do anywhere else in the country?" I asked.

"Like what?"

"I don't know like what, that's why I'm inquiring." There was a pretty long wait and to help it along I ordered beer for everybody. It cost me thirty-five cents and worried me. Pa expected expenses, that's what he gave me the twenty dollars for, but treating in a saloon with somebody else's money might be going a little far. I don't think it's embezzling, but I've heard tell it can start that way.

The beer and my buying it changed the talk away from buildings, anyhow. They picked up flour and iron. Milwaukee marketed more wheat and made more flour than anywhere. It was so important they had a factory right there that didn't make anything but millstones and shipped them all over the country and had railroad sidetracks right into the plant. Milwaukee made locomotives too, which was more than Chicago did, and had an ironworks that squeezed out railroad rails the same way saus-

125

age squeezes out of a press. You work it right, there's a lot more information in beer than in books.

I was about ready to leave to take a look at such wonderful goings-on and then my beer tasted bitter. Progress had gone so far, with sidetracks right into the plants, they didn't use any harness at all. Millions of tons of wheat and flour and millstones and rail iron moving in and moving out and not a farting horse in the whole process.

They changed from talking big business to stories about odd businesses. A fellow on Juneau Street who sold wooden shoes, a professor telling fortunes by reading the bumps on your head, how magnets built in a belt around the waist draw rheumatism right out of the joints. It made good listening, but mighty poor prospect for harness.

"By gosh, kid, you want to see something clever, come on next door, the guy has a patent on it and always tinkering around making it better yet. Ever see a machine that'll print type just by spelling out what you want and poking keys for the letters? That thing is going to have a real future." The man talking hadn't said much before. He was a loose-jointed roll-headed fellow who made me wonder how much alcohol there was in that beer, it dizzied me so to watch him. "I'll take you over there, I know him."

A machine to print type! I've watched printers. There's one across the street from our factory back home and he has to pick each letter out of a little cubbyhole and line it up in a little rack he holds in his other hand. Some of those letters aren't any bigger than pinheads and they're backwards and it's a slow miserable job. A machine that would do that, why, every printer would buy one. Think of the hauling!

"Let's go," I said.

"Wait a second," the barkeeper said, "you've got one coming on the house." I told him I didn't have time.

The place next door was a wonderful fine machine shop

126

with a treadle lathe and fine grindstones and all sorts of hand tools to shape and size things, just what you'd expect of an inventor. The fellow who'd brought me hollered around a little, but whoever was supposed to be there had gone out. "Here it is," he said, "this is Mr. Sholes's type writer."

It was a kind of box with a keyboard in front like a good accordion. Each key was a letter, as he said before. I saw it, but they weren't arranged a-b-c order. They were all mixed up without especially spelling anything, but among them was a sort of word I could read up near the top toward the left. If Q W E R T Y is a word I never heard it used or knew the meaning of it. The keys were on the ends of levers that ran back into a round wire cage. It had wheels and rollers on it no end and was a right well-made patent. "How's it work?" I asked.

"What's your name?" he asked.

I spelled it out. He took a finger and skipped all over poking keys down as fast as he could find them. Every time he poked, something inside whacked. Every key he poked down jumped right back up again. "There," he said and quit. I didn't see anything and told him so.

He grabbed hold of the paper and pulled it out which made a whirring sound in the gears. He showed it to me. It said:

```
EMIL ROHLAND
CHICAGO, ILLINOIS
```

"Gimme that paper," I said. Lord, it was nice, just like a calling card. Better than that, just like a handbill, my name in neat black letters all in a nice row I could save and use any time I needed style. "Put another paper in there," I said. "I want to see that again."

He rolled another paper in and after it set a second I

127

pulled it out and got that same businesslike *whirr* like he'd done. There wasn't anything on the paper. I asked him what happened to the type he'd set up.

"What do you mean?" He rolled his head at me.

"Why didn't it print?"

"Because you took the paper out."

"But it went through the machine, just like the first one, and nothing happened."

"Of course not, you didn't wait until I spelled it out again."

"But you did that before."

"Sure, and you got it in your hand. Now gimme the blank one and I'll put it back in and you wait until I write it out again."

"You mean it doesn't stay set up in type? You mean you have to poke all the keys all over again for every sheet you want?"

"Of course you do. What's wrong with that?"

"Well, it won't be very popular. What printer could use a thing that only gives one copy? Why, the littlest order they get, for invitations and such, they need anyhow forty or fifty copies."

"This isn't for printers, this type writer, it's for writing letters. Look, I'll show you again." He put another paper in it and poked all over the keys and stopped and hunted letters he couldn't find and was at it a considerable time. When he pulled it out, there was a letter all printed, right from the "Dear Sir" on down through the "Most Obedient Servant."

That disappointed me something awful. That machine cost anyhow twenty dollars, it was so complicated and made so precise, but who could afford that much for a clever toy? "How many of these has he sold?" I asked.

"Not any."

"I thought not."

"This maybe is his sixth machine. He hasn't tried to

sell any until he gets it foolproof. Then you just watch how fast they'll turn them out."

"Who'll want them?"

"Business and commerce. Neat letters anybody can read. This type writer will be a sensation. You mark my words. It'll revolutionize office work. Why, even a girl can be trained to operate one of these."

I guess he was a pretty good friend of the people working on that thing and was prejudiced. Letters in business, how much does that amount to? Pa's been making harness all his life and grew rich on it and our plant is respectable big and there's no letters to go out from one month to the next. Last I heard of a letter had to be sent was when Pa wrote back to Prussia for more harness makers to come over and even that could have been let go because he didn't get any.

I thanked the fellow kindly and left. There wasn't any use waiting for Mr. Sholes. I couldn't see as he'd have use for any of my harness.

Back at the livery stable I inquired how they were fixed. Darned if I didn't sell two sets without any argument or excuses or anything and got cash for them, which was sixty dollars.

8

Rudolph wasn't in his room to hear about my good luck at the livery stable. His bed had wrinkles and a sag in it from where he had been thinking. While I waited for him I put the day down in my journal, which took until ten minutes to seven. I went down to the dining room to look around for him, but he wasn't there and hadn't been, they told me. It smelled wonderful in there and I should have eaten without him I was so hungry, but I figured if I did that he might get back in the room and wait for me. He wasn't, though, so I waited up there for him. I did a lot of looking at my watch. It ticked all right, but wouldn't go ahead to speak of. I wound it, but it was wound and kept on acting like there was mucilage in it.

By and by I dug through our gear and found what was left of our box of lunch the milliners hadn't gone through, and came up with a bent and pretty dry sandwich which was the best I ever ate. I finished up Sarah's fudge too and was grateful for it, but rich and sweet and so much of it going down all at once in swallows like I'd ordinarily handle mashed potatoes didn't set so good. It didn't ache or get violent, but I could feel it pushed aside, sort of,

130

down there for a considerable wait whether it should go through or be sent back.

Rudolph came in at half-past eleven with powerful talk and a powerful breath. I tried to tell him I'd sold sixty dollars' worth of harness, but that wasn't anything compared to his excitement. He didn't even bother to listen, he just pushed his hand out even with his pants buttons to flatten me off for silence for his news. Milwaukee wasn't the place for us at all, he said he discovered, because Milwaukee had finished organizing and had settled down with everything fitting together too precise to leave room for new opportunity. Milwaukee was tamed, when what we needed was some place wild that we could help tame, and by God he'd found where that was. "The Chippewa Valley," he said.

"What's the Chippewa Valley?" I asked.

"It's five or six million acres, that's what it is, and most of those acres have at least four thousand board feet of white pine worth sixteen dollars a thousand. Pines two men can't get their arms around, growing so thick you can lay your hand against one and reach out and touch another without taking a step. They're sending out four hundred million board feet a year and they're just getting a good start. There's two men here in the hotel from up there, came down to buy a bigger steam engine for a new sawmill they're building. I went out for supper with them and between the bragging they did and the pumping I did that's where we're going next. We're leaving tomorrow. You know what? They're still using oxen in a lot of the lumber camps. That we got to change. Think of the market up there for harness."

I thought for a minute such talk was all whisky, it'll do that, but then I remembered that our getting to the logging business was exactly why Pa wanted us out while it was still winter. Rudolph was right, that's where we be-

131

longed, not here. My time was wasted with that beer and selling two measly sets of harness afterward looked pretty foolish compared with the prospects Rudolph lined up working with whisky.

The longer we stayed in Milwaukee the more time we'd be wasting, so first thing next morning we ordered our boxcar on to the Milwaukee & St. Paul, and moved out of the hotel and took a train for Eau Claire, which was practically a day's trip northwest across the state. That was a pretty good bite because the Milwaukee & St. Paul only went twenty-three miles past Eau Claire and stopped. The St. Paul part of their name was only bragging. They weren't there yet. Imagine a big railroad talking like a little kid does when you ask how old he is and he says he's seven going on eight.

Out of Milwaukee a half hour there were some right fine lakes on both sides, one after another, all with Indian names the people I asked could say easy enough but got kind of unsteady trying to spell for me, because they had so many odd-sounding syllables strung along it was hard to tell for sure when to stop. Indians don't give a hoot for spelling, or they wouldn't have peppered the country so full of knockdowns like Chenequa and Okauchee and Nogowicka and Oconomowoc. I looked sharp on all of the lakes I could see, but I didn't find the one where they were cutting ice like Mr. Schmidt said. That was odd because if they were doing anything like that they ought to be right next to the railroad. First the type writer and now the ice—things that sound so promising with beer sometimes don't seem to have any more body to them than the foam on the glass.

By the time we got to Portage, Rudolph said he'd had all the scenery he wanted and could make better use of his time finding Chippewa Valley people and getting them to talk. He didn't want me along.

At Portage we had to wait for the train from Madison

132

to make connections with us. I got out. At the depot, my watch was seven minutes fast, which was something an expensive railroad watch shouldn't ever do. It made me sick and worried that I'd been careless and let harm come to something that was so perfect when Pa gave it to me. I didn't know what I'd done to ruin in a week a watch that should have lasted twenty years. Less than that, it was hurt in the last hour because at Milwaukee I hadn't noticed anything wrong.

We crossed the Wisconsin River at Kilbourn. We were out of Kilbourn a ways winding through pine trees and rocky knobs with a peek at the river here and there, just enough to thrill but never enough to satisfy, when Rudolph came back to interrupt the view and order me to turn over the sixty dollars. Half an hour later he came back again for all the money I had left, which was twelve dollars and thirty-one cents. I'd used it pretty fast in Milwaukee for the livery and such out of the twenty Pa had started me off with. It puzzled me a minute why he needed it, but then I remembered we hadn't started any bookkeeping which is a necessary thing to do and here he was taking on all that tiresome job without bothering me.

"You want some help?" I asked.

"No, I guess not," he said, glancing at me kind of nervous, and then hurrying off again to his work. I could understand that, getting figures to balance is a touchy thing. Somebody just breathing over your shoulder can sometimes make you lose a dime it takes five minutes to go over the column to hunt it down again.

At Tomah we had to change trains. Before we pulled in, Rudolph came back sweating and white. "What's the matter," I said, "lose some money?"

"How'd you know?"

"I can see it on you're face. Don't worry, though, next time you sit down you'll see your mistake. How much are you off?"

133

He wouldn't tell me. "Are you sure you haven't got a dollar or two you forgot to give me?"

"No, I haven't got a cent."

"Can I borrow your watch?"

I didn't see how that could help balance his book. Besides, we were going to have pretty near an hour's wait at Tomah and I needed my watch to use that time to hunt up a jeweler to see why it was running fast.

At Tomah where I expected Rudolph to roam off finding things and people to interest him the way he likes to do, I couldn't get rid of him. I didn't feel like telling him I had let something terrible happen to that wonderful watch. He'd have chewed me out good and I'd have had it coming, but first I wanted to find out just what I'd done wrong so that I wouldn't do it again. He stuck to me as if he depended on me, which was an awful strange way for him to act. I had to tell him outright I didn't want him with me. He let me go then, but he looked downright uncomfortable to be left alone.

I found a jeweler. The clock in his window showed my watch eleven minutes fast, four worse than it was at Portage two hours before. A man came by. I asked him if the jeweler's clock was right. He took his own watch out and looked at it and said, "Yep." I had time and was going to go in to have the jeweler open it up and tell me what was wrong, but doggone, that costs money, and I hadn't asked Rudolph to give me mine back. By the time I got back to the depot and found him, there wasn't time left to go out there again and get the jeweler to look at it.

Something had taken the starch out of Rudolph. On the new train he sat there quiet with me, looking as glum as the landscape. That had been cut over and had lost its spirit too. Mile after mile there wasn't anything but big black stumps sticking out of the snow. Your eyes squinted for relief and there wasn't any. Snow and stumps stretched

134

across the flat places and down the valleys and up the hills until the sameness made you close your eyes to shut it out. Once in a great while there'd be a log cabin suffering lonesomeness so hard it seemed to make the train drag. The engineer did what he could, he'd whistle. Sometimes there'd be a man with a bucket he'd set down to wave back, the poor fellow.

The trainboy came through with a coffee pot and sandwiches. I didn't have time to eat at Tomah and Rudolph hadn't said whether he did or not. I was hungry. I asked Rudolph for my money.

"There ain't any money." He said it so painful I knew he was telling the truth. "Eighty-five dollars those sons-of-bitches took from me. Emil, we haven't got one nickel for a cup of coffee. We're strapped."

"You been robbed? What happened?"

"I been robbed all right, but that wasn't what happened. Couple of well-dressed, nice-talking fellows who said they owned a plow works in La Crosse got to discussing business with me. They had a bottle and a deck of cards. Now they got our eighty-five dollars, damn them, and just when I got on to the way their faces showed what they were holding—why the hell didn't you have another ten dollars? You must have been spending plenty reckless back there in Milwaukee."

He wouldn't talk any more. The trainboy came back. His coffee smelled so good my stomach rumbled like an empty barrel rolling on bumpy ground. I had to turn away and look out the window. It was getting to be that lifeless time when it isn't day any more and dusk comes soaking in to settle sadness all around. It's a discouraging, dying kind of time that takes the spice out of whatever you're doing and makes you think how old your pa and ma are, and how you haven't come up to what they had in mind you ought to be.

135

We were out of the stumps and in a worse dismalness where a fire had gone through the woods. All you could see in the gloomy twilight was a wilderness of naked tree trunks tangled together in the snow that tried to hide them. Big black sticks tilted every which way. In the distance they stretched on and on, but tiny and spindly and ever so tall and tapered. I wanted to shut my eyes, but the awfulnes of it wouldn't let me. Then all of a sudden in the middle distance there was a space. It led to a single dark pine tree, big and high, that hadn't been touched and had kept all of its crown and the snow that settled on it since the fire. It was a regular old Pa of a tree. After that a whole living forest came thick and spread toward our train. Next we were in it, flying past big healthy trunks and then the dark of the woods joined the dark of the dusk. A trainman came through and lit the lamps and I couldn't see out any more. Night is a wonderful relief.

Night also requires supper and a place to sleep. Those come easy when you're home where they're free, and you don't give them much of a thought either when you have the cash they take anywhere else. We were in a fine pickle of a state, speeding bankrupt into the wilderness. A couple of big businessmen with ideas for changing the logging trade from oxen to modern times and when we'd get there we'd have to beg at a barn for permission to sleep in the haymow. Rudolph dressed like the president of the railroad and the only supper we could afford depending on some kind lady handing us each a plate off her back stoop. It wasn't much to look forward to. The more I thought about it the more terrible it looked. I got good and scared. I got so scared I got mad. Red-hot mad.

"Listen you, Rudolph Rohland," I said, "you want to play games you do it from now on with checkers, not ten-dollar bills. Eighty-five dollars, and not yours in the first place, what's the big idea?"

"I feel worse about that than you do, so cut out your

136

complaining. It's gone and that's that. I don't want to be reminded of it.''

"You don't want to be reminded! That's two sets of harness gone I got to put in my journal because I sold them and how am I supposed to take care of that? I'm sure not going to put down what really happened, I'd be ashamed to, but darned if I'm going to blame Pa for it by charging it off to a short count in the car, either. You got me in a hole that worries me.''

"Forget it. Everything is a gamble. The only time there's anything wrong with gambling is when you lose. If my eighty-five dollars troubles you, look at the size of Pa's bet. Five thousand dollars he's gambling on that harness that it can find a market.''

"Pa isn't either gambling. He's counting on two of his sons.''

"I counted on two aces. They weren't big enough. Hell, Emil, big men play big, like I told you back there at the Plankington House, and you just got to get used to it.''

"Yeah. What we got to get used to is not eating and not sleeping. You played big all right.''

"Plenty more where that came from. We'll be all right as soon as we sell one or two sets, that's all it takes.''

"Maybe you forgot, but those harness are all in a box-car, and freight takes switching and waiting on sidings. The four days that'll take are going to be plenty long and hungry.''

Rudolph laughed. "You just leave that to me. We'll be quartered elegant and we'll never miss a meal. You worry about details too much.''

At Eau Claire there were sleighs at the depot like there always are with the drivers hollering the advantages of the hotels that sent them. Rudolph picked the best one and had me pile our luggage in just as though we were going to stay at that hotel. They don't charge for the ride but they expect you to patronize the hotel. I supposed we'd go in and wait until the sleigh left to go behind to the barn and then we'd sneak out again and stick them for the trip, but no, Rudolph marched right up to the clerk. My watch I noticed, was sixteen minutes ahead of the hotel clock.

"Your best room for me," he said, "and a small connected one for my man, if you please."

I'd forgot, but Rudolph hadn't. Good hotels don't ask for pay until the end of the week. Our being broke wouldn't show until Saturday, which was an arrangement to be mighty thankful for.

"Never mind that little second room," I told the clerk, "we're partners and we'll share one room, alike." Pa didn't tell me I had to be Rudolph's hired man.

Rudolph looked at me kind of different and let out a breath without using it.

"Well now," the clerk said, "I'm awfully sorry, but we're filled up tight. I haven't another bed in the house."

Rudolph jerked back glassy. "Where's the other hotel?"

We carried our grips to where he directed us, but they were full up too. So was another one and that was all the hotels. We inquired about boardinghouses. The second one of those we tried, the landlady had room, but when we said okay we'd stay she asked five dollars for the two of us for a week in advance, which was the style in Eau Claire.

I felt myself melting into my shoes, I was so embarrassed to have to tell her how we stood. She wouldn't see our side of it, I could see that. Like as not she'd say that's what she had in mind wanting her money right then and there. I didn't know how to go ahead or how to back out.

Rudolph fixed it. He asked to see the room. After we got up there he said it wouldn't do at all. She came down to four dollars, but that didn't help any, and we got out of there.

Those grips got awfully heavy no matter how often we changed hands. It was a lot colder than Milwaukee too.

138

We came to a big sawmill sprawling dark all over the premises with light in one big sort of a shanty a little ways off from the rest of the sheds and lumber piles and sawdust.

"Look," Rudolph said, "that plant has its own bunkhouse. If we can get jobs, they'll put us up."

We went in and found a foreman. Sure, he said, he needed help. He looked us over. "You," he said with his eyes on me, "I'll take." He looked at Rudolph's clothes and the way he kept his beard. "Got nothing for you."

"You take it," Rudolph told me. "I'll hunt you up about noon."

"You go try and find the preacher here," I whispered to him. "That's his job to help out the needy."

Rudolph snorted as if I'd asked him to trade his pants for a petticoat. He went off into the night.

It was too late for supper and too early for bed. That big old barn of a place fed and slept a lot of men, but most of them right then had gone uptown and there was only a handful around reading or playing checkers or sewing on buttons. A big lumpy-fingered man sewing on buttons sure looks out of place at such work. It's like belting up a flywheel to turn a screwdriver. The foreman showed me my bunk. I puttered around a little and then crawled in, but I couldn't get sleepy or even comfortable wondering about Rudolph. When I wasn't churning my belly was. By ten o'clock the bunks had filled up and the last lamp blown out. I slept some and woke up a lot and just when I was sleeping real good somebody hammered a gong and yelled and stretched it out long, "Five o'clo-o-ock. Breakfast."

We had a breakfast worth getting up for. Pancakes and fried pork and eggs and fried potatoes and doughnuts and bread and butter and coffee and prunes. There was a sign up, No Talking at the Table, which I wondered about,

139

but was glad to obey. I ate until it hurt me to breathe. It was wonderful. After breakfast there wasn't anything to do except sit around and yawn and let the wind out of all that eating, and wait for six o'clock starting time. When the whistle blew my watch was still sixteen minutes fast. It hadn't gained a bit overnight.

My job was in the engine shack helping a fellow named Ole run the steam engine. He looked at the gauges and blew the whistle and listened how she was running and walked around with the oilcan. All I had to do was keep the fire from going out which is harder than it sounds. Fire is crazy stuff that always acts contrary. Out on the loose you can't stop it, but in a firebox it takes all you've got to keep it going. I pretty quick got a different idea of steam from the respect Pa holds for it. Sure it's powerful, but the work I had to do pitching those heavy slabs in would saw a few boards too without any steam at all.

In a little it got light. In between pitching I had a chance to look out and see what Eau Claire was like. It was hilly and rivery and steamy and loggy. Log piles and lumber piles and sawdust piles helter-skeltered all over the place. Houses and sleigh tracks and trees and bridges and wide bare places mixed themselves together ever so careless. It was a man's city, you could see that. It didn't have any more order than bachelor quarters.

About a block away a blacksmith was just swinging his doors open. I'd noticed before he had some wheels on axles standing upright in his side yard and a sleigh with a built-up box on it, but half far away like that I didn't at first catch their size. Those wheels came up to the eaves. The blacksmith walked in front of them. The hubs were as high as his head. When he crossed in front of the sleigh, the runners were two strides apart and the box went up I'll bet three feet above his head. I'd like to see the wagon those wheels were for and the man who could use that

140

sleigh. I planned to get over there for a close look as soon as I could. I also planned to be on guard around that crazy blacksmith.

I got a kick in the pants. It was Ole. The steam was going down. Next time I had it up and there was time again I asked Ole what nature of man that blacksmith was. Ole said it wasn't the blacksmith. Those were special gear for a special man. He knew I was a greenhorn in that country and spun a yarn about a lumberjack who was eighteen foot tall and had habits in proportion and those things were made for him. The giant owned a big ox that worked winter and summer pulling those rigs—an ox that had a distance between his eyes the length of an ax handle. It was a regular old Jack-in-the-Beanstalk kind of a story Ole took pride in, but he didn't need to lay it on like that. The plain truth about that sleigh and those wheels couldn't help but be a pretty good story by itself, it seemed to me. That's the trouble so often, somebody has something wonderful interesting he sets out to improve and first thing he's spoiled it.

When Ole sent me off to the boarding shack to eat dinner and hurry back, Rudolph was waiting. He hadn't missed any breakfast or sleep. He hadn't slept in his clothes either. He was spick and span, and it must have been after dinner for him because he had a prosperous cigar started.

"Found out a lot about this town," he said, "and what's going on up in this Chippewa Valley. Boy, this is really new country, everything is bustle and expansion. Our harness is going to make us rich."

"You got a place to stay?"

"Sure. Right off. Thought of my railroad passes and found a pawn shop. He loaned me eight dollars on them, and in a week my loan is due, which will be ten dollars, but by that time we'll have our car, and cash from what we've

141

sold, and we'll be on our feet again. I'm in a boarding-house now, but as soon as there is a room I'll be in the hotel, that big first one we went to."

I didn't have time to talk and eat too, but I took a minute to point out and ask him if he'd looked at those roof-high wheels and that sled.

"They use them in the woods."

"Regular? All the time?"

"Sure."

"They got railroad engines to pull them?"

"No, just oxen or horses, whichever they have."

"Well, then, we might just as well go back home. Gear that size, those brewery horses in Milwaukee would be too puny. Our harness is going to be too little again."

"Quit your worrying. I never saw a kid such a worrier as you are. You keep that up the place for you is in your own one-man shop like Pa started out, where you're safe from seeing anything new. Ordinary horses handle those wheels, they aren't part of a wagon, and that sled they put two teams on, maybe three, all the more market for harness. I'll let you know when our car gets in, then you can quit here."

It took five days. The pay was a dollar-and-a-half a day, and they took out fifty cents a day for my board and bunk. They didn't give me my money though, it was just a piece of paper that said it could be exchanged for five dollars on the first of July. I asked how come and was told as long as they wouldn't get their money until then it was up to me to wait too or take it up town to a saloon or a store or any place, and I'd get four dollars in trade any time I wanted it.

My watch was still sixteen minutes fast, you don't go changing a railroad watch yourself, so the store I looked up was a jeweler. He complimented me for having such a watch, and said it was the best in the trade. I told him how

142

I'd got it from Pa who was also the best in the trade, and I wanted things right and that's why I came to him. He asked how fast it gained.

"That's the funny part of it, it gained all sixteen minutes in one day and has been holding steady since."

"Where you from?"

"Chicago."

"That's your trouble. It was the train ride."

"It gains when it's on a train and runs perfect everywhere else? That's a dickens of a habit for a railroad watch to get. Can you fix it?"

"Depends whether you stay here or travel around. It'll gain going west and lose going east. If you're going to be here a while, I can set it to Eau Claire time, and you'll be all right. There's nothing wrong with your watch, but you don't want Eau Claire time if you're going back to Chicago. North and south it doesn't matter, but every place east and west has a different time. Your watch right now has perfect Chicago time, just the way you started with it."

"What kind of a troublesome system is that to tangle people up? They better do something to straighten it out."

"Can't. It's nature. The world is a ball, you know that. When the sun is exactly over a north-and-south line from you it's noon wherever you happen to be. In Chicago that's fifteen minutes and forty seconds before it happens here, and when you bring Chicago time here to Eau Claire, you're that much fast. If you're traveling much you'll always be wrong. How do you want it?"

I told him to give it back to me the way it was. It would be nice to look at those hands and know I was on the same time with Pa no matter what it was all around me. It was a connection I wanted to keep.

That jeweler was a fine man to tell me all that knowledge. He didn't charge me anything when he could have taken

143

the whole four dollars for resetting it and acting like it was something serious. I'd have never known the difference. I asked him how the railroad men handled such a complicated business when every town had a different time.

"It's a mess," he said. "I don't know how they keep it straight. I hear there's thirty-five different correct times used across Wisconsin. They must have it worked out on a chart they memorize or tuck in their watch pocket showing how many minutes and seconds local time at each station is ahead or behind the time they carry along from the division point where they headquarter. Then they must add or subtract in their heads every time they pull into a station to tell them whether they're on time or not."

"Why don't they just have every station clock carry headquarter time? Then all their time could be the same."

"Sure, and have local people depending on their local time miss the train thinking they had three or four minutes to spare? That's no good. I told you it was complicated."

It sure was. I left it to them to figure out. I knew my watch was as good as Pa meant it to be and that satisfied me. I wasn't going to worry about railroad troubles, the ones in the harness business are bad enough.

I moved into the hotel with Rudolph. He had a lot of work lined up which he divided into big business he'd handle and little business for me. Big business was to go to the men who owned the sawmills and the lumber camps and the landholdings and the booms where they sorted out whose logs were whose. Those fellows, he figured, should buy harness by the gross and they were the ones he was after. My job was to go to the stables behind the stores, and visit the preachers, and hunt out the doctors, and all such people with single teams. That looked fair enough to me even if his part sounded more adventuresome and exciting. At least I didn't have to be his servant any more

144

and had my own territory where I could be boss. That was a wonderful improvement.

I did like Pa said for selling single customers, I put on a full load of harness and piled the bags high in the box sleigh I'd hired, and laid one open and spread it out over the top to show off what I had. I was going to replace the harness the livery team came with and put ours on for demonstration, but they were such poorly made miserable-looking leather, I left it be to argue against itself. That was contrary to the way Pa had said, but he also said I should get new ideas. It made me feel so good I didn't feel a bit like I'd been worrying I would ever since South Water Street. Selling, it seemed to me right then was the same as wheelbarrowing to the manure pile, sometimes there's a load and sometimes there isn't. You keep sweeping and shoveling, you can't help but come up with something. Besides, I already had sold harness without hardly thinking about it, back there at the livery in Milwaukee. The first time is always the hardest, and that was behind almost before I'd noticed what I'd done.

Just the same it was a little hard to say whoa in front of the gristmill and get off for business without being sure how I should start. A lot of teams were there waiting their turn. They had all kinds of time to inspect my sample set. It gave them something new to talk about. I had five or six around me right away. All of a sudden with so many of them standing and looking at me waiting expectant-like for my performance to begin I felt foolish and out of place to be bragging up my own goods. It didn't seem necessary or good taste to stand over Pa's product and make claims as if it had to be forced on people like patent medicine.

But they expected so hard, those fellows. Hungry to hear practically anything. Attention for anything I wanted to say, and I was letting it slip away no better than Rudolph with our eighty-five dollars. Eyes that should have been

145

helping fingers were magnetized on me—a farmer closing his coat got it cross-buttoned to hang like a barn door on one hinge. Aside him a mouthful of tobacco had stopped chewing to hear better. Not tended to, it trickled. A big nose on another face hung sad and discouraged that so many smells have to be stinks. The crowd had a blinker too, overworking his winks instead of letting them come natural. There was also a new hat floating around wherever the man underneath walked, but the blend between hat and man was missing. You thought hat, or you thought man, but you couldn't quite get the combination to team. It was a good hat. The man was handsome. The fit was fine. I don't know what was wrong.

I also didn't know what was wrong with me, why I couldn't start. I thought of Pa, and my feet standing apart and supported so solid on Rohland workmanship. By God, me and that harness weren't going to be like that man and that hat. I started, but it wasn't selling. I just talked about harness, the right way to hang it in the barn, what hurts leather and what's good for it, how to clean it, how often to oil it, the places to look for in getting a good fit, differences in builds of horses and how to make them comfortable, where the pull and strain is heaviest, and just about everything I know, I guess.

I didn't have to sell anything. They came up and asked where I was from, and fingered the harness and peeked in the bags, and showed each other the stitching, and argued how long it would take a harness maker to make what was in the wagon now with no waiting and edged around to ask what my price was.

"Would ten dollars a set cheaper than you can get them from any harness maker in town be all right?" I didn't know what that would come to, but figured they would. Whatever it was would still be a profit.

The man with the unsettled hat didn't have any such trouble underneath it. He said, Hell, that was right fair

146

and he was taking a set. He opened half a dozen sacks to make up his mind which to take. I sold one other set too, to the farmer whose overcoat was buttoned kitty-corner. He handed over two twenty-dollar bills which were wonderful to see and asked for four dollars' change. Lucky I had the order on the sawmill for five, which was worth four. He took it and seemed satisfied. So was I, that was six dollars a set better price than the livery in Milwaukee had paid. I liked Eau Claire, it was a fine city.

The hat man found the set he had decided on. "Scrip all right?"

He handed me an order made out like mine from the sawmill, but instead of a company, it was on Chippewa County, which was just north of us. A county is government the same as the United States. Greenbacks are only orders too, come right down to it.

"Sure," I said. "But I've lost twenty per cent already on a five-dollar sawmill order I had which I can't blame you for. If I can take ten per cent off on your county scrip, it's a deal." I felt a little crooked saying that, a county is sure a lot more reliable than a sawmill, but when you're supposed to be paid five dollars and then only get four it makes you mad and you try overhard to get it back.

"By God, kid, I like your spunk. If you say so, that's what it will be. Tell you what, I've got three teams I'll be working mighty hard this spring and I don't want to lose time repairing old harness. I'll take three sets."

Two others were interested too, but didn't have enough money with them and asked if I'd be around awhile and would drive out to their places in a week or two.

It went good all day. I drove from one place to another. Every so often I'd sell a set or a single, but the best of all was to circle back to the gristmill and to the blacksmith every two hours or so to catch the changes in who was waiting. It was fun the way they must have talked my stock over while I was gone because by the time I'd get

147

back the new ones were downright eager to inspect my goods. Once I had to go back to the boxcar to add more sacks to keep the load looking full.

By dark I'd got rid of thirteen sets. I had a hundred and twelve dollars in cash, ninety in sawmill orders, and three hundred and twelve in county scrip. That country seemed awfully shy of ready money. Lacking it didn't seem to hold anything back, though: the sawmills whined steady, the trains hauled out big loads and unloaded other stuff all day long, there was draying all over the place which is the best sign of good business, and the hotels were crowded. It just goes to show that people who trust each other can use anything they agree on for money. I suppose even sawdust would work. What money is doesn't matter a bit, it just has to mean the same thing to everybody.

I felt tired and wonderful good. Rudolph felt better yet. "I've been studying this country ever since we got here," he said, "finding out who the big men are, how they operate and what they're planning next. That's hard to do. It takes time. It means talking with workmen, and men standing in the saloons, with the depot agent, the hotel owners, the county treasurer, and hanging around the land office. I put this and that of what I hear together and now I've got it."

"What have you got?"

"There's a Pine Ring who run everything. They control the timberland and the sawmills, and even have a majority on all the county boards around here to vote exactly what they want." His eyes sparked above his beard as if he was happy that things were like that.

"My gosh," I said, "I knew that the second night I was in the bunkhouse. How many harness you sell today?"

"That isn't the point. Key man for the whole Chippewa Valley, I found out today, is a fellow named Roger Roberts. He's a clerk in the land office here."

148

"How much harness would he be good for?"

"Probably not any, directly. But he'd be the man who could tip me off where the next developments will be and who will run them. Then I move in for their harness needs. Going to find out all I can, next day or so, about Mr. Roger Roberts and then meet him and get him off for a few drinks to make him friendly."

Next morning I dropped in at the bank as soon as it opened to have them make out a cheque I could send to Pa. They discounted the sawmill orders twenty per cent like I knew they would, but the county ones they knocked off a whopping forty per cent. No wonder I had so much of that paper. I'd been giving a lot better bargain on our harness than I intended or needed to.

"Why do those orders say one amount and pay a different one?" I asked. "If I owe a man a dollar he's going to get a dollar, not eighty cents or sixty cents. Why don't they make out those orders for what they really mean and be done with it and not mix people up so?"

The banker pulled his mustache. He pulled only the left side of it which must have been a pretty regular habit. He'd got himself so his right side didn't match any more, the left was stretched and polished so bright from handling. "The orders are generally good for the full amount if you can wait until the due date. If you can't, somebody has to advance cash, and you have to pay for that service with the discount."

"Why then are the counties discounted more than the sawmills?"

"Because the counties manage their affairs so poorly. They don't collect their taxes businesslike and they let their contracts for courthouses and roads on bids that are too high. When these papers come due, there might not be enough to pay them in full."

The check I sent Pa was a lot smaller than I'd have liked on account of those terrible discounts and because I had to

149

hold out cash for our expenses. What I sent Pa came to twenty-one dollars a double set, which was so dirt-cheap it was awful. But even at such a crazy price, Pa would get his investment back ten times over when we got rid of all of them. I didn't know whether I should be ashamed or proud.

An idea came butterflying through my head, but wouldn't quite light. Those orders were a kind of paper money. The sawmills and counties used them for money when they didn't have real money on hand. Why didn't they do like business in Chicago does, borrow it and pay interest? I remember Pa saying money is easy now, only seven per cent. That was it, that seven per cent. If they borrow it, they have to pay it. But if they put out orders instead of paying money, they get by without interest. Why, those smart, scheming scoundrels, they were using their help double, once to do the work and once to put up the money they operated with. The workmen, instead of getting interest, had to accept discounts that are downright usury.

I was a fool to cash in that paper. Pa's got a good big bank account. He doesn't need spot cash. I should have sent that paper directly to him and let him hold it the few months until it was due. Twenty per cent for five months, at that rate holding the orders would be just as important as selling the harness.

9

From then on I changed my policy. I still took orders in trade, but I discounted them the same rate as the bank did. It didn't cut down my sales hardly at all because that harness was still a good bargain and a bargain is prized anywhere. After a few weeks though, it began to be the same people coming back to the gristmill and blacksmith again and I'd been all over Eau Claire and worked the country around it some. Most of the men who'd wave to me from a load, or whoa to talk a little, held Rohland lines in their hands which was satisfying to see. It made it darned hard to find new customers, though.

Then one night after a day when I worked the hardest of all and sold only two sets Rudolph was stomping impatient around the hotel lobby waiting for me. "Thought you'd never get in."

He had a fire and confidence to him exciting to see. "Finally got that Roger Roberts to open up. Worth all the work and waiting. Now let's get a quick supper and go up to the room where we'll be private. Won't dare tell a thing until we're alone."

I edged around to catch his breath. What he was saying

was genuine, there wasn't anything on it but onions and cigars. All that excitement cold sober, well, I didn't notice what I ate for supper.

"We're moving," he said. "Right quick, too. We're making an inspection way up the Chippewa Valley. How much harness left in that car?"

"Maybe five hundred sets. Why?"

"Don't sell another one."

"My gosh, did you—?"

He grinned like Pa did giving me my watch. I never saw him so happy. "That's all, now. I tell you I won't say another word until we get up in our own room."

Up there he laid down on the bed and stretched out and worked a couple of fingers lazy-like through his beard to explore his face for itches. It was a natural thing to do. An itch you bring out patrolling around relaxed like that is a pleasure to take care of. It's a kind of insurance against emergency scratching in public. That was all right and a necessary thing to do for a fellow who goes so strong for appearance, but I didn't feel it was worth rushing through a good supper and neglecting it just to hurry up there to watch him scratch.

"All that hinting before supper, you couldn't hold yourself," I said. "Well, now we're alone. What's up?"

"Roger Roberts. The Pine Ring. I told you how it's all one clique from timber cruising to settling the stump land with farmers. You know who's just today got himself into the Ring? Me." He got up to comb out his beard. Half the time he looked into the mirror to admire their choice and the rest of the time he made main ideas more important by waving the comb. "Roberts has all the Government survey notes for the whole Chippewa Valley in his land office. It's his say who looks at them and who can't. Anybody who wants to buy Government land has to get it from him. Now the Pine Ring, as soon as it lumbers off one good part and needs another, Roberts hauls out his surveys that show which sections have the best pine and are close to the good rivers and they pick out what they want and he sells it to them. All they need to buy is a little in the middle. You see, Roberts is also the government agent to prevent logging trespass, but he can't be in two places at once so they log off all around what they've bought."

"He told you that himself?"

"Of course not; that's the talk in the saloons, but it's true just the same. You'll see as I go on."

"Why, that's just like that Communist back in the Government warehouse in Chicago said. Why, that's giving away Government property."

"So? Well Congress wants it that way. Look at the land grants they give the railroads. And to the colleges. Why, Cornell University way off in New York owns half a million acres of the finest timber spank up the middle of the Chippewa Valley. Anyhow, it's all mixed up, lots of the Valley is still Government land, lots of it the Pine Ring owns direct, and big chunks are owned by dozens of speculators. Many little pieces belong to settlers, though, and more and more of them are coming in all the time. They need roads and schools. This is the part Roberts and I had a long talk about. This is the part where Rohland harness comes in.

"What is the first thing you need," he went on, "to change primitive land to civilized land? You need roads, that's what you need. Roads bring people in and take products out. Back home in Illinois, a road comes easy, you just run it across the land. Up here in the Valley it doesn't come that easy, the timber is even in the way of the loggers. They need roads. After the timber is logged off the settlers need roads. The Ring is going to cut those roads through. Roberts is going to tell from his Government surveys where the best pine lands are, it doesn't matter who owns them. It'll take a whole new company, and I'm selling them the harness it takes."

"You been working on this three weeks," I said.

153

"You've had time to study this out. I don't get it the first time through. I never heard of building roads as a business anybody made money at."

"Emil, it's a dandy, the way we're going at it. It's a way for the Pine Ring to get free timber anywhere they want it and get it legally. Roberts had it in mind for a couple years, and I've sparked him into getting it organized. Here's the way it'll work. When the land was surveyed and laid out in sections, each section became a square a mile long on each side. It's right in the law that roads four rods wide are supposed to be run along the section lines any time they are needed. It's also in the law that the timber in the road belongs to whoever puts the road through. It's part of his pay for benefiting the land. Now then who's got the authority to order those roads built? The town boards. Practically all of the town boards in the whole Chippewa Valley are men owned by the Pine Ring."

Rudolph took a deep breath. "Naturally the roads they'll order put through will be where the pine is most valuable. Clear it off and that's the road. Besides the timber, the contract with the town also pays five dollars a rod for the improvement, that's an extra sixteen hundred dollars a mile and there's five or ten thousand miles that can be worked like that. No bridges or grading at all. When they pull the log sleighs through that's proof it's an open and usable road. It'll take fast modern equipment because there's so much distance to cover and get it done before tax time a year from now. That means horses instead of oxen and every single harness will come through me."

"Why, that's downright crooked. We don't need that kind of business. Our harness is going fine. All it takes is a little work. Why don't you forget about such stuff and come out with me tomorrow and help me look up new territory and find out for yourself how nice it goes?"

"What do you call this plan, if it isn't new territory?

And it's not crooked, what do you think I am? It's helping develop this country. It takes initiative and spirit and forcefulness. Somebody has to do it. Common people never will, that's why they're common. Look at the railroads, they call them crooked too, but think of the good they do. This is big, you keep forgetting that. You don't handle million-dollar operations with Sunday school rules."

"Pa would."

"Oh, would he? Did the War Department advertise the harness he bought for open auction? They could have got ten dollars or more a set that way. No, sir, Pa looked up a colonel and a congressman and slipped his deal through the back door of Grant's Cabinet. Sure it helps the country, but it helps Pa first. You don't call Pa crooked, do you? Well then, trust my judgment a little too."

We hired a good team and a light sleigh and told the livery we wouldn't be back for maybe two weeks. We took our luggage and stuff, but none of our harness bags, Rudolph wouldn't have it. "We're going to visit lumber camps and sawmills and look at that timber. A big supplier like I'll be has to know those things first hand. I'm no peddler," he said. "I'm looking over an industry. Appraising its resources. Reviewing its methods. We don't need any harness along."

We took a set along just the same and he couldn't do a thing about it. They were on the team we rented. I had sold them to the livery the week before.

We followed the Chippewa River to the north on a surprisingly good road with a telegraph line running alongside. Cutters and light sleighs and heavy-loaded bobsleds came and went in both directions so frequent it surprised me until I remembered Chippewa Falls was up ahead fifteen miles and was a big place too. There wasn't any railroad to Chippewa Falls. Everything to or from there had to come over the road we were on. We got there in

155

about two and a half hours, which was a little faster than a team should be pushed, but we were traveling light and Rudolph was in a hurry. "We want to inspect that sawmill up there."

"I been in a sawmill. Five days of it."

"You can't see a sawmill by working in it. What did you learn from it?"

Rudolph was right. I hadn't seen anything except the slabs I threw and the roaring fire I pitched them at, and Ole hollering for steam. "You had plenty of time," I said, "why didn't you see what you wanted to at the mills in Eau Claire?"

"Because the one at Chippewa Falls is bigger and turns out more and is the most up-to-date sawmill in the world. Why waste time on anything short of the best? How can I tell what's a new idea and what isn't unless I go where the latest improvements are?"

Chippewa Falls was just like Eau Claire without a railroad. They had a new courthouse which wasn't paid for; I had some of the paper out on it. Back in Eau Claire I heard there was a water closet in it cost ten thousand dollars so the county board wouldn't have to drop their breeches out in the cold. I wanted to see if it was any better than ours at home, but Rudolph wouldn't let me drive up there, he was all hot about that sawmill.

His clothes got us right into the superintendent, who took us personal through the plant. We started in the enginehouse. They had a man to watch the steam just like Ole did, and they had a man responsible for keeping the fire hot just like I had to, but he didn't have to pitch slabs. He didn't have practically anything to do. That boiler fired on sawdust carried automatic all the way from the saws. The superintendent was so proud of that patent he must have been an old fire feeder himself. I knew just how he felt. They had so much steam they ran the extra into the log pond to keep it open all winter.

156

He must have been an old hand at every job they had in the whole mill, he was so quick to point out the improvements. That man was downright improvement-crazy. He showed us how quick the carriage shot the log back for the next run through the saw, that was twice as fast as last year, he said, and cost them a fortune. "We'll gladly pay a thousand dollars for every ten cents we can save on a thousand board feet," he said. "We'd get it back in a hurry because we turn out two million board feet every week."

Rudolph's forehead wrinkled upward. It surprised him as much as me to learn what a high-paying business inventing for a sawmill amounts to. If I wasn't committed to the harness trade, I think I might look into it.

The logs they were sawing were beautiful, straight and even and three foot across. One circle saw wasn't big enough to go through them so they had two, the smaller one above lined up to make exactly the same cut on top as the main one below. Together they sliced those logs into planks and boards something perfect. Every little while they'd whine coarse and shoot off sparks where gravel had got into the bark. It wasn't dangerous for fire, the wood was too wet, the superintendent said afterwards, he couldn't holler loud enough in there, but it was a worry the saw would rupture. It also was the reason they had to be sharpened so often.

You could see all over why it was the foremost sawmill in the world. There wasn't anything I guess, they hadn't thought to have steam power do. Once the logs got in there, power moved them along, turned them over for fresh cuts, sent the boards through smaller edging saws, ran the scrap side pieces into lath and carried the finished products one way and the waste another, and all the workmen had to handle were the levers. They went along for weeks at a time without so much as a sliver in a little finger.

"This is a lot different from what it used to be," the

superintendent said, holding up a hand with the thumb gone. "Sign of a shingle maker. Our new machine turns out six thousand shingles an hour without anybody having to get closer than six feet from the knives."

It wasn't just one sawmill. Really it was a row of sawmills aside each other under one roof, the plant was so big. They had one room keeping busy filing circle saws of all sizes. Up close to the big ones you could see how big they really were, four or five feet across and half an inch thick. When the filer cut across the edge of a tooth it would ring like a church bell.

The superintendent changed his smile to a troubled look. He put the thumb and forefinger of his good hand to a tooth on the big saw to show how thick it was. "These fellows are our hogs. Every bite they make is a board half an inch thick chewed up into sawdust. For every four planks we get, the saw gets one. Inch boards, every two that go to the lumber pile, one more is sawdust. It averages out every fourth log belongs to the saw. To get the lumber there is in three trees, four have to be cut down. Every forty acres logged off, ten acres are eaten up by hogs like this. Lad—" he put his crippled hand around my shoulder—"there's a problem and I wouldn't be fair just showing you the things we're successful at."

A man treats you decent like that, you try your hardest to help. I would have spoken right up advising them to buy thinner saws, but it seemed to me anybody would think that way and there was probably mighty good reason why it couldn't be done. Maybe they could slice instead of saw, a cheese knife for instance doesn't make any cheese dust. I didn't say it, though, he was too smart to have missed any easy way.

All the lumber was carried by rollers out to a big shed without any sides. There were men all over that place. Where the automatic machinery ended it was surprising how much back and arm and leg work it took in manpower just to take care of the lumber brought there by steam

158

power. They didn't just pile it up, they laid it crisscross in cribs twenty boards high or so snugged up tight, and snaked them down with tandem teams to a low yard stretching acres and acres along the Chippewa River. Next spring the high water would come up, the superintendent explained, and float them. River drivers would string them together into rafts and float them down the Chippewa, down the Mississippi, to Davenport and Rock Island and to St. Louis.

"Last year," he said, "one of our rafts carried two and a half million board feet. It was four acres when it was assembled out on the Mississippi, enough lumber to build a respectable village. Makes a person sick, though, to think that the sawdust from it would have been another raft an acre and a quarter big. Sawdust. Ghost lumber I call it, with its dead dust stealing a quarter of the timberland, stealing a quarter of every man's work from camp cookee to head sawyer here, stealing a quarter of the price every Kansas farmer has to pay for his barn. It's a hell of a way for me to wind up your visit to the finest lumber mill in the world, but it's the truth."

Rudolph and I drove away from there silent for quite a piece. After a while Rudolph couldn't stand it and swore. "That superintendent makes me mad, running down the lumber industry that pays him. We got scrap leather at the Rohland works too, but I'd be dead before I'd complain about it to a stranger. The damn fool, if there wasn't sawdust there wouldn't be lumber."

"That wasn't his point, you missed it altogether. It's improvement he wants, and ideas. Maybe some stranger with a smart head can help and besides, that's just what you said this trip is for, reviewing the methods. Seems to me we got a dandy from him to review. Twenty-five per cent more lumber would be twenty-five per cent more hauling which would be a pretty good boost even for Rohland harness. Your Pine Ring going to do that for us?"

"How the hell do I know? Everything is a gamble, Emil,

I told you and told you. Pa is only going to be part satisfied for us to sell our harness a set or two at a time. That could be done easier than you're doing it, right in Chicago. What he wants most, what I want to give him, is business he never thought of.''

We stayed at Chippewa Falls that night. It was too late in the afternoon to continue up the valley.

Next morning was gray and dull, one of those days that doesn't want to get on with itself and nine o'clock isn't any brighter than seven. They come like that ever so often to give lie-abeds a chance to feel they're early once in a while too. We set out up along the river again, this time really toward the wilderness. North of Chippewa Falls there isn't a village for a hundred fifty or two hundred miles until you get to Lake Superior. There's exciting names on the map just the same, the rivers where the timber is. The main Chippewa River, which farther up splits to a West Branch and an East Branch, the Thornapple, the Jump, the Flambeau, which splits also to a North Fork and a South Fork. That's what makes the Chippewa Valley so valuable, along with the timber there always are good rivers to take it out.

I always had the idea a lumber camp was sort of an outpost and once the winter set in they had to get along by themselves without word or outside help until spring. It wasn't that way at all. The supply road we took was a hard-used highway with smooth, thick-packed snow tramped practically into ice. Bobsleds used it to take grain and hay in, and loads of strap iron and bars and shoe metal and hardware for the camp blacksmiths. Traveling light like we were, we passed a lot of them. Other loads were all grub, quarters of beef, bags of beans, boxes of prunes, barrels of flour and sugar and pork. Chopping down trees takes plenty of food. There were other fast rigs like ours too, people from upriver having business at the county seat, owners visiting their camps. There was

160

even a stage. Nobody was cut off, mail and newspapers went right along with the rest of the traffic. Almost every load had an extra rider or two of men or boys going both ways from the camps. I guess they didn't stay put anything like I thought they did. It was mighty good harness territory, and we didn't have a single set along we could sell.

We headed for the junction of the Flambeau with the Chippewa about twenty-five miles upriver from Chippewa Falls. Just about all the trip was stump country. There were nice patches of good-sized hardwood and enough evergreen left to keep it from being all bare. I asked Rudolph why they skipped them.

"Weed trees," he said. "The maple and oak sinks in the river, so there's no way of getting it to market. The evergreen is hemlock, slivery splintery stuff nobody would buy for lumber."

The stumps made me anxious to see the pine. Most of them were big enough to serve a picnic from if there hadn't been that backbone of splinters sticking up where the last of the trunk broke away.

In the middle of the afternoon it started to snow and got pretty. Big lazy flakes drifted down. They seemed to hush everything and take the hurry out of being alive. Some of the worry too, a nice quiet snow is so clean and innocent it whitewashes you too. I suppose that's why the best post cards for Christmas always show it snowing. One thing snow doesn't hush, though, is sleighbells. They seem to jingle a lot more noticeable in a snowstorm. The livery hadn't hung any yet on the new harness they got from me, and they don't ordinarily attach them to the tongue for a team like they do on the fills for a cutter. We were without bells ourselves, and I didn't particularly notice them on the other rigs before it started to snow, but once the snow came I kept hearing them all the time. Up ahead there'd be a faint ringing, but nothing in sight

161

through the snow. The bells would get a little stronger, and then maybe your eyes could pick out a filmy shape that would get clearer and darker while you came up on it. It would be a heavy-loaded bobsled to pass, its bells a jangling, black and clear, and driver smiling while you were opposite. When you pulled ahead it hardly took any distance at all to fade it into the snow again and disappear it, but you could hear the bells for a long time afterwards. Sleighbells are the nicest connection, and downright dependable, in a snowstorm.

After a while we were the only team on the road. We had passed everything that had started from Chippewa Falls the same day. We weren't meeting anything any more either, because people don't start on a long trip like that in the afternoon. It got dark. We lit the lantern and Rudolph held it in his lap. It got to be a little uneasy, a strange road and a destination we didn't know we could find and no telling how much snow there'd be. The horses picked up a little faster and turned off the road. Rudolph got down and walked ahead with the lantern. "It's a branch road. The horses seem to sense something. I think we better let them have their heads."

He climbed back on. The horses plodded ahead determined. In a little one of them whinnied. It wasn't but a little after that two squares of light showed up and got brighter and there we were, at a cookhouse with the lumberjacks just going in for supper. I've been around horses all my life and I still don't know how they do it. So far as I know that livery team from Eau Claire had never been up there before and yet they picked exactly the right turn-off. Maybe it's thinking. Whatever it is, Pa and us Rohlands have an everlasting good trade supplying smartness like that with the gear it works with.

I'll take a lumber camp every time over a hotel. A hotel calls you a guest, but you aren't, they charge you. A lumber camp puts up your team, sets you up to their table until you can't breathe for food, and gives you a bunk any time you feel like visiting. They're downright sociable all around and everything is free even if you load your plate three times at a sitting, but for big braggy talkers like they are the table rules are surprising. You can reach all you have a mind to, and take the last piece on the platter because they'll bring another platter anyhow, and pick up your meat to bite off a mouthful, and belch, and wipe your whiskers with your fingers, but you have to do it all in silence. It was just exactly like the sign at the sawmill where I boarded at Eau Claire, No TALKING AT THE TABLE.

That hit Rudolph a little unfair. For the kind of work he gets results with, such a sign padlocked his tool chest tight. Supper without words was tougher on him than supper without salt. He was hit and had to stand for it, but they really weren't aiming at him. There's Norwegians and Swedes and all kinds of foreigners pretty touchy against each other in a lumber camp. With Paris in the shape it is on account of Bismarck, and Germans and Frenchmen across the beans and doughnuts from each other, they have to have such rules because we're a neutral nation and choose to stay that way. It also helps the cook and his dishwashers keep from having to work half the night. As it is, they're the last ones to bed and the first to have to get up, anyhow.

In the bunkhouse after supper it was altogether different. There they took their conversation in portions as big as their food was a little while before. Those big men did everything big. Because it was snowing outside they hashed that over and then remembered record snows. One hairy-armed fellow locked his fingers across his knee and lied about a winter when it snowed blue. Could he ever lay it on. Everybody knew it was a yarn, that was the point of it. Then a thin preachery-looking one with deep-in eyes sang a solo about a girl whose lover pried out the key log in a jam, and all the logs above it clobbered him. She was the one who found his body later on one moonlight midnight and fell in trying to fish it out and drowned too. They all ached for her and enjoyed it so much he had to do the last verse over and over.

Once, when it dulled a little, I asked a question which is something a stranger should never do around a lumberjack, it seemed. They got more ways of avoiding a straight answer than a horse trader. Near the door somebody had leaned a long heavy pole with sort of a loose fishhook attached backwards near the end. I'd seen such a thing used to guide the logs into the mill at Chippewa Falls. I asked what they called it.

A fellow with blue-black hair and a red-checked shirt made out he didn't quite get my question and egged me on until I had to walk over and touch it which was just what he wanted because by that time the whole bunkhouse had hushed to watch me.

"Oh, that. Bring it here, will you? Nothing but a toothpick, lad. Belongs to a rather big fellow works with us. Say, Paul must still be out. Anybody seen Paul since it started to snow?" Two or three frowned and shook their heads.

"Well, that's common. Walks alone every time it snows hard, nothing to worry, sometimes he's gone days at a time. Paul was bothered considerable with tartar building up on the inside of his teeth. Couldn't find a tool anywhere that could touch it. Made this and it works like a charm. This business end goes into his mouth and rests on his lower teeth. He sets the hook—see how it's turned inside pointing at itself—he sets the hook under the tartar with his tongue, his teeth making a solid pivot he can rock on. He puts his hands out on the handle and pries down and, well, something has to give. The tartar plows off in chunks. Of course it leaves a lot of rough edges, but he fixes them easy enough. Rolls a grindstone in a bed of

164

wintergreen, pops it in his mouth, and moves it around considerable while he sucks and dissolves it.''

Everybody was watching me to see how I took it. If I swallowed it green, they'd be amused one way, if I got mad to be taken for a sucker, it would be even more fun for them. I had to think fast how to respond. As long as we'd be in that camp my reputation and my standing would depend on what I did next. I picked up the tool and gave it a good close inspection. I sort of set it up for the kind of pry he described. I discovered something.

''Mister,'' I said, ''that's a right good yarn, and I'd believe it except for one thing. The way this hook is attached it would catch him under the tongue, not the inside of his teeth. I think I know the party you refer to, though, isn't he the one owns the ox whose eyes are the length of an ax handle apart?''

Well sir, I couldn't have done better passing around a box of cigars. When lumberjacks laugh, it's like a locomotive laughing when the engineer throttles too fast and the puffs interrupt each other and the driver wheels slip. The whole bunkhouse shook. There was knee slapping, and faces turned orange, and eyes squinted shut and shoulders shaking. The blue-black one who'd tried to rib me roared as loud as anybody, which was good to see. You never know, he could have got mad just as easy.

After a bit when it calmed down again he dropped his mouth open and wiped winkers out of his eyes with one finger and said, ''Guess I can't hook you on that cant-hook story so I might as well tell you straight. This thing is called a cant hook. That's its name. The hook is for biting into a log to get a good solid hold on it, and the long handle is to give the leverage. Anything else you ever want to know around here you just ask. If anybody tries to spoof you again, I'll leave calk holes all over his ass.''

Next morning I didn't have a thing to do which is a

165

pretty wonderful way to visit a lumber camp. Rudolph hung around the superintendent like he did the night before while I was with the fun in the bunkhouse, so I had nobody to bother me. I could walk and look wherever I wanted to.

When it got daylight the snow had stopped. It was clear and cold and quiet and none of the shapes or colors or sounds oozed into each other like they do when haze or unsettled weather ruins the edges of things. The camp was downright peaceful with snow on the two big buildings we ate and slept in, and on the barn and all the smaller ones like the blacksmith and carpenter shops. Smoke came straight up from the cooking shanty and didn't dissolve into air, but stayed sharp blue. The blacksmith was shoeing an ox. The steam from its nostrils came out in two sharp plumes that traveled a couple feet before they disappeared. The ring of the hammer on the anvil was a sharp, solid thing like any other object with weight and body to it.

The camp set in a little pocket. They hadn't disturbed the pine trees, which surprised me. I expected a camp built to log off the timber would start with the handiest ones close by and work farther and farther out, but I guess they don't like a landscape of stumps either, and if they don't they're in a better position than anybody else to avoid it. Those pine trees were elegant. As far as I could see they sprung black out of the snow, maybe as close together as five or six feet, maybe once in a while twenty feet apart, most all of them as big around as engine boilers. I never knew God made trees like that. When I raised my eyes to follow one up I stopped breathing like you do when a good choir aches your throat with the Amen to a powerful hymn. Black and straight they went up and up and up without a fork or a crook or a branch for maybe six stories. Above that their dark-green tops went on another four or five stories and held a little snow and gave little peekholes at

166

a bright blue sky they must have been brushing. I stepped up and touched one. I followed it up from close like that. It went so far and weaved a little way up there so close to infinite space the awful size of it reeled my eyes. I backed away in a hurry from such an uncomfortable feeling.

If God drove Adam and Eve out of the Garden of Eden for taking an apple out of just a common ordinary orchard tree, it sets you to thinking how He maybe feels about such prize pine. No wonder the Pine Ring people have to be so cold-blooded. No wonder lumberjacks have to be so rugged and rough and tough. It's like Rudolph says, I guess, sin is for the strong.

I was anxious to see how they took down and handled such monsters. It was easy to find where to go. I just followed the path the lumberjacks had tramped from the camp through the new snow. The walk through the timber was something eyes were made for. I wished Pa was there. He'd have fit because those trees and him were exactly the same stuff. They were ever so old and straight, and strong and solid and spread out so firm where they came out of the ground and stood so grand and reached so far and were still green and growing up on top under the snow. That's what Pa was too, and that's what he expected of me some day. I felt like an ant feeling around the bottom of a telegraph pole.

After a ways there was brightness up ahead. When I got there the timber stopped. Naked snow and black stumps with mushroom snowy tops stretched dismal ahead and over a hill as far out as I could look. Nothing to raise my eyes to. It was a sick, robbed feeling. It made my feet so heavy all the fun of walking bogged down. The tracks went on and on under the empty blue sky. The coldness of it stung my breathing. If they could only have left every fourth tree or so that got wasted anyhow. Two hundred years a growing to end up in sawdust, by God, that could happen to me too if I'm not careful. The saw takes a

167

twenty-five per cent discount, the wages men get up here take a twenty per cent discount, it seems to me from the few people you hear about that really amount to something the discount on a life can get worst of all.

Up over rises and down through low spots the lonesome openness kept on. Once in a while I caught a sound like sleepy far-off thunder rumble. Maybe a quarter mile farther I heard faintly a man's voice, lifted high for carrying and long-drawn-out for attention, give a singing yell. When it died out a crack came from over that way, then a swishing clatter speeding up to a short roar and ending in a thump with a bounce to it. The faster I walked the more sounds I heard. Chopping, lots of it, steady, regular *ziss, ziss, ziss* of saws from five or six places, voices. I came over a crest and there the whole works spread out harvesting a forest, taking down a landscape. I got there just in time to hear a singing, "Ti-i-i-m-b-r-r" and watch men scurry away and stand waiting. A piece of the dark-green cover high over their heads cracked itself slowly free and swished up speed on a long curve toward the ground. It took ever so long to fall and knocked snow and boughs into a silvery commotion. The trunk spanked along the ground raising another snow cloud to hide everything for a second. The butt kicked back out of the cloud and raised higher than it had ever been in the tree and then whipped down again and rested dead. After it was all done and still, the sound came crashing up like it was the soul of the pine rushing past to get out of there.

It came to me for all that turmoil and work and noise down there it was only celebrating a tiny little instant of time, but God, how important an act can be. I was looking square into the middle of four hundred years. Two hundred years old those trees were, and it would take two hundred years again to raise the next crop like that.

168

10

Ahead there, they were taking down a forest, slick and clean like a boy getting a head shave. I always thought a barber shop floor was a mess. It can't compare to lumberjack leavings. I saw why they didn't lumber off right where they built their camp, the clutter around would have driven them crazy. First there'd be the stumps sticking up as big as boulders to go around, and in the space between, the branches and tops laid crisscross and tangled so tight a rabbit would have had trouble to get through. Those tops looked skimpy way up in the air, but on the ground they were big as hay loads. The men and ox teams from a distance looked downright puny against the wall of forest they pecked away at. What they were accomplishing didn't look possible. When men organize and go after what they want, well, no wonder God got worried at the Tower of Babel and had to mix them up to protect himself. There the men were messing around looking for an easy way to heaven which, of course, is a different thing altogether from what lumber people have in mind even if the job they're at is maybe just as big.

Down among them it was exciting and a million things

to ask about and smelled sweet. A pine tree is perfumed extra nice, in the needles, in the chips, in the saw cuts and it drifts ever so far. It's a good thing it does. Lumberjacks have a carrying smell too that needs something to dilute it. Too bad some of that nice pine smell didn't penetrate into the bunkhouse. It sure would have been welcome, especially to an outsider.

When I got amongst them, and walked around to see what each one of them was doing they'd pick me up with their eyes and keep on working and maybe grin a little, but none of them would stop to talk. There were plenty of sounds, the men hollering directions, guiding the oxen, chopping and sawing, skidding the logs around, grunting and heaving to load the high-piled log sleds, chains rattling and zinging tight, snow squealing cold under the runners, but not a word of visiting. When lumberjacks are working, words are tools they wouldn't waste careless any more than they would go at a boulder with a two-handled crosscut saw.

Bishop George, he was the lean, sharp-faced preacher sort of fellow who sang that sad song in the bunkhouse the night before, was on one end of a saw that took all his wind. Gabby Pete, the one who told me that long cant-hook story, had only two outdoor words, gee and haw, for his ox team. The one they'd called Whispering Jens because something was wrong with his throat sure didn't have anything wrong with his back and arms the way he could make that ax of his sing. Every last one of them saved conversation as if it was whisky—something wonderful to have fun with when time hangs heavy but no good on the job. I had to get my questions answered by looking, not listening.

Those giant wheels that had worried me at the blacksmith shop at Eau Claire were just the right thing in the woods. They had four pair a going and they were fourteen feet high and the slickest things ever to handle a big log. They'd get a chain around the butt end of a log that was

170

maybe four foot across, and roll a set of wheels in place over it and grunt and pry until the butt was hung from the axle and held up to clear the ground. Then they would start the oxen pulling, and they'd lean into their yokes slow and powerful and those high wheels would turn slow and grand and crunch the snow until it hollered and drag off the log a bumping and a thudding to where a double-width, double-length sled was being loaded double-high.

I thought they'd maybe use those high wheels some way for their leverage to roll the logs up, but they didn't, the wheels were just for snaking. At the sled they had heavy timbers running up the side of the load at the front and back and set at a slant like roof timbers. They took ropes and pulley blocks and another yoke of oxen and rolled that log up the timbers, men on each end guiding it with heavy poles with iron-spike tips. When it got up there it was a pretty touchy business to keep that big round thing resting solid when all it had for foundation was other logs that would roll any chance they got. I wouldn't want the job of those fellows up on top. If anything gave away and those round logs started rolling, those men would be flattened out like pie dough under a rolling pin. They were pretty careful, they had to be, and once the load was heaped up beyond anything I ever saw pulled they snugged it tight with chains. How many yoke of oxen will it take to pull a load like that? I asked myself. They had a trick for that too. They did it with one yoke. The trick was in the road. The ruts the runners ran in were iced. Solid, hard, slippery, thick-blue ice. I scratched my head how they arranged that. That ice was as important as the rails are to a locomotive. One ox yoke moved away with the load. Ahead I saw a little rise as the ice tracks went over a little hill and wondered how they handled that. They just hooked on an extra yoke of oxen stationed there and walked it over, the extra yoke unhitching at the top and walking back. The load disappeared over the hill. I'd have liked

171

to follow it, but there was too much to see where I was for the time being.

You take any job big enough so there has to be more than two men at it, it never seems to go right or get done without somebody in charge to say "Start here," "Easy does it" and "All together now," and make the crew all go in the same direction. Funny how anybody, almost, knows how to work, but how it never gets started or moves along without a head. That foreman never touched an ax or a saw or a log or a whip, but because he had the say of it all there was a steady procession of log sleds moving that forest up the ice road and away forever over the hill. He did all his work by pointing and hollering, and was the only one a visitor could turn to for talk. I didn't really turn to him, he got around all over and saw me standing and took me for one of his crew and thought I was loafing and came to see about it.

"Oh," he said, "you're the kid with the harnessman visiting the superintendent. From Chicago, ain't you? Well, what do you think of this; ever see anything like it?" He swept his hand in a half circle from in front to behind him as if he owned it personal.

"A lot going on," I said, "but couldn't you work better with horses?"

"Horses got too many nerves, and take veterinarians and we'd have to keep them over summers. Oxen maybe move a little slower, but they're as durable as a range of hills, and in summer all we have to do is turn them loose to forage for themselves."

"Say," I said as long as I had him handy there, "how is it that back there where the old stumps are there's no rubbish left like there is here where you're working?"

"It burns off. Fire always gets in when dry weather comes in summer and fall. Ever notice the haze that time of year, even down as far as Chicago? Well, that's from miles and miles of the last winter's slashings burning off."

172

We were standing among some tops they'd sawed off. They would have been good-sized trees all by themselves. The one I laid my hand on was maybe a foot or fourteen inches where they'd ended the last log out of it. "Big stuff like this you let lay?"

"No good. Who wants it? You fellows in Chicago want a board, it has to be clear. This stuff would have knots peppered all over it and who'd want to line a room like that? No market for it." He had to leave then to holler, "Ti-i-i-m-b-r-r!" for a big one. My, how that man could yell.

At noon a horse team came trotting along from camp with covered boxes and cans in the sleigh bed and the cook's helper driving. There was another sleigh behind it driven by a tall lean fellow whose knees stuck up so sharp even his lap robe couldn't hide their angles. The two sleighs pulled a little ways up in among the standing trees that would go down before the sun would. "Knock off," the foreman hollered. "Grub time."

The cookboy threw off the canvas. The cans steamed. A wonderful coffee smell drifted around to remind a person how hungry he was. Along with it another can steamed out a peppery stew to drive my mouth a watering. All around the teamsters set out oats buckets for the oxen. Men came determined from all directions until there must have been half a hundred circling in toward the grub sleigh. The cookboy passed out tin plates and tin cups and tin spoons and ladled out stew and coffee. The line picked up bread from the boxes. Men stood around balancing their plates and cups with one hand and ate with the other. Some sat in the snow, some leaned against trunks. Here and there one balanced on a rock. The trees towered above everything, silently reaching upward their last day of life. The foreman and the stranger and I wound up the line. We weren't in any danger, one thing a lumber camp never runs out of is grub. I hear the cook

173

is the highest-paid man in the place because if he's no good they just can't hold a camp. We must have struck a top-rate outfit, there was even an apple for everybody. An apple in one hand and a slice of bread in the other is a mighty fine dessert. Hurts your teeth, though, the way an apple can store cold.

The day was lots better than anyone could expect for late February with new snow, and warm sunshine streaming down between the big pines and getting right to the bottom. You could stand around without mittens or earmuffs and not feel uncomfortable after you'd eaten a little, or even sit with your back to a trunk in spite of the cold. Food inside you warms up the whole country. It was downright cozy and friendly in the couple of minutes before the foreman would end the resting. The cookboy gathered up the tinware and banged and clattered it into the sleigh box.

The stranger whistled over to his sleigh and banged around lots more than he needed to, opening a box. He pulled a couple of nails and they squealed all the way out, then he grabbed the board they had held and pulled that up and back so that the nails on the other end squealed louder. "Gather round," he hollered, "and I'll show you woodsmen a thing or two about axes. Come one, come all, the Bates ax makes boys into men and makes men independent. Gather round, I say, you've never seen what an ax can do until you've watched a Bates."

Some eyes raised, but nobody moved. Everybody just kept on resting and belching and minding his own business.

I don't know if he got mad or not, but he just stood there on top of his sleigh looking all around and not hollering any more. Standing up high like that he looked seven feet tall.

After a minute, he reached down into his box and came up with half a dozen axes. First thing I knew, all six of them were flying through the air in different directions.

Whack, an ax struck a trunk behind Gabby Pete, who was examining a tear in his jacket, and quivered there, the handle hanging down within three inches of his head. "Why, you!" He jumped up and took out toward the sleigh.

Another one hit above four of them talking together. One whacked so hard it loosened a gob of snow big enough to make two or three wet necks. All six axes hung handle down from different tree trunks. The Bates man got his crowd quick.

"Now, just a minute," he drawled. "This isn't to pick a fight, it's just to study the nature and character of the ax." While he talked he had one sailing around in a circle, swinging high and dipping low. He was safe in the middle and knew it. The lumberjacks just stood there. They knew it too.

"No harm done, friends, and none intended. Those axes were not thrown in foolhardy, reckless anger. They were thrown with the utmost precision."

"Precision, hell. I felt the wind of it and you're going to feel something of mine that isn't wind. I don't miss."

"Brother, if you thought that was a miss, I don't blame you for getting mad. But a Bates ax lands where you want it to, every time. It's a matter of balance. Like this."

He threw an ax high into the air, spinning like a windmill, the double-bitted head flashing in the spots of sunlight it cut. While that one went up he pitched one after another until he had four up and every time one came down he reached out, grabbed its handle and sent it wheeling again. I'd like to know what kept him from getting his hands cut off grabbing into them so quick, but he never so much as nicked a finger even when he had to reach out to stop them and gather them in. Four axes passed from one hand to the other so fast you had trouble to see it done and he never even clicked one blade against another. Somebody cheered, then I guess everybody. I know I did.

175

"That's what I mean by balance in a Bates ax." He grinned.

"Balance? You're a damn juggler. Best way to test an ax is on a tree."

"How right you are. Here, take this ax and go off about forty, fifty feet and put a blaze on one of these pines."

Bishop George marched his red-plaid shirt off through the snow, hefting the ax as he went. He chipped off a four-inch blaze about shoulder height in one flourish. He fingered the ax edge a little on the way back.

The Bates man on the sleigh picked up one of his axes, sighted on the blaze, hollered, "Left" and let fly. The ax flew, and bit into the blaze an inch from its left edge, burying itself an inch deep. The handle hung straight down, its end vibrating about a foot out from the trunk. He picked up a second ax, hollered, "Right" and landed it on the blaze, about the same distance in from the right edge. "Now," he said, "I'll put the third one square between the other two, and the ends of the handles will all be level and the same distance out from the trunk."

He did it too, just like he said he would. All three axes hung from the blaze as if somebody had measured and marked and made a rack for them and hung them in it. I never saw anything like it, and I guess a lot of those woodsmen hadn't either.

The foreman lifted his hat and scratched and said, "Well now, tricks and fancy skill is right interesting and pretty to watch, but mostly we buys our axes for chopping."

The man on the sleigh grinned, his blond hair almost colorless in the bright sunshine. "That's right, friend, but balance is the secret of accuracy in getting results from an ax. Now that you know every Bates is balanced, we can go on to show how every stroke depends on that balance."

He got off his sleigh, walked over to a sound three-foot trunk, stepped back the distance he wanted and braced his

176

feet just so. One cut went in and down from about the height of his shoulder and the other went in and up from about his knees. I'll bet that was the fastest any tree ever opened up. There weren't any chip ledges either, those cuts couldn't have been smoother if he'd gone in and planed them.

"Now," he said, "watch the back face between the two cuts."

It had been fairly straight and smooth, but not anything like the upper and lower surfaces, and now he chopped big ragged chips as if he was making it rougher on purpose. Pine juice saved up for a hundred years drifted out in the sunshine and made a fresh, sweet smell. He took out big chips and little chips and seemed to have lost his knack altogether because he wasn't laying the ax twice in the same place. Pretty soon he slipped his hand up the handle not over nine inches from the head and took tiny chips, one here, one there, and finally just pulled the blade along sort of chiseling and gouging. All of a sudden I saw something that wasn't there a minute before, and it just made me gasp. Abraham Lincoln, with his deep, sad eyes looking at me from the middle of a pine tree. Beard, high cheekbones, the quiet thinking, it was all there, chopped and shaved out with an ax.

The Bates man leaned back, not saying anything, just fingering his ax head. Nobody else said anything either. It was the quietest bunch of men you ever saw, looking at that tree from one side, then crossing over to the other and looking again.

Pretty soon one of the old fellows spoke real low and positive. "I'll take one of those axes, mister."

Well sir, all his axes sticking in the trees where he pitched them went first and then he emptied his box. Two dozen axes, sold just like that.

The foreman ordered the men back to work. The cook-boy drove off, his tinware clattering loose in the boxes on his sleigh. Chickadees lighted and chirped their kind of gossip over the crumbs we all had left wherever we ate. I walked over to the Bates man.

"Mister," I said, "you ought to be on the stage. People would pay good money to see what you can do."

"That's what they all tell me, so I tried it. Hell, boy, there's more people need axes, I discovered, than spend money for entertainment. I got a better, steadier living this way. Giddap, Bill, get along there, Oscar, got to get to the next camp by night."

I felt kind of discouraged watching him go before I could get a little advice from him. Sales always go better if there's some kind of show along with it, I learned that from the way the Negro and his banjo helped me out that day so long ago on South Water Street. If there only were some hair-raising tricks a person could do with a harness. I puzzled about it a long time. I couldn't think of anything except the way Rudolph can throw them on but he even quit that since we left home.

About three o'clock there was a lot of jabbering and jawing at the edge of the timber. The next tree to be cut was the one Mr. Lincoln was looking out from. They had to call the foreman to decide whether the tree should be cut above Old Abe to save him in the stump or below him so they could float him down the river to surprise the sawmill. The foreman squinted around from one angle and then another and decided to cut below him, he liked that idea of sending him out in the world and maybe reading about it in the paper and have a clipping to carry along for those who hadn't seen it and wouldn't believe it. He supervised the whole process, but it didn't work out. When the tree fell, and bounced, Old Abe split all to pieces. The foreman got so mad he couldn't even swear which is a pretty tough shape for a logger to be in.

I wanted to study for myself the reason an up-to-date business like lumbering stuck to such pioneer ways as using mostly oxen. Oxen are such mild, slow-moving things they don't even use lines to guide them. A yoke around the neck and a chain around the yoke running back to the load is absolutely all there is to the harness for a team of them. That's a dickens of a note for our trade. I haven't any use for oxen. I'd like to see them all skinned and their hides made into harness leather, which is the only quality I care for in the beasts.

Best way to find out about oxen I know of is to watch them handle a load so I walked over again to where they were heaping up a log sled. This time I went in front to take a good look at the yoke of them that would pull it away. They were chewing their cuds. They didn't chew up and down like a horse does, but rolled their jaws sideways and chewed forever between swallows. Maybe that's why they'll stand better than horses, they always have busywork eating their food twice like that. Enjoying it all over again, they probably are too occupied to ever make trouble. What I wouldn't give for that in a team of horses sometimes when they're so all-fired skittish.

They had big mild eyes and lazy, heavy heads. Their thick weighty yoke on the backs of their necks was a burden by itself. It looked like nobody thought of a new pattern since Moses came out of Egypt. An ox is built with plenty of muscle, but his legs are short. That puts his power closer to the ground than a horse's is. It makes them slower, I never heard of an ox race, but it also should make them stronger on a hard pull. They're geared down, it seems to me, just like a freight locomotive has lots smaller drive wheels than a passenger engine.

The men were chaining down the last logs way up on top. I asked if I could go along on the trip. There were three men up there already, but somebody said, "Sure, scramble up," and I did. When I got up there it was Whispering Jens in charge. I never rode so high on a load before. Whispering Jens wasn't driving, that would have

179

been an insane place to handle oxen from with no lines and way out of distance for a whip. The ox driver was another man altogether who walked along controlling them by yelling. Strong as those oxen were the load was so big they couldn't start it alone. They had to hitch on another pair for a jerk team and even then it took a man with a crowbar prying at each runner to lever us into moving. "Sixteen thousand feet on here, the scaler says," Jens whispered.

As soon as we were moving, one yoke of oxen kept us going until we got to the rise and another one had to pitch in. We went up smooth on those ice ruts, but pretty slow. On the downhill side we picked up speed. The runners started to thud. The logs grumbled a little. The faster we went the higher up it seemed I was. I didn't like it to be traveling downhill with a load like that and no lines in anybody's hands and no breeching straps, or even a tongue for the oxen to hold back on. We had about as much control as riding a house roof carried off in a flood. What a dickens of an idea, I thought, to put Whispering Jens, a man who couldn't even yell, in charge of a job like this. Those oxen had to trot to keep from being run down by their own load. The driver down below swore and hollered, "Ice Monkey! Where in hell is that kid? Hey, Ice Monkey!"

A boy came tearing out of the woods with his breeches hobbled around his knees. He grabbed a pail from somewhere with a fire shovel in it and threw sand ahead of the runners. His red underwear had the drop seat down. His bare behind poked out naked every time he stooped to aim a shovel of sand under the runners. He slowed us down so good with that sand the oxen even had to pull a little on the downgrade. As soon as we were safe, everybody in sight laughed at that poor kid. They nicknamed him then and there, "Two Cheeks to the Wind," and they ribbed

180

him something fierce while he tucked in and buttoned up.

The men up on the load with me laughed and kidded at what they'd seen, and repeated it all over again and clapped their legs and didn't mind the height and pitching at all. To me it was a dangerous ride, so dizzy high, the logs grumbling against each other, sometimes opening, sometimes squeezing. If a person slipped a foot into one of those openings between the logs, they would have mashed it. The others dangled their legs, but I wouldn't take a chance like that, I kept my knees up and my feet on the same log I sat on which wasn't a very good position to feel solid at, but it did keep my feet out of the way of those grinders.

The ice road wound around through the fresh stumps. I felt sorry for the poor farmer who'd have to take them out before he'd have decent crop land here. Rudolph and the Pine Ring and all the big talk about getting the lumber off to open the land. Lumbering doesn't open any land, what it opens is only the sky. A stump is ten times more work to chop out and get rid of than sawing off a tree, and a hundred times more lonesome. When that poor farmer comes along, he won't have a jolly gang around, or sit at a table for sixty, or spend his evenings in a company playing jokes and singing songs and spinning wonderful yarns. No wonder the farmers in the cutover are so bent-backed and sad-faced. No wonder there were so few of them. I wished I had a few sets of Rohland harness along to hunt them out and give them a good bargain. They'd need the best they could get to haul stumps like those off once they got them loose.

The men on the load didn't mind such lonesome scenery. They talked about a box social and spelling bee at the Flambeau Settlement schoolhouse the whole camp was invited to that night which was Saturday. There'd be girls there and it was only a seven-mile walk, which was worth

181

while even if you were a poor speller because there was a saloon at the settlement too and a little whisky could improve anybody's spelling.

The ice road ended at a landing on the frozen river. A landing is a storage yard where all the logs a camp cuts are piled up in a wide high row all along the bank so when the river opens in the spring they can tumble the logs into the water and float them downstream to the sawmills. Piles and piles of logs stretched on and on, lying there dead as far as I could see, and pretty near as high as anything can be piled. A board is a pretty thing, and a tree is a pretty thing, but a log is an ugly, clumsy thing between the two. I don't know, maybe a tree is like a living person with a duty to grow big and strong and after it's done with that has its own afterlife as part of a beautiful building and has to die to get from one shape to the other. If that's the way it's supposed to be, a log landing is, in a way, like the job at the halfway point where a thing isn't alive any more and isn't a soul yet, and all those lumberjacks were sort of jolly undertakers. I mentioned that viewpoint, but nobody could see it. They got mad at me.

Lumberjacks, I found out, don't like to talk about undertakers or have anybody remind them of that trade. They come near to needing one in just about everything they do and it gets too close. A tree that doesn't fall all the way when it's cut off and hangs halfway on another tree is apt to kill somebody when it does break loose. They're so dangerous they call them widow-makers. If a chain around a log sled pulls apart and the logs break loose, the men on top and anybody walking alongside are goners. A man can go under in a river drive and the churning logs will grind him to sausage and drown him to boot. The most dangerous of all is piling up the logs at the landing, because there they are all piled loose, they have to be to roll easy down the bank when the ice goes out. The man who builds up the pile is called a top loader because that

is where he has to stand. I wouldn't want his job for anything. If he makes the tiniest mistake where a log should
be put, the whole pile under him gives way. If he slips
on a little snow, it could be the trigger to tumble the whole
pile. If a log coming up twists or slips, it can knock him
over, or dislodge everything under him. You just take
thirty round clothespins, for instance, and try to pile them
six wide and five high on a table. After you see them roll
down you say, "No, thank you," if anybody offers you a
job as a top loader.

Back at the camp where we could talk again—everybody keeps pretty mum around a landing—Gabby Pete
told about a top loader they lost last year who was the
carefulest man ever and hadn't made a move out of place
and nobody could figure out how it happened until one of
the teamsters came in and said what he'd heard. "You
know what that damn fool top loader did? He forgot himself and let one go. First thing a top loader has to learn
is never to fart on the job. It's that touchy."

I wanted to see what the landing looked like from the
river side. I could have walked through where there were
aisles between the piles, but that would have put me in
front of them where they're meant to come rolling down
when the drive starts. I wasn't going to fool around near
any hair trigger for such business so I walked way around
the end and out on the ice. Those log piles stretched as far
as I could see.

Out on the ice was one of those monster big boxes like
the blacksmith at Eau Claire had standing in his yard. It
was built over runners as wide as the log sleighs. Horses
were hitched to it and a man was with it. I walked out to
find out what it was.

It was a wooden tank. The man was on top working a
cistern pump up there, filling it up from a hole in the ice
where a hose was poked in. "What's this kind of rig for?"
I asked.

"Cook sent me out. Soup tomorrow. Go around to the front, will you, and boost up that sack of rice. She should go in about now."

I walked in front. There wasn't any sack of rice.

"Damn, it must have dropped off. Here, you come up here and pump a while, I'll walk back along my tracks and find it."

I pumped until I heated up and had to take my coat off. While I rested and looked around I saw smoke curling up from a bush on the bank. Under the smoke, when I followed it down, was the man I was helping, sitting there puffing his pipe and watching me. Soup! One of those lumberjack tricks worked on me, that's what it was.

I climbed off in a hurry. The man knocked out his ashes and came back. He grinned a little and I grinned a little. We both felt foolish. On my way back I took a look at the rear of the tank. Two valves back there. It was the rig they made those ice roads with.

The man who owned the camp had some expenses I'll bet he never found out about. Everybody knocked off an hour early on account of the box social and spelling bee. The cook planned on going too. He had supper ready early. There was plenty of it but not much variety or especially appetizing. A man could get what he needed, but it sort of discouraged him from needing very much. Anybody who hadn't decided for sure whether he was going or not, that supper made up his mind for him. It even seemed like it was planned to help the camp owner get back part of what the men quitting early cost him. On top of that it also would account for some mighty good bids for all of the boxes that would have any size to them at all. A camp cook is the schemiest kind of a schemer.

He was a good sort, though. He had lots of hot water for anybody interested and pails to lend and dippers and basins which a few of the men borrowed and carried to the bunkhouse. Nobody did anything dangerous like taking a

184

bath and going out and catching pneumonia. Mostly it was singing and jabbering and neck scrubbing and wrist washing where it would show. A few washed their feet which wasn't any risk because there a lumberjack is always used to being wet. Riskiest of all were the five or six who lathered up and shaved. In there with so many of them crowded together and milling around, and every so often some cutup wadding a soggy towel into a lump and socking it across the room for a joke, it was downright dangerous for a man to have a razor open with the blade against his face and that long touchy handle exposed to be bumped. There were a few nicks, there were bound to be. What surprised me most was nobody losing a lip or slashing a cheek open.

They cut a little hair for each other and trimmed some beards and had a jolly time. One blue-black fellow went back to the cook shack to dip his fingers in the stove polish, Gabby Pete told me when he saw him go, to put a shape and shine to his mustache. "Cook won't have any stove polish, he don't have time for polishing no stoves, so the guy will have to do like Cook does himself, run his fingers around the ring left in the dishpan to get his mustache wax."

Those fellows dressing up did it Christmas tree style. Nobody had a whole change, but everybody had one kind of ornament or another to switch working clothes into visiting clothes. A rainbow scarf, an unfolded checkered shirt, here and there a clean pair of pants, a fresh pair of red knit sox to turn over the tops of their boots, maybe a mackinaw too new to wear in the woods, whatever they could dig out of their private pack. Those packs they tugged out from under the bunks were in more styles than you see on a baggage cart at a depot. Some were just sacks, some were satchels, some were fancy wooden chests. There were saddlebags and plain blankets either rolled army system to hold a fellow's possessions or maybe just gathered up careless by the corners. When I saw how

185

they were beginning to blossom out I left to head for the superintendent's shack where Rudolph was with our gear.

Rudolph had heard of the party too. He was just as anxious to go as I was. We were alone in there and while we cleaned up lumberjack style I asked him how his deal looked now.

"Far as I'm concerned, everything fits. Been with the superintendent all day, visiting crews, estimating the next stand he's moving into, talking horses against oxen. This new trick they're using of icing their logging roads will make them switch to horses, they'll have to because horses can be controlled better and have so much more speed, and time costs money. He's been wanting to make the change himself. I didn't breathe a word about our road plan, that's none of his business. What I wanted from him was high-speed methods and short cuts and production tricks so I know what I'm talking about when I sit down with the big shots of the Pine Ring that Roger Roberts is passing the word to who can put this thing across."

"Did he help you?"

"Who, the superintendent? He's been hatching new lumbering ideas all winter long and couldn't get authority to try them. That ate on him terrible, there's nothing harder on a man than a brainful of ideas that have to be held back. When I got to him he was dancing, you might say, like a kid waking up in the middle of the night and can't find the chamber pot. He spilled out to me like I was the angel Gabriel sent special to listen to him. It's all ammunition I can use."

We hitched our team and started out for the settlement. The stars were Christmas-night bright. The moon hung halfway up the sky, clear and blue-white and cold. Only part of it was up there, a thin slice of moon shaped with a round outside and a round inside like ice freezes in the bottom of a pail when there's only a little water in it and the pail sits on a bad slant. It was a night to tuck the lap

186

robe snug and careful and pull your neck into your shoulders.

Every time we overtook anybody walking they climbed on. They didn't talk, lumberjacks are like crickets, the colder they are the less they chirp. By the time we got to the settlement it would have taken a top loader to accommodate another one. First place we stopped was the saloon. Rudolph treated. They had sawdust on the floor which was handy for spitting, but miserable for anybody dropping part of their change. We all warmed up pretty nice. Rudolph treated again, which made three or four of them who'd been there before we came, and in on both treats, look curious but grateful and ask who he was. Rudolph liked that, he'd have treated again, but while he was introducing himself the saloonkeeper set one up on the house. He could afford to. I'll bet he gets quite a handful back every time he sifts that sawdust.

It began to buzz awful nice in there with the whisky warming up a person inside and happy fun talk making everybody friendly with everybody else. It was a good substantial party taking shape right there. Rudolph and I broke away, though, and drove over to the schoolhouse.

They'd built the schoolhouse with ambition the settlement would grow a lot of large families. It was half as big as a barn, and lit up cheery. People were going in so steady the stoop just boomed from their stomping to knock the snow off their feet. Rudolph went on ahead while I tied the team to the rail. My, he looked grand, so straight and solid, his clothes so sleek and black there in the light from the door that picked up their quality without showing the hard use they'd taken since Chicago, his silk hat high and confident just a gleaming back the yellow from the lamplight he headed toward. By golly, it struck me, so what if our harness is an everyday sort of thing people naturally take for granted? I know the quality to it, but it takes Rudolph to remind everybody that the trade can be aristo-

187

cratic too. I got to respect him for it, that's a point he's
better on than any of us Rohlands, even Pa. I threw the
horse blankets over the team and snugged them on careful. Poor things, they'd be standing out in the open cold
for hours before the trip back could warm them up again.

We were early enough. Nothing had organized yet,
everybody was still in the Howdy-do, what-do-you-think-
of-the-weather, my-but-it's-been-a-long-winter, is-this-
your-little-Alice-stretching-out-so part of the evening, and
nodding and shaking hands and looking where a cap and
coat could be stored. A family would come in with all its
girls and the mother, each carrying a generous-size package ever so careful. All the packages were disguised under
hemstitched covers or newspapers, or anything so nobody
could see what it was and recognize it later to know who
brought it. That would have ruined the bidding. Some
of those packages belonged to girls no box social had ever
helped before, you could see that. Hope is a wonderful
durable thing. Especially with a good-size logging camp
near by bringing all kinds of new men into the area.

In order not to give away which woman went with which
lunch, they had committee women to take the packages and
disappear behind the screen up front. There'd be paper
rattling back there and gurgling noises women make together complimenting something, and then a committee
lady would pop out, her face beaming with smiles but
blushing from all the attention bouncing off of her. She'd
put a pretty box all done up fancy with ribbons and color
and decorations in with those that already were on the
table and back off to look how it showed. Maybe she'd
decide its position could be improved. She'd lean over
and touch it and maybe turn it a little east, or fluff up a
bow, and be satisfied. By that time another committee
woman would come out with some other girl's box which
she'd worry around a while. Rudolph circulated here and
there getting acquainted wherever three or four men
talked. Whenever he faced the front and a woman would

188

put another box on the table, I noticed, that box got mothered around something awful.

Seems we were in there half an hour without anyone getting up to take charge. The boxes had stopped adding at the table. No new families had come in. The schoolteacher walked around worried. She was a woman, they couldn't get men teachers up there because the woods paid better. One of the committee women tried to calm her down a little. "Now, Miss Waterpebble, you just relax, we've got everything going along just fine."

"But we ought to be starting, and Mr. Schmahl hasn't shown up. Where is that man?"

"Dearie, he'll be here. He's never missed a meeting yet, that's why he's been elected school clerk. My, what a fine attendance we have. There's people here come twelve miles and some—" she looked at Rudolph— "from a lot farther than that I'm sure. We'll have a wonderful program."

That schoolteacher was the oddest girl. She was pretty. She had nice clothes. She was trim. She looked smart. She used all the cute little ways of talking and moving a woman uses to make you pay attention and she smelled as fresh as a cedar chest. The trouble was, she couldn't seem to blend all those good things together. Things she moved she moved too much. Her neck, for instance, willowed so free her head took the darnedest tilts to stay up there at all. She'd shift a shoulder, then her elbow would adjust to the shift and be wrong for her wrist. Her wrist would try to correct to it and then her fingers would add their opinion and total up a position so awkward she'd have to start all over to feel right. She did such things with her mouth too, and her eyebrows, and whatever she did always started out the same as anybody else moves to keep themselves loose and comfortable, but for her it never got to the place where she could rest and forget it. I couldn't keep my eyes off her, and neither could the other men, I noticed. Rudolph was fascinated.

"Here's the clerk. Now we can begin," somebody said.

The man stomped snow off his feet and peeled out of a woolly buffalo coat with his back turned to me. When he turned around with his cheeks cold-bitten red it was the cook from the camp. He moved right up and stood behind the teacher's desk and appointed the captains for the spelldown. "Each of you can choose a team of twelve," he said. "If we make it any bigger it may take too long, there's other parts to the program too." He waved his hand toward all the boxes piled up on the table.

The outside door opened again. About eight lumber-jacks we'd left at the saloon tramped in. Right away one of the captains chose Bishop George for his side. The other captain picked Miss Waterpebble. She whispered to her captain. Next time his turn came he picked a twelve-year-old-boy. She must have recommended him. Both captains squinted over the room looking for talent. They'd consult with some of their team before every choice. Any-body who'd ever been a preacher or a printer, or had a reputation from spelling bees before, was picked pretty early. Toward the end of the choosing, the teacher's cap-tain picked Rudolph, and after Bishop George whispered to his captain, I was called up to that side. Mr. Schmahl, the clerk, laid down the rules and pronounced the words from a long list he pulled out of his pocket. He'd probably been writing that list for a week between rolling piecrusts and stirring stew. He wouldn't have needed to limit the teams to twelve. He knocked us down on both sides, be-cause his list was sneaky and came out of a cookbook in-stead of a speller. I can spell as good as anybody, and always put both *c*'s and both *m*'s in *accommodation,* and know my way around words that get tricky with *ie* or *ei.* He got me on a word which he defined as a way to fix meat, only I spelled it *brazed* like you fix a harness ornament. What he wanted was *braised.* Rudolph went down on *mousse* which isn't the big animal it pronounces like, or the little one the word sort of looks like, but is a name for something made out of whipped cream. *Meringue* worked like a shotgun, knocking down three on each side. The twelve-year-old got it right and stood there proud enough to bust. He did bust too, the next time around on *mussels* which is an altogether different thing from *muscles* even if they both are meat.

That left Bishop George and Miss Waterpebble opposite each other alone. The Bishop was unsteady on his feet from staying at the saloon too long and the teacher was unsteady just about all over from her habit of overcorrecting her motions. At their spelling they were both rock solid. They spelled like Kingdom Come. *Purée, bologna, torte, sauerkraut, sherbet, spaghetti, goulash, appetizing, cereal, tomato, soufflé, canapé,* they kept on and on.

Rudolph stood against the side wall sizing up Miss Waterpebble like the timber foreman planning the next pine to fell. I don't think anybody noticed the wanting look on his face, the contest was going too hot. I wouldn't have either except for his lecture back there in Milwaukee and this being the first time we'd been together with women around since then. I watched him edge back quiet like and lean down to whisper to one of the committee women. They whispered fast awhile, him smiling and reasoning, her undecided but tempted. That's all I saw, it got so tense up front. The teacher was stumbling on a word. "B-a-n-a-n-n-a."

Cook looked at the Bishop. "Banana, a Central American fruit."

"B-a-n-a-n-a."

"You're right! You're champeen of the Flambeau Settlement spelling bee for 1871." The Bishop bowed and pretty near fell on his face, the load in his head was so heavy. He got under himself in time, though, and once he got upright again he could balance fine and walked around all right.

"You've won fair and square," Miss Waterpebble said

twisting her head like a colt exploring the feel of its first halter, "and I congratulate you, but—" she looked at Cook —"you interest me with that Central American fruit. Can you tell us a little about the banana?"

That was darn nice of her. I was curious myself and so was everybody else. We all listened quiet to be educated. Mr. Schmahl hemmed a little and got red. He didn't know a thing about the fruit. A school clerk and not knowing, and being a cook and not knowing, that hit him in both places he wanted to be proud of.

The Bishop spoke up. "I ate one once in New Orleans last summer. They're good. Shaped like an ear of corn, you husk them the same way only instead of kernels inside it's in one piece, soft and sweet and creamy, kind of like custard but more solid."

I don't know if I'll ever get to New Orleans or not, but when I do I'm going to try a banana. Another group of lumberjacks came in just then, must have been a dozen. They hadn't picked up a ride and had walked the whole seven miles.

"Speaking of food," Cook bellowed out, taking charge again, "we'll start the box social now. Fellows, you'll have to bid up sharp or go without a partner, seems to me we got maybe twenty more gentlemen here than ladies. It's a good cause, the money will be used for a globe and a dictionary and some wall maps." He picked up a box prettied up with wallpaper and tinsel. "What am I bid for this gorgeous creation?" He weighed it in his hand. "This epicurean expression of culinary craftsmanship? Gentlemen, food is my life work and if you were standing as I am to waft the delectable aromas arising here you would confirm my judgment, this is surely a masterpiece. Do I hear a bid?"

It started with a dime which worked up to forty-five cents. That was a lot for a farmer to pay, after his wife and maybe two or three daughters had all fixed up boxes which cost him something too.

That cook was a right fancy auctioneer. He got the prices up good and joked like they all do that the bidding wasn't just for the wrapping, but what was inside part and parcel, the whole thing. He made me wonder whether our harness wouldn't go good that way too sometime, but darn it, auctioneering is a trade all by itself you have to be top rate at. He whittled that pile down fast. First thing I noticed there weren't but about a dozen left and I hadn't bid once. Rudolph hadn't either. I pitched in for all I was worth on the next box, but so did a lot of others. It was about the size and shape of a shoe box and had a red apple and pine cones on the top gathered into a bouquet that sat in the middle of a green hairbow. All the rest of the package was plain brown. I had to go way up to ninety cents to get it. That was exorbitant. It served me right for watching instead of speaking up while they were going for a quarter or thirty-five cents.

Rudolph watched like an owl at the next six boxes, but never so much as nodded no matter how hard Cook wheedled for a bid from him. The next box was all done in gold paper. It was like the sun coming up when Cook lifted it.

"Five dollars," Rudolph sang out before Cook had a chance to ask for the first bid. Everybody turned and stared to see who would slam-bang that way into an auction. A little ten-year-old girl giggled. She giggled a little and started to cry. The committee women looked happy, I guess such a bid would buy a pretty good globe all by itself. Some of the men looked a little mean, they thought he was poking fun at their thirty- or forty-cent buying. Cook tried a little for a second bid. He couldn't put any heart into it. He gave up and turned the box over to Rudolph.

The rest of the boxes went pretty quiet. Cook seemed tired and the bidding seemed tired. A quarter, thirty-five cents, forty cents, and another quarter, and it was all over. "Unwrap your boxes," Cook ordered, and stepped down.

That was the exciting part, to find out whose box you'd bought, from the name inside, and find her and pair off and go to a seat and sit together and eat. I got a gray-haired little pony-whip of a grandma with fried chicken and pickle sandwiches and angel-food cake and blueberry sauce screwed up tight in a jar.

I looked over at Rudolph. His face was the color a depot stove takes when the agent fires up and goes away forgetting he's left the drafts open. His partner was the little ten-year-old and she was bawling her head off, scared to eat with him. Her ma tried to argue her into it. Rudolph tried to calm them both down, and said it was all right, it didn't matter, and tried to look like a gentleman, but nothing worked. Her ma said see here now, and whacked her across the bottom and promised her more. That brought over the schoolteacher who'd been bought by her twelve-year-old speller who was also in sort of a stage fright at who he'd got. She suggested a trade that worked out to suit everybody. They made a nice couple, Rudolph and her.

The committee unpacked baskets they'd brought and charged twenty cents to everybody who hadn't bid a box and fed them sandwiches and cake and stuff. They passed around coffee separate because there's no way to keep that hot in a box.

Grandma said, "Eat, boy, for goodness sake, eat," and handed me a chicken leg. It was roasted juicy brown and tender. She had a whole shoe box full of good things, all packed careful and separated with napkins so they wouldn't squash together or mix flavors. They didn't mix flavors either, I noticed at the first mouthful, because a brand-new flavor had become boss since she'd packed. Shoe-box flavor. I didn't say anything, I didn't want to hurt her feelings. She noticed it too, but what the dickens could she do then, so she didn't mention it either. Shoe-polish chicken. Shoe-polish sandwiches. Shoe-polish angel food cake. The blueberries probably were all right, but by that time I had a shoe-polish mouth to ruin them too. Poor old lady, the last time she could have been to a box social must have been before shoes came in boxes.

After we finished eating, and while some of the courting-age couples who'd been lucky enough to match up interesting to each other were still mooning together over their lunch, the committee appointed volunteers to move the furniture back. Two fiddles and an accordion showed up. A dance started. The extra men weren't extra any more on account of the saloon being so handy. There were always about as many gone as were extra. It let all the men with double interests enjoy their dancing and their thirst too, and gave all the women and girls lots of variety in partners. Cook called the square dances. Golly, he made them fun. That man had a talent for everything. They were a lucky school district, if you ask me, to have him handy. I danced with Grandma, all the committee, Miss Waterpebble and everybody, even the little ten-year-old who wouldn't eat with Rudolph. We stomped that school-house down solid on its foundation. Slivers flew up from the floor kicked loose by the hobnails the lumberjacks wore. When they dance in the Chippewa Valley, they dance.

Once, on the way back from the saloon, Rudolph and I were together. "Lord," he said, "how I'd like to pop that schoolteacher. All those jerks and motions, they need to be educated for a purpose. Think I'll try it."

I laughed at him. "A schoolteacher? Even if she would be willing, how you going to get in her room?"

"Don't need to. She ate with me, so I get to take her home. That's all I need."

"In this cold?"

"There's deep straw in the bottom of the rig. There's the horse blankets and the lap robe. I'll get her away a little before the dance breaks up, or any time she wants to go. You stay here and I'll drive back to get you."

"You talk as if it's as easy as buying our boxes tonight."

"It is, Emil. Like I told you last month in Milwaukee, you just have to know what you want and go after it. Thought I was stuck with that brat, though. Damn committee woman, I slipped her two dollars to blow her nose for a sign when the teacher's box came up. When she blew, it was the brat's. Why the hell can't people be honest?"

Back at the dance I looked special for that committee woman. She was blowing her nose again. She had a cold. A regular old apron-filler of a cold.

In a little while Rudolph took Miss Waterpebble home. I wondered and wondered. I didn't feel like dancing or going back to the saloon to pass the time. After a long while Rudolph came back. There was a little straw on him. It didn't tell me anything. There's always straw in a sleigh.

11

AFTER we were back in Eau Claire again, Rudolph wouldn't let me go out with any more harness. He went out to wind up his deal and sent me to our boxcar to count exactly how many there were left. I had to root them all to one end—I'd been taking them from the middle where they were handy to the doors—and then carry them from the full end to the empty end in order to count them accurate. I reported five hundred and ten sets when I went back to the hotel to meet him at noon.

"Good," he said. "You get right back there, because this afternoon there will be teams coming around to load them up. After they've gone, go over to the freight agent's office and release our boxcar."

It was about dark when I got back to the hotel. Rudolph marched around the room like the Czar of Russia must have pranced when he got word that Seward had turned over the seven million dollars and took Alaska off his hands. "Emil," he said, "roll your eyes over this once."

The paper he showed me, but held onto while I read it, was an order on the Chippewa Valley Road Development

Company, payable at no interest one year from date. The amount was twenty thousand, four hundred dollars.

"Pa's total investment back four times over in one sale," Rudolph said.

I looked at the figures again. They made me swallow dry. Enough money on that piece of paper to let a person be a spendthrift the rest of his life and still die rich. There were two more carloads just as valuable waiting in Chicago to be shipped to us to get results like that twice more. I thought what a mighty smart pa I had to have figured out how this was going to work and what a mighty smart brother to pitch in and do it. Glory be, what a difference there is between big business and little business.

"Rudolph," I said, "what a wonderful thing you can put in your journal tonight."

"Journal, hell," Rudolph said. "This calls for sending Pa a telegram."

He was right. Before we could telegraph Pa, though, we had to figure out where we'd go next. We had more harness in the Chippewa Valley, I think, than there were horses, but of course that was the idea, to pasture off those slowpoke oxen.

"Next carload," Rudolph said, "should go to a well-settled farming area. Spring's coming on any day now. We should be there before the plowing and the planting starts."

We picked Sparta. I'd have liked to stay a little longer in the Valley to see those logs go thundering into the rivers and watch the drivers ride them down the high water spring brings, but that wasn't our business. A fellow can't have everything. As soon as we picked Sparta we sent Pa the telegram. What a supper we had to celebrate. Champagne, and fresh buffalo tongue expressed in from Omaha. We earned it or, to be more exact, Rudolph did.

We left winter when we left the Chippewa Valley. Sparta is seventy miles south of Eau Claire, which makes a difference in March. Most of the difference, I suppose though, came with the thaw that started the day we moved. There was lots more difference though, than weather. Sparta was built on ground instead of sawdust. Like every town, it had a river through it. There were some logs, and of course a sawmill for local trade, but mostly the banks were used by boys fishing. People bought and sold with United States money, not scrip. The saloons were quieter, at least in the colors the men wore. Farmers dress pretty dull compared to lumberjacks. The talk was wheat and corn and oats and railroad rates. They bragged some, of course, but corn and such doesn't provide much of a jumping place for imagination to take off from like a pine tree does. Sparta was old and tamed down compared to the Chippewa Valley. There wasn't a bit of talk about new townships, or fast-made fortunes, or overpriced court-houses. What interested them was freight rates and form-ing a kind of a club to do something about the railroads. From the way they talked, that club which was named the Patrons of Husbandry, was a kind of farmers' ring hoping to run things for agriculture like the Pine Ring does for timber. They also talked about the Grange which I took to be another club in competition, but they both were the same. They didn't have any such clubs around Sparta, the ones they were talking about were in Minnesota where they were strong, and in Adams and Waushara counties where they were just starting, which was pretty far away too. It's darn easy to travel by tongue.

Sparta was horse country. Oxen were scarce. That made harness go good. The *Sparta Herald,* their news-paper, every little while ran advice about harness like how a collar should fit, and whether checkreins were good for a work horse or not. In the army the head must be kept up, that goes for a horse as well as a man. Our harness had checkreins. For farm work anybody not wanting check-reins could unsnap them and take them off. Mentioning

199

harness in the paper helped, people take pretty serious anything they read in their own paper.

We divided into big business and little business again, Rudolph and me. My work was just the same as before, hiring a rig and carrying harness and driving out to talk to people. Rudolph visited around the hotel, and thought on the bed, and called on the *Herald,* and got well known in the saloons trying to find some kind of an outlet in Sparta that would be as exciting as the one he organized in the Chippewa Valley. That was hard to do. It didn't seem to be much of a country for big business. Little business was better than anything I'd done in the Chippewa Valley, and every bit of it was good dependable cash. Rudolph studied and worked at his problem and used up a lot of whisky.

"I got it, Emil, I got it," he greeted me one night. "Bigger than what I did in Eau Claire. The one thing that bothers all the farmers is freight rates."

"Bothers me too," I interrupted. "Nine hundred dollars just to haul our harness around."

Rudolph laughed. "You should be a farmer. Four carloads of wheat from, say, here to Milwaukee would cost as much as Pa paid for hauling our harness wherever we want it for ten months. We got a railroad bargain like has never been heard of. For a farmer, his rates eat up his profit."

"How's that tie in with selling harness?"

"The Grange, Emil, the Grange. In Minnesota they're so strong they got a department that buys farm machinery wholesale for the farmers. Well, if I help organize Granges in Wisconsin, I don't care about their railroad rates, I just want to get them started and plant that idea that they can buy wholesale too, and then I'll step in with a harness contract. I got to get right over to Minnesota to find out all about it."

"Move again when I'm doing so good here? Besides, our passes are only good for Wisconsin."

"We won't move. You don't have to go along, I'll go

200

alone. Once I get this organized, Emil, it won't be a sale and done with, like the first carload. When this gets going they'll take harness by the carload, year after year. It's exactly what Pa told us to look for.''

Rudolph stayed in Minnesota two weeks. He joined over there. When he came back, he took to Grange work full time and got to be an expert on their laws and by-laws and made speeches and visited the few there were in Wisconsin and got all fired up about a state convention in June. It got so I sometimes didn't see him for a week at a time. He'd come back with all kinds of reports of important people he met and things he saw, but big business works up to results awful slow. It kept me humping to keep him in expense money. That was all right, because that's the way we operated in the Chippewa Valley, and the results he got up there were exactly what he was building up to with the Grange and maybe even a whole lot better.

In a way, I sort of hoped he'd take all spring to line up the Grange, I liked my part of the harness business so well. Farmers are wonderful fine people to visit and talk to. Every time I'd come back to the hotel I'd be half afraid Rudolph would be there ready to say, ''Emil, lay off selling now, the rest of this carload is spoken for.'' I got to piling in a few more sets every time I went back to the boxcar and got to driving farther and farther out of Sparta. Sometimes I'd stay out overnight, the farmers were so cordial. It was so pleasant with them, and I got so nervous that any day Rudolph would show up to stop it all that I hired a bigger rig and loaded it full and set out to be gone a week.

The place I stayed that night they had a mortgaged mare ready to foal and it looked like twins. They'd got word to a neighbor, and he'd come there two three hours early it looked like. After supper the neighbor and the farmer pushed back their chairs and talked weather and crops, which I tried to swing around toward harness with-

201

out much luck. It wasn't the kind of thing either of them had a mind for right then. The dragged-out farm wife quietly cleaned the table and piled the dish work around the dishpan and I had to think how she fit in exactly like Sarah said, a slave to one drudgery job after another. Her little girl watched the neighbor and me, shy for a little spell and when she shadowed from one place in the room to another she took as big a circle around us as she could. They had an old grandpa living with them, gray, fuzzy thin-whiskered with just as much of it on the back of his neck as on his face. He sat on the edge of the couch, bright-eyed to listen as long as the talk was interesting, but ready and handy just the same, to roll on his hip and stretch out for a doze when the fancy would hit him.

Little girls can't stay shy very long, it's against their nature, I guess, anyhow the circles got shorter and shorter until she stood in front of me, her bashfulness used up and forgotten. She gave me a long steady look and decided that I wasn't dangerous or even interesting. Anyhow, she left and hunted around until she found an old cooked-off chicken back, dry and white with a string tied where the neck had been. The old rooster that first owned it never got the use out of that bone that she did. First it was a puppy on the end of a rope. She couldn't have squealed happier with a real one. Next it was a grasshopper jumping when she jerked. After that it was an engine, *choo-choo*-ing through a forest where the trees were her pa's legs, and into the depot under the table. She tipped the bone over and used it for a sled to haul spools. When her pa and the neighbor went outside to look at the mare again she called it her sewing basket and filled it with bright little patches of cloth. I'll never sell any harness here, I thought. A family too poor to own their own mare or to buy one little girl even a single toy won't have money for anything else either. Funny thing though, I never saw a happier little girl.

202

I should have gone to the barn too, anybody selling harness it just isn't good business to be cold to anybody's mare and colts, but the little girl playing with practically nothing but her imagination fascinated me. She got more fun out of that chicken bone in ten minutes than I can remember in the whole box of truck I had when I was little. I was hoping she'd friendly up to me pretty soon, I even tried to set a little bait taking out my watch and dangling it and putting it up to my ear, but girls are contrary. It was her grandpa she left the bone and string for, to tease him out of the drowsiness his supper was sneaking over him.

"Grandpa, you say no and I'll say yes."

The old man's knobby knuckles twitched. A faint gleam started somewhere far behind his eyes and brightened steadily like the lights in a front door do when somebody brings a lamp up the hall to answer it. "No-o-o," he yawned.

"Yes," she ordered.

"No," he roared making believe he was mad.

"Yes, yes." She clapped her hands. Her eyes danced.

"No. No, no."

I never heard two little words get such a workout, such a batting back and forth, such a squeezing out of their juices in all my life. You wouldn't believe there were that many dozens of different sounds saying the same thing. That old grandpa was as smart as a whip, thinking back over a lifetime of different styles and reasons for saying no, but every time he dug out a clincher to end the argument she built her yes into a new pattern and he had to think up another. I can't imagine where that little three-year-old who'd never been anywhere picked up all the wisdom and experience she had at the tip of that busy little tongue. I guess maybe it's like Sarah says, they're born with it ready to use as soon as they need it.

She and the old man never used one other word. The

203

way they played it, I guess, one would lose if they said another thing except yes or no, but they didn't need to, they got a hundred more things out of those words than the dictionary says and they did it so plain there was a story standing out in each back-and-forth. A sick person being begged to take his medicine and refusing. A lady trying on a hat, a girl wanting a different dress, a conductor finding a passenger without a ticket, a farmer selling a cow, a storekeeper turning up his nose at a tub of butter, a preacher pounding away at sin, an auctioneer trying to build up the bidding, why, it was just like the best kind of play acting, the expressions they used.

It was the hottest debate a person could listen to and when you boil it down that's all any debate is. That's the point of it, to see whether the negative or the affirmative wins, that's what they try to get at no matter where they start.

They used up so much energy, those two, and whooped it up so loud it got too strong for the mother doing the dishes and she stopped them, which was too bad. I'd like to have seen the finish. It was about time though, the grandpa was about as worn out as if he'd done a threshing alone. He'd built up a good red color and his breath was coming hard, but I think he would have stuck it out a little while longer anyhow. The little girl stopped, but pretty unwilling.

"Well then," she said, "let's do it the other way. I'll say no and you——"

"Shut up," her ma ordered. "I've had enough of that goose gabbling."

I never did find out whether that mare had twins or not. She didn't have anything at all that night in spite of keeping the farmer and his neighbor up until morning. By the time we had breakfast, which those two took in shifts and I had to drive on, that mare had upset the work schedule on two farms. Nature is sure unpredictable.

204

The middle of that morning on a long stretch over a rough ridge where there hadn't been any farms for two or three miles, and it was one long pretty view after another across different valleys, I caught up to a boy walking in my direction. I saw he was about as old as me. I asked him if he could use a ride, which he could and climbed up.

"Where you from?" he asked, looking over my rig.

"Chicago," I said, which wasn't exactly up to date, but a lot more powerful way to start a conversation than any other answer I could give him. "Rohland harness out of Chicago. I'm Emil Rohland."

"You mean you come from a factory?"

I like people who light up like that. I like people you can say something to and it starts the wonder turning inside them. "Yep," I said, "a big factory."

"Tell me about your power." He said it so eager he pushed his face way over toward mine to meet my answer quicker.

"Power?" I said. "All that a team can produce and then some. Why, Pa's taken our standard trace strap and hitched two teams to each end and they couldn't pull it apart. A Rohland harness *is* power."

"Huh-uh," he said. "I mean the power in your factory. How do you run your machines? What kind of an engine do you have?"

"Ten Rohlands, Pa and my brothers, and besides us we hire dozens of harness makers. We don't need any machines. We don't need an engine."

"Only handwork? I thought you. said you had a factory?"

"We do have a factory. That's what I just told you." Doggone if that kid from such back ridge country wasn't digging out the very thing Pa wanted the worst way, steam and pulleys and whistles and belts. There I was, having to argue for the side I wasn't for myself. Runaway words get a fellow off the road he wants worse than a runaway

205

team. That kid wasn't running down the quality of our harness. I didn't have to fight him. "I like engines myself," I said, "and Pa would give anything if there was a way you could stitch leather with them."

"My gosh, all they'd have to do is make a heavier sewing machine."

"That's what Pa says, but nobody makes them, he's tried."

"Well, they will, it's just bound to come. Say, your pa's all right, looking for something that isn't even planned out yet. Mostly people are the other way around. An invention is finished and works, and could save time and make money for them, and they won't have a thing to do with it. That's why I'm eight miles away from home up on this ridge and walking, because so many people don't want to change when something better comes along."

"It's pretty up here. I can see it isn't that, though. You got a reason for being up here sort of the same, maybe, as I have. What's your name?"

"Henry Stonesmith. My father's a thresher. You've sure heard of him around here. Maybe no, though, that's right, you said Chicago."

"Threshing? That's a long time away yet."

"Yes, but there's plans to be made ahead. We're buying a steam engine and you know what? Some of these farmers say they'll pull out of the ring if we don't stick to horsepower. Say they won't let the steam engine on the place. Scared of fire. There's enough like that we have to spread out pretty far to get a season's work. I'm up here to see whether we can haul the engine up the grades. I also look at the bridges to see if they'll be strong enough. We're getting a big engine. It weighs tons."

"How's your pa fixed for harness? Ought to have strong new harness for a load like that on roads like this."

"Guess maybe we should. I'll recommend you to him. But you know what? We shouldn't have to need harness at all. The engine power should get to the wheels and drive itself. A locomotive does, and a steam engine could be made to do the same, that's all a locomotive is."

I told him about the one I'd seen at Racine. He was good and interested until I had to describe the belts that ran from the engine to the wheel. "That would never do for a threshing engine," he said. "Belts give too much trouble. It should be geared."

"You haven't even got your steam engine yet and already you want to improve it. Where'd you learn all that machinery stuff?"

He laughed. "I don't know anything about it. Someday I'm going to, though. This fall I'm starting at the University of Wisconsin. I'm going to be an engineer and work with power."

Poor kid, I told him the way to be an engineer was to get a job on the railroad and work up to his own locomotive.

He laughed again, this time at me a little. "A man running an engine is one kind of engineer. That kind gets its name from handling engines. The kind I mean plans the engines, and figures out where the strain comes and how strong the parts have to be. That kind of engineering teaches how to handle different kinds of natural forces."

"Natural forces? Steam isn't a natural force. You have to fire up a boiler. That's a manufactured force, it seems to me."

"A natural force is anything that always acts the same way when the conditions are the same. The trick in engineering is to find out what all the conditions are and control them. Steam is only one kind. There's dozens of natural forces. There's power in all of them and most of them nobody knows hardly anything about using. You're selling harness. That only harnesses horses. Someday men will learn how to harness rivers, and the wind, and the tides in the ocean, and stuff like kerosene that explodes, and gravity, and electricity, and sunlight, and I don't even know how many more."

"Hold on now. We *got* windmills. We *got* waterwheels.

207

We *got* the telegraph, we *got* burning glasses. Why, they even catch sunlight to take pictures. And harnessing explosions, they do that now every time a man pulls the trigger of a gun. Henry, you'd make a first-rate locomotive engineer being so wild about force you can control, but where can you go with that other engineering? Things get discovered only once and everything you said has already been discovered.''

He was the arguingest person. ''Oh, has it now? All right, take the telegraph. I admit it settles the problem for good for getting word from one place to another, that can't be improved on. But the telegraph is only maybe a tenth of the use there is in electricity. They've built electric motors—I've never seen one—but they will turn anything a small steam engine will. They've also built dynamos which are things that make electricity when they're turning. Now, supposing a big dynamo would be turned by a waterwheel, and you'd run the electricity it makes over some wires to one of those motors. Why, man, you could put it up on top of a hill and get power up there as if your water wheel was up there too, out of the way of a flood. Wouldn't such a thing be a new discovery worth studying about?''

''That's the point. It isn't necessary. If you want power up there, put a steam engine up there. What's the use of going into something different when what there is gives the results you're after?''

He was a smart kid and I liked him no end, but, Lord, how odd his thinking was. That's the trouble out in the country where people are apt to be alone too much. I think I was able to help him some. If he sticks to steam, he'll be all right. There's a future in steam.

I let him off down in the next valley. I hoped him and his father would do all right with their new threshing rig, I like people with good business gumption. I kept on thinking about him all day and those different kinds of power. I think maybe he had something there when he mentioned sunlight. You take a burning glass making a white-hot spot no bigger than a pinhead, it will burn a hole in most anything without having to warm up. All they'd have to do is make a big magnifying glass, maybe sixty feet across or so, and set it up and put a boiler at the hot point. You could run the biggest steam engine and never have to haul in coal or wood. Why, you could run it for nothing. Something practical like that is going to come pretty soon, I'll bet in a year or two. Electricity! Running water uphill through wires! If that's what they try to teach at a university, Sarah was lucky they wouldn't let her in.

12

It was a wonderful spring morning. The air had a fresh washed smell, and you wondered how it could be that the world is so old and still looks and feels so brand-new. You thought of Genesis and how they tell you it was six thousand years ago, but your ears and eyes and nose and the tingle in your skin said it couldn't have been farther back than while you were eating breakfast. The slant of the sun, the wet on the grass, the buds popping out, a glistening plow rising out of the furrow to make its turn and the long first black mark behind it being explored by robins—how could anything ever have been newer? The littlest things underfoot couldn't have known a yesterday, slick polished ants, as black as a careful woman wants her stove to be, were ringing their holes with neat piles of sand crystals. I drove past a sweet-smelling big tree the bees were humming around and if someone had come up and warned me to go by quiet without disturbing anything, I'd have known right off that God himself was taking a nap on the far side of it with His back against the trunk and His hat over His eyes satisfied with what He'd done.

A shadow came over. It wasn't anything more than one

of those fleecy clouds playing tag with the sun, but when they're in front they lose the white and for a minute they're pretty black. Funny how they must be the same thing wherever they are and can still be any color they take a mind to. I looked all around the sky wondering about clouds and storms and stuff and what it is that makes one change to the other and how big the whole thing really is and if there'll ever be a way to use it, and why the world is so crowded with stuff down here and so empty up there. Away off to the south, just over the rim of hills, a smoky spot shimmered and trailed off in the distance behind. I couldn't tell what it was. As I watched it would melt all together and get bigger and rise higher but ever so slow.

The next time I looked it was lots darker and bigger and seemed to be unrolling itself from behind the hills. I thought I could see specks in it. The bigger it got, the faster it came. The specks came plain then, it was all specks, easy to see in the front and dissolving into eye strain farther back. They were birds, by the hundreds, by the thousands, by the millions maybe, flowing and spilling across the sky like wheat shoots out when a sack is emptied. There weren't any leaders, they came on abreast and they didn't cackle or honk or chirp or anything of their own noise, but so many of them churning up the air made the sound of a big wind ahead of a storm. It was spooky to hear blowing like that and not see a bush pitching or a tree swaying. They came overhead and passed and they were still coming as far as I could see. They made a shimmering river across the sky, wide and full and deep. It twisted and made sweeping bends as though there were valleys up there to follow just like there are on the ground. Long after the front was out of sight the steady solid stream behind kept almost the same position, bending where the ones ahead had bent, flying low or flying high, however the first had done.

I don't remember that I had stopped the team when I

211

first noticed them coming in the distance. I probably did because when you look far you need a base that doesn't jiggle. I dropped my head to take the kink out of my neck. I saw the horses had just as strange a feeling as I did. They stood with their heads together and their back ends spread as far from each other as the tugs would let them, trembling and nostrils wide and uneasy as if a train was going by. I got off and went to their heads and patted them a little which seemed to help all around.

The pattern of flight changed some. Overhead it seemed they covered the whole sky but if I judged by the width they kept in the distance ahead and in the distance behind they still followed their river, maybe a hundred feet above me and maybe a quarter mile out each side. Some of the solid was breaking, they seemed to be coming in waves that overlapped like shingles on a slant. They went by like bullets. Once in a while when there'd be a particularly good space between the surges, your eyes could look head on into the next wave and it would be tier after tier maybe fifty feet thick and so tight together their wings could have knocked feathers off each other. Inside where I couldn't see it must have been so thick I'll bet there were coasters riding with their wings folded and carried along because there wouldn't be space under them to fall through.

I tried and tried to pick out single ones to see what they were. I couldn't make it work, they blurred together so and looking straight up with them overhead was a risk too. Spatter fell all around, so much of it the air began to smell musty sharp.

I heard a gun go off, and in a little while another. Pretty soon guns were booming ahead and behind and all around and then so often you could hold your breath and count up to ten different blasts before you'd have to blow out and suck in new air. It came to me then what they were, they

212

were those passenger pigeons people tell about. It kept up like that maybe an hour.

As sudden as they came they were gone. The wind roar died out far away. The guns stopped. Silence seemed so unexpected I wondered if my ears had quit. After a while some little bird experimented with a chirp and other spring-chorus sounds picked up. One of my horses whinnied and on ahead a strange one answered. I climbed back on the wagon and slapped the lines.

All those pigeons. Where did they come from? Where were they going? How many were there? It must have been all the passenger pigeons in the world and in one flock right over my head. Maybe they are a common thing out in the country like this when the land wakes up for another season, but never having seen anything like that before they thrilled me. I had to find somebody to talk to about them.

I drove a little piece and came to a field where there'd been plowing going on. The horses were tied to a fence rail with nobody around. I waited and then a man came over a rise coming back from his buildings, I suppose, with a double-barreled shotgun up to his shoulder, sweeping at the sky with nothing to pull the trigger for.

That man was mad. His hat was jammed down mad. His feet stepped mad. His shoe-blacking eyebrows crouched down so mad his eyes looked ready to squirt. A man in that shape doesn't take time to explore you with a "Good morning, boy," he spills his mad like a barrel bursts when the hoops snap.

"Salt pork until our tongues are pickled," he roared, "and a thousand tons of pigeon pie go overhead and my gun two forties away. For an hour I gawk with my mouth hanging open."

He tramped around excited explaining how he'd never have a chance like that again, and wondered where they

213

had headed for and damned them and told how these were his last two caps he'd been saving for a chicken hawk and by Jupiter he'd rammed in a charge this time that would bring down a tubful if they'd only come back, and who in hell was I.

I mentioned harness a little, but it didn't seem to interest him. I expected to lose him any minute to get back to his plowing, but he wasn't holding that very urgent right then either. A gun hangs in the hands a lot more exciting than a pair of plow handles. "Look there, look there," he shouted, "here comes another flight. By Jupiter there *will* be pigeon pie today."

Sure enough, over the hills where the first had come from, the sky spilled out again and the wind sound came on again like before. This time they were even wider and thicker and the under side darkened up solid. It looked as black as a storm, and made me feel funny without knowing exactly why. Clouds made from birds isn't the way a person is used to things.

Their coming so solid like that unhinged the farmer too. They're all handy with guns, they have to be living out alone in the hills and pockets, and I'll bet any other time he could make his shots count. He fired head-on at the pigeons while they were still out of range, and both barrels, one right after the other. People don't shoot like that when they go after meat, they only act like that when they're crazy excited or scared shaky or try to drive off something they don't want any closer. Those pigeons never even noticed they were shot at.

They came overhead and on to hide the sun and spread sidewise until we couldn't see out. They were even lower than the first flight. They skimmed just along the treetops, and I don't know how much higher, but it must have been awful thick to build up such a wind noise and dim the light on such a bright day. The farmer held his empty gun with the barrel drooping toward the ground, his head

214

raised and his mouth open. Beyond the field, to the north, the flight seemed to dip down into an oak woods. They were lighting. At first all I could see was the curtain of birds dip down behind the trees. As the trees got full and couldn't hold any more the lighting place moved closer and closer to us until it was at the edge of the woods. Birds in the air got so thick they made a haze between us and the trees. The haze took on a pattern of puffs and billows dropping out of the sky, turning up just before they reached the ground and landing in the trees with a graceful upward swoosh. Branches filled up and sagged with the weight and more pigeons fluttered in the air without room to light and landed anyhow and crowded off those that were already there. Pigeons landed on other pigeons and sometimes a whole branch would crack and go down. The whole woods was full of motion as if a fire was in it and every tongue of flame was a pigeon, pigeons on the ground darting their heads as they fed on the acorns, pigeons whisking through the spaces between the trunks, pigeons shimmering and hovering over each branch, pigeons in the sky above the trees like the dense smoke of a burning that can't get enough air.

There were more pigeons than woods to hold them, it looked like, and still they roared overhead, landing if it was at all possible, going on if they couldn't. Bare ground they skipped mostly, except where the furrows were turned. The new plowing right where we were standing had angleworms in it which they seemed to know about, but its being open and us there watching bothered them. They'd swoop down to land, and change their mind and go back up again to look it over and drop down again and scare themselves up once more and finally make a hovering decision to take a chance. Those that were down made a regular whirlwind of the plowing, as they beaked into the clods. Birds from in back flew ahead to get an open spot and as soon as they lit others lit ahead of them until

215

it was a rolling, boiling storm of wings and leaves and dust and noise. They twittered and squawked like recess at a crowded school. We stood there forgetting everything except how to watch. They'd work up close, maybe fifty feet or so, and then get cautious and sound a warning in their throats which would be a surprise to those about to light ahead of them who would have to stand on their tails and tread air and decide quick and shoot off every which way like blue sparks. They turned so quick they'd leave feathers to add to the litter being whipped up. They were elegant birds. Even if they were called pigeons, they were altogether different from the clumsy pigeons that hang around barns and livery stables looking sleepy. They were as different as a soldier is from a beer-wagon driver. They were trim and pretty and quick and bright.

Mostly they were gray-blue and brown-blue. When they pecked at the ground, you could see a brassy shine on the backs of their necks, sometimes green, sometimes purple, it changed right while you looked. When they raised up, their throats and breasts were wine-red, dark and rich, some of them duller than the rest, though. They had uncommon long tails and red feet. They had little heads and big eyes, red eyes that caught the light and flashed it back. The bull's-eye in a switchman's lantern doesn't have as red a red, they just don't make a red like those pigeons' eyes.

We stood and looked and looked. I could have easy picked up a rock and killed three or four, it wouldn't matter where it landed, but I didn't feel like it and the farmer never thought to, he was standing so still. Sometimes a thing is so big and so grand the only way to gather any part of it in and own it is with your eyes and ears. Right there, right then, passenger pigeons held title to the plowing, to the woods beyond the fence, to every tree in sight, to all the air and all the space. A hailstorm couldn't have covered the landscape more thorough or beat up all it hit like those pigeons did. Seeing and hearing and feeling it all crowded inside me so tight it felt like the stuff I think with was tramping down too. It was a scary feeling. It was a relief to have harness to think of as a kind of comeback medicine.

No matter how thick the pigeons were, a mile off the line they followed should get me out of them, and put me among people going about their regular business. There just had to be an outside edge of pigeons. Anything else would give you indigestion of the brain, which is what happens when a piece of thinking starts common and gets out of control and builds itself up to a horror.

I got out of them, and yet I didn't. My first move toward the horses put panic in the pigeons. The near ones flew straight up beating their wings together to make sharp cracking sounds which the others took as a danger signal and rose making the same kind of racket. The whole flock thundered. Right amongst them like that it sounded like a reunion of drummer boys celebrating the Civil War all over again.

The disturbance I started circled out about the length of a six-car train all around. I never had that much influence over a landscape before, or anything else for that matter, of such a size. People seeing the pigeon cloud I kicked up from a distance could easy mistake it, I bet, for a barn and a couple of strawstacks going up in smoke. I traveled in the clear space in the middle of the commotion for twelve minutes, I timed it, before I drove through the thickest of the pigeons. After that it was spotty and then all clear.

I had a poor day. Anybody that had a gun, or could borrow one from a place where the man was gone or sick, was out in the woods. I could hear them banging in all directions. When I did find anybody at home all they wanted to talk about was pigeons, pigeons, pigeons. They kept going over all day in ribbons and streamers across the sky, sometimes thick, sometimes thin, sometimes high, sometimes low, and every time you thought they were gone and there couldn't be any more if you raked the continent, another river would start flowing out of the south or sometimes west of south.

Back at Sparta the coming of the pigeons controlled all the talk and pepped up the business. At the livery stable they asked me outright whether I planned to use the team and wagon tomorrow because if I didn't they had call from three or four more shooting parties than they could handle. I told them I wanted it the same as always. That made them a little huffy because the day rate brings in more than booking for a week like I'd done, not to mention the extra dollar or so they can always add on top, and get, when everybody wants a wagon at the same time.

A buggy came in, and the box behind was so solid full its lid was propped straight up. The two men who'd hired it had to ask for two feed sacks to carry off the pigeons they'd shot. The stiff dead things they threw into the sacks head-first and tail-first and every which way, feathers matted bloody and smelling gutty, packed together until the sacks were so solid they couldn't lift them and had to drag them off.

All over town it was the same way. Boys came walking back from the woods with pigeons dangling wherever they could hang them. Every woodshed door had a woman or two or an old man sitting on chunk wood plucking feathers. Men walked out of hardware stores with shotguns they'd just bought. One had a sign tacked up, "Sold out of shot." Kids in yards whittled at slingshots. Down at the depot the telegraph operator had a circle of men around him anxious to know what Chicago and Milwaukee markets were paying by the barrel. In between he grumbled because he couldn't get his own messages out to the professional netting companies he had the names of in St. Louis and Peoria and Chicago. He said they pay a good reward to the first operator who wires them for sure where the big flights settle. I wondered why he didn't keep still and send whatever messages he wanted to. The people crowding him wouldn't know the difference unless they could telegraph too, which didn't seem very likely to me.

They didn't have a cooper in a little town like Sparta and a butcher was dancing around trying to get his message to the operator to call La Crosse for a supply of barrels. The mayor of the town was in there too, not crowding in to send a message or anything, but crowding in to prove how right his politics were. I never saw a man fit himself more plain with an I-told-you-so gleam to his expression. "This is what happens," he pointed out to some of the men who'd tried to crowd into the operator and couldn't make it, "when there's such limited telegraph outlet for Sparta and for the whole area Sparta serves. It's a disgrace to the country that the telegraph, which should be a universal service, is left in the hands of commercial enterprise. Why doesn't Congress act to establish postal telegraph? I've always favored it and I'll keep at it until we get it. Telegraph service for the public in every post office, why, think how the country could prosper linked together in such a network."

Over at the blacksmith shop, which stayed open because the smith was extra good on guns, anything that had ever been shot was all of a sudden brought out for repair. There were a couple twins there, about thirty years old, I guess, and bachelors, you could tell by the buttons gone they had replaced with horseshoe nails. Those brothers had stopped to show off their pigeons and tell how they'd got them.

"Twenty-six in a single shot," one of them bragged.

"Got pretty near a hundred here," the other said, "and weren't out over twenty minutes."

"Well now, Canada Bob," someone else said, "or are you Canada Bill? Never could tell you two apart, not that it makes any difference. Weren't you scared having all them pigeons come at you and you two alone out there with only shotguns to defend yourselves? You must have pooped your pants. Seems I can smell it.''

"Hell.'' Somebody else laughed. "I know how you got your pigeons. Those were stragglers you stepped on while you were running away from the shadow of the flight.'' Everybody laughed loud and rough. The twins walked away sad. " 'By now, Canada Bill, Canada Bob. Be lots of shooting tomorrow, you'll have to go north, way, way, north where you can't hear it.'' The laughing wasn't fun laughing, it was tear-apart laughing that scratches blood and leaves salt in it. Along with it the blacksmith drummed his anvil and made it laugh too, sharp and irony.

"What you got against foreigners?'' I asked one of them I knew because I'd sold him a set of harness the day before.

"What foreigners?''

"Them two, the two you've just been so mean to.''

"Canada Bob and Bill? Hell, they ain't no foreigners, they're born and raised right here.''

"Aren't they smart or something?''

"They're smart all right, too damn smart. When the rest of us around here marched off to war and the draft got to them they sneak off for Canada and made good money in the wheat fields, and 'sixty-six or so they had guts enough to come back to inherit their old man's place, the yellow cowards. Be a long day before we'll ever let them forget it.''

Supper at the hotel was wonderful better than usual. We had pigeons. They pan fry crispy brown and the breast isn't just a V of meat around the bone like a layed-out old hen, but round and plump and juicy and sweet. I ate two of them and finished off with little morsels that fall off the bone and settle tempting in the warm fat on the bottom of the platter.

220

Everybody else at the table lit into those pigeons just as hard as I did. They knew a lot about them too. When I said how good they tasted the man opposite who was in town to put together four mowers he had sold to the Sparta dealer said, "Sure, but if they nest near here you should taste the squabs, they'll be ready in about a month. These are all right, but they're nothing like squab."

The high school principal from Tomah who'd come on business to see the county superintendent and would go back on the night train taught about pigeons in his science class. "They'll nest somewhere near," he said, "because the acorn crop last year was extra good and there's oak and lots of it in a band across the whole state through here."

"A strange bird," the man next to him said. He had black fingers and terrible around the nails on his thumb and first finger because he was a printer and ink is made not to come off. "Think I've set more type on passenger pigeons than on any other kind of creature. Everything about them is spectacular. For instance, they're not a water bird, but they'll light on water to drink and hold themselves up by spreading their wings and take off again just before the water soaks into their feathers."

"A miracle," a thin man with a voice made for Fourth of July said and popped in a forkful. "They come in glory, power, and infinite number to prove God's watchful care over His world. Remember how it was a dove that brought word to Noah that the flood had abated? Just so, they come now to assure the fertility of another season." He was an evangelist there to start a revival, his posters were tacked all over town.

"Beg pardon, Reverend," the mower man said, "but their fertility is a little hard on the farmers. With pigeons in the country it takes an extra peck of wheat seed for every peck a farmer would ordinarily plant. Just because they taste good, we shouldn't forget when they come this thick they're bound to hurt the crops. Why, they've been known to clean out the acorns so completely the hogs can't pasture for forage.''

"Well," the principal said, "they are a crop themselves. Think of all the meals they provide. Probably every single table in town tonight and maybe five miles around, I don't know how far, has pigeons on it and maybe that will last a month. The feathers rate next to goose for bedding and pillows, and there's cash for birds that can be salted down and shipped out. The squabs render out a shortening that's cleaner and tastier than most butter this time of year, and the thick droppings under the roosts process out a high grade of saltpeter.''

I sat there looking at the platter with a few pieces of pigeon still on it getting cold, but what I was seeing again were those sweeping flights across the sky and those proud living colors when they worked the fresh plowing. The meat I had just eaten would be gone by breakfast. The performance out in the open I'd been in that day I knew I would remember as long as I can think.

"They sure must have killed a lot of pigeons today," the mower man said, "all that peppering around we been hearing, and all of the dead birds I see brought into town.''

"Dead birds," the printer said with sort of a squint that looked back inside him more than it looked out. "Funny how so much of what's in this world can't be made use of until it's dead. Pork, beef, wheat, sugar cane, why, damn if we don't have to kill constant to keep alive, even the vegetarians.''

He'd discovered something interesting up in the attic of his mind and trotted it out to the light to see what all it could be used for. "This tablecloth, comes from killed flax. The handle of that carving knife—bone. The leather in our shoes. The horsehair in a mattress, and the cotton ticking it's covered with.'' He raised his eyes to the ceiling. "The

222

rafters and roofboards and shingles, ripped out of trees. What is man, anyhow, some kind of maggot that can live only in the presence of death?"

The evangelist's lips quivered more excited the farther the printer went. That printer was getting into preacher territory but he didn't notice. "Reminds me of a report I set up for the Legislature back in Madison four five years ago. Said when you take off the trees you get fire and floods and wind and loose soil blowing around and the land dies. All our killing, we're even killing the land and then where'll we be? Comes a time when there's nothing but white bones and even the maggots are gone."

He scared me. He gave me that same awful feeling I get poking around in the Book of Revelations.

The evangelist boomed out as if there was a back row he had to reach. "It is all a part of God's way." Such a confident, ringing voice, it was a comfort he was there. "The Good Book tells us the earth shall be destroyed and there shall be a new heaven and earth. Perhaps it shall be a slow, long-time destruction, as you visualize, in which man is a part of the process performing according to divine plan. Most authorities, however, believe the end will be sudden rather than prolonged."

He wasn't as comforting as I started to give him credit for. Slow or fast, the destruction of the world isn't my idea of table talk. I got goose pimples racing all over me. I got to feeling like castor oil was pushing.

"I'm not proposing a theological doctrine, Reverend," the printer said. "I'm just mentioning what everybody knows when they think about it, that generally a dead thing is more usable than a living thing."

"You're forgetting man, the most important of all. Living, moving man in God's image. Man with a soul to be developed and perfected."

"Sure, Reverend. With heaven as the goal. And where

223

is heaven? On the other side of death. Not much use to us until we're processed, the same as a lumber baron fells his trees, or a farmer salts his pork.''

''A vale of tribulation,'' the evangelist said with his chin dropped on his vest and without using hardly any of his voice. He said it sort of complaining to himself. I don't know if it was on account of how things are down here or on account of the printer.

13

Next morning was foggy and so thick it was dim. I started out like usual figuring it would clear up in an hour or so like it commonly does after the sun works down on it and thins it out. A fog is a cozy thing because nothing has any distance to it. A thing is either close by or isn't at all. Your eyes can't wander. Your ears don't go out very far either, I suppose noises get soggy and damp too and dissolve away pretty close to where they're made. Things get kind of dreamy and stand out alone and surprising and nothing has any connection with anything else. There isn't any livery stable, there's just a door where a man goes in and a team and rig comes out. There's no schoolhouse, there's just a boy and a girl walking out of the mist with straps around their books and walking into the mist. The fog ahead seemed so thick it made a fuzzy wrapping around a hitching post I could just see, but where I was it had a hole in it, and sharp, and my own team was as clear as they had ever looked. When I got to the hitching post, it was clear there and I'd brought the hole along with me and where I'd come from was all fogged in. I've tried and tried, but I've never been able to catch up to where fog is the thickest.

I figured it would be good to get going before the fog lifted because it would help me catch farmers at their barns with plenty of time to talk harness. I didn't know if the pigeons could come over or not in fog like that, but it didn't matter, nobody could see them if they did. I was thankful for that fog, those pigeons the day before were as bad competition for the harness business as I ever met.

Maybe two miles out of town—it's hard to tell how far you come in a fog—the road must have gone into an oak woods, anyhow there were trees all around dissolving away into fog ahead and behind and to the sides and up. Looking up in a fog is more mysterious than any other direction, it eats a thing away so fast. Branches would zigzag up ever so strong and plain and divide and fork three or four times and above the last little crotches I could make out the wood just melted away wispy and ghosty. I never rightly heard just how high up a thing has to be before you call it a part of the sky, but it must change with the weather. Those big old pines up on the Chippewa high enough to make me dizzy looking up them seemed like they only sort of brushed the sky and yet these ordinary scrub oaks popped themselves right into it for sure. Maybe that's what a fog is, the old sky getting so worn-out tired it has to come down awhile and rest and get its strength before it can go back up and sail around again.

The sky wasn't the only thing resting. I drove slick and clean into more of those pigeons again before I noticed them or they noticed me. One minute the oaks were bare and lonesome. Fifty feet farther it was as if you'd gone quiet through a henhouse door in the twilight and caught the roosts filling up and some still pecking around in the feed. My horses were quiet, walking slow. The ground and the old grass and leaves that rustle so in dry weather were misted silent. The fog had moistened up the boards

226

in the wagon so there wasn't any rattling or squeaking. I sat still on the load so there wasn't anything to rile up or scare those pigeons. They took the horses and load and me for something natural to be expected in a fog, I guess. They didn't pay any attention at all.

Pigeons sat shoulder to shoulder on the branches, bright and sharp where they were near, gray and foggy and almost out of sight on the higher places. Way up where the twigs were dimmed out, the shape of single pigeons could be made out, blobs of gray against a little lighter gray. On the ground they pecked away at acorns. The ones changing places flew skillful, twisting and wheeling around the trunks as if there was nothing to it. The team walking along disturbed the ones in the road. They'd fly up and hover overhead until I'd gone by and then light again where they'd been. Some of them even lit on the endgate, their pretty red feet gripping the top of the board, their bodies rolling to keep their balance with the pitch of the wagon, their necks shimmering purple into green and back into purple again, their red eyes like sparks popped out of a fire and ready to start their own. Those pigeons were enjoying the coziness of the fog just like I was. They were using it for protection too. Nobody else had discovered them there, I never heard a gun or met another team or saw anybody since I'd left Sparta. I drove through them a long time. They gave me a delight with their endless numbers and their pretty looks and the skill they used to handle themselves.

Funny, though, I either saw them by the thousands or else I didn't see them at all. They sure must have liked each other's company. You take a blue jay, for instance, he can get along happy whether he's alone or not, usually he'd rather have a little territory to be boss over where he can drive off any other blue jay who pokes around too close. A passenger pigeon must be like a honey bee or an ant the way it can't seem to feel comfortable unless the whole relation is right there with him. Worse even, ants and bees do strike out alone once in a while.

I drove and drove through them. They set me to thinking. They were probably all over the whole country today just like they were over the whole sky yesterday. The reason I wasn't hearing any guns was because the swish of their wings around me and the fog drowned out any distant shooting. Pigeons roosting all around like they were would be lots easier to knock down than to pepper out of the air. That fog wasn't rising, it looked like an all-day affair. See here, I asked myself, what farmer or anybody else is going to stay home today and buy harness when the woods are full of wonderful tasty meat like this that a person can fill a wagon box with if he only has a club?

The more I thought about it the more it looked like a hopeless day. About half-past ten I turned around and headed back to Sparta. After dinner I dropped around to the gristmill. A foggy day is most generally a heavy day at a gristmill, but today I expected it would be pretty light on account of the pigeons. I was wrong. There were a lot of wagons waiting. A lot of talk of pigeons too and how they were slick and clean gone out of the country. I sold three sets of harness. Maybe that wasn't fair, taking their money and not telling them what they wanted to know, but I wasn't going to tell on those pigeons.

It surprised me nobody had come the same road I had been on. Come to think of it, I hadn't passed a driveway and the road was hardly used. It must have been just a backwoods trail. Such country and the fog too could swallow up a lot of pigeons without anybody knowing a thing about it. I was glad they were hid. It made my harness important again.

I found farmers I hadn't got to before around the saloons and at the machinery dealer. I headed for the depot just before passenger time from La Crosse counting on finding a few farmers there too. Everybody likes to watch

228

a train come in. In the fog, though, there wasn't much track to look down.

A station platform is always interesting to poke around on, there's so many different barrels and kegs and boxes and things standing around. The dogs like it too, there's rats to chase under the platform, and smells to sniff on the planks, and kegs of herring to puzzle over and raise a leg to. A big black mongrel came trotting out of the fog and growled off a little yellow one. He wouldn't let him anywhere on the platform. That black dog took possession like he was the station agent. He checked all the barrels. He discovered other dogs' brands and squirted his own to cover them. After he made the rounds he sat down to scratch his ear. Soon as he had that taken care of, his piles must have started itching or maybe he had worms, anyhow he stuck his back legs out ahead of himself and hunched his rump down and started to pull himself along with his front legs to scratch himself by dragging. I don't know how he avoided getting slivers. He dragged himself across a puddle one of the barrels had leaked without noticing what he'd done. That barrel was turpentine, it had it stamped across the head. I never saw a dog turpentine himself before. It worked the same though. He got up puzzled. After a little he made a dodging jump and wheeled around to snap at what had bit him. From there on I can't just say what did happen, that dog went into such a yowling bouncing blurr. First thing I knew he'd streaked off ki-yi-ing into the fog and the little yellow one lit out behind to act like it was him the black one was running from. It wasn't long before the little yellow one came trotting back stiff-legged and head high to put his own brand back again on all the important places. I don't think herring is to be trusted any more. I've lost my appetite for it.

The passenger was twenty minutes late. I can understand why they call a train a passenger because that's what it carries, but it's a funny name for pigeons, come to think

229

of it. They aren't passengers, they have to carry themselves. Passengers in the air, whoever heard of such a thing?

The train came out of the fog as spooky as everything else that day. First there was nothing and then a fuzzy outline whispering at you that got darker and darker until it was a rumbling, clanking black engine. Pieces of fog were wound around the driver axles. The steam boxes leaked out more fog. The stack smoke and the steam in it didn't carry up very good, it all drifted back down again to thicken the fog and give it a rich wood-smoke flavor. Bright yellow cars were bright only one at a time as they came oposite, the ones pulled past grayed up as soon as they were by and the ones behind and coming up yellowed out of the gray a different shade for every car length. The men on the brake wheels on the vestibule platforms pulled like sixty and made the shoes screech against the wheels. It took ever so long to stop and when it did it was a thump stop like a train always does.

Trainmen all along the passenger and from the station started running toward the engine, brakemen, switchmen, conductor, agent, and everybody. There was something wrong up there to make them all do that. I got up there as fast as anybody. What it was, they'd hit some sheep back a ways in the fog. What I'd seen wound around the driver axles and the connecting rods wasn't wisps of fog like I'd taken it for. It was pieces of sheepskin and gray wool and it was a dickens of a mess all tangled tight. It had got hot. It stunk burnt and gutty. It was meat and mutton tallow ground and scorched tight like a frying pan gets when it fries dry. It was wool balled up like burdock burrs catch on a collie. Sheep are the worst thing a locomotive can hit. It was lucky they didn't ball up underneath and derail them.

They had to untangle that locomotive. That's the interesting thing about depots and yards and tracks and stuff, you never know what might happen and it's always worth sticking around. Everybody knows that, that's why there's always so many visitors come traintime. They were working and we were watching when somebody grabbed my shoulder. It was Rudolph.

"Didn't expect you here," he said. He could scarcely talk, he wheezed so with a cold. "Was going to try to catch you tonight at the hotel. Better this way, we can talk while they're repairing the engine. Then I can stay right on this train and save a day. Let's get off somewhere where we're alone."

"You better stop anyhow, and go to bed. You sound sick. You look sick too."

"I'm all right. Every hour counts. By tomorrow I might not be able to get a room, they're centering in so fast."

"The Grange? You got the Grange lined up?"

"That can wait. How many harness you got left?"

"About half a carload. Around three hundred sets, I guess."

"Ain't very many, but enough to start on. I'll go through. You lock up the car and get it shipped to Kilbourn as fast as you can. Pack up our stuff and check out of the hotel. Settle up and take the first train tomorrow."

"What's at Kilbourn? What's going on?"

"Pigeons, Emil, passenger pigeons. A harvest out of the sky. A fortune waiting to be cropped."

"Pigeons? They aren't any help to selling harness. People go pigeon crazy. They're around here too, by the millions. Everybody stops working to go hunting. My sales have fallen off something terrible."

"That's because your pigeons here are just a sport. All north of Kilbourn it's a nesting of them. The commercial hunters are moving in, the telegraph office at La Crosse is directing whoever asks them over to Kilbourn. It will be a regular packing house for a month or so and

231

heavy hauling, gear into the woods, pigeons out. There's netting business and crating business and salting business and barreling business and Lord knows what else they'll need lots of harness for. Got sixty dollars? I'm about out of money.''

I gave it to him from the sales I'd just made at the gristmill and hadn't had time yet to bank off to Pa. Rudolph sure uses money up fast, but, man, I thought, can he ever get results with it. But pigeons, how could he expect them to pay off like the pines in the Chippewa? I don't know, it seems the harder a person works at little business, the harder it is to understand big business.

I didn't have much time to figure out such a thing that should have had a lot of time to work on. They'd got the wool unsnarled and the sheep scraped off the locomotive and the conductor had yelled, '' 'Board,'' and Rudolph had swung on before I even started to realize how fast things change nowadays. But I did like he said and sent the car on to Kilbourn and paid up at the livery stable and went back to the hotel and packed.

Next morning I took the first train for Kilbourn which is pretty near halfway back to Milwaukee. It wasn't foggy any more, but it was a miserable cold rainy day. It was the kind of a day you like to catch a farmer inside his barn puttering around pleasant with a hammer and some nails and a board or two, but in no hurry. It was the best kind of weather there is to put a man in the mood to listen about harness. I enjoyed the train ride, though, and as for losing a good day, I didn't worry too much. Most all of Wisconsin spring, I noticed, is made up of that same kind of weather. The warm, balmy, stretchy days are wonderful comfortable, but they're as rare as holidays.

From Sparta to Kilbourn is sixty miles. You get out of the hills at Tomah and then there's a long stretch of marsh with warty gray-yellow bluffs sticking up here and there

232

right out of the marsh. Then the bluffs get thicker and blend into ranges of hills, but the railroad is smart, it runs along on the level in the valleys between without having to punch into the hills until it gets to the Wisconsin River where they've cut out a sort of shelf for the tracks to follow until they have to cross which takes a bridge and there you are in Kilbourn.

In the rain like that and from the train, with everything looking dismal, your thinking gets as unhappy as what you look at. Such things connect a lot more than a person is liable to notice offhand. I got to feeling how long it was since I'd left home, and if Ma was still fighting smells from getting into our new house. I wondered how business was going at the factory and if Pa had found any machines yet that would work in a harness factory. I imagined what a walk would be like today starting at one end and going through and stopping at each of my brothers for a word and what they each might be saying to me. I wondered about Rudolph and that awful cold of his.

He shouldn't have gone on, the shape he was in. Weather like we'd been having, one day so summery you'd lather up if you didn't peel off to your shirtsleeves and the next few when the buds would pull back hurt because they'd been fooled so, why, he could get lung fever being so careless on days like that. Maybe it wasn't the days. The night air is a hundred times worse, and with his habits, girling around like he always brags, who knows where he'd been laying out? That stuff opens your pores something awful dangerous, I've heard tell. Wisconsin spring and girls and open pores could be the worst kind of combination.

I didn't know why I was thinking like that, there on the train. At first I blamed it on the dismal weather, but the reason was more direct. I was in a whole carful of girls. Girls my age, girls a little older, girls up to maybe as much as where they start disguising with hair pieces and high

233

collars and rats and things so you don't know how old they are, but you know it's somewhere up there for sure just because they try so hard.

So many girls all together surprised me. It isn't usual for them to herd together so. I started talking to the one across the aisle who was sitting there pretty holding a cardboard box on her lap. "You all going on an excursion or something?"

Her eyes opened big. She smiled. She liked me to ask because it wasn't fresh or anything like when there's only one girl and you start talking. With a carful it's different, she was honored I picked her out. "No," she said, "not exactly, we're going to Kilbourn to work."

"What's at Kilbourn? I mean for you girls to work at?"

"Pigeons."

"Pigeons? Doing what?"

"I don't know, exactly. Pick and pack, I suppose. Two years ago my sister did awfully well at Kilbourn, didn't you, Bertha? Now I'm old enough to go along and earn money too."

"The pigeons come there regular?" I asked.

"It wasn't pigeons in 'sixty-nine," Bertha said. "Hops. We picked hops. They had such a bumper crop they had to bring in girls by the trainful, why, I met them from Milwaukee and all over and even then we scarcely had enough pickers. My, the money we made. Things change in a hurry, though. Last year the hop lice got in and there wasn't a crop. Sure hope we can do as well with the pigeons."

We must have been about twenty miles or so from Kilbourn and I was having the nicest time talking to those girls and hearing from Bertha about the dances they'd had in the evenings, that was where the hop waltz started, she said, when the whole car began squealing. Gee, but girls are high-pitched. The train was cutting square

234

through a flight and the girls were getting their first sight of the pigeons. Blue bullets whizzed past the windows on both sides and what trees we could see all had some too. The train slowed down until it hardly moved. At first I thought the engineer was being nice to the girls to give them a good view, but then it came to me it wasn't that. I'll bet he was scared of those pigeons, scared they'd get into the spokes and bearings and ball up with feathers like he'd had trouble the day before with the sheep.

There were plenty of pigeons, but they weren't near as thick as some of the flights I'd seen out of Sparta. They weren't as tight-packed on the trees like I'd seen them in the fog. Those girls went wild. They crowded the windows. The ones I'd been talking to and two others pushed tight against me and shoved their heads over my shoulder to look closer. Maybe it wasn't ladylike, but I didn't complain, I kind of liked it. Some hair brushed my face. It smelled good. It tickled too, all the way down my back and across my chest from just touching my cheek. Golly, how powerful a quick little touch from a girl is, to spread out so quick and so far.

What is there to a girl anyhow, I wondered, to make Rudolph lead such a risky life just to enjoy them? Was I missing something important, or worse yet, was there something wrong with me? Come June I'll be sixteen years old, and I'm all developed and mature and I'd like to find out for myself just once whether I can handle a girl proper or not. Some day I'll want to get married too and wouldn't that be terrible to be a husband and have something wrong when it's too late? I heard about a stallion once, that looked good and acted smart all around and when they led a mare up to be served he wasn't no more than a natural-born gelding. That isn't going to happen to Rudolph. He knows for sure it isn't. That should make him satisfied and contented, but it don't just quite work like that either, I notice. I don't know what it is.

"Aren't those pigeons pretty?" I said. "All those pretty colors and gay wings and long tails."

"Go good on a hat," one of the older ones said.

"Money, that's what they are. Five cents a dozen they're paying for clean picking. I guess we'll all keep busy."

I thought of the printer. Nothing is any good until it's dead. Not even to a girl who's supposed to be fragile and delicate herself and love beautiful things. It made me wonder if beauty is only for wild flowers and butterflies, and sunsets and such stuff that can't be changed into money. All those pretty girls after pigeons, I thought. Well, with Rudolph in town they'd better watch out or some of them will be pigeons themselves, the kind Rudolph collects.

We crossed a high bridge over the Wisconsin River where it was deep down between rocky walls. The conductor poked his head into the car and hollered Kilbourn and there we were at the station. I asked where the Tanner House was and hurried toward it. Kilbourn wasn't a very big town, I could see all of it from the station, just about, but it was lively. There were lumberjacks, which surprised me so far south, and farmers—they're always around. The townsfolk were on the streets too, which was a good sign the place would be exciting. There were Indians, and the La Crosse girls from the train. There were dozens and dozens of strangers from all over pulled there for business like me. They weren't hard to pick out because it always takes time to blend any man into a different town.

The teams in the streets were thick, they hauled boards and barrels and stuff every which way. The saloons all had little groups of men standing around outside. Wherever there was a store or a lunchroom, its door would never quite shut between people pushing it to go in or out.

Every town has two or three sheds scattered around

they once had use for, but afterwards get to stand empty. They weren't empty in Kilbourn. The first one I came to was made into a pigeon-packing factory. Dead pigeons were dumped high on a long table. A man chopped with a cleaver cutting off the wings. A woman next to him jerked off the tail feathers. Another man slit the bellies and tossed them along to a couple of girls who pulled out the crops and guts. There wasn't time to pull off the feathers. A man on the end packed them tight in layers in a barrel with a layer of ice every two or three layers of birds. I didn't peek in there very long, it stunk so, that and the pig yard they were next to. It took one man handying around to drive on the barrel head and roll away the full one and bring out another empty and scoop shovel up the guts and blood to carry over and dump to the pigs. When I turned to go, a grain wagon drove up. The box was only one board high, but it was loaded solid, tight full of pigeons. That shed factory, I figured, must be working around the clock.

A little farther on another shed was a carpenter shop where three men hammered crates together as fast as they could saw and pound. They had half a carload stacked up finished outside. Funniest crates I ever saw, only three inches high. They were for shipping pigeons live for sportsmen shoots, I discovered, for other parts of the country where there aren't any pigeons wild and they'll pay good money for a chance to pepper away when the pigeons think they've been turned loose. Such thin flat crates looked mighty uncomfortable, it seemed to me, for a bird that likes to stand straight up and stretches pretty near a foot high not counting his tail. Sandwiched flat like that I was told, keeps them from fluttering around and breaking their wings because they are a nervous bird. Seems to me they got good reason to be nervous with every person in the country after them one way or another. It made me think of the roost of them I'd found alone in the

237

fog and got me to wondering if they were still there secret and safe, or if somebody had discovered them too as soon as the fog lifted.

At the hotel I found Rudolph laying in bed. He wasn't sleeping and he wasn't thinking. He was sicker'n hell. His cold had gone in. He was hot and shivering. When he talked he was hoarse and short of breath. He scared me.

"You had anything to eat?" I asked.

He shook his head no so I chased down to the kitchen to order up some soup. They were busy down there, new action like that in a little town is always a strain on a hotel. They had all they could do just to dish up whatever they were cooking and carry it in the dining room and bring back the dishes and wash them. They didn't have any soup on hand and didn't have plans to make any. I had a terrible time. I had to find the owner himself and tell him what the matter was and then he went out personal to the kitchen and put on some bacon quick and stirred in a little flour and when it was brown, thinned it out with milk. He said soup was ordinarily made in a kettle and took hours and hours to build up a flavor, but bachelors and campers and such people who have to eat too without time to cook proper, and nobody to do it for them, having an appetite for soup they can always depend on bacon and milk because the flavor is in there already and comes out quick.

I took the bowl up to Rudolph. All he got down was two spoons of it. He was just too sick to even eat. He dropped his head back all tuckered out and waved me away weak not to bother him.

"You been to a doctor with this?" I asked.

"Didn't have time," he whispered.

He was in poor shape the day before when I saw him at Sparta. He had got terrible worse. "I'm going right out to find a doctor," I told him.

I found where the doctor was supposed to be, quick enough, but he wasn't there. He'd gone out shooting pigeons and wasn't expected back until after dark. I left word for him to come and hurried back to the hotel. Rudolph was sleeping. I piled the blankets on him good and started to unpack our gear.

Like usual, Rudolph had chosen more elaborate than we needed and had two rooms again. I don't know how he managed that with so much going on in town and so many extra people here, but this time it was the right thing. Sick as he was, he needed a bed alone. I did what I could for him and looked at my watch every five minutes or so waiting for that doctor. It was half-past nine when he came.

He took his pulse and looked at his tongue and down his throat and stuck a thermometer in him and listened how his chest sounded when he tapped on it. Doctors can tell something that way like some people know when a watermelon is ripe by thumping it. Whenever I've tried it it just sounds like a watermelon instead of whether it's green or not. The doctor tapped and listened and tapped some more. I guess he wasn't sure either. He opened his bag and pulled out a hearing thing he put in his ears that had tubes to a little knob he held all over Rudolph's chest and listened some more. They don't haul out instruments like that unless it's pretty bad.

It was bad. The doctor took the tubes out of his ears and said, "He's got a bad throat and a tight chest. I'll leave some medicine. Keep him in bed and warm for a couple of days or it might swing over into pneumonia. I'll drop in again Monday."

Next morning, which was Sunday, he seemed a little better. His throat wasn't so sore any more. I brought him up some breakfast. He ate fair and sort of enjoyed it. He asked how the pigeon business was shaping up in town

239

and when I thought our car of harness would get in. After that he was tired again and dropped off to a pretty good sleep.

Along about the middle of the morning I washed his face and hands and pulled the wrinkles out from under him, and made him a little more comfortable. He dropped off again to sleeping more natural and all of a sudden I got a powerful hunger to go to church. Sickness can go any which way, you never know for sure until a person is up and around again or has died. Somebody close to you going through it you need all the help there is and it's no time to neglect your praying. I'd have walked seven miles, I think, to get to a church. It wouldn't have been more than I owed anyhow seeing I hadn't been once since I left home. Counting Rudolph, I guess we owed up to quite a hike because I don't remember when he'd gone last. Like most times when I owe God something I got off easy, there was a church just up the street. Close doesn't always count, I was late. I edged in while they were singing and was taken to a pew about a third from the back. Churches are nice that way, they treat a stranger with the best they've got and hand you a hymnal opened right on the song. The lady next to me who did it even ran her finger down the words for me to catch up to where they were which was the second line in the second verse. It was a six-verser.

I couldn't help noticing the man right in front of me. The way he sang, head up high and tilted back, the book in one hand and held high too, the organ voice coming out of him, he should have been in the choir. He was a little fellow the years had packed down littler yet. The coat he wore hung tired and greenish burnt, like black does after years in the sun. I wouldn't have noticed him special, lots of old men look like that, except for his other hand. Standing up like we all were for the singing, it was his free hand held across the small of his back that kept me from looking around much at the other people. The palm side faced me. All the time he sang, his hand kept opening and shutting, hunting the empty air for the feel of another hand to grasp. It was a slow, lonesome motion, like it had been going on for ever so long never finding what it looked for, but still aching with hope. Open and shut, open and shut, I don't think the rest of the man knew what his left hand was telling back there. How far back, I wondered, was it looking, and who for? A sweet little old lady with her name carved in marble? A yellow-haired little dickens whose fingers don't ping the cookie-jar cover any more? A son in blue who went away to join Grant and never came back? It wouldn't say. A hand can't talk. But it did talk. It talked so sad my throat hurt. If something happened to Rudolph, that hand hunting helpless could be Pa's.

I had to look off somewhere else. I wasn't the only one not paying attention to the hymn or its singing, I discovered. Up ahead three pews the cutest little girl, maybe seven or so, had her head and shoulders turned square around examining me. Her mouth hung open so far I could see the pink inside. Her lips pulled dimples into her excited cheeks. Her eyes looked two blue holes into me. At first I thought something was the matter with me, my face dirty in church or something, but it wasn't that. It was a happy, expecting, questioning look—just as if I was somebody who had promised her a pony and her face was asking did I have it tied outside. I'd never seen her before in all my life, which made it downright puzzling why she'd pick me out to look at like that.

The hymn ended. The little old man pulled his left hand away from its hunting and brought it around in front to settle down for the sermon. The little girl never turned frontwards at all. She pulled her knees up on the pew and hung her elbows over the back of the bench and held her head in her hands to watch me. The lady with her didn't approve of such a position. She scowled at her in a lecture

241

that didn't need any words and nudged her to square around the way people in church are supposed to face. The girl turned. As she brought her head around the light glistened in her hair like sunshine on fresh oats straw it shined so pale yellow. That kind of hair has to be kept scrubbed to look like that. She leaned over to whisper to the lady she was with. Then the lady turned to look at me.

I couldn't figure it out. I couldn't follow the sermon either, because ever so often that little head would sneak around and those blue eyes would claim me again. Her face would puzzle and puzzle trying to push some of its happiness over to me. You can't get looked at like that without trying to help back. I grinned too, and gave her a great big wink. It was a wrong thing to do, like petting somebody else's puppy, the way she squirmed then. She had to be nudged again, hard, which made me feel bad because I was the one who started it this time. It isn't much fun to be the cause of getting a pretty little girl into trouble, you feel terrible. Best thing I could do to repair the damage was not to look any more and concentrate on the sermon.

I discovered I was a little late to pick up the idea the preacher was working at. He'd already finished sixthly and started on seventhly. I couldn't follow him any more than I could have followed the stitching in a piece of fancy crocheting. My eyes and my thinking stole back to the little girl. She had made me feel important to be picked out. Maybe it's the Rohland in me, the same kind of attraction Rudolph gets them with. It's wonderful to have a girl do that, but I wished it was one my age. That idea didn't work out. There were girls my age in that church, quite a few of them, but they were following seventhly, not looking me over.

When church ended, the little yellow-head ran to me. "What's your name?" she asked breathless.

"Emil Rohland," I said.

The sunshine left her face. "Did you ever have a baby sister?"

"No."

The lids came down over those big blue eyes. They opened again slow. "Where you from?"

"Chicago."

She looked at me ever so lonesome. A little smile flickered out tired. "I thought you were my brother." She turned and walked away without looking back.

14

Come to notice, while church broke up and people were talking to each other and being nice to strangers, it was mostly women. The preacher and three or four others and the little man whose back I'd seen and me were all the men there were. The others were all out pigeoning. It put the preacher in kind of a fix. He had to be against it because they were doing it on Sunday and he had to be for it because he'd announced a pigeon-pie supper the Ladies' Aid were putting on for Monday night and one of the parties out were shooting for that, he found out. Churches, I guess, have right hands too who don't know what the left hands are doing.

Somebody introduced me to the little man. He had deep eyes and careless hair, the kind that looks the same whether it's combed or not. His jaw snugged up squarelike under the porch his coarse gray mustache made. Altogether he had a proud old head that could have bossed a body twice as big as what he had. His name was William Wilcox. He was too old to have been a soldier himself. He looked like a father of a soldier to me. There's no medals or uniform to judge by, but sometimes a man's face flashes like a medal itself and you know before anybody tells you.

I walked down the steps with him and toward the hotel. We talked a little. He struck me as a good one to know, right away I knew I could trust him and learn things. "Did you have a boy in the war?" I asked.

He stopped and looked square at me. "Yes," he said, "I did. Never came back from Antietam. My only son." Then he said something that made me feel awful good. "You remind me of him, a little."

Me reminding somebody of somebody else reminded me of the little girl in church. I told Mr. Wilcox about the excited way she acted and why in the world she'd take me for her brother.

"She's adopted," he said. "She was about four then and remembers her brother. She hasn't the slightest idea who got him or where he is, poor child. Tell me about you."

I told him about Pa and our factory and how Rudolph and I were agents for Rohland harness and followed the pigeons here for business. I asked him what his business was and if the pigeons helped it.

Asking saddened him. I guess sadness was catching that day. Mr. Wilcox told me he was a photographer. He wouldn't have anything to do with the pigeons. It was downright slaughter, he said, and a dirty cruel business that hurt his stomach just to think of what people will do for greed. "Have you been out to the nesting?" he asked.

I told him I just got into town and had a sick brother and our car of harness hadn't come in yet so naturally I hadn't been anywhere.

"Well," he said, "the excitement of it and doing what everybody else is doing will harden you to the terrible destruction so that it probably won't bother you at all. Why should it, man's instinct is to kill and destroy. But after you've been there come back and talk to me. My gallery is right down here on Broadway with my sign in front."

245

When I got back to Rudolph he seemed a little better. I brought his dinner up and he ate pretty good, but he still breathed fast and felt weak. I tried to get what he had in mind for selling harness here that might be especially good, or would have to be different from the way I'd been working, but he was still too sick to care and couldn't help me. In the afternoon when he went to sleep again and seemed all right I took another hour to look over the town.

The sun came out and warmed it up pleasant for sight-seeing. I walked down Broadway which was the main street. I found Mr. Wilcox's gallery, but of course it was closed, being Sunday. He was a right good photographer, the pictures in his window were as clear and sharp as any I've ever seen. More interesting too, they weren't just people, they were scenery. Rocks and water and pine trees, my, they looked like wild places exciting to climb around and carve your initials in. They were pictures of the Dells of the Wisconsin River which were right there at Kilbourn and worth while to look at direct as long as I was there and handy to them.

Mr. Wilcox's gallery was about the only place closed. So many people in town, and the pigeon nesting to be harvested made Sunday business extra good for the lunchrooms, the stores that sold shot, the livery stables, the saloons, the picking and packing places, and everything. It seemed more like a Saturday afternoon than a Sunday. I stopped a man I took to be a native and asked him where I could see the Dells the best.

"There's seven miles of them," he said. "It's all Dells, all along the river."

"Are they pretty?" I asked.

"Pretty?" He scratched his head. "They're all right, I suppose, if you like scenery and have the time for it. Go out on the bridge, that's a good place. See all you want from there."

"The railroad bridge?" I didn't favor that, stepping

246

over the open places between the ties and maybe being caught out there with a train coming.

"Sure. It's a double bridge, trains run on top and teams go through underneath. What you can see from there the rest is all just like it, more or less."

I'd seen that part from the train, but it was so quick it was just enough to whet me for more. The bridge would be a fine place to stand from to take time to look. I walked down there. There were quite a few Sunday strollers stopped to lean and look. It was a fine place up high, pretty near a hundred feet above the water I'd guess.

Other towns sitting alongside a river, like Eau Claire and Chippewa Falls and even Sparta, get some good out of their location because the ground and the water come together at an easy slope and have a shore and they can put up buildings that use both. Kilbourn couldn't. The rocks ran straight up and down and the river ran along in the bottom of the gorge. Anybody wanting to get at it had to go upstream or downstream to find a landing. I never saw a town with a more useless location as far as the river was concerned. It was pretty, though, in its layers of color. Christmas-tree green of the pine trees on top, yellow brown of the old rocks torn through like a spice cake, and way down at the bottom, the water silvery where the sun hit it, or blue a little farther off reflecting the sky, or coffee-brownish slipping deep past bulby rocks and their shadows, it made a person wonder. Wonder what ever happened that could crack a bed of sandstone wide open that big, and spread it apart so far and make it so deep it could hold a whole river. Wonder how the river found the crack, and why the crack went all the way through so the river could run out again on the other side. Golly, such things are mysterious. Whatever it was must have happened a long, long time ago. The edges were all worn round and dark. The rock was in layers like irregular building stone with the mortar between dissolved out.

Some of it was straight, some of it was tipped so that it looked like old castle ruins. There were rows and rows of holes where swallows sailed in and out. You could look and look and the longer you looked the more there'd be to see.

It wasn't like most high places that give distance to looking. It really wasn't a high place at all, the ground at both ends of the bridge was just ordinary and it only was high compared to the river down below. A little bit upstream the river hid around a bend and a little bit downstream it did the same thing, the gorge was so crooked.

While I was looking downstream the people on the upstream side set up a commotion like when they've been waiting for a parade and finally it shows up. I crossed over. Coming out from behind the rocks was a lumber raft, something like I saw them make up at Chippewa Falls, but it seemed awful tiny so far below. It floated as careless as a chip in a gutter. More like a waterbug with only two legs left, one sticking out ahead and one behind. What they were were oars, with two men on each one. They weren't used like oars exactly because the men didn't row them. They steered, sort of, both men pushing on each of the oars to move it and leaning into it with their full bodies and walking back and forth across the raft in slow, leaning steps to sweep the oar the way they wanted it to move. The current carried the raft along and, my, but those men were expert to keep from touching any of the rocks jutting out from the banks as they rode along so powerful and silent.

What a wonderful platform they were on to enjoy the scenery, right down in it like that. Golly, how I envied them. As they came toward the bridge they looked up. We waved and they waved and then they passed under us way down below. We all rushed over to the other side to watch them come out. That raft was going all the way down the Wisconsin, I heard, and join the Mississippi at Prairie du

Chien and go down the Mississippi way to St. Louis, and they'd be riding it for more than two weeks yet. For sleeping there were four little hog houses built on it and rowed up like houses on a street. They had draped extra pairs of pants over some of the roofs to dry out. River drivers get splashed pretty often.

Downstream the river widened out before it went around the bend. The rocks valleyed out a little and part of one shore made a beach with room for a few buildings where they'd built a water mill and cribbed up a log dam across the river. In the middle the spillway rolled smooth fast water and dropped it about three or four feet to rile up into choppy rapids that spit foam. No wonder that bridge was so popular. Every raft that ran the river had to aim into that spillway square and true. If it slewed through a little cornerwise, it could knock the dam out or smash up the raft or get stuck crosswise in the spillway. Anything like that would be mighty interesting to see. Even if none of them happened at all, the way the drivers would have to target that raft through the spillway would be a kind of trick anybody would cheer to see done. Everybody likes to watch experts be successful.

The men on the sweeps pushed them slow one way and then the other. Their work didn't seem to have much effect on the raft, it rode so deep it was only a plank or two thickness out of the water. Big, heavy things like that raft was, no matter how puny it looked from way up where we were, don't turn short or respond quick. It worked more like a locomotive where they have to have long sweeping curves in the track to change direction rather than like a wagon that will take a square turn in the road. Just the same those raftsmen made it through that spillway as precise as a farmer brings a load of hay through a barn door. Better, it didn't even brush the cribbing. It slipped over grand, and ducked under the white water on the other side. The front end disappeared, then the waves and foam washed the whole length of the raft and for a minute before it rose out again the four men were knee-deep in water hanging onto their sweeps. No wonder they have to carry extra clothes along spread out to dry. Last we could see of the raft going around the bend, one of them looked to see how wet the stuff they'd draped on those little roofs had got.

Next morning Rudolph was some better, but not good enough to get up. I puttered around with his breakfast and slicked him up a little. For a particular one like he is, ordinarily, and troublesome about the way he looks and the way he feels, he was easier on me than I ever expected. Being sick improved him which was the biggest surprise that happened to me since we left Chicago.

"I'm all right," he said. "No sense you tying yourself down too. Go on out, take the whole day. Learn something about the country around here. It won't be wasted, whatever you find out. You mark my words we can use it for our business later. Now get."

I went to the depot first. Like I expected, our car hadn't come in and they had no idea when it would. I'd just like to know what happens to boxcars that take them so long. Sure, they have to switch, and a freight train goes a little slower than a passenger, but to use up extra days like that they must haul them off somewhere and let them sit.

The livery stable was no better for service. Pigeon people had rented all they had. All they had left was an old buckboard and two horses in the stalls. They couldn't give it to me because there wasn't a harness left in the place. That I'm going to fix, I thought, but I didn't say anything. It might have given them a sudden idea to go out and buy another from the harness maker up the street. Business as good as they were enjoying I wouldn't have had a chance to get them to wait until our supply would come.

That friendly little man from church, Mr. Wilcox, was in his gallery. I knew I shouldn't be bothering a businessman just to talk, but I was a little lonesome and he was the only one I knew.

He seemed to like it that I dropped in. Come to think of it, taking pictures is lonesome too. People only have it done about twice in a lifetime, once for a wedding picture and once just before they die to sit proud with their hands on their knees to show how big a family they'd raised. It struck me Kilbourn was a pretty little place to keep him in business. No wonder he had to wear his coat until it turned green. No wonder he took pictures of the Dells—maybe they were just practice so he wouldn't forget how. I wanted to be nice too, so I complimented the scenes he had in his window and told how I'd seen the Dells from the bridge.

"You should see all of them," he said. "There are canyons and beauty spots and rock formations you wouldn't believe. Look here."

He put a card into a stereoscope like we have at home to look at Niagara Falls and handed it to me. "We call this the Navy Yard." he said. I could see why. A row of rocks nosed out into the river, each one of them big and solid and curved like the front of a ship sticks out of the water. The picture was so real it seemed like I could reach out and put my hand between the different rocks.

"We've got deep pictures like these at home," I said, "but I never knew there were such dells here or pictures of them. Why, this is almost as pretty as Niagara Falls."

"We've got more to show off here than there is at Niagara Falls," he said. "People know about it. I've got an order here for six dozen of my best views to ship off to the London International Exhibition." My, his eyes were proud. They took a far-off longing. "If we only had a steamboat."

"You talk like my pa," I said. "He thinks steam is the answer for everything too."

"Well, isn't it?" He put another card in the stereoscope for me. "That's Stand Rock, at the far end of the Upper Dells. To see it a visitor would have to rent a livery rig and go by land, or get somebody to row him five miles upstream which takes too long and costs too much. But a steamboat!" He breathed it like it was an old, old wish he'd slept with every night for years and years. "Sixty people at a time could sit on her decks and turn their heads from side to side to see wonders they'd remember the rest of their lives. A steamboat would put Kilbourn on the map. Make money too."

I picked up another view. "You sell a lot of these?"

"Pretty good, but nowhere near what I'd sell to the visitors we'd get if we had a steamboat."

"Say," I said, "I've seen this one drawn in a magazine somewhere." It was labeled *The Hornet's Nest* and was a rock hanging like a hornet's nest from another rock.

"Sure. They drew it from my picture of it. *Leslie's Illustrated Weekly,* and *Harper's,* they both buy views from me for their artists to work on."

Those magazines were the best known in the whole United States. It came to me Mr. Wilcox was a lot more important man than a person would guess to look at him. *Leslie's* and *Harper's* don't fool around with anything unless it's the very best they can get. Smart too. By putting Mr. Wilcox's photographs in front of one of their artists they saved all the time and money it would cost to send him here to draw it.

"Two years ago the biggest hop boom the country ever saw happened right around here," Mr. Wilcox went on. "The pictures I took of the crowds of girls picking hops sold well too."

"Well," I said, "you sure get where things are exciting. Bet you're planning to do the same thing with the pigeon nesting that's bringing all us strangers here. My, but those magazines would pay you nice to have that."

"Maybe so. But there's too much killing and cruelty in this world without using the camera to help it along. I'm

252

not interested in making a name for Kilbourn as a slaughtering house, and that's exactly what pigeon pictures would do.''

''But gosh, think of the money.''

''What kind of money? Thirty pieces of silver? The pigeons are here for a season. Next year they'll nest somewhere else. It may be ten years or a hundred before they stop here again, maybe never, they're such a far-flying kind of bird and gypsy in their habits. Pigeons are temporary, pictures are permanent. No, Emil, there's little enough in this world that's inspiring and beautiful and makes a man wonder by what lucky chance he's privileged to be in its presence. The Dells do that. They've been here before man was made and they'll be here after he's gone. The Indians come to them for meditation. They make a white man meditate. I like to think that my pictures start a tiny bit of meditation too. Maybe plant a hunger to come and stand among them and really feel what Dr. Smith who wrote 'America' wanted us to feel when we sing, 'I love thy rocks and rills, thy woods and templed hills, my heart with rapture thrills.' If we only had a steamboat.''

''I wish you had a steamboat, too. I'd like to see all of these Dells myself.''

''Well,'' he admitted, ''if you really want to it doesn't take a steamboat, but it's a lot of work. I've been at it six years now and I haven't photographed a third of all there is. If you want to help me carry equipment, I'll take you along sometime. Had in mind quite awhile now to try to catch some of the power and rushing when high water comes a little later on.''

I thought that was pretty nice of him and told him I sure would go along. I had to leave then because I didn't want to keep him from his work too long. A person can do that pretty easy when you haven't anything pushing yourself and you forget.

Outside, the first morning catch of pigeons was already

253

on its way toward the packing sheds. Limp birds piled high in the wagon box, their necks stretched long, their heads smashed. The ends of the reins, the slack ends behind where the driver held them, rose and fell among the pigeons in time with the plod of the horses. Each time they rose they dangled blood and stuck feathers. People sure are different. If Mr. Wilcox would have been watching that wagon, it would have been the pigeons sickened him. If it was Pa, and one of our drivers, he'd have sulphured the air to see a man soil leather like a horse does. It all depends, I guess, on what a person holds to be important. And who you've just been talking to. Made me uncomfortable both ways.

A flight of live pigeons went over as if they came to cheer me up a little. It was a thick flight, but only lasted a couple of minutes. I gawked as if I'd never seen them before. The driver of the wagon never raised so much as an eyebrow. I wondered if those up there might be part of the ones I'd seen in the fog back out of Sparta. Seeing them up there gave me a powerful hankering to roam amongst them in the woods all by myself again. Rocks aren't the only thing a person can meditate among.

Like I expected, there weren't any rigs that had come back to the livery stable. "I don't want to bring any pigeons back," I told them. "You've got horses left, just saddle me up one that walks good in the woods and doesn't get nervous."

I crossed the river and headed west away from town. It was sandy country no good for farms and left wild. Scraggly pine trees too little and knotty for lumber, and scrub oaks stood thin on the slopes. Sandstone ledges and low bluffs rimmed little valleys. Sometimes there'd be open spots of sand on the higher rises. On a sunny day it would have been pretty country, but it was chilly and gray. Spring that had started so nice for a few days back at Sparta had stood still ever since. I didn't see any pigeon nestings, but there'd be flocks once in a while feeding on the acorns on the ground. They were wilder than at Sparta. I couldn't get anywhere near them.

Ahead a ways I could see two men raking a garden-sized patch of ground in the space between a few dead trees. That's funny, I thought, making garden on such worthless ground and no house around. There was sort of a house, though, like a camper's lean-to and made out of brush, I saw later. I rode over there.

It wasn't any garden. Those two men were pigeon netters. They had a spring net on each side hid in the brush all spring-poled and triggered. The reason they were raking was to clean away the feathers and to work the blood from the last catching into the ground so the next pigeons couldn't see any evidence.

"All right you," one of them grumbled, "either you move on or hide in the blind with us. They're getting wary. If you want to watch, that's all right, providing you help."

"What'll I do with the horse?"

"Take him into that thick grove of pine ahead a piece. Tie him up in there where our team is." He looked worse than if he'd butchered a pig. So did the other one. Their clothes were blood-stiff from their chests down to their shoes.

When I came back they had their plot of ground baited with wheat soaked in salt water, a whole bushel of it spread out. Pigeons like salt like a lumberjack goes for whisky. They set their stool pigeon on his platform out by the bait.

"We can use a third man. Ever do any netting?" He walked me toward the lean-to.

"No. How do you expect to catch pigeons here? I don't see any nests or any of them roosting or anything."

"The nesting starts about two miles north and goes for fifty miles, all the way to Grand Rapids. Netting's no good in the nesting because they won't feed where they nest. They save that for the squabs after they leave them."

There was half a wagonload of dead pigeons in the

255

lean-to. It smelled strong to be packed in there with them like that. A good deal of it came from the men. "Well, if you never netted, you can't work the stool pigeon or the fliers, that's for sure. Here, you take the trip ropes and when I yell 'Trip' you yank them. But not before or we'll have an hour's work shot to hell without getting anything. Both together, mind you. Understand?" I nodded.

"O.K. then. Now no talking. No coughing. Don't even clear your throat. And no moving around, they can see better than eagles. Understand? What time is it?"

"I got a watch," I whispered, "but I got to move a little to pull it out."

"That's all right, I mean sit still when a flight is in sight."

I looked at my watch. "It's eight minutes after eleven. Why?"

"About time for the change. Sure enough, there they go."

I could see out without moving. The sky was full again, all going north. They didn't pay any attention to the bait. I sat without winking or swallowing, but those two netters didn't follow their own orders. They fidgeted around and scratched and even talked. Naturally, no pigeons landed. I got the idea. Those netters were just like lumberjacks, playing a trick on me because I was a stranger to the business. It seemed funny, though, to let a whole catch go by just to fool me.

"What's the idea," I said, "you talking and motioning when you tell me I can't move a muscle?"

"These are toms, due back on the nests to relieve the hens. Couldn't draw them down now with any kind of attraction. In a little it will be all hens, coming off to feed. That's when we have to sit still."

Off in the distance to the north the sky a little above the woods shimmered and darkened as the flights coming in hovered and settled and the flights starting out rose and

256

organized. Those pigeons timed themselves better than railroads schedule their passengers to change trains.

"*Now* we'll sit still," one of the netters hissed.

A whole sheet of pigeons headed toward us out of the north. One of the men held two live pigeons with cords tied to their legs. The other held a cord that ran out to the stool. I held my trip ropes. I held my breath too, if I'd do anything wrong now no telling what might happen. I was part of a team. It was a powerful feeling. I wanted to do a good job for them.

· The pigeons came straight over us. They put us in shadow. The netter holding his fliers pitched one of them out. It flew up to try to join the flight. He let the other one go. They went out and up as far as their cords would let them and then he pulled back. They beat the air trying to go up and being pulled down. It made them look as if they were landing by their own choice. The flock above broke its pattern. The netter operating the stool pigeon pulled his cord. The stool and its pigeon rose up two or three feet and dropped sudden. The stool pigeon fluttered as if he was landing too. Pigeons came out of the air and landed in the dead trees to look the situation over. They landed and landed and landed and made the branches crackle and drop a shower of broken twigs.

The stool pigeon and the fliers worked again. That was just the confidence the wild birds needed. They left the trees. They came out of the flight. They made a spinning funnel of birds dropping down to land, a funnel as big and as solid as Mr. Wilcox's hornet-nest rock. They landed on the bait. They spilled out over the ground. They covered the ground. They made a second layer and a third, and still the funnel whirled, drawing birds out of the flock.

"Now," came yelling into my ear.

I yanked one rope. The net came sailing from the ground all along the side on the south. The spring poles quivered straight. Wings whirred like thunder trying to

257

escape to the north. I yanked the other rope. The north net came up and over catching a wall of pigeons and overlapped the net from the south. A million pigeons just out of reach beat the air and swerved off free. Not all of them though, the whipping spring poles knocked dozens of them down.

A hand whacked my shoulder hard enough to topple me. "Good boy, we've got 'em, we've got 'em, good boy."

Out in front the nets rose and fell like mush bubbling on a stove. Birds broke loose from the edge where the north net overlapped. They left like bullets. The nets were a good two feet off the ground, the pigeons under them lifted so hard trying to fly. Both men ran out trampling over the nets to peg down the loose edge. They sunk in and had trouble stepping as though they were walking in a hay mow over loose hay. One went down and rolled full length before he got his footing again.

The nets billowed lower and lower to an uneasy rest. In a little I couldn't see the meshes at all. Pigeon heads with red scared eyes stood up like a thick bed of strange spring flowers. One little hillock stood up higher than all the rest. It was the stool, the stool pigeon prisoned like all the rest of them. I wondered what he was thinking. Poor fellow, he couldn't see anything to think. His eyelids were sewed shut to keep him calm.

The netters went at those heads sticking up as though they were strawberries in a bed. They each had a pair of pinchers. They went from head to head cracking them.

"Here, take my pinchers. I can use my fingers. Us two alone here, we'll be at it till dark."

"No, thank you," I said. "I've got to get along."

"I guess you're right. You ain't exactly dressed for this part of it. Wait, here's a dollar."

That was good pay, the little I'd done. Of course it wasn't anything like the profit I could have been earning if our harness had come, but you get a good feeling making wages outside your own calling. I walked back to my horse as satisfied as if I'd have sold a set to those fellows.

I got to thinking they were rough ones, those two, and such a business, dirty and stinky as the fish wharves along the river in summer back home in Chicago. Cracking those heads, that was too much for me. Something inside started to speak up. It said I was just as dirty to jerk those ropes. What kind of person was I anyhow to enjoy discovering pigeons in the fog and keeping their secret and then turn around and enjoy springing those nets? I didn't have to do it like the stool pigeon, tied down and blinded. I walked into it free, with my eyes open. What kind of person was I, agreeing so honest with Mr. Wilcox, who wouldn't even take pictures of the pigeons, and then catching enough to fill another wagon? Thirty pieces of silver. I sold out and got a dollar, and only a greenback at that.

Pay like that got me to thinking of Judas. I don't remember if he was the disciple who used the net or not, but some of them were fishermen, I remember that much. Hauling in a netful of fish or hauling in a netful of pigeons, what's the difference? Jesus Himself, seems to me, told them where to cast once and they got the biggest catch ever, it says so right in the Bible. I was all mixed up.

New country from horseback and places to get into and talking to people doing their own business is wonderful fun when you know where you stand yourself, but if that platform is shaky you don't get any more good out of it than the horse that's plodding under you. I didn't care to go on the two or three miles to the nesting. I went back to Kilbourn and checked the freight depot again. My car was in. That cheered me. I took a set along and rode back to the livery stable with the sack slung across in front of the saddle. That was a right good idea Pa had to pack them in sacks, it's the handiest all around.

I took the old buckboard they had left at the livery stable and my harness and their team and I was in busi-

259

ness again. It seemed wonderful good to be at the one thing again I was sure of. Good hard selling to unwilling people, that's what I needed because thinking is like a fire that gets out of hand and hard work is the only extinguisher that can handle it. I sold harnesses all over town. Rudolph sure picked good again when he decided on Kilbourn. I told him so too, when I came in that night.

He was up and had his clothes on and was all cleaned up, but he looked peaked and didn't feel so good. I could see that right off. "You didn't go out today, did you," I asked, "on such a chilly day?"

"Only to the barber shop. I just had to get cleaned up."

"And you took the works, hair wash and bath and everything?"

"I couldn't stand it any longer, I could even smell myself."

"Rudolph, you shouldn't have. Now you've gone and opened your pores again and chilled yourself walking home. No wonder you feel bad."

15

A PERSON's body is a contrary thing. It gets chilled and then goes to the other extreme and heats up out of control. Rudolph burned up all night and couldn't get any sleep. By morning he had worn himself out and me too and had the bedclothes pulled every which way and was mumbling steady and nothing he said made sense. I was scared. He was too sick for me to leave, but he needed the doctor bad so I asked the hotel people to send somebody right out to bring him.

"Pneumonia," the doctor said. "He was coming along fine, but he's a mighty sick man now."

"What can I do for him?"

"Nothing, really, except to get yourself ready to sit up with him tonight. I'll have to stay with him all day, so if you've got things that need to be done you better go and wind them up because this man is going to take steady care for quite a spell."

I telegraphed Pa.

After that I didn't have anything to do. It didn't seem right to go out with harness, I don't think the doctor meant me to do that. What I needed was to be with somebody I

261

felt a little close to. I headed for Mr. Wilcox's gallery. What a lucky thing for me I happened to drop into that church that Sunday. It isn't always the sermon where the best good comes from.

He was standing on the walk, looking up at the sky. Just when I got to him the sun broke through. "Pretty important to a photographer," he said, "to have the sun out. Looks like maybe there'll be enough today I can get some work done."

"I could use a little sunshine myself," I said, and told him about Rudolph.

He was ever so nice, and sorry such things had to be, and told how all Kilbourn had wonderful confidence in that doctor. "Good you came by. How'd you like to come along and help me photograph an Indian camp?"

"I'd like to. But I thought you said beautiful scenery was what you wanted your pictures for. No Indian camp I ever saw made me feel like meditating. Why, Wisconsin Indians don't even have wigwams."

His eyes looked like Pa's when the talk is about making Rohland harness better. "The Dells are more than landscape. To get their full story in pictures it takes river drivers and rafts. It takes the Indians too because their spirit gods inhabit the water and rocks, this is the homeland of their legends, this is Winnebago country. You hear the talk all over town, the farmers coming in feel strong about it, move the Indians out. That's bound to happen and soon, so I've got to get my Indian pictures while they're still around."

Of all the bulky gear he needed. His camera in its carrying box was only a tenth or so of what we had to load in his wagon. A heavy box of glass sheets, half a dozen gallon bottles with solutions in them, different pans to pour the different stuff into, funnels to get it back in the bottles again, a stand for the camera, a black cloth to cover

262

it with, holders to put the glass sheets into the camera, a kind of tent thing of more black cloth to keep the light out while he worked inside, and a red lantern to put in it so he could see while he worked. Towels to wipe on changing hands from one solution to another, a basket of lunch, oats for his horse, presents for the Indians, a canvas for covering in case of rain. A photograph is just like any other kind of manufactured thing, it has to have a factory behind it to produce it. When you have to take the factory along wherever you go that's rough.

"My gosh," I said, "you should have a peddler's wagon, closed in and a lot of your stuff set up permanent inside."

"Like Brady used in the war? Trouble is, most times I need to work from the water."

"Well, fix up a houseboat."

"And how would I get into the narrow glens? Some of those won't even take a rowboat."

I stopped talking. I didn't want to hurt his feelings, but if I was in his business I'd get sick and tired of having to carry clutter like that around wherever I wanted to go. I think I'd practice drawing. All he'd need for that is a pencil and a board with a paper tacked to it he could rest on his knees wherever he sat down. In the long run he'd probably turn out more pictures.

We plodded along, over the bridge and along the river road upstream. I couldn't help noticing the harness. It had been a good one, but it was older than I am, seemed like, and patched in a dozen places. I wanted to suggest he should have a new one, but you don't talk such things to a friend, it looks too greedy. I thought of giving him one for a present, but that wouldn't have been fair to Pa. Besides, that little old fellow was proud. He might be insulted and think I thought he needed charity. A man could hold that against you the rest of your life. Charity. That reminded me of something. There's a poor farm in every county and I never thought to go see any of them. Why, they need six to ten times the harness an ordinary farm does.

Sometimes it's best to talk around a thing instead of directly at it. "Being in the harness business," I said, "a fellow has to learn what his competition is. Who's the best harness maker in these parts?"

"Ringling, August Ringling, used to be over in Baraboo. Seems I heard he lives over in McGregor, Iowa, now. Mine is one of his, lasted since before the war. I hear he's not doing so well now."

"What's the matter, doesn't he have help?"

"Yes and no. He's got seven boys and they help him a little. Most of the time, though, they're off somewhere training a dog or a horse to do tricks, or practicing on horns, or trying to juggle. Most boys gets over playing circus, but his oldest is just as bad as his youngest and precious little he gets out of any of them."

It set me thinking what Pa would do if any of us Rohlands played a trick like that on him. Poor Mr. Ringling, with just as good a chance to make a reputation and get rich as Pa and then have boys like that to wash him out. It's just a shame.

We got to the Indian camp, but we didn't get any pictures. I don't know what it was, not understanding their language, but they ran us off. Probably heard they were going to be moved way out West and blamed us for it, and made up their minds they'd do the chasing. Mr. Wilcox didn't think so.

"I went at this wrong," he said. "Setting up the camera, and draping the black cloth over it probably made them think I was going to release an evil spirit. No harm done, I'll just have to come alone three or four times without the equipment and get them used to me."

"You got patience for all that rigmarole?"

264

"Why not? I need those pictures."

"For *Leslie's*?"

"No, just for myself. I want my pictures of the Dells to be complete, the full story."

I was beginning to get edgy about Rudolph. Just because the doctor said he'd take over was no reason for me to light out for an all-day tour. "Suppose we can go back now?" I asked. "I'm worried about my brother."

"Why sure. As long as the Indians aren't willing I'd just as soon get back myself. Got some ideas for a faster shutter I'm making. I want to get pictures of the action as the drivers make their runs through the Narrows. With the shutter I'm using now the water would be just a blur when what I want is the churn and splash as the rafts go awash."

My, but Mr. Wilcox had a clear-cut idea of what he wanted. Steamboat, Indians, rafting, scenery, hops, whatever made the Dells important he'd fight for as if it was a private empire he had to spend his life improving. Just a black box, but with it he can gather a tree or a forest and still leave it standing, with it he can send his Dells to thrill people in London without disturbing a single rock here. In a way that's more powerful than the whole Pine Ring and the river drivers and the pigeon netters and the Indians all combined. Nowadays that's quite a trick to earn a living and build up a business and make a reputation without cutting anything down, or killing anything, or using anything up. Those Indians were more right than wrong, there is a spirit in Mr. Wilcox's black box and a mighty powerful one. Their only mistake was not knowing a good spirit from an evil one. Can't really blame them much, though, us civilized Christians aren't too sure of the difference either until somebody like Mr. Wilcox points it out. He was a whole Dells Ring himself.

He didn't ask me if I'd been out to the pigeon harvest

yet. I hoped he wouldn't. He'd understand my springing those nets all right, I was just one more of the kind of people the world is full of who like to look, but get more tempted by a chance to gather something in, no matter what, and get ashamed afterward instead of before. Mr. Wilcox was greedy too, but what he was greedy for was beauty, which doesn't hurt anybody or anything and never yourself.

We crossed the bridge again. "Water's coming up," he said. "And look at the boys downstream fishing lumber below the dam. A raft must have sprung off a dozen boards. Pirate's Eddy will be rich the next few weeks. Shingles, lath, lumber, sometimes enough to frame up a house drifts around in a circle down there."

Back at the hotel the doctor looked worried. Rudolph looked terrible, so quiet and breathing so funny. Nobody could do anything, the doctor said, except wait. Pa couldn't possibly get there before sometime after midnight, but I went to the depot anyhow to meet everything that would come. I got a wonderful surprise on the seven-fifty-five express.

There he was, good old Pa, stepping down from the passenger car, big and powerful and solid, but maybe not towering quite so much as I thought I remembered.

"Emil," he said.

"Pa," I said.

"Rudolph, how is he?"

"Awful sick, Pa. Since last night he's out of his head, his fever is so high."

"Ach, so bad is it? Good I come."

You can remember a person for all you're worth away from him and when you see him again, your remembering didn't cover ten per cent what it could have. Hearing his beard whisper against his lapels as he'd turn to look over a shoulder, the dutchiness to the way he strung his words together, the little bit of yellow stain in his whiskers at

266

the edges of his mouth, the faint smell around him, part leather, part soap, part wool, part tobacco, part sweat, that's Pa's combination, and nobody else's. How those things do bang back at you so familiar again.

Pa talked to the doctor. The doctor shook his head. "He's sunk into a coma. Only possible chance is to pack him in ice."

"Emil," Pa said, "you get ice. Ice and oilcloth."

I cracked a washtubful of ice. We put oilcloth over the mattress and rolled it under Rudolph and packed him solid with only his head out. Pa sent me off to get some sleep and said he'd watch through till the fever broke, if it could.

Rudolph packed in ice. You can't sleep much when you know you're losing a brother. I heard of packing corpses in ice in hot weather to keep them until the funeral. I never heard of doing it on anybody still alive. That doctor was experimenting, they do it every chance they get. I didn't like it, but sick like Rudolph was, what else could he do?

That doctor worried just as hard as Pa and me. I went in about midnight and there he was, sitting there with Pa, the both of them watching. The ice and the oilcloth were gone. Rudolph was wrapped in blankets, still breathing. Seems he was breathing a little easier.

"Fever is broke," Pa told me. His eyes were ever so tired.

"Yes," the doctor said, "but he's got a long slow repair job ahead. He should have a woman's care at his bedside, day and night for the next few weeks. I guess I can go now."

Pa looked at me. "I telegraphed Momma to send Sarah."

"Sarah? After what he——" I shut my mouth quick.

"I know. You think it was mean he treated her, turning his back on her good-by present. I think so too," he

267

whispered. "But a good woman is kindness, and kindness for a few close weeks, ach, how that can change a man."

Rudolph improved fast enough the next few hours, while I spelled Pa so he could sleep a little, to relieve the worry in both of us.

For Pa's shift the next night, he didn't need to plan on worry to keep him awake. "So I don't nod off, now I study how my Rohland agents work for me. Your journal Emil, and find me Rudolph's." Pa settled down between Rudolph and the lamp and took his glasses out and hung them on the end of his nose. He needed them to read as bad as anybody. He always keeps them loose on his nose and loose on his ears so they won't look permanent as if he had to use them for everything.

I relieved him about midnight.

Pa met me outside the door sizzling sulphur and trying to talk low not to disturb anybody at that hour. That was tough on him to hold his mad down to indoor size and midnight size. "A sick man I cannot ask. A carload of harness gone. There should be records. Here. Read out to me from Rudolph's journal."

I felt a sting on my palm as he whacked something down onto my hand. "It's dark out here."

"Under a chandelier yet it still would be dark. One sentence since last January he wrote. 'Sold five hundred ten sets harness.' Sticking in the journal a slip somebody owes him twenty thousand, four hundred dollars."

"It's an order, Pa, like those I sent you for some I sold."

"Yah, yah, but nothing in his journal. Maybe nothing in the order too. Worse yet, maybe nothing in my Rudolph."

Pa kind of choked up. I was glad it was dark. "To my room now I go. Sleep I don't expect. Think, I know I do. You talk with me tomorrow?"

That was an odd way for Pa to put it. He never *asked*

268

me before, his way was to order me to listen or to talk, whichever way he wanted it.

Sarah came on the first train next morning. She pitched right in putting the room and Rudolph in order and taking charge like a woman always does when she knows she's needed. She was a wonderful relief.

Pa and I had his talk alone in my room. He had my journal. Every little while he'd run across something I hadn't put down clear and ask me about it. I'd thought I'd forgot most of the details, but having the germ down made all the missing parts leaf out like spring does to a tree. It sort of worked out, there was more come out of my journal than I'd put in. Pa laid it aside. "Tell me, now, about these harness Rudolph sold."

That was harder because I hadn't put it in my journal, being Rudolph's work, but I described the Chippewa Valley, and told what Rudolph had told me about the Pine Ring and his joining it, and Roger Roberts and the day the wagons hauled off the five hundred and ten sets.

"I go to Eau Claire," Pa said. He left on the afternoon train.

He came back in three days, his shoulders a little more rounded, his eyes more concerned in what his feet were doing, his voice without the roar he most times had to hold down before. "Is a Pine Ring, maybe, but none of the names on the order does anybody know. Roger Roberts I found, but no Chippewa Valley Road Development Company. Saloon card players, not lumbermen that harness disappeared to. Rudolph talked big. Looking for an investment, he told, and more than once hinted that a deal on the shady side he could wink along at, too. Always such talk makes scheming men scheme faster. A man willing to cheat is easy to cheat."

Pa leaned forward on his chair and held his head in his hands. I never saw his head need support before.

269

"Can't we get the law out and take back the harness?"

"Five hundred different people own it. The ones who sold it, for a few quick dollars a set, like buckshot are scattered now."

"Couldn't you hold Roger Roberts?"

"With a lawyer I talked to him. As outside he is to this as me." Pa pulled out Rudolph's twenty-thousand-dollar order and tore it slow into snowflakes. "Back to home I should take Rudolph along, and make you my agent alone. For that, even, pneumonia cheats me now."

"Pa, I know somebody here you ought to meet. Mr. Wilcox. He's the best medicine ever when a man feels low. Why, he can show you comfort and hope just watching a chipmunk, for instance, and funny thing, remembering that chipmunk, or maybe Mr. Wilcox—it gets all mixed up—sort of has something to do with how you talk the next farmer into the good there is in a Rohland harness."

Pa didn't say yes or no. I don't know if he even heard me through all the disappointment crowding his head, but afterwards it worked out we walked along the street aimless and as we got to Mr. Wilcox's gallery he didn't even notice my maneuvering him in.

I introduced Pa to Mr. Wilcox and Mr. Wilcox to Pa. I felt so proud of both of them and felt so good to show them off to each other my voice went scratchy and swallowy. When they shook hands Pa was the Union Pacific and Mr. Wilcox was the Central Pacific and I was driving the golden spike.

They mentioned the weather. They looked at me and agreed I was a likely lad. After that both of them ran out of what to say. Mr. Wilcox asked Pa how Rudolph was, which didn't open Pa up any. Us Rohlands don't go around complaining about each other. Pa asked Mr. Wilcox what he thought about business. I figured that would get them rolling, the way Mr. Wilcox invents devices for

270

improving his equipment and wants a steamboat like Pa wants steam-run machinery.

"Excuse me just a minute," Mr. Wilcox said, "I've got thirty prints that have to come out of the hypo," and disappeared behind his curtain. He didn't mean it to send us off, he's just precise and photography goes by the clock.

Pa walked out. He didn't mean it disrespectful either, but the gnawing on his brain of what Rudolph had done turned him inward, it seemed. All the wonderful power those two had in ideas to trade and instead of meeting they just rumbled by each other like two freights on separate tracks.

"Walk with me, Emil, back to the hotel for my satchel and to the station with me."

I looked at my watch. "Pa, it's three hours yet till train time."

"Good. Empty the station will be. I want to be alone with you."

Up in the room Sarah sat in the sun next to the window. We caught her thinking worried, too. I had never told her what Rudolph did. Pa wouldn't, I know that, and it wasn't something Rudolph would mention himself.

Pa said good-by to Sarah and held her hand and patted it and looked into her eyes a long time. "In two weeks, maybe, I see you in Chicago again? My Rudolph in good care he is."

She sort of choked up and didn't answer. I don't think she could think more of her own pa. Pa walked over to Rudolph's bed. He rested his hand on Rudolph's. He looked long in his eyes too. He didn't seem to find what he wanted. "My Rudolph, my Rudolph," was all he said.

I tried to cheer him up at the station while we sat in there alone on a bench. "How's your stitching machine coming?" I asked.

"Not my machine, Emil, the Rohland machine it will be. An old man I am, I discover here in Kilbourn. More and more testing now I have to give all my boys to find do I know them as good as I know my harness. Maybe I got more Rudolphs, no? A stitching machine already is for shoe leather, otherwise how could we buy shoes in a box? Such a machine I have seen, such a machine they are working to change for harness stitching. Maybe by next winter we get it. But it is nothing, if men from my Rohlands I have not built.''

''Pa,'' I said, ''you don't have to test Gottlieb, or August, or Casper and Jacob, or any of them back home. You know how dependable they are.''

''Yah. Yah,'' he said slow after each name I said. ''You have right. And Emil too, I find is dependable.''

That made me feel good. But, darn it, I wanted to make him feel good. He needed it, not me. ''Aw,'' I said, ''Rudolph will——''

Pa interrupted. ''Maybe not so long, who can tell, *Rohland and Sons* comes down from the sign and up goes *Rohland Brothers*. A good factory you will get. A good name you will get. But not from me comes all your inheritance. Property can go quick, that the five hundred harness left in the Chippewa Valley should prove. A name you think is gold can be only brass rubbed too much. In my heart now is no happiness with what Rudolph makes of Rohland.''

Those things hurt to hear. ''Pa,'' I said, ''you can't give up being boss, you just can't.''

He swelled up straight. His beard poked out. He opened the drafts to his eyes and his voice. ''I give up nothing. I am boss. I stay boss.'' He said it like a locomotive eating up a grade.

''What I say is only, look ahead, Emil. Harness is important, but it is not all. From every man you meet, from the land, from the times, from what you see that makes you think, from what men have built or found out or neglected ahead of you, you also are inheritor. Up in the pine country is a special trade. Strong men that walk alone in the woods to only look and decide. You know, Emil, the name of the trade?''

''Sure, Pa, that's the landlooker. He goes into the timber ahead of any crews or even before it's been bought and makes up his mind what it amounts to and whether they should go after it or not.''

''Exact, you put it. Emil, you too must be such a man. Not for timber, not even for harness, but for you. The thinking men do, the discoveries they make, the government they pick to live with, the waste and the saving of what there is to work with, all is for you to put a value on. You must look, see, decide. Much it can mean to a man, or nothing. Depends is he a landlooker or no.''

''That isn't going to be too easy, Pa, figuring everything out right.''

''Who says everything is to come clear? A Washington and a Lincoln already we have had. From you, that I do not ask or expect. Only not to be blind around you, that is all.''

Maybe we were there in the station a long time, that's what the depot clock said, but it went way too quick. The train came. Pa got on. Awful quick, it seemed, he was gone again. I walked back to the hotel as lonesome as I ever want to get.

16

WHAT Pa said was so. That looking-around business and judging was the way he worked himself. It brought results for him. It built up the Rohland factory, and the Rohland reputation, and put him on Michigan Avenue, that's what it did. There's dozens of harness makers in Chicago, and hundreds of them in Wisconsin, and thousands of them in the country, but just being good with leather and linen hasn't raised any of them up like Pa climbed, I notice. Why, the whole plan with the army harness, anybody could have stepped into that any time in the six years since the war ended if they'd have seen it. Pa was the only one who looked. No wonder he was so earnest there in the station. He was opening up the secret of his strength, that's what he was doing, and handing me the key to go in and help myself.

From Pa to Rudolph was too much of a difference for me to take all at once just then. I stopped in at Mr. Wilcox's again and had to think how much like Pa he was in such an altogether different way. They were alike only to me though, I guess. Not to each other, that was sure, unless alike things go against each other sometimes just because they are alike, I don't know.

"Want to show you something," Mr. Wilcox said with his eyes excited. "Hold this shutter up to the light. Now watch close while I squeeze the bulb."

Something clicked. I couldn't see any parts move, but the thing made a hole in itself and shut again all in the same click. "How fast would you say that it opened and shut?"

"It didn't take any time. It was all at once."

"Lightning even takes time. Nothing is instantaneous. Go ahead, guess how long that shutter was open."

He clicked it again for me. My watch ticks five times a second, the jeweler in Chippewa Falls mentioned that. His shutter and a watch tick were the same. "A fifth of a second," I said which was as small as time divides as far as I'd ever heard.

"No sir," he said. His voice scarcely whispered. "I made this shutter, near as I can figure, to operate at a hundred-and-fiftieth of a second. Now I can photograph fast water and stop the spray in the air. I tested it yesterday on a buggy going past with the horses trotting. The spokes in the wheels and the hoofs of the horses are as sharp as though they were standing still. Figuring speeds and distances, anything less than a hundred-and-fiftieth of a second should have given a little blur, and there wasn't any blur."

"You got it done just in time. The high water is churning through right now, I notice."

"That's right. A week or so and it'll go down and the rafts can run again. There's a lot of them tied up above the Upper Dells where they're taking them apart into separate rapids pieces to take through. I want to visit them tomorrow, if the weather is right, and get pictures of what's going on up there. Like to have you along."

"I'd like to see that. But with Rudolph sick and Pa here I haven't been very steady in getting around and selling." As soon as I said it I figured a way I could do both. Those

275

rafts were part of business in Wisconsin and pretty important business. Pa would want me to see them. "Suppose I take my harness out," I said, "and work the forenoon and meet you at the landing at noon when the sun is brightest and after you get your pictures I can sell again along the road back." That's the way we left it.

Next day it was sunny and nice like we wanted it. I got an early start and headed north toward the pigeon nesting. When I crossed the bridge the water below was fast and high and just sang. Foam whipped wherever the rocks poked out and made resistance. Branches and dead wood spun along. Little whirlpools started anywhere and sucked along spinning. If there were fish in that water, they were sure being slewed around some. There weren't any rafts, of course, in such a suicide.

Word at the breakfast table was that the nesting had broke up the day before and the old pigeons had all gone and everybody was heading for the squabs now. There'd be a lot of people up there, I figured, and some of them for sure would be needing harness.

A pigeon nesting is an altogether different thing from a pigeon roost. I expected the nests to be as thick in the trees as apples in an orchard. They weren't at all. Nesting is the only thing those birds ever do spread out and separated from each other. Sometimes there were only ten or a dozen nests in a tree, a few times only one or two. The most I counted was forty-eight which made the tree look like sort of a hat rack a whole schoolhouse had thrown their caps up into. For passenger pigeons like I'd been seeing them pile up on each other those nests looked mighty far apart. No wonder the nesting area had to spread all the way up to Grand Rapids and all the way out to the other side of Black River Falls like I'd heard.

There were people everywhere, more than I'd ever seen out in the woods before. Men and boys and teams and Indians and once in a while a woman even. They all had sacks hanging heavy around their knees. Squabs were dead easy to get just about any way a person went after them. Those I ran onto on the ground that were learning how to fly were in flocks like the old ones already, but they didn't know how to manage themselves. They could only rise a foot or two and they couldn't wheel or turn yet because the tail which they need for a rudder is the last thing to grow. They were fat and heavy. A boy with a club could fill his sack pretty fast and what his club missed the squabs themselves seemed anxious to finish up for him by smashing into a tree trunk and knocking themselves out or by tumbling over themselves when they landed and couldn't right themselves. The ones that were too young to fly could be picked up off the ground. The ones still in the nests, they poked out with long poles. Everybody had a long pole.

I was in the wrong place again as far as harness was concerned. Things were too much in a turmoil and exciting. Anything anybody did turned out to be a good way to harvest squabs. Nobody needed to organize their equipment or improve it or even wanted to take time to talk about it. Out there you either talked squabs or didn't get listened to.

It was dirty and messy from the pigeons splattering all over everything while they had been nesting. It was smelly from rotten eggs poked out of the nests with the squabs. It stunk from dead pigeons shot while the old ones were nesting and never picked up. One place somebody had disturbed a skunk who had been squabbing too, and he had set them right as to who was in possession. Some crazy fool had lit three sulphur smudges figuring he would dizzy them out of the nests, but all that did was choke everybody who came near.

If a tree was little and had lots of nests in it, they wouldn't even bother to poke the squabs out with poles. A couple of men would get together to shake it until the squabs were pitched out. Larger trees they'd take an old log and three or four would drive it like a battering ram against the trunk. Squabs just hailed down. A real high tree especially well loaded they'd chop down and while it fell the squabs would drop and thud like soft big apples.

The dirtiest of all the tricks to get squabs was by a couple of half-breeds I watched specializing in birch-bark trees. They'd spot a paper birch and look up to see if it was good and loaded with nests. They'd set fire to those pretty wisps of thin bark curling off all over like shavings. The fire would zip up the trunk as fast as Mr. Wilcox's new shutter goes and flare along all the branches and explode out over the whole tree in one big roar. Smoke would billow up to the sky. Scorched squabs would plop out by the dozens. The half-breeds never bothered to pick them up. They had boys along for that who'd gather the squabs while they went on to the next good birch bark.

The dirty clothes of everybody, the splatter on everything, the sickening smells, the rags people had tied over their heads, the black jagged skeletons of birches that had been fired, the pigs some had driven in to eat the rotted birds, the crows hovering around to get their fill, it was as dismal and horrible as anything I've ever been around. It was more miserable than the creepiest parts of *Pilgrim's Progress,* because in that you're only reading and when you look up you're away from it.

A nesting is supposed to be a nursery where the little ones can hatch and play and learn to be expert pigeons. Ordinarily anybody feels good toward young things and takes care of them when they need help and protection. The boys banging away with their clubs, they were the same ones who took care of puppies and kittens at home. The farmers in there poling the nests just as like as not smile kindly and speak soft when one of their setting hens comes clucking out of the strawpile followed by a dozen downy chicks. But pigeons are different. They're free, they are a crop without any investment. Nobody knows them personal. Kindness and protection is only for something you're raising yourself. Anything with a value to it that could grow up and get away the idea is to get in there and take it while you can. It made me think of the printer at Sparta again and how right he was. It made me think of Mr. Wilcox and how right he was too, to not bring his camera to such a place. I got out of there as fast as I could and wished I'd never come.

I came out to the Wisconsin River upstream of where I was to meet Mr. Wilcox and there it flowed, wide and quiet and clean and peaceful. It was too big for people to harvest, which was a thing to be thankful for. There it was, just like God made it, a permanent thing nobody could kill. It washed the air, you could smell the cleanness. It washed the bluffs that sat with their feet in it, it washed the sand, it cleaned away the scum from the way I'd been thinking. I never knew before what repair there can be in a river. My, how wrong the printer was for a thing like that and how right Mr. Wilcox was.

I hurried the team up, because pretty as a river road is, it winds awful and takes time and I had no idea how far upstream I was from where I should be. I drove for half an hour letting my eyes taste little samples. Green whispering pines, clean old knobs of sandstone with ferns hanging lacy, chipmunks jerking here and there with nobody or nothing chasing them, cool clean air feeling good in my nose and ever so often a cozy peekhole through the trees or around a knob showing the river lying there grand. My, but it did me good. The road curved in closer toward the river and dipped down and there I was at an open place with a yellow sandy shore. If Kilbourn had a place like that, it could be a real river town to get some good out of its location.

There they were, acres of rafts, all of them, I suppose, that had come down from Jenny Bull Falls and Wausau

279

and Grand Rapids since the water had come up and were stuck there waiting until they could run the Dells. Most of the drivers had gone on for a high time in Kilbourn to pass the time. There were only a few puttering around breaking apart the latest raft into its separate rapids pieces which were rafts by themselves only smaller, of course. Mr. Wilcox's developing tent was put up on the shore near where I tied my team. His camera was out on the platform of tied rafts pointing toward the one they were breaking up. It had the black cloth over the back end and the bump squirming around under the cloth was Mr. Wilcox, I could tell by the legs.

"Am I glad you came, Emil," he said when I got out to him. "Scarcely enough drivers here to make up a crew. What I want to show is the two men on each of the sweeps of a rapids piece, and the way the ropes are thrown from one raft out to another to bring them together to tie up. You want to get out there and catch the rope? For the picture you can be part of the crew."

I liked that. I jumped out there. The two on each of the sweeps kidded me friendly and welcomed me to the crew. The one left standing on the main body took a heavy pole and pushed one end of our raft out and then the other so there would be water between for the picture.

The space between us opened out nice. Those powerful men on the sweeps took my eye. It took strength and brains to pilot a slow clumsy thing like that raft to put it where they wanted it against the whole strength of the Wisconsin River. Of course they were just making believe right then for Mr. Wilcox's picture, but for the real thing they'd be handling themselves exactly the same. What a respectable rival to work against, I was thinking, all the power the Wisconsin River could collect and put together from the three hundred miles behind it. What a different thing it was from a man working his force against baby squabs.

280

"Ready now." Mr. Wilcox directed with the bulb in his hand and standing aside his camera.

The raftsman back there sailed out the rope. It spun high, uncoiling itself from the loops in the air coming toward me. I marched up to get it. "I got it," Mr. Wilcox yelled.

I didn't catch my end. I tripped on one of the bundles of lath laying all over the raft. The loops plopped on the raft. The rope between slapped the water and started to sink. Rope uncoiled loose from my end and slithered into the water. I grabbed, but the last end of it went over the side ahead of my hand. Those men bullyragged me something awful.

The one back with Mr. Wilcox reeled it all in and looped it again to throw. One of them from the forward sweep came back where I was and got himself braced for the catch. The rope came sailing out again. It didn't reach the raft. We had drifted out too far.

He and Mr. Wilcox scurried around fast getting another length of rope and tying the two together. The two ropes together were too heavy to throw. Mr. Wilcox ran to the upper end and untied a rowboat and pulled it around the outside of the rafts. That was faster than getting in and rowing it around to the man with the rope. It wasn't fast enough. By the time the man got it and rowed toward us we were out in the current. The rope playing out slowed him in spite of the way he bent those oars. When he got to the end of the rope, there was a hundred feet between us. He let the end of the rope go and got in the current himself and pulled like sixty to get to us to take us off. By the time he reached us we were moving awful fast. The water we were in swirled faster than anybody could row no matter how strong they were. It was too late to take us off. By that time the rowboat was more dangerous to be in than on the raft. I was scared.

He clambered onto the raft and ran to the forward

281

sweep and motioned me to help on the back one. "Our only chance now," he yelled, "is to try to steer her to the side and out of the channel."

You don't steer when you're being poured into a funnel. You can't ground a raft along the sides of a funnel. We angled those sweeps almost crosswise and all it did was make more bearing surface for the current to push against. The shore on both sides narrowed in. The rocks got higher and higher. The water speed doubled itself. There was seven miles of sudden death ahead.

A raft can't go around bends as sharp as water can. Those masses and masses of curved rock were horror closing in. The rowboat swirled ahead of us, the emptiness of it as horrible as a coffin gaping open. The beautiful Wisconsin Dells. We were all going to be killed by something supposed to be beautiful. Killed by scenery. We were as helpless as pinfeather squabs. I was dripping wet. It wasn't the Wisconsin River. It was my own sweat.

The only help the sweeps gave was something to hang onto. Straight ahead was the first bend where a solid cliff turned the river. Maybe the sweeps did help. Maybe it was the current zipping us along its middle. Maybe it was my praying and maybe all five others were praying too, but we made the bend as neat as the water did. Our end of the raft skidded past within three feet of the cliff and caught the rowboat and crushed it to kindling. It relieved me to see it go.

So close to shore and no shore to jump to. I made up my mind the minute we brushed again so close I'd jump to a ragged place and climb straight up with any fingerholds I could find. I looked up. Where there were finger- and toeholds the cliffs above hung over in porch fashion. Where they went up straight they were smooth. There wasn't any more chance of jumping and catching than if I'd try it from a freight car rumbling through a tunnel.

282

We made a few more bends and made them clean. Awful close, but clean. I began to have faith in those drivers handling that raft. I began to respect those sweeps and what they could do. I prayed they'd keep on working so fine.

"We're going to make it," I yelled.

The two drivers on my sweep weren't red and wind-burned any more like they were when they jollied me as I jumped on. Their hands on the sweep were turning corpse gray. Their faces faded to bearded lead. "The Narrows. Listen to her roar. Jesus God, the river's on edge through there, three times deeper'n she's wide. And halfway through we have to make the Devil's Elbow. Hang on, Jesus God, hang on."

We were in a roar where we were. Such speed as we were making there'd have been roar to a top buggy on a dusty road. Up ahead the roar had a whine to it. A whine like a pipe organ with all the stops out and all the keys held down, like the sound on a platform when an express goes by, like a saw relishing a log, like the pigeons roared when the net sprung. The gorge narrowed so fast the rocks themselves sprang at us like a net, too. The sight and sound took my stomach and all its connections and knotted them around my neck and pulled them tight. If it wasn't for those five drivers manning their sweeps so brave no matter what happened, I'd have laid right down like another bundle of lath and given up.

We hit the rock at the elbow head-on. The forward sweep blade splintered. The sweep pole lifted off its pivot, knocked its three drivers pitching. The one who'd jumped on from the boat sprawled and staggered all the way back where I was before he got his balance. The whole front section sprung boards loose, but didn't break clear. The raft spun around the hung part. Our end cracked into the opposite wall. That snapped the back sweep. Boards on our end buckled and splintered. Right there in front of me I couldn't hear those boards crack loose in all that roar. The raft stopped and tilted upward, wedged tight between the walls. The water couldn't stop. We weren't a raft any more, but a dam. A wall of water knocked us down and would have swept us off if it wasn't for stakes we grabbed that pinned the boards together and stuck up a foot. The loosened boards went. The broken sweep poles went. All the lath roared off. Bundles of it raked me. The water pulled me straight out like a flag whipping from its staff. If I'd have breathed, I'd have drowned. All I could think, over and over, was, we didn't make it, we didn't make it.

The water set me down again easy on the raft. I opened my eyes. My head was out. I could breathe. The water pressure had broken the raft in two where the cribs joined. We were moving again. We were all alive. Four of us hanging to my two-thirds, two on the other third bumping us. No little shanty, no more sweeps, our two rafts now were swept bare. We were racing again and turning end for end, bumping the sandstone knobs on one side then the other. I recognized those knobs. Mr. Wilcox's Navy Yard. Stone ships standing still in all that roaring force. Swallows played fork-tailed over us. I never wished for wings so hard. Not the angel wings I'd be judged for any minute, but real wings to get me out of there.

The river widened out again. The whine left the roar and then the roar quieted down. We still slid along pretty fast and without sweeps we'd bump and turn around and around as we went along. Our two rafts traveled the same speed within talking distance of each other. Those drivers could stand now without anything to hang onto. Only when we bumped rocks did we have to hold onto those stakes. "Bet that's the highest water anybody's ever run the Devil's Elbow," came booming across from the other raft.

"Whadda ya mean run it?" one of our drivers hollered back. "We had about as much control as a calf with the shits."

I didn't feel like kidding. I had to look for my hands and feet, seemed they weren't reporting to me any more at all. I tried and found I could stand too. The raft was solid and level again. The drivers couldn't get over complimenting themselves and me that all six of us had come through the Narrows without a single man washed away or even a broken leg. After that they started bragging and laying plans which saloon was going to hear it first. The Dell House won because it was in sight, right ahead of us at a natural landing. "Always tie up there," one of them explained to me, "after we get a rapids piece through the Narrows. Get a snifter or two and then set out on the walk up the road after the next piece to bring through. Feel like I'll take a half-pint for a starter."

That Dell House was going to have to set up six half-pints the first round, we were so wet and cold. And thankful.

But our rafts wouldn't go where we wanted them to without sweeps or poles or anything for control. The current still had us. It didn't go toward the Dell House which was on wide quiet water. It kept us skimming along under the bluffs opposite.

We set up a whooping and a hollering. I did my part, but those five river drivers really knew how to roar. I didn't dare shut my eyes. It would have been too much like being in the Narrows again. Trouble was, with nobody running the Narrows the Dell House was dead. There were no other drivers to row out to take us off. The folks running the place must have gone to town. There couldn't have been anyone there, that's for sure, or our roaring would have tumbled them out to see what six bulls all at once could be up to.

The channel funneled in again fast. The rocks were higher than ever. The roar built up again and it wasn't the drivers. The same thing over again. My chest felt like a thousand spiders crawling all over it and down my arms to my elbows. I threw myself down again and hung onto my stake.

The driver who had rowed out to us came over to me. "It's all right, kid. There's no place ahead anything like the Narrows. With two rafts now instead of one, the shorter length is probably an advantage. Sure, we'll spin and bump, but the rest of it is just a lark."

It wasn't a lark. He hadn't any more than said it when we hit hard again and knocked him down. He got up right away, but only as far as a sitting position, and next to a stake he could hang onto for the next bump. I sat up too. The water looked too awful, low down like that.

Those terrible rock walls, sometimes smooth, sometimes jagged, made me want to yell. Going through straight would have been bad enough. The dizziness from the raft going round and round pitched and spun the cliffs too, until they were toppling and crashing down without ever reaching us. Mr. Wilcox's beauty. Mr. Wilcox's scenery. A steamboat through a hell like that? Big masses of broken-off rock lay along the edges. They had to fall to get there. Others could fall any time, some of them were only balancing while we rushed past. Take strangers in there to risk that? Women would lose their babies right on the boat. Or mark them for life. Beauty? The most beautiful land I ever wanted to see was good old flat Chicago and Pa's dry warm factory out of sight of any water except our bucket and dipper.

It didn't matter any more whether there were bends or not. We turned and bumped along just as bad on the straight shoots. We never crashed as hard as in the Narrows, but one grinding bump after another and always on the corners began to loosen the stakes that held the raft together. Grinding bumps changed to squealing bumps. Separate boards began to stick their ends out, splintered and split and splayed ends. Sometimes the other raft and ours would engage like two slow turning wheels. We'd both bang kindling off each other almost as much as when a bad knob would rake us.

Both rafts were coming apart fast. Not a board at a time, but over-all loosening like an empty old barrel gives up when the hoops and heads that hold it together start springing. If we only had some kind of a pole left to shove ourselves away from the grating places. What made it so awful was the way we were swept clean. There wasn't even an ax any more. My three drivers tugged and grunted to work a board out, but the raft wasn't that loose yet. It was loose enough to get a hand down for a good grip on a board, which the one from the rowboat did. The strain of turning in the current clamped the gap sudden and crunched his hand. He screamed. It held him thrashing. It held him until the next strain opened the gap again. What he pulled out could never be used for fingers again. He buckled down and sat there straight-legged with a surprised expression, looking at his hand and not believing what he saw. There wasn't any pain in his face. Must have been the hand had gone all numb. It did that to me just seeing it. Numb all over.

The two on the other raft set up a shouting and pointing ahead. Happy shouting. I turned to see what it was. The railroad bridge. We were tearing past Kilbourn, and not a bit of it showed, we were down so deep. That bridge, up there so high, so solid, so safe. I didn't know what they were shouting for. We could just as well expect help from the moon. That bridge spun around as dizzy as the cliffs. I had to grab my stake again to hang on.

I hadn't been noticing the roar especially. The driver

getting his hand crushed and feeling the raft lose its solidness was more to worry about. As we came to the bridge the roar built up powerful again.

The dam! We had to go over the dam. No sweeps. Out of control. The raft as loose now as a baby's spools strung on a string and we had to go over the dam. I looked for the spillway. It was all spillway from bank to bank. The spiders started crawling my chest and arms again. Up the back of my neck and across my head. I hung onto my stake for all I was worth.

I thought of Ma and how she worried Wisconsin was going to be dangerous and how she was so right and we laughed at her. And Pa, with nine boys and never lost a one, war or anything. Last one come and first one to go, that wasn't fair. I choked up mad.

"See here," my brain ordered, "the very first time I took a good look at this river I watched a raft go over that dam. It had to find the spillway. We don't have to, there's a cushion of water so thick across the whole dam now it doesn't matter where we go over. The drop is exactly the same because the dam didn't rise any, only the water. High water above the dam is also high water below the dam."

My brain didn't predict what our spinning would do, or what would happen not having any sweeps and having been banged squeaky with the front end smashed off and the raft broke in two.

We picked up speed. We rode onto the dam. For one long second the sight ahead was sky and us sailing toward it. Sky and three drivers lying flat, hanging hard to their stakes like me. Not exactly like me, one of them had only one hand to do it.

The raft plopped. Out of the sky into mad churning water. We went under. Way under through water that cut and tore and pulled. It seemed so foolish to hang onto my stake that was holding me under. If I'd only let go I could rise and breathe again. The solid pressure changed to chopping stings. I opened my eyes. A water wall shut them again and near wrenched my head off. In between the chopping I could breathe.

We'd made the dam, but to be in the horror below was worse than the Narrows. The raft was breaking up. The stakes tilted every which way. Boards were coming out and bobbing away. Another five minutes, it looked like, there'd only be boards and no raft. Five minutes, the space between two numbers on a watch face, what a tiny weak thing to have the power to say when you'd drown.

The other raft ground in close. Its two drivers walked its edges looking into the waves and foam and boards and litter chopping around. My drivers were doing the same thing. My drivers? There should have been three of them. The man with only one hand to hang onto his stake, he was gone. The terror crawled my chest again.

I got up and started looking too. We were in rubbish so thick there hardly was room for a man to come up. Lath and boards and shingles and branches, and foam pushed up and sitting there sudsy, but no sign of a man. No sign of any current either, that was boiling along a hundred feet off. We were in a little pocket in quiet water. There were men on the shore who'd come there to rescue boards and stuff. Pirate's Eddy, that's where we'd come to rest.

We fished out a few scantlings we could use to pole in as far as we could get. The men on shore planked out to us the rest of the way and we were on solid ground again. I'm never going to leave it.

"What damn fools would run the Dells in water like this?" they asked on shore.

"We broke away, that's all. Six when we started, five of us left. George Cramer swept off."

He was the man who threw the rope I didn't catch. He

289

was the one who rowed out to save us and got drowned himself. Is that the reward a man is to get for being brave? How do they handle things up there, anyhow, to let a wrong like that go through? George Cramer. It's a creepy thing to be so close to a person so intense for a while and never hear his name until he's dead. I'd have liked to know who the others were, but it seemed kind of silly to be introduced and shake hands so late.

"Lost him at Devil's Elbow?"

"Hell, no. Split in two there, but we run the whole goddam Dells as personal safe as a litter of kittens in a basket. You saw him go, didn't you see us go over the dam?"

"We're below it, how could we? You were all lying flat when we see you bob up."

"That's right. You couldn't tell. It was the goddam dam. Run safe through the worst the Old Wisconsin could throw at us by herself but, no, that wasn't enough, they have to build a goddam dam to kill us."

"You're all wet and cold. Look at the kid shake and shiver. Better get something warm into you."

"That's right. We got to move to dry off. Anybody got a bottle on you?"

Nobody had a bottle, so we all lit out, us and those who'd gathered, for Kilbourn. We had to walk back up to the bridge and cross it to get to town. On the bridge we all stopped a minute to look down at the dam and argue where it was, exactly, we'd gone over. Everybody got madder and madder at that dam.

"Why the hell's it there anyhow?" one of the drivers asked. "The law says you can't close off a navigable stream and I'd like to know what else that goddam dam does. We ought to rip her out. For George Cramer we ought to rip her out."

We stopped at the first saloon. The whisky helped like everything to warm us up and help us tell what all had

290

happened. It got pretty lively. I didn't like to leave, but I didn't like any wet clothes either and excused myself to go change.

"Don't ever do that," they warned me. "Too much of a shock. Let them dry off on you, then you'll always be tempered."

I thought of something else. My watch. When I pulled it out it had a bubble between the face and the crystal and had stopped. When I shook it, it gurgled. I got out of there fast and hunted up the jeweler.

"Tch, tch, tch," he said. "Don't you know enough not to let a watch get wet and especially not a fine, expensive one like this? Fell in the river, huh?"

"Never mind that, can you fix it?"

That depended, he said, on how long it had been wet and he'd have to take it all apart and clean it and then adjust it and test it, and it would take weeks and be expensive.

"Never mind that either," I said. "You get right at it." He promised.

Weeks without my watch. I felt empty and lost. It took Pa so far away, not having my watch. I just couldn't get myself to leave. The jeweler was friendly and liked to talk too. By the time I did go my watch was all in pieces. I had half dried out myself.

The street churned with men, mostly river drivers collecting from all the saloons and places. Anybody who'd bought a bottle, and there were a lot of them, passed it around in honor of George Cramer. Two of the drivers had kegs on their shoulders. It wasn't whisky. It was powder. Powder to blow out the dam. They spotted me and took me along so that all of us who'd been on that wild run were together to lead the march back to the dam. "Tear out the dam," we roared and whooped. "We're coming, George Cramer."

You don't go tearing out a dam, we discovered, when

you can't get at it. We were stumped by the water spilling over so powerful. The whole Wisconsin river protected that dam and buried it deep from one rocky bank to the other. There wasn't any place we could get at to fuse a powder keg and sink it against the cribbing. The force of that water would have spun an anvil over before it could have sunk. We all stood around foolish.

There was a little talk about blowing up the mill which was the reason for the dam. That petered out, though, because it was on land, and private property, which we didn't have any quarrel with. If I'd only have caught that rope. George Cramer would still be alive then and nobody would have been in trouble. George Cramer. It wasn't really the dam, it was me. What kind of a mixed-up murderer was I anyhow feeling sorry for those squabs and getting sick to my stomach over how they slaughtered them and then turn around and drown a man? I felt terrible.

A rig came charging up with the horses all lather. My rig from the livery stable and Mr. Wilcox sawing the lines. He looked scared to death. He saw me. He just sank together with relief.

"Thank God, Emil, thank God. What happened? Why's all this crowd?"

"That man who tried to take us off. He swept off going over the dam. They want to shoot the dam out now."

"Shoot it out?" a man near me said. "The kid's got the answer. What we need is artillery. That cannon and its pyramid of balls in the park uptown!"

If that didn't put organization into the crowd. The veterans took charge. An old sergeant, who said he'd been in the Tenth Wisconsin Battery and fired all nine days at the Siege of Savannah, took over as commander. He sent a platoon of twelve to go get the cannon. He set three more men to fish out a pole and fashion it to a ramrod and another for a swab. There's never any of those with a park cannon. He sent into the mill for sacks for swabs and for wadding. They got them easy, the owner and two helpers cowered in there scared to death, they reported.

"We'll make a picture for you, Dad," they kidded Mr. Wilcox. "Blowing out that dam is a part of our rafting too."

"I've caused too much violence today already," Mr. Wilcox said. "If it weren't for me, none of this would have happened. That cannon like as not will burst and kill half a dozen more of you."

"It wasn't your fault, Dad. But the dam has to go. Take a picture as we rake her, we'll all buy one."

"I'll leave your team here, Emil," he said and walked away shaking his head sad.

The cannon came rumbling over the bridge and complaining down the road hitched on behind a lumber wagon. In a park they don't grease cannon wheels. They hadn't turned for six years. It wouldn't roll by itself even downhill.

They dug some wheel holes and positioned her. They dug a bird's nest out of the barrel and stones and rubbish the kids had chucked down in. It took a long time to ream out the fuse hole. If it weren't for the whisky, I think they'd have given up.

"Funny," somebody said, "I haven't seen the village marshal, all the commotion we're making."

"Hell, he came out while we snaked the cannon from the park. Tied him up so he wouldn't get hurt. She's clean now, as clean as we can get her, bring over the powder and let's get this thing loaded. Take your team up the road, kid, way up. If she busts, there'll be brass flying half a mile."

I took the team out of sight and tied them. I wasn't going to stay there and miss the fun. When I got back, all of the crowd had gone behind rocks and around bends except

293

the artillery crew. They put a long fuse into the hole and lit it. We all ran for distance and cover. Where I was I couldn't see cannon or dam or anything.

After a long time it went off. It made my ears buckle. Before they buckled back the echo came bouncing over from the wall across the river. It rumbled back and forth ever so long before the gorge let it sail away and die out. When we ran out the cannon was as good as ever. So was the dam.

"Good old fieldpiece," the commander sergeant complimented. "I knew she could take it. Now we'll get down to business."

They swabbed her out and reloaded. No long fuse this time, just down the touchhole. They aimed her careful so the ball could strike the most amount of dam. "Fire," the commander yelled and touched a torch to the hole.

The roar liked to tear our ears out. A chain of splashes spanked across the smooth polish over the dam. A little spot of crumble scarred the rock wall on the other side, ten feet above the dam. That cannon ball had skipped along the top of the water like a stone a kid throws.

"Damn ricochet. We've got to punch a hole through her broadside."

They grunted the cannon around and pointed it square into the dam. The next ball tore into it so hard two big pieces of cribbing timber poked their ends up. They cheered to see it and passed a bottle. "We'll put some more in the same place."

By the third ball things started moving. I don't know how much ripping those cannon balls could do down under there, but they must have punched a starting hole through for the river to get a finger into. The straight line across the river buckled a little V into itself at the spot they'd been hitting. The V widened. Timbers like railroad ties stripped out and end-over-ended downstream. The whole

294

Wisconsin River took over to finish what the artillery started, and relished the job.

What a churning terrible force a river has when it breaks loose. Once it got a place to grab at it ripped that dam slick and clean away like a rotten picket fence. It cleaned out Pirate's Eddy and lifted the rafts and all the rubbish and pulled it into the current and around the bend. The whole river rushed by free again. The rivermen whooped and cheered a little more and then tramped uptown to celebrate.

Next morning I dropped in to Mr. Wilcox and found he'd walked all the way back the road, after he left my team with me, to collect his gear and his wagon and bring it back. I felt guilty I hadn't thought to drive him back and help him.

17

Without pigeons uprooting people and without a dam riling up the river drivers, Kilbourn made the finest kind of headquarters to work out of for selling harness. With Rudolph getting better and Sarah taking care of him, there wasn't any worry there for me any more, nor bother from him interfering where I went. I had the nicest set of weeks ever, just moseying along, a new road every day and calm steady people to talk to who weren't excited about anything special. That's the best kind, they got time and brain space to plant excitement into about harness quality and bargain price. I did real good.

South of Baraboo I came onto one of the places Mr. Collins had described to Pa where his North Western was building a brand-new line up from Madison. My, if they weren't splitting up the landscape. The roughest, rockiest country I ever saw, and darned if they weren't slicing through it instead of going around. Some places they'd be cutting so deep through a hill and the folded rocks inside they'd have to blast. Two hundred feet or so farther they'd have to use what came out of the hill to fill up a deep pocket because railroad tracks have to be practically on the level and if the level isn't there it has to be made. I never expected such busy hauling. The place just crawled with teams and scrapers and wagons and men with wheelbarrows. Everybody lived right there on the work, like lumberjacks do, out of a camp. They had a cook tent and a horse tent and a bunk tent. They also had a lot of old, poor harness. I picked out one of the teamsters to work on while he rested his horses for wind. They weren't his own team, he said. They didn't belong to the North Western either. All the horses and harness and wagons and gear belonged to a man in between who undertook on his own to get the work done. He was a contractor for building a roadbed like Pa was a contractor to build harness for the army. I asked to have him pointed out and hunted him up. Talking to one man is lots better than having to reach sixty, but of course it's riskier because if he says no and sticks to it you're all done. In a way you have to be sixty times more careful.

I was careful. Twenty sets he bought, without taking as much time as a farmer takes to buy one. I had sneaked over into the part of our trip Rudolph had divided out for himself. Big business. I think Rudolph has been pulling my leg. Big business isn't much different from little business.

Next morning was the day Rudolph was supposed to get out a little to build up his strength. He should have looked happy about it, but when I asked if there was anything I could do for him and Sarah before I'd start out for the day he was glum.

"Where is Sarah?" I asked.

"I told her to walk around an hour or so and get a little sunshine. She needs it. Mostly, though, I sent her off so I could talk to you a little alone. Don't go out right away, I got something to say. Sit down."

I sat down and waited. I waited quite awhile, but he didn't start. Something was bothering him. He laid there

297

with his eyes shut, not sleeping I could tell by his breathing, but thinking hard. Afterwards he opened his eyes and looked and looked at me.

"Emil," he said, "I don't quite know how to begin." He looked at me some more and shut his eyes. When he talked again they were still shut. "No use to begin anywhere, that's done and can't be changed. I'll just tell you outright. Sarah is going to have a baby."

My ears started ringing. All of a sudden there wasn't any water in my mouth. "Oh, no," I said. "How can that be? She isn't big or anything."

"She'll be big all right. Told me two days ago, as soon as she thought I was strong enough to stand it to know. I don't know what to do."

"It's you, isn't it?"

"Of course it's me. What do you think she is?"

"Well then, marry her."

"A Rohland marry a servant girl? Dishonor everything Pa has built up?"

I felt like reminding him he'd dishonored Pa and everything Rohland already and sleeping with Sarah was maybe the easiest thing in the whole business to correct. "You aren't thinking of Pa," I said. "You aren't thinking of Sarah. All you think of is you. Well, the best thing for you and Sarah and everybody is to get married and you should be proud to get her no matter how you had to do it. When's the baby coming?"

"In October."

"Well then, it's only the start of June now." I counted on my fingers. "June, July, August, September, October, five months for everybody to forget and all this blow over. I can get a preacher for you and you can get it done today and wire Pa and that's all there's to it. Pa'd be happy, he thinks a lot of Sarah. So do I."

He sat up straight in bed. "That baby is hers to worry about. I'm not going to be saddled down with a woman

298

and a brat. Good God, Sarah herself hasn't even asked me to do that. I'll thank you to keep your nose out of it too.''

"Well, I thought you were worried and wanted help."

"I do, dammit. I want some real help, not to be tied up for the rest of my life.''

"That's going to be a problem.''

"You're mighty well right it is. I'm thinking of Sarah. She's been good to me these weeks here. I'd like to do something for her. For me, I can just let it go, women have babies every day without being married, nobody holds the men especially unless once in a while a woman takes it to court. Sarah'd never do that so I've got nothing personal to worry about. I'd just like to make it easier for her, that's all. Maybe three or four hundred dollars would do it, I never thought of that.''

"She'd throw it back in your face.''

"I don't know about that. Money talks. With four hundred dollars, for instance, she could easy buy a substitute like any of the drafted boys could during the war. A war is a lot more serious thing than a girl in trouble.''

"You make me sick.''

"We just have to be practical about this, that's all, and get a little help to Sarah. You got four hundred dollars, haven't you?''

"No, I ain't,'' I lied.

I wasn't so sure inside as I tried to sound. Principles are one thing and offering Sarah money would be the most insulting thing a person could sink to, but in a way getting four hundred dollars would be a lot better bargain than getting Rudolph. As a husband I wondered if he'd be worth four dollars. "I'm getting out of here, out where it's clean,'' I said.

I didn't go out with harness. I walked and walked. Lucky I didn't meet Sarah anywhere. I wouldn't have known how to face her, I was so ashamed. I tried to think.

It all jumbled up. Without planning to I stopped in to Mr. Wilcox.

"All sold out of harness," he joked, "that you've got time in the morning for a visit?"

"I don't feel like meeting new people today," I said. "I'm all mixed up."

"Want to tell me about it?"

"No, I don't. It's something I have to think out." I didn't mean to be short with him, but I wasn't going to blat out Rohland troubles either. Especially not a mean, dirty one like we were in now.

"Every man worth his salt has private thinking to do," Mr. Wilcox said. "I do mine best out among the rocks and the pine trees and the solitude left over from when this old world had its own turmoils. Going to Congress Hall today. If you like, you can help me carry in the equipment."

"I'd like to help, but I'll never go on that river again."

"I wouldn't ask you to. Congress Hall isn't on the river, it's about six miles south of here and it's a dry canyon."

That suited me fine. Just being with him helped. I didn't think out any answer, it didn't help that much and I didn't expect it to, but just being around him and climbing around those rocks in the peacefulness and quiet was soothing. We poked around and puttered in there all day. It was late afternoon before we got back to Kilbourn.

I didn't want to go back to the hotel. Being alone again made it just as bad as when I started out in the morning. A whole day gone and who did I comfort? Just myself and now that was gone too. I dropped into a saloon for a little whisky to take the sag out of me. I didn't expect it to help. I just didn't care. I took it alone way off on one end of the bar. Wild talk like you always hear in a saloon, especially where they have a river-driver trade, drifted over from where a half dozen of them were listening while a stranger treated and bragged.

"Women?" he said. "We've got eight of the best beauties you ever laid eyes on and I promise we'll bring them out without a stitch on so you can see for yourself. After that you're on your own." Loud laughing drowned out the rest of what he said.

I got curious. I stood a little closer to find out what was going on. The stranger was telling of a show he was putting on that same night and what he was there for was to advertise it so he'd have a crowd. He was a hard-looking character. Tiny red veins ran crisscrossed all over his cheeks and nose with his skin under the veins instead of over them. If he'd cut himself shaving, he'd half bleed to death. His eyes were bloodshot. His bottom lids pulled away an eighth of an inch from his eyeballs so that the red hung out open. "For a show like this," he said, "I don't dare put up posters or pass out handbills. You boys pass the word along and come and enjoy yourselves. We're out where we won't be disturbed. Show's in a tent on the right past the last house on the Portage road."

Women. A show with bare naked women. I wondered what it would be like. Maybe if I went I'd understand Rudolph better. Myself too and why I felt so funny pleasant and hungry when those La Crosse girls brushed their hair across me in the train to look at the pigeons. Girls in such a show were bound to be whores, how could they be anything else, and I'd find out once for sure how a man can tell them from ordinary girls. Seems to me that should be a help for anybody to know. With women being such an important part of a man's life, no difference if he's a heller like the river drivers, or one to ruin a girl like Rudolph, or just to plain get married without any trouble, a man should at least find out what he's dealing with. I was sick and tired of Rudolph making all the

301

trouble and me trying to pick up the pieces and patch them together again. I got just as much right to poke around finding out about girls as he has. I made up my mind I was going to that show.

I didn't even go back to the hotel for supper. I couldn't have faced Sarah. They'd charge me for supper anyhow at the hotel because I didn't give them notice, but I figured reckless one place, reckless another, and ate in one of the lunchrooms. Pretty soon after supper three or four men strolled out of the livery stable and headed up Broadway away from downtown. More came out of the saloons and moseyed toward the Portage road. A steady stream came out of the hotel and from the Railroad House down near the tracks. The advertising had worked. I'd have found that tent just by keeping my eyes open and following the walkers even if I hadn't known its address. It cost me a dollar to get in.

There wasn't any place to sit down. The tent was bare except for one big platform and two little ones up on horses. We filled it just standing there, maybe a hundred or a hundred and fifty men and boys sort of squirting their eyes around noticing who else was there. The word had got around fast, there were three or four farmers I'd sold harness to from as much as four miles out and all kinds of hired men.

The canvas back of one of the little platforms pushed open and a man came out. "Girls are taking a beauty nap," he said. "You'd want them fresh as daisies, wouldn't you? Of course you would, so just be patient for a few minutes more and while we're waiting let's talk about something pretty important—masculine virility."

A burly big river driver guffawed. Three four others from different parts of the tent roared out laughing too.

"Now just a minute," the man on the platform warned. "Sure, you fellows are perfect specimens, now. Perfect, and yet unknown to yourself you may be nourishing a condition that may lay you in your grave when you should be in your prime. Or worse yet, make a raving lunatic of you, a burned-out nothing gibbering and jabbering nonsense behind the bars of an asylum. You can tell. You can tell, oh yes, you can. That is, if you know the symptoms."

The place was so quiet you could hear your own heart beat in your ears.

"The symptoms? Well, you're sleeping sound. You dream. Oh man, what you don't dream. Wrestling with a redhead, or some beauty you've been thinking about— oh, those thoughts, those damning thoughts—and, man, how you pay for them. You awaken with a start and a throbbing and there—gone from you forever—soiling the bedclothes—is a vital part of your manhood. You haven't lost anything, you say? It's a normal, natural occurrence? Well then, are the awful consequences natural too? Maybe ten years from now, maybe a year, maybe next week, your back aches so you can't rise from your bed. If that's all, you're blessed with luck. Paralysis is more common— idiocy—even suicide—are the awful consequences. Your vital male fluid—you know what it's worth to you? Every drop—every single drop of it—takes an ounce of your blood to make. How many drops do you lose at a time? A hundred, gentlemen—more than a hundred. That costs you a hundred ounces of your lifeblood. There's thirty-two ounces in a quart—three quarts of blood burned up in just one attack of spermatorrhea. Bad cases have attacks as frequently as ten days apart. Would you cut your wrists once every ten days and let three quarts of your precious blood spurt away? No, you bet you wouldn't— that's what it means, though. Spermatorrhea is simply another name—a medical name—for suicide."

He scared the living liver right out of me. Exactly what he said has happened to me. A cold rush came over me like the water when our raft stuck in the Devil's Elbow. I had just as bad a time to breathe. I've got that disease,

303

I know I have. I looked around. I wasn't the only one. Most of the hired men were whiter than sheets and worked their Adam's apples like corks bobbing when a fish bites. A disease ending in *orrhea* is the worst that can happen to a person, anybody knows that.

"Men, you don't have to face the terrible consequences," he went on. "Medical science has a remedy." He whipped out a bottle. "Hembold's fluid extract Buchu cures spermatorrhea. It's advertised in all the papers with a money-back guarantee. You can get it in any drugstore, but, boys, who of you wants to have it known in your home neighborhood of your affliction? That's why I've brought a supply so that you can be treated and cured without embarrassment or shame because we men will keep this occasion to ourselves. One bottle—a complete cure—your lifetime assurance that they'll never put *you* in an insane asylum—one dollar."

I'd have got hold of a bottle somehow if it was twice the cost, but I wasn't going to label myself in front of people who'd bought our harness and the rest of that tough crowd. Nobody else needed the cure bad enough for that either. He never sold a bottle.

He had thought of that too. A person didn't have to buy while everybody else was looking. He told how he'd be right there aside of his private platform all through the show and anybody could drift over and get their bottle on the quiet whenever it would be handy for them. "Now, bring on the girls."

The man with the bloody eyes I'd seen in the tavern started squeezing an accordion. Out they pranced onto the big platform, eight of them like he said. They *were* naked. Their hair was down in front of their shoulders, and they held their hands around to cover other places like all the naked paintings and statues do. The river drivers whistled and stomped and yelled to get their money's worth so once in a while one would roll her eyes and hold her mouth devilish and use one hand to sweep her hair aside. They got more and more reckless as the music went on and pretty soon tossed their heads to switch their hair so it hung behind and after that they put both hands on their hips and just posed. Gosh!

Another man with the show came out on the platform to explain. "These girls," he said, "lead a pretty full and active life." That made the crowd laugh. He laughed too. So did the girls. One of them winked.

"But look at their stomachs. I said *stomachs,* not where you're watching. Notice how flat and trim they all are? Now, gentlemen, you all know that accidents do happen. I shouldn't wonder but a goodly share of you right here, right now, might be a wee bit worried about a stomach somewhere that's beginning to round out a little? And if you're worried, how do you suppose she feels. You're thinking maybe of putting her in a buggy, the same buggy, maybe, where it all started, and driving off two or three towns away to pay twenty-five dollars to some drunken doctor? Or worse yet have her dose herself with castor oil and quinine? They try everything, even hairpins, and what does that lead to? Blood poison and a horrible death."

Poor Sarah, that's who he was talking about. My palms got so wet I had to wipe them on my pants. What an awful thing Rudolph had done. But I knew a thing or two about selling, that man was another crackerjack at it and he was leading up to something.

What it worked out to be was a medicine called Emmenagogue which he had for sale in bottles for women who were going to have babies, but really shouldn't. Like girls who weren't married, or married ladies that already had all the family they needed. The girls in the show, for instance, that's how they kept so trim in their business, he said. He promised there wasn't anything in it the slightest harm because any paper you pick up advertises it, which

305

was so, I'd seen it dozens of times, but I never rightly understood what it was for because nobody'd ever explained it to me before. He recommended a man should have a supply handy just in case his lady friends might start complaining.

Why, it was exactly the thing we needed for Sarah. It would take care of her, and of Rudolph's worry and mine. What a lucky thing, I figured, that I happened to go to that show.

The first bottle he held up for sale I pushed up toward him. I felt ashamed doing it, but if I was in trouble I know Sarah would help me no matter what she'd have to face so I jerked a quick breath and told him I'd take a bottle.

He looked down from the platform. He complimented me being so young and said he was surprised I had use for it so early. I didn't figure he'd joke about it. I wouldn't go around embarrassing anybody I was selling a harness to. Somebody laughed. I felt terrible. I got so mad I was just about ready to tell him a thing or two and put him straight I wasn't buying for myself but for my brother. I cooled down in time. If I'd have said that, they really would have hooted. It was bad enough the way it was. I took my bottle of Emmenagogue and tried to hide myself back farther in the crowd.

After a while when a few more had been sold and he couldn't raise another dollar no matter how hard he tried they went on with the show. I snuck back to the first platform and bought my bottle of Buchu and hurried out of there to get back to Rudolph and Sarah with the help I'd found. Pa was right, there's more good things to be learned by looking around than anybody who doesn't try it could ever imagine.

When I got back Rudolph sat downstairs in the hotel parlor with a tailor from Baraboo going over goods samples for a suit. It was the best sign ever that he was

306

well again. It also was a sign that I couldn't get at him to give him the Emmenagogue, because Rudolph deciding on clothes would be harder to interrupt than the Wisconsin River. I had to give it direct to Sarah herself.

I rapped on her door. She let me in. She was packing. I asked her why.

"Why? Because my work is finished, that's why. Rudolph is better, isn't he?"

"I suppose so. My, but you took good care of him. You can tell Pa I said so."

She got a little whiter. "Emil, I'm not going back to Chicago." Her voice broke a little. "I'm going home to Peshtigo." She didn't say why, but I knew. That reminded me why I'd rapped on her door. I didn't quite know how to begin.

"Rudolph told me," I said. "Told me this morning. I've been thinking all day."

"Yes," she said, "so much thinking now, so little thinking before. Thinking. The whole population of the whole country could pitch in and think their brains hot for me, and it couldn't change one iota now. Why didn't I think when it could have counted?"

"I got good news for you. Here." I handed her the bottle.

"What's this?"

"Read it."

"Em-men-a-gogue," she read. "Friend to the distressed female. Starts monthly flow and brings on regularity. Especially effective for obstinate cases of several months' standing. Particularly suited to—— Emil, where did you get this?"

"I bought it. For you."

"Did Rudolph tell you to?"

"Why, no. I found it myself. Rudolph doesn't know anything about it. Take it. You don't have to worry any more. It's guaranteed."

307

"Sit down, Emil." She started to cry. After a little she braced up again and looked at me. "You know what this will do, Emil?"

"Why, yes. You just won't have any baby, that's all. It says so, like you just read."

"You dear, innocent boy. It isn't as simple as this. You don't know what you are doing. I take that back, you do know. As far as clean, simple, honest, unselfish love can tell you, you know precisely what you are doing. I'll remember that and take a joy in it no matter what hell lies ahead. I'm going to hurt you, Emil, hurt you as the innocent are always hurt. I can't touch that bottle."

"Why not?"

"I can't *prevent* a baby any more. There *is* a baby, a living, developing baby. I think I can sometimes feel its faint, ever so faint, moving. Emil, could you poison a baby in its crib?"

"My God, no."

"The baby is lying in me. I am the crib."

She handed back the bottle. My hands burned. I threw it out the window. I heard it crash. She cried and kissed me. We mixed tears. I gulped out of there to my own room.

My mind made pictures faster than Mr. Wilcox's camera. The Irishman back on South Water street and the coffin I gave him for his little girl. Springing the net on the pigeons. Not catching that rope on the raft. Offering to poison a baby. First I give a coffin away, then I start filling them. Sorry for pigeon squabs, and kill human beings. On top of all those troubles I had that terrible disease the agent at the show described. Jesus God, I prayed, I'm busting up my life like a raft in the Devil's Elbow.

I wondered if my bottle of Buchu was a poison like Emmenagogue. Well, I figured, I'm poisoned mind and body anyhow, so I took a big dose.

I tossed for hours trying to think. I also tried not to

think, but it didn't work either way. When I did doze off a little it wasn't sleep, but dreams. I was at the show again. One of those girls and me. We Rudolphed. It woke me up. The Buchu didn't work. My case was too far gone. I lay there trembling scared I was going crazy. I never slept again all night.

After daylight I couldn't stand it any longer for worry and went in to Rudolph and woke him up.

"You look terrible," he said squinting at me fuzzy. "What the dickens is the matter with you?"

"I got the spermatorrhea."

"You got the *what*?"

I told him what happened. He lay back laughing. "Kid, there ain't anything wrong with you. You just had a wet dream, that's all. Every man has them, it's perfectly natural."

"Honest, Rudolph?"

"It's the truth, Emil. I wouldn't lie to you about that. It's nature's way to let you know some of the things your body is ready for. You're just growing up, that's all. When it happens again just relax and enjoy it."

"You mean it isn't a disease? I don't have to take a cure for it?"

"Of course not. Believe me, I know. Now go back to bed and go to sleep. You're all right."

What a relief that was. I believed Rudolph. If there was anything he was expert on, it was that. Experts don't need to lie, they know. I went back to my room and heaved that bottle out the window too and climbed back into bed. I was so tuckered out I slept solid until noon. I missed saying good-by to Sarah and seeing her to the train and everything.

18

WE STAYED longer at Kilbourn than the harness business was really good for. Two things kept us there, waiting for my watch to be adjusted perfect and waiting for the Baraboo tailor to finish Rudolph's suit. We had to travel farther and farther to find business.

Rudolph rode along with me, at first only a little trip sometimes in the morning, sometimes in the afternoon. After a while he gained enough strength to take half days of it, and then he felt his old self again to take a full day. Mostly he was quiet and let me do all the talking to farmers and folks.

"When you going to pick up again?" I asked him one day, "and get out by yourself and start up again on big business?"

"You know, Emil, I been thinking about that," he said. "Funny thing, but you've had all the good luck."

"Me? Good luck? How so?"

"That's what I want to find out, how so. Come right down to it, we're two-thirds through the second carload and except for that deal up at Eau Claire which doesn't count, I guess, I haven't sold a single harness."

"I noticed that," I said.

310

"So did Pa notice it. How do you suppose I can make it up to him?"

That was a change. Rudolph never asked me for advice before. I wasn't prepared with any. "Gosh, I don't know. I can get my watch tomorrow. Then as soon as your suit is done you ought to be deciding where we should go next to headquarter out of."

"My suit will be done the end of this week. Suppose you pick where we should go next."

I didn't say anything, but I sat there pleased. Where to go can be mighty important. Letting me decide that was a lot different from the way we'd started out when I was supposed to carry his baggage.

I didn't get to decide. That night we had a long letter from Pa telling what a dry July it was in Chicago, and how he'd had a talk with Mr. Collins of the North Western. Their new road from Green Bay was pushing along toward Marinette in good shape. Pa ordered us to Green Bay. Green Bay, he said, had farm trade and Fox River trade and Great Lakes trade and railroad trade and railroad construction. He made it sound like a little Chicago.

Our last day at Kilbourn Rudolph took a few harness and went out alone while I wound things up and paid our bills and stuff and went in to say good-by to Mr. Wilcox. I don't like good-bys. I kind of dreaded it.

"Well, well," he said. "So you're going to leave our city? When will you be back?"

"Back? I don't suppose ever."

He looked at me steady. "I thought you did fairly well here with your harness."

"I did. Real good."

"Didn't you tell me the whole idea of this tour of yours is to see how much of a market there is and where it is?"

"That's right."

"Well then, you'll be back. Probably not selling from a wagon again as your company grows, but instructing your agent in the things you already know. Good luck, and see you soon.''

Why, of course that was the way it would be. That was the whole point and reason why Rudolph and I were out and I'd forgotten it. Coming back was as important as Pa's stitching machine we'd have by next winter, the market we were exploring now was what would keep that machine running.

"You bet I'll be back," I said. "Back and watch your steamboat chug through the Dells.''

At suppertime Rudolph came in to the livery stable whistling with an empty wagon. That surprised me because I thought I'd reached all the market there was out of Kilbourn, and back, in a day's drive. He looked twice as healthy as when he'd started out in the morning.

"Look at this, Emil." He grinned. "Solid cash. It's wonderful the way the quality stands out in our harness. If we didn't have to pull out, I could do the same tomorrow and every day.''

"Big or little business?" I asked.

"How'd you mean?"

"Why, the way you divided it yourself, remember? All at once or one at a time?"

He laughed. "Never thought to notice. Sort of in between, now that you bring it up. Damn if I know whether a threshing crew is one or the other and what's the difference, anyhow. I work on the men together, but they buy separate. This dry weather is perfect for threshing. Everybody is hurrying to take advantage of it before the next rain comes. Hurry makes them load extra big and heavy. Big loads and hurry is a strain on harness. It's a perfect time to bring around Rohland harness.''

I wished I'd have thought of that. I should have too, they'd been cutting and shocking grain all week. Wouldn't they pick the one day I stayed in and he went out for starting the threshing and now we had to leave.

312

"Too bad," I said, "we have to lose this valuable time now while it takes four five days to get our boxcar up to Green Bay."

"No," he said, "Green Bay is quite a bit farther north. They'll be four five days later starting. It's just right. We'll get there for their full threshing season and it won't be a worked-over territory like you've finished this one off."

Green Bay was just like Pa said and Rudolph predicted. The dry weather stayed which was more than anybody could predict. We didn't investigate new business at all, but concentrated on the threshing crews in the open farming country south on both sides of the Fox River. By September we had sold out and telegraphed Pa to send the last boxcar to Green Bay.

It got so dry it worried the farmers. They couldn't fall plow because the ground got like rock. The bugs thrived, though, the grasshoppers sprayed ahead of the team wherever we went and the horseflies bit and the crickets chirped and the trees throbbed with that loud, dry-weather buzzing some insect you can't see does. The Green Bay paper had accounts of chinch bugs and seventeen-year locusts and potato bugs and army worms ruining things one place or another all over Wisconsin. Only thing that wasn't bothering was mosquitoes. I didn't remember, come to think of it, being mosquito bit since the Fourth of July. Farm business dropped off bad. Their buying quits sudden when they're worried.

The railroad builders on the North Western up toward Marinette, we discovered, looked on the dry weather as extra good luck they never dreamed of. They were working considerable north of Green Bay past a town named Oconto. It was a scorcher of a trip through the dust to get there. Worth while, though, because where they were working was ordinarily marsh country, reeds and bogs and tamarack and stuff, but dry weather so long as we'd been having had dried it up so they could work in it without getting wet. That job just sang along. Hundreds of men and teams scraped the marsh dirt and sand together to make a grade down the middle and a ditch on each side. They didn't have to haul dirt along anywhere, just ditch enough to give them what they needed for their grade. The contractors were making money faster than they'd planned with no sticky muck to bog them down and hold them back.

They were looking for more men and more teams and more equipment, anything they could get to speed the work faster and get it done before a rain would come along and make the swamps marshy again. Every few miles was a different contractor. They all bought harness from us. We sold all we could load on a wagon three trips in a row, but it took a day to drive out and a day to drive back each trip it was so far north of Green Bay.

I was for hitching our boxcar to a work train and working from it direct, business was so good, but Rudolph voted against it on account of the risk from fires. There were fires all over. The tamarack trees they had to grub out and snake to the side, they burned those to get rid of them. Every so often, the marsh grass would catch fire and run itself out, maybe a mile or two along the grade on both sides. Some places the marsh ground itself was old grass settled down, each year adding a layer, and that would burn too, right in the ground. It put a haze in the air and a stink in your nose. Once in a while it would burn up a pile of ties before they got them laid. They had trouble all along with the telegraph line, sometimes a dozen poles in a row would burn off overnight. "I lost two-thirds of a car of harness once before," Rudolph said, "I'm not risking our last carload out on this line."

Just the same, he pushed me awful hard and drove himself like a section boss to reach the contractors at the head

314

of the line and get out of there. "What's all the rush?"
I asked.

"We got to get to those contractors before they get into
the next town. That's Peshtigo. It's damn near October.
I don't want to be bumping into Sarah now."

"But Pa said we should go to Peshtigo that very first
night when Sarah described it, remember?"

"Yes, I do, but Pa's forgot it by now. We aren't going
there."

Pa hadn't forgot. Back at Green Bay there was a letter
from him. He'd been talking with William B. Ogden, he
said, who practically ran everything in Peshtigo because
he owned its sawmill and woodenware factory and a private railroad eight miles long to Peshtigo Harbor and a
fleet of ships to market his goods to Milwaukee and Detroit
and Chicago. Pa ordered us to Peshtigo to see Mr. Ogden's
different superintendents who would have notice to expect
us. He also said Sarah had never come back to Chicago and
we should call on her home to see what was the matter. "I
like that girl," he ended, "and didn't expect she would
leave us so careless."

"Peshtigo," Rudolph said. "Hundreds of places in
Wisconsin and Pa has to pick the one spot I want to
avoid."

Rudolph is strong-headed, but he isn't strong-headed
enough to disobey a direct order from Pa. Next morning
we loaded up again and padlocked the boxcar and started
out.

It was dusty and dry and hot. The wagon squeaked, not
in the axles, they were greased, but the spokes in the hubs,
and the spokes in the felloes and the boards in the box.
After a while it quieted down some, maybe the dust working in and packing, or maybe just that everything else was
so discouraging too we couldn't listen to a wagon very
long and care. We passed dried-out gardens and given up,

315

and people's flower beds all dead and brown, and horse troughs without any water in them. We saw rain barrels dried out and fallen together, and dogs raising dust just scratching themselves. We passed a hog yard and none of them were lying down because they had forgot how to wallow. One was trying to root, but all she raised was ashy dust and she had to lift her snout to sneeze. I never saw a hog sneeze before, but I never saw any country so dry before either.

Mostly all I could smell was dust, and when I got used to that, smoke. Those two things fixed up everything you could see too, the dust crowding into everything near and the smoke oozing up the distance and blotting everything dim. There weren't any clouds, nor any blue sky either, even that looked dried-out and sickly. The sun was dim, I could look right at it with both eyes open and they wouldn't water any more than the grit in the air made them. The sun itself had little more energy than the rest of the sky and wasn't any brighter than the bottom of a polished copper kettle. The whole world was smudgy.

"That unnatural sky makes me uneasy," Rudolph said. "Looks ready to explode. Reminds me of the way the firebox of a cookstove looks when the ashes are still warm and you douse a little kerosene and kindling in and gray smoke curls around thick and drifts out from the cracks around the lids. All of a sudden—*poof*—it catches and blows the fire door open and rattles the lids and roars yellow." He looked all around. "Emil, I don't like it."

I didn't like it either, but it wasn't such a risk as he said. Talk always exaggerates. Sure, the marsh we watched smoldered and once in a while a little patch of tamarack flared up like it *was* kerosened, but a whole landscape can't blow up no matter how dangerous the sky looks. There were people out in that smoldering country, farmers and settlers, and landlookers for next winter's timber and all those railroad crews. Sure, they were nerv-

316

ous and worried, they couldn't help it, but they weren't pulling out afraid of everything going at once.

We pushed on too and the farther we went the more burning we saw. Some of the farmers were burning on purpose and using the dry weather for a good chance to fire a forty or two they wanted cleared.

Along about noon we came to a fork in the road. "Take that one to the northwest," Rudolph said.

"That's the wrong way," I said. "Peshtigo isn't northwest, it's northeast."

"I know it. I'm sick of this flat country. Let's go up in the hills for a day or so. Monday will be time enough to pull into Peshtigo. I have to think awhile before I want to face Sarah."

I couldn't blame him. I wanted to see some hills again myself. They do something for a person. That fellow in the Bible who said he looked to the everlasting hills where he got his strength, he knew what he was talking about.

After a couple hours the road started to climb and an hour after that we were in the hills. They flared spotty too, sometimes a whole slope would be burned out and dead, sometimes we'd see the orange eating along the underbrush like a big ringworm disease scabbing the land.

19

THE road took a dip into a little valley toward evening and everything changed. Beautiful green pine trees, lush with water they were getting somehow, stretched up all around and crowded the road. The air smelled clean and sweet. Rudolph and I both took deep breaths of it and it was nourishing, like a meaty sandwich and a cup of strong hot coffee, honest to goodness. The horses perked up, and not just because it was downhill either. They snorted and sucked in and blew out and pranced and farted like they'd just been turned loose in a tasty pasture.

Birds and bugs and animals and things are smarter by an awful lot than people. Out in the smoking, smoldering, stinking places you saw men and women once in a while, and horses and pigs and farm stuff that people owned, but anything that was its own boss cleared out ahead of the burning. Here in the valley you heard chirping and singing again, and saw chipmunks ducking under rock ledges and kicking up the needles and scurrying around to the other side of trees. It made you pick up interest again, and let your eyes and ears and skin enjoy themselves instead of discovering new ways of getting scared.

I'd have clean forgot there was anything in the world like we'd come through except that it showed up so plain on us. Burn holes in the gunnysacks the harness was in, and on my sleeves and Rudolph's shoulders. Gray ashes and charcoal cinders on our hats. Red stinging spots where sparks got their licks in before I could slap them off. Rudolph's eyes were redder than the day after a binge, and gritty, looking out of two sooty holes. I must have been just as beat-up, because when I blew my nose and looked at my handkerchief it was like I'd cleaned a stovepipe.

The valley was heaven. We came to a bend where the trees on one side dropped down and we could look out. Over their tops in the distance more of the gray blanket we'd been driving through smothered out the horizon and just above that a lonesome spooky sun, red and bloodshot from the fire, seemed not to know where he belonged just like us. Below, the trees stretched down and down, and at the bottom sat a clearing with a healthy, growing color to it and a shiny stream running through. Away off on the side some log buildings peeked through the trees, three or four maybe, and from two of them smoke crawled where you were used to it, out of their chimneys.

We couldn't look long, the trees closed up the view right beyond the bend. It didn't matter. We had a promise now we'd be out of the fire for the night, with a chance to wash, put up the horses, get a meal and a bed of one kind or another and maybe find good talkers and a harness sale too. You can always depend on a road down a valley, anything it gives you a peek at it will bring you to.

"*Hsst.*" Rudolph put a hand on my arm to make me pull in the lines. "Look there, will you."

A doe! Head level and stretched way ahead, she walked out of the trees onto the road. Two more smaller ones followed, heads up, then down, then up again, each step quick and ever so sure. No wonder their tracks are so

319

sharp and pretty. For a second all three heads froze high and still, looking at us, and then *zip, zip, zip* the show was over. Not really over, it goes where you keep your special things that never dim.

It took us just a few minutes to get to the clearing and the buildings. A man puttered around the well sweep in the yard like he'd heard us coming and was waiting. A woman and a girl about my age stood at the kitchen door looking whether we'd drive past or turn in. Soon as we turned in they were gone.

"Nice valley here," Rudolph said, "can you put us up?"

We had to wait while he looked us over. When they do that you know they're foreign. It's either trouble with the language or suspicious what you're up to, or both, and you just stand there. I guess we looked so scorched and done-in it would have been a sin in any kind of religion to say no to us. "You stay," he said without much expression. He tried to smile, but it came pretty weak, and faded away troubled. "Where comes today more fire?"

"About to the edge of your valley, but I can't tell which way it is spreading. If it stays quiet like this, maybe it can burn itself out outside your valley."

"I know. I walk out day behind yesterday. For rain I thank God, but it never come. For wind I am afraid. It make me sweat standing still." He turned his hands outward, strong, willing, helpless hands.

"I'm Rudolph Rohland. The kid here is my brother Emil. Heading for Peshtigo."

He motioned he understood and said his name, Vale Holonen, and then had me unhitch and take the horses to the creek. They drank deep. I envied them standing hock-wet in the cool stream, touching their noses to the surface, the swallow surges sweeping all the way up their necks and landing in a muffled splash way inside. I wanted to jump in the creek with them to rinse off a layer or two.

Mr. Holonen's log barn was just so, everything neat and

320

spic and span, better than lots of houses we'd been in. Stall room you can usually find, but it isn't very often the harness pegs to go with it are kept empty too. Most times I have to clean off all kinds of old straps and ropes and clutter. I saw a good currycomb and brush on the shelf, and not all dusty either. I didn't think he'd mind so I gave the team a quick rubdown. They sure needed it.

At the washstand outside the kitchen door all the rest of me throbbed for what my face and hands were getting. I don't think I said anything, because you don't ask for such things, but Mr. Holonen answered just as if I had. He even smiled just a little watching me splash and spill. "Comes more tonight. Eat first, then hot bath."

I thought that was pretty nice of him. It isn't everybody that will heat up water and get out the washtub and turn over the kitchen to strangers. I'd have never expected a quiet one like him to open out like that.

Inside the women were curious about us like they are most places we stop. There was a mother, trim and slim and blond, and a daughter just like her and another one about my age. They all had blue eyes, not washed out like most, but rich and deep like a baby's. Mr. Holonen told them who we were and us who they were. The mother was Aila, the older daughter Hilma, the youngest Signi. Every one of them would have been a compliment to a calendar.

The mother didn't talk English at all. I think she could have, because she sure understood it. Foreigners are like that sometimes, when they don't see many strangers and their own folks are always around to handle what has to be said. Nothing ever pushes them, and I be darned if it was me if I'd take the risk either of coming out with something funny I didn't mean that way and get laughed at. She sure jabbered away in her own talk, whatever it was.

Hilma and Signi talked just as good as I do. Mr. Holonen sat back letting them, proud as anything because they could do it, his eyes just a shining at us for being there to listen to them. Rudolph pretty quick concentrated on Hilma, the oldest. First he listened, mostly, because you can look a person over all you want while they talk and it isn't forward and brash as it would be any other time. You get a woman to talk, Rudolph told me a dozen times, and you can always go on from there. It's the starting place, he says, for whatever you're good enough to work up to.

When the right time came, Rudolph has that down pat too, he started his own tune to give her a chance to see how handsome and smooth he was. Hilma had been through such ceremonies before, you could see that. She knew just how to lead him on, and keep him thinking he was doing all of it. In a little while he was as at home, and important, as a big old buzz fly let through the kitchen door.

They didn't have hardly any store things except the dishes and oilcloth and clock and lamp. The chairs and table were homemade and good ones. So were the rugs. Everything was as clean, and in its right place as Ma used to have Sarah keep our house.

Rudolph kept Hilma so occupied with their talk she pretty much neglected her share of getting the supper, but the mother and Signi didn't mind. Signi carried and talked too, a word or two to me, and a lot of foreign jabber with her mother. I showed her I could handle another language too and just for the dickens of it spouted off a question in German I learned in catechism, and darned if she didn't snap the answer right back, in German too. Imagine that, living in the woods and keeping three languages straight. That takes brains. "Say," I said, "where'd you folks come from?"

"Finland."

"Where's that?"

"Just east of Sweden."

"There isn't any country east of Sweden." I was good in geography. I can still see the map of Europe, and where countries touch each other. "There isn't anything east of Sweden except Russia. You come from there you're Russian."

"So right, so wrong. Even in America they keep us from being Finns." Mr. Holonen's face went sad, a long-time kind of sadness you could see he'd been through over and over. "Signi, you're young. Maybe live long enough until there be Finland again. Tell him Finland, so he knows, and you never forget."

Supper was ready. While we ate they were all as solemn as at the Lord's Supper, and I kind of believe it sort of was. Lord's Supper is so you can keep your soul alive; well, these people, the way I got it, felt responsible for keeping a whole fatherland alive in their hearts when all the rest of the world figured it was dead. Signi told it like Lincoln must have done at Gettysburg and it was so sad and brave and forlorn and beautiful you wanted to go over there and fight and all you could do was sit there trying to keep your eyes from running. Why is it that sometimes when things make you hopping mad and you got reason to swear like a lumberjack you have to reach for your handkerchief instead?

The way Signi told it, Finland worships freedom and liberty even more than the United States, and had it long before Columbus got restless. Then one country after another came at them with armies bigger than any little nation like them could fight off no matter how brave they were. The last one was Russia, so long ago even her grandfather back in the old country never had a Finland. Taxes going to Moscow, saluting a hated flag instead of flying a loved one, songs they daresn't sing, sons drafted into the same army that killed their fathers and if somebody so much as makes a speech criticizing anything, off to Siberia. Beautiful lakes and forests, but everybody starving to

323

death. Patriots for Finland from little girl babies to shriveled-up old men, every last one of them, and nothing they can think or do can help. Over there you're born homesick, and grow up homesick and die homesick without ever leaving home. The Holonens came to America, over here freedom has a reputation, but they got hurt again because we don't give a damn for anybody's but our own. Last year's census wouldn't even let them say they were from Finland, but put them down as Russians. I felt mad and ashamed. A fine, big, wonderful country like ours blowing out the last little flame of pride they could have kept. That's mean and cheap, I don't care who does it.

I looked over at Mr. Holonen. The lump I couldn't swallow pretty near busted my throat. Everything where he came from gone to hell and buried under a load of sorrow, trying to make his own little go of it in a new place with a new language almost too tough for him, but none of that was too much when a man had a daughter like Signi to hold up what he believed in. He hadn't eaten a thing, just listened and watched, his eyes full of love, his big hands resting idle on the table because the job being done was in a different class from what *they* could do.

"I go," he said, pushing himself away from the table, "I look how comes sauna."

Sauna? What was that, I thought, maybe the fire? It came to me how much this valley must be like the Finland Signi described. They say history happens over again. I got an awful feeling, maybe the fire would come in and run all over like Russia, and the valley go just like their Finland.

Rudolph told Hilma about Chicago and dressed it up a lot more than it really is. He always uses Chicago when women are listening, and I've never seen the time yet he couldn't make the dishes wait.

"Chicago," Signi said, like that answered everything.

324

"Oh, we've waited so long until we could ask someone. Where'd we put that paper?"

Her mother busted out all grins and pointed to the clock shelf, and spilled out a lot of excited Finnish. Signi lifted up its doily and came over to me with a piece she'd cut out of the news. She walked in front of the lamp and it lit her up something special, the light splashing into her hair and gleaming out again like the sun does on a milkweed pod that's just fluffed open.

"The magic comb," the clipping said. "One dollar. Will change any color hair to black or brown. Box 1152, Chicago."

"Coming from Chicago yourselves," Hilma said, "you must have seen them. Are they any good? Do they really work?"

I don't think Rudolph knew about those combs any more than I did, but here was somebody asking him some expert advice and he's not one to turn down that kind of invitation. "It's just like it says," he said, "and it works like magic. But are the women buying them? Not on your life. They want hair like yours and will pay an awful price to get it, but there isn't much for sale. Most girls that have it know what they got, and keep it themselves. You ought to be mighty proud of yours just the way it is, all three of you."

"Well," Hilma said, taking back the clipping. She tried to act disappointed, but gave it away, the way she felt the shape of her head. She tucked a couple of strays back in place. Signi didn't show anything one way or the other. She hunted up a mirror and looked and moved it around and looked some more trying to figure it out for herself. Gee, but her head had a pretty shape.

Mr. Holonen stomped back in. "Sauna is ready." He beckoned to Rudolph and then me, and picked up two lanterns from the kitchen and lit them.

Outside he didn't say anything as he walked ahead of

us to the nearest other building made of logs too. "Mr. Holonen," I said, "you've been saying sauna two or three times, but we don't know what you mean. What is a sauna?"

The shadows of his legs from the lanterns at his knees scissored across the pine needles and sand off into the darkness of the warm night. "Sauna is Finland bath you never forget. So clean. So rest. So strong. I show you. Signi tell you."

"A bath!" Rudolph said, and talked for both of us. "I could use that."

Mr. Holonen hung a lantern outside each of the windows of the log house. We went in.

Inside was a little vestibule. Mr. Holonen started undressing and had us do the same. He was big and well built like Rudolph. I was glad to see he didn't have any more hair on his arms and legs and chest than I have. It goes to show that a man can be strong and powerful without looking like an old buffalo robe no matter how much Rudolph brags about it. The two of us naked white, and Rudolph as near to it as he could get without somebody shearing him, Mr. Holonen picked up his clothes. "Here they maybe get wet," he said so we all carried ours out and put them on a bench outside.

It was moonlight out there, dim from the haze up above and the trees stopped a lot of it, but moonlight just the same, besides lamplight streaming toward us from the two lanterns and from the windows in the kitchen. It's a risky business prancing around naked, but it didn't take more than a few seconds and we were back inside.

Mr. Holonen took us through the vestibule to the room inside, a sort of empty shed with a sand floor where a fire had just gone out and the ring of stones around it were still scorching hot. Benches climbed up one side from the floor almost to the top of the wall. He motioned us to sit. There was a tub with a dipper floating on it in one corner.

There were some fresh-cut little branches with the leaves still on and that was all. It was so hot I felt I had walked into an oven. He dippered up some water and splashed it lightly on the stones. I expected steam. It sizzled and wisped but the room was too hot for steam to show, I guess. It got hotter. It was soft and pleasant and gave me a nice pliable feeling. Mr. Holonen dribbled on another dipperful.

He came over and sat down with us. "More high, more hot. You go where you like." He climbed up two rows higher and sat there a minute and then climbed down to trickle on another dipper. It must have been just right because when he went back there he stayed. I climbed up there, and Rudolph tried it, but it was too hot for us and we backed down a couple notches. I could feel the heat even in my windpipe. If I breathed fast, it burned all the way down. I itched and trickled and scratched and rubbed and couldn't keep up at all with the places that needed me. Rudolph ran like a windowpane in the rain, the wetness plastering his hairs tight to him all over. It wasn't so much the steam making us wet, it was the sweat cooking out.

The door opened. Signi, Hilma, and the mother walked in, bold as you please, and without any clothes on either. I expected to hear some terrible screeching, the mistake they made, but they saw us, and smiled, and kept coming right in. The screeching came all right. It was me.

Rudolph let out a roar.

I grabbed for something to cover up with. There wasn't anything but those few branches with their skimpy leaves. I'd have shied a couple rocks at the windows, but I knew those rocks were hotter than stove lids. I clambered up to the top row where the light was dimmer and got scalded and came tumbling down, right in front of Signi. I wished I was hairy like Rudolph. I wished I was dead. I wished I didn't care.

Signi smiled and reached for my hand. She led me over
to the bottom bench and had me sit down. She sat beside
me. Her mother dippered a little more water on the rocks.
Hilma sat down a little ways away from Rudolph. His
eyes were out an inch. It would have taken a lot dimmer
light to keep me from seeing that.

"Wh— why, why do you come in here," I stuttered,
"wh—while we're in here?"

Signi looked at me puzzled. "Why, what's wrong with
that?"

"Holy Moses," I yelled and the heat scalded my throat
again, "because we're men and you're women, that's
why."

"You're men and we're women?" she puzzled. "It was
that way before. You knew it and we knew it, so why
should that make any difference now?"

"But we got our clothes off!"

"Can you take a bath with them on?"

"Good gosh, do you always do this, with anybody?"
This was worse than the show at Kilbourn. Looking at a
naked show is one thing, being in it is another. Such nice
people as I thought they were, turning out to be a whole
family of whores. It hurt me so I felt sick.

"Look, Emil. We eat together and it makes us friends.
We talk together, and each gains by what the other says.
We sit together and the same fire makes us all warm, the
same lamp lets us all see. Togetherness is always stronger
than singleness, it is what keeps Finland alive while there
is no Finland. Our people must have strength and pre-
serve it, that's why the sauna means so much. From it
comes strength to the body and to the spirit. Strength
and togetherness, that is the sauna. Tonight you are with
us, tonight we share our sauna with you. There is nothing
to be ashamed. It is fine and good as when you sit at our
table."

I never sat naked before as part of a religion. I wondered what kind of heathens they were in Finland, anyhow. In a way it was a relief. Being heathens is altogether different from being whores. I was trying to puzzle it out when I remembered the catechism I'd tried on her before supper and the way she popped back the answer. Why, they were Christian just like I was! A Finnish girl and a German catechism? I asked her how that was.

She laughed the nicest chuckle. "We're the only Finnish family anywhere around. The nearest church is German, so I had to learn my catechism in German and learn the German too. It was kind of hard."

I know how hard it was because that was the way I had to learn it too, but I didn't think very long about that. There's boys in a catechism class, that's what I was thinking, and I couldn't help but wonder whether she might have had the class over for a sauna too. I didn't dare ask. I'd still like to know.

When I got over the shock of it, it was nice. A sauna is wonderful practical at that. It doesn't mess up the whole kitchen and crowd you into an awkward little space like a washtub does. No water to heat on the stove, and no mixing a pail of hot and then a pail of cold until you can touch your toes in it, you just move up or down on the benches until it suits you. It saves time too, everybody together like that, if you live through the dying you do when the others walk in. I got to feeling lazy and peaceful and cozy and careless and recognized it for one of those times that only comes once in ever so long and gets to be the kind of thing you'd like to stretch out to make it last and last.

The less I moved, I noticed, the less the heat scalded. I turned my head slowly to take in the beauty of Signi sitting there aside me. Golly, a girl is a beautiful thing, the way they're put together all over and everything looks so soft and has such nice shades and curves. I wanted to touch her. I put my hand on the back of her shoulder. She turned

329

her head and puckered her mouth a little and leaned over and blew on my shoulder. It was like a red hot poker sizzling a hole into me. I pulled my hand away quick. She kept right on talking as if nothing had happened.

Signi told me the sauna is the first thing a Finnish family builds. They live in it while they build the barn and then the house and all the time it's such a center of their lives that the mothers always pick it for the place to have their babies.

Babies! Signi near me like that. Me just as naked as she was. I had to think of something else and quick, and concentrate.

I told her about the doe in the road, and the other ones with her in all the detail I could bring back. Signi said she saw them every day and watched them grow from speckled little fauns. A sight of them, she said, made her feel the whole world was beautiful. She talked about pine trees, and chipmunks, and walking around the rocks on the rim of the valley, and smelling clover, and which birds sing best, and walking barefoot in powdery dust, and tasting blueberries out in the dew.

I'd have liked to tell Signi I thought she was as pretty as any of those things, and worth a thousand times more for remembering, but while I studied how to do it her mother and father came over carrying those thin little branches and passed them all around.

They started switching themselves and then each other and all of us. The reason for it I found out later is to put tone and toughness into you. After that we all ran outside and down to a pool in the creek and jumped in. Took my breath clean away. I thought I'd catch my death of cold, but it doesn't work that way. It tempers you like a blacksmith chilling a horseshoe.

Rudolph and I couldn't take that cold water like the Holonens could. We excused ourselves and shivered back where our clothes were and started to dress.

330

"What a setup," Rudolph whispered, "what a setup. Passing it to us on a platter. If I don't get a piece tonight, and you too kid, you ever have a piece?" I was glad my teeth were chattering.

Up through the dim moonlight the Holonens walked the path and came to us, refreshed, at ease, strengthened and cleaned. They dressed without a care in front of us, the girls simply holding just a dress over their heads, letting it fall, and they were done.

Back in the house the mother poured wine and passed a kind of coffee cake. We sat around and talked. Weather and fire and crops and railroads mostly, until the yawns took over and they showed us our bed. Rudolph never once mentioned harness, but that was all right. I had looked Mr. Holonen's over when I put the horses up. They were old, but cleaned and oiled and in fine shape for a good many years yet, the way he takes care of things. Maybe it was my being worn out from all day through the fires, maybe it was the relaxing in the sauna, I don't even remember hitting the pillow.

Somebody was shaking me, hard. By the way they were doing it I must have been gone a month. "Get up. Get up, boy, get up."

It wasn't Rudolph. It was Mr. Holonen. It was night, he had the lantern. His face was terrible to see, grim and deep-set. I rolled out in a hurry. "The fire get into the valley?" I asked, looking at my watch, and grabbing my clothes together. It was a quarter after midnight.

"Devil from hell in valley," Mr. Holonen growled. "Go to barn. Hitch up." He handed me the lantern. In the kitchen Hilma was crying. All alone, crying, and wouldn't answer me.

Outside I couldn't see any more fire than the glow it had before, so I knew it wasn't that. I wondered where Rudolph was. Rudolph and Hilma, that was it. Rudolph, for all his big talk and tomcatting around, hadn't he learned any-

331

thing? Mistaking a clean, beautiful thing like the sauna for something low and dirty like that show at Kilbourn. How could a person be so blind?

I harnessed and got the horses out and was hitching up when Signi came out of the house to me. "What happened?" I asked, and then was ashamed I'd asked it. You just don't ask people to describe things like that.

"I don't know," she said, "nobody will talk about it. They only say it was bad. Something that came out of the sauna. Never, never, never again, my father says, will a visitor come into our sauna. With hot water and scrub brushes we must scour it out, he says, before daylight."

The lantern was on the ground while I hooked the last trace chain to the doubletree, on the outside away from the house. Signi came around the wagon. We stood close to each other. "My brother misunderstood," I said. "Maybe things can get too beautiful, I don't know. Oh, Signi, Signi," and then I couldn't talk.

My lips were dry and hot. Hers were sweet and moist. Somehow I felt like I was the fire and she was the valley. This hungry kiss and then what? Ever so slow, not wanting to, it seemed, she pushed me from her. "Good-by, Emil." She picked up the lantern and walked slow to the house. Lord, it was dark.

When I climbed up to the seat, Rudolph was sitting there, grunting and groaning. Out at the road I had to dig out our own lantern and light it to see which way to go. Rudolph was a mess. One eye puffed shut, a hole in his beard where part of it had been yanked out by the bloody roots, his cheeks gouged and clawed.

"Mr. Holonen kind of took you apart, I see."

"Mr. Holonen, hell. Hilma. I can't understand it, I can't understand it."

332

20

THINGS had happened so fast to kick us out of the Holonen valley my head had trouble to catch up and figure out where we were or where we were going. Neither one of us had had time to square away our direction, which was a bad way to be in the middle of the night on a strange road. The only thing we knew was that we were headed on rather than headed back the way we had come in.

"Now what?" I asked.

"Head east when you can. Might as well try to find that damn Peshtigo and get out of this corner of the country."

"East," I said. "How can I find east in the dark from a road that winds? We been coming northwest. By rights I should turn right the next crossroad, but from a winding road in the hills like this turning right could take us north or south or even west, you never know."

There wasn't a crossroad for about an hour until we'd climbed out of the valley. One guess was as good as another. I turned right. After a while we came to the end of the hills on a ridge we could look down and see ahead. It was grand and awful all at once.

It was like being up in the bell tower of the courthouse

back home in Chicago and looking off in the night over the street lamps, seeing the downtown offices lit up and the twinkling windows in the houses as far off as the city goes, locomotives puffing sparks and men swinging lanterns in the yards, foundries glowing red, it was grand. But we weren't looking over a city busy in the night. We were heading into the fires again. Far off it had reached big timber, towers of yellow flame built up and up. In the half distance a haystack flared. On the slope, eating upward slow, a rim of glow spread toward us through the ground cover. It was weird and beautiful and dreadful. The night had turned cool, but it smelled hot. The smoke was back in our noses again.

"I guess we're going east all right," Rudolph said. "If we could only see the stars, to know for sure."

"Lucky thing," I said, "the fires are patchy and not one big blaze. Funny, why isn't it burning all over? Everything is dry enough."

"No wind," Rudolph said. "And been at it so long, a couple of weeks now. Nothing to drive it any one direction so it just eats wherever it can spread easiest. In between it's either burned out already or hasn't been reached yet. No telling where it may be cutting across the road and we'll have to either wait it out or run it."

It didn't get any better or any worse. Sometimes off to one side of the road there'd be fire creeping and crackling, sometimes the other. Sometimes a whole tree or three or four in a clump would catch and flare horrible all the way up and if they were close enough, light up the road for hundreds of feet. We were just lucky those flareups didn't happen right next to the road or on both sides at once.

At dawn we still couldn't tell which way was east. The smoke had got so thick what little daylight there was didn't show where it was coming from. Sometimes we could scarcely breathe for coughing. All we could tell was that we were down in the flats again which at least was the

334

right kind of country for where we were supposed to be going.

We got to a burned-out spot that would have been a marsh in ordinary weather. The road had a hole in it two wagons long and four or five feet deep. There should have been a bridge, but it had burned out. The creek under it had been gone for weeks, even the bottom was powdery. We just drove off and around and up again.

Down in the smoke like we were since the last hill leveled off we couldn't see ahead any distance at all. Fog is bad enough in a country you've never been in before, but smoke is worse. When fog lifts, the land and the crops haven't been hurt. When thick smoke like that lifts, there's scars, bad scars. We went through ever so many of them, that Sunday. Gray, powdery ashes that had once been fields, black stubs instead of rail fences, barns that had gone a day or two before with all their strawstacks. A few still smoldered.

At noon we came to a farm with fences of neat piled stovewood running from the house and around to connect all the outbuildings. We stopped to eat, but they wouldn't stop to feed us. A light wind had sprung up. The whole family were out there throwing those fences down and clearing spaces so that if one place caught, those pretty fences wouldn't be fuses to the other buildings. They let us pump a drink and fill our jug and said the road would get us to Peshtigo, but it was a long way off.

Late afternoon the wind rose strong. "It'll clear the air," I said.

"It'll connect the fires," Rudolph said.

Soon as the wind rose we came onto a fresh fire climbing the tamaracks on both sides of the road. What little we could see ahead looked like a haymow flaring up before the roof puffs off, it was so yellow hot. Those tamaracks went like a spark in a box of matches, a few minutes' wait and it was all over and we could drive ahead. The air was still

335

hot, but everything that could go had gone and we were probably safer than anywhere else because a thing can burn only once.

"What's that ahead?" Rudolph squinted. "A rig?"

It was a rig. It had stopped. An open wagon something like ours.

"Probably waiting like we just had to," I said.

They were waiting, all right. When we started to pull out around them their horses were lying dead in their harness on each side of the tongue. The wagon wasn't burned. A man and a woman sat on the seat, their gear piled up in the box behind them. They sat there faced straight ahead and leaning against each other so discouraged they didn't even turn around to look as we came alongside. Our horses reared up wild. I had to hold the reins tighter than that team had ever strained them before. They settled down and stood trembling.

"Poor things," I said. "I guess I'd be scared too if I came on dead people sudden like they came onto those horses."

"God Almighty," Rudolph cried, "those people *are* dead, look at them."

The skin dissolved straight off of me and left my clothes rubbing my bare nerves. Rudolph got down off the wagon and walked in front of theirs, stiff-legged as a dog edges around to brave out another dog. He looked up at their faces.

"Not burned, their clothes not even scorched, and they're dead, stone-dead." He climbed up and lifted the woman's arm. I couldn't have done that for anything. "She's still limp. Must have just happened."

"Rudolph," I begged, "I can't stand it. We've got to get out of here."

"Not until I figure this out. It was that flash of fire, but why aren't they burned? Couldn't be the smoke or we'd been dead ourselves long before this. The flames suck all the air away from them? Put a poison in the air maybe? That's it, there's poison gases drifting around cooked out of the marshes. Gas at home, remember that's poison too. They been gas-poisoned, them and the team both. Could just as well been us."

I shuddered so I made the seat squeak. Could just as well been us. That's what I'd been thinking. Rudolph saying so too made it double worse. "What are we going to do?"

"Go on," he said climbing back up. "Can't help them. If there's water left in our jug, we can soak our handkerchiefs and make masks."

That's what we did. It felt gruesome to have my nose pressed against such clammy cold.

By suppertime we passed a lot more farms. Prosperous farms in maple clearings. No pines or tamarack or marsh, but the fires were in the grain stubble and in the tindery pastures and in most of the meadow haystacks. The wind was running it in fast. The smoke was thick enough, it seemed, to be a gas itself that could catch any minute. All the light was yellow, sickly dirty yellow that made everything you looked at sickly too. We couldn't bother those farms for a meal either.

About an hour later we went through a mile or so of pine again, completely burned-out right up to the edge of a good-sized town.

Between the town and the burn they'd plowed and shoveled a path of ground twenty or so feet wide to make a firestop. It ran off on each side of the road. A tired sooty man dragging a shovel and holding a lantern patrolled it. We met him where it crossed the road. "What town is this?" Rudolph asked him.

"Peshtigo."

"Well, we made it," Rudolph said and let out a breath that sounded like it emptied him complete.

"Damn near didn't have anything to make it to. We

337

mighty near lost her three four different times the last
two weeks. Got her licked now, every way the fire could
possibly get in has been burned over so wide we're safe.
Even if a fire in town happens careless, we can handle
that. We got two fire engines, the town has one and the
woodenware factory has its own. We got fire barrels all
over town and we keep them full.''

"Where's the hotel? We're mighty tired and hungry.''

"Ho,'' he said. "That ain't too easy. Peshtigo's pretty
prosperous. Drummers and dealers and buyers got the
hotels filled. Couple three hundred railroad workers just
came up from the harbor this afternoon. You gonna be
lucky if you get your supper without standing an hour
for it.''

We thanked him and drove up the street. "Well,'' I
said, "we can find where Sarah lives and drop in there for
supper.''

"We will not,'' Rudolph said. "I'd rather go hungry.''

"Well, I'm going to see Sarah. Pa said we should.''

"Haven't we been through enough last night and today?
We're dog-tired. We've been through hell. Sarah left us
in June. Emil, this is October, the eighth of it. She might
be propped up in bed right now with a brat at her tit.
Think I want to drop in on that? Here's a saloon. Let
me off. I'm going to get good and drunk.''

"You are not. We're going to eat.''

"The hell we are, drop me off, I say.''

I couldn't do anything with him. He worried me, no
sleep for two days, clawed by Hilma, choked with the
smoke, horrored by the couple we found dead, afraid of
Sarah, running away from himself. A person can stand
just so much. I shouldn't have tried to push him like I
did. He wasn't in any shape to go loading himself with
whisky. I felt terrible. Well, I figured, I know where to
find him. I'll just go to Sarah and make my call quick and

338

come back and by that time he'll probably have treated half a dozen times and talked important. He'll have worked somebody into finding a meal and a bed for us.

I watched him cross the street. There were maybe twenty men in sight and Rudolph looked the roughest and most worn and grandest of all of them. Ash dust on it, and holes burned in, and sweated through at the brim, a silk hat is still a silk hat.

The wind stopped sudden. Not a gradual die-down like wind always acted before, but a hushing, thick-acting quiet like a blanket settles down. The smoke thickened. Men stopped their talk and looked up puzzled. Far off, out of the smoke and gloom I heard a boat's fog horn like from the harbor at home. It was a Chicago sort of sound, like a blast for a bridge to raise up and let them through. Peshtigo has a harbor too, I remembered, downriver a ways, and it was probably smoky out on the bay too and they were signaling because they couldn't see.

I asked a man and got the directions where Sarah's folks lived. I tied the team loose like and rapped on the door. Sarah came. She didn't know me. I hardly knew her either, she'd got so out of shape and big-bellied. She hadn't had her baby, that was plain to see.

I didn't know what to say. She looked and recognized me. "Emil, it's Emil. But what's happened to you?"

"The fires," I said. "We've been traveling through the fires all day."

"Rudolph, did he come?"

"Yes, but he had to stop off uptown first," I said.

She had me come in. She was alone. Her mother and father, she said, were to church services. She dippered out some warm water for me and had me wash. No wonder she hadn't recognized me, I soaped twice and rinsed and still got her fresh clean towel all black. She set out a lunch for me and a cup for herself. We talked. Once, right while

339

she had her cup to her lips waiting while she listened she *mmmm'd* funny and sloshed her coffee and doubled up a little bit and got a scared look.

"What's the matter?" I asked.

"Nothing," she said. "Go on about the people on the wagon."

Something outside splintered. Horses neighed and a wagon rumbled and hoofs thudded off and away.

"A runaway," I hollered. "Somebody's having a runaway."

I ran out to my team. They were gone, and had yanked off the picket I'd tied them to. Sarah came panting up behind me.

"All our harness," I yelled. "A whole wagonful we were supposed to see Mr. Ogden's superintendents with. What's the matter with that fool team, they always stood before."

"Look," Sarah said. "In the air. Like snow. And listen."

Big flakes of ashes came settling through the dead still air. Off in the distance from the southwest came a roar like the Narrows at the Dells. It was coming toward us. A couple of dogs streaked by us like they had been shot at. The roar came louder and nearer. Sudden-like, there was a startled deer standing in the middle of the street. It took off away from the roar, and headed uptown.

"You have deer right in town?" I asked.

"No-o," Sarah said. "I never saw that before."

I wanted to run myself. I couldn't have said what from or what for, but I wanted to run. Animals are smart, I remember thinking, that team had a reason to run away.

"Look!" Sarah shrieked and sucked her breath in. Over the roofs and over the town trees, cutting through the smoke, a wall of fire rose solid from the southwest. A climbing orange-yellow thunderhead of fire with rolls and billows and towers of flame. It rushed overhead. Out of it

340

fire fell, pieces of bark, slabs. The burned-out acres around Peshtigo, the firestop plowing, were no holdback. This wasn't a forest fire boiling across the land, this was the sky exploding down. Angry orange and purple bulges dipped down. One brushed a shed. It blazed instant.

Steam whistles howled. Church bells rang. They weren't confident sounds like usual. Whistles and bells shrieking and clanging pulled the people flying into the streets. The wind came at us from all sides. A howling, lifting, tearing, burning wind. It pitched us like a baby sweeps clothespins aside when it's tired of playing.

"We've got to get to the river," Sarah yelled. "There isn't a building will stand through a fire like this."

She was right. This wasn't like a fire gutting a building in Chicago or even a whole block where you could back off and watch. It wasn't like our trip up here through the fire either, where you could pick and go around, this was all hell moving in, and fast. One second it would be dark with smoke and night, the next bright as day as a house near by would flare up and explode and go flaming off in pieces, the roof flying away into the sky, burning timbers sailing every which way and the crash of it never coming, the way the wind roared.

Sometimes there'd only be two or three people I could see inside the circle my eyes would reach, and sometimes a dozen, running, yelling, carrying, dragging, coming into view and out, everybody with a different idea of what to do or where to go. Sarah moved the slowest, but she knew where she was going. Uptown. Out of proportion like she was her swollen stomach kept her legs from working right. We had to hold hands to get along. How she'd changed since the Dells.

It wasn't all people. Fences burned and let out hogs. A sow with a litter cut across in front of us, her mind made up where to go and bee-lining for it faster than you'd think a hog could go. Loose oxen and horses, geese and chickens, milled right with us. The stink choked me. Blistered paint, scorching wool, smoldering manure piles, pine resin, crisped leather, the sawdust they made the streets out of, everything made rasping choking smoke.

Sheets of flame played in the sky like lightning, firing up big black balloons of smoke that sometimes sailed out of sight twisting and burning, sometimes dipped down to touch off whatever was below. Gusts along the ground picked up sand and threw it like bee stings, ripped off porches. A blast of heat and wind sandpapered my face and spun me to my knees. Sarah pulled me up. I had to wonder how she got wind enough to do it when the air itself had burned-out holes in it that sucked the breath right out of me.

We came aside a yard. A little boy not over seven or so came running out of a house and took the idea he'd be safer climbing into their big apple tree. A tongue of flame reached out and blew up into the dry dead leaves. The whole tree flared like the birches the Indians fired to get the pigeons. The boy fell out all ablaze and thumped sprawling like a squab. He never moved again. For a minute it looked like he did, the way the flames weaved and ate and fought over him. I threw up.

"Oh-h-h-h!" Sarah shrieked, and doubled up holding her belly.

In a lull in the wind as we reached the main street, a deep voice behind me raised goose pimples on the top of my head. " 'For behold, the Lord will come with fire and with his chariots like a whirlwind, to render his anger with fury and his rebuke with flames of fire.' "

I stopped dead in my tracks. Sarah moaned and raised it to a shriek. When God Himself talks to you that's the last end of it.

I sneaked a peek over my shoulder. I turned square around to look. I saw him ask, " 'To whom will ye flee for help? And where will ye leave your glory?' "

342

He was seven feet tall, and as broad as a bull. An arm like an oak limb stuck out about four feet, holding a Bible open flat on a hand big enough to be its own altar. " 'Therefore I will shake the heavens, and the earth shall remove out of her place, in the wrath of the Lord of hosts, and in the day of his fierce anger.' "

His voice could roar a wall down, but he wasn't God, I was relieved to see. God doesn't read out of Bibles. He makes them. Just the same, it was awful. His head was about a bushel basket of white hair, springing out every which way and his beard reached pretty near down to his pants. " 'Behold the day of the Lord cometh, cruel both with wrath and fierce anger to lay the land desolate and he shall destroy the sinners thereof out of it.' "

Behind him two girls walked in white nightgowns, their uplifted faces wearing sort of I-told-you-so expressions, and happy about it. " 'And shall consume the glory of his forest, and of his fruitful field, both soul and body. . . . And the rest of the trees of his forest shall be few.' "

Sarah and I should have been moving, our little time was wasting away. The old man and girls had me hypnotized. Behind them the sky was a big belly ripped open. Yellow and bloody bulbs of giant fire looped and twisted through rolls of green-black clouds. The guts of heaven were being ripped out. " 'Therefore is the anger of the Lord kindled against his people, and he hath stretched forth his hand against them and hath smitten them.' "

Cinders fell on his hair, ate holes in the nightgowns. A handful of his pages flamed up. " '. . . the heavens shall pass away with a great noise, and the elements shall melt with fervent heat, the earth also and the works that are therein shall be burned up.' "

They were getting pretty close now. They didn't see us, or anybody else or the fire. They were as good as in heaven already, I'll swear it. A little flame spitting up from a piece of shingle, it was scarcely more than a puff

343

you wouldn't notice in all the rest of the end of the world, caught one of the nightgowns and flared all over the girl. In a flash she was naked, her body pink with heat, her breasts glistening with scorch, her head and the hair below her belly flaming.

I didn't see her go down, or whether those with her ever knew. Panic dissolved me. I came out of it running, so scared I wet my pants and left Sarah to get along alone.

God was mad, damn mad. Made a beautiful world for us, and what do we do? Slash it away and tear it down. Make rafts out of the pine forests. Burn off the railroad clearings. Blast through the hills. Slaughter the pigeons. Lay the women. All right then, if we wanted it that way, He'd step in and do it right for us.

Why did He have to go after me for it? I didn't cut any trees. I didn't start any fires. I didn't ruin any girls. I netted some pigeons, but that was a mistake I didn't know I was doing. I ran for all I was worth.

I came across the fire engine. Men were holding hoses that turned limp in their hands. As long as a trickle came out they pointed those nozzles. The man tending the boiler couldn't keep his fire up. His wood on his platform blazed, but bare-handed he still tried to grab those flaming chunks and pitch them into his firebox. He stayed there until the spokes burned out of the wheels and dropped the engine and pitched him off.

A drygoods store with fire up its walls still stood. A big man staggered out of it with an armful of woolens. Rudolph, that's who it was, his hair flying, his face blistered and hard to recognize over the puffed eye and scratched cheeks Hilma gave him. The wind tore at a blanket and billowed it out from his load. It whipped and cracked trying to pull loose. He carried it all, flapping and spanking into the street and made everybody going by take an overcoat or a pants or a blanket and then ran back in for more. I got a pain in my chest and up my throat to

344

see him fight his way back into that burning store again. He didn't know those people. He didn't have to risk himself like that. I felt cheap and ashamed, but wonderful proud of him.

I ran back to Sarah. She was going slower and had terrible trouble to do it. She couldn't take three steps without stumbling now. It was her feet giving out. I looked down at her shoes. The laces were burned off. Her ankles had stretched the leather as far as it could go and the heat we kicked through had burned it as stiff as stovepipe. The uppers were giving way from the soles. I looked at mine. Brand-new boots a few days ago at Green Bay, they were done for now, the stitching burned out, the leather scorched. I hadn't noticed it before, but my feet felt as if they were one big blister apiece. Once I knew it, I could hardly walk either. It seemed ages ago we started through the fire.

Sarah looked and handled herself like an old person ready to die. Come to think of it, she was only nineteen, three years older than me. Shoes or no shoes, she would die if I couldn't get her to that river.

By the time we came even with the drygoods store, at our slow pace, Rudolph was out again with a bigger load than before. Parts of his beard were scorched off and holes smoked all over his clothes, but he was still all right. Nobody got by him without his making them take something.

"For God's sake, Sarah," he roared, "pull on these men's pants, and here's a thick overcoat, and one for you, Emil."

"Come with us," Sarah panted. "I need you with me."

"I can't. People are roasting. Enough things in there to help them cover to get through."

He dashed away to knock down a girl running with her shirtwaist on fire and smother it with a jacket and got her up again, and ran back to us.

345

"Get those pants on," he yelled at Sarah. "Get to the river."

"Rudolph," she gasped, "it'll be any minute now. My baby."

"Well, then, you each take a blanket. Cover your heads. For God's sake, the river, the river. Get to it."

Sarah threw her arms around Rudolph and clung to him. He pushed her away. "Emil, if you don't get her to the river, she'll have her baby right here and all of us will burn. Now get moving, you hear?"

A baby? Now? With no place to have it? "Sarah," I yelled, "hold it back, hold it back."

She viced my hand. "Just get me to the river."

"Yes, but who will ..."

"You, Emil. You'll have to."

"Almighty God," I prayed, "what are you asking of me?"

"Everything, Emil. Everything."

It numbed me. It numbed me like the fire itself.

Those blankets helped like everything. We could hood and mask ourselves to strain out a little of the heat and smoke. They kept the heat off for a while, and when there was a fire barrel I could get at I would dip our blankets in it. People that were still moving, I noticed, most all had thick woolen coverings of one kind or another now like we did. The wind pulled and sawed and you didn't dare let it get in under or it would rip you naked. Once in a while somebody's grip would give way. Off their blanket would sail, and then it would blaze into the distance. Maybe they'd go down after that and maybe they wouldn't, but the ones that hung onto their thick stuff had the best chance.

The going got harder and harder, so much stuff cluttered the street. Pieces of trees rolled along with the wind and burned fierce, stretches of boardwalk blazed, bodies to go around, rigs that couldn't get through and abandoned,

their loads on fire, boards blown off and jackstrawed together flaming. A cat picked her way with a kitten in her
mouth, her tail switching. A rat ran along with her for a
little piece without either one noticing the other. We used
every barrel we came to now, if we could get at it, to splash
what water we could on each other.

Back at the sunken-together fire engine even part of the
hose that had fed it was on fire.

At the mud where the burned-through hose had leaked
its last water Sarah flopped down and had me swill our
blankets in it.

"Look there." She gasped. "The sash mill. The river is
on the other side. If we make it, it's a bigger miracle than
everything we've come through yet."

The mill was one big factory of flame. Off a little its
lumber yard was another, the flames connecting the two
solid. The slash pile was a bonfire, the sawdust pile a
glowing mountain. The wind bent the flames out flat.

"By the road, twenty rods to the bridge," Sarah said.
"Never make it. Baby. Nearly here. Take mill yard.
Shortest way to river. Crawl along fire hose." She brought
her knees up to her belly in pain.

I looked along the hose. My belly cramped too. The
hose looped right into the yellow hell between the mill and
the lumber yard. Nobody since the Book of Daniel had
gone into a fire like that and come out alive.

Sheets of flame whipped thick and fast along the street.
There wasn't a living thing in sight any more. The little
mud we lay in let us breathe, but that would bake away fast.
It steamed already. We'd die if we kept to the street, we'd
die if we stayed here, we'd die trying to make it along the
hose. Sarah slapped my face, pounded her fists into me,
pushed my head down to make me breathe the little air next
to the ground. She worked along on her hands and knees.
She reached back to pull me along. "Crawl, Emil, crawl
along the hose."

347

We inched along side by side under our mud-heavy blankets. Blasts of fire swooshing down stopped us again and again. We'd lay flat and still, the blanket edge in our fists pulled tight to the ground at our noses. In between we'd hunch ahead just a little more. Ahead to a fire a thousand times worse. It didn't matter. How could it? That's what the old man walking with the Bible was trying to show.

I peeked along the hose. Ahead of us it was burning, beyond and under the fire it wasn't. Flat now, with no water in it, it still wasn't burning. That wall of fire burned from the *side,* carried out straight from the mill by the wind. There was space under it. That's where Sarah planned we'd go through. Every bit of the fire we'd come through came down from up above. This was the closest down yet, but the hose still wasn't burning. If it was a chance at all, it was our only one. We crawled along slow.

Our mud-soaked blankets dried out crisp and baked us under them. Maybe five feet further under that blast would be the best we could do. I raised my blanket just a slit off the ground. Right ahead of me the hose dipped down into a ditch. A fresh ditch, wide enough to crawl through single file and three feet deep. Mud on the bottom where the hose couplings had leaked. I pushed Sarah into it and tumbled in behind.

Thank God, somebody had ordered that ditch dug, probably thinking it could be a fire stop to save the mill and the lumber yard from each other if an ordinary fire got into either one these last terrible days. It didn't amount to anything for that, but to us it was life. At the bottom there was decent air, it was under the worst of the wind, and down three feet further, below the fire, made such a difference it was hard to believe. For a little we just lay there moaning. I didn't have any terrible burns, but my face was raw and my hands were blistered and my feet stung so they throbbed, but I felt there was hope. It was a wonderful feeling. Hope in the bottom of a ditch. Hope in a tunnel through Hell. Life if we kept our heads down.

Sarah crawled ahead of me with her blanket over her. Sometimes I had my head under mine, sometimes out if I could stand it. Dragging her feet along even with my face like she was, I saw what a narrow squeak we had to get here at all. Neither of her shoes had any bottoms.

We had to stop twice for her cramps. One of them was so hard she had to yell. We crawled under two timbers crossed over the ditch, and burning, but they didn't burn through and fall in until after we were past. The worst of all was a dead hog in the ditch. He was way too heavy to lift out. We had to crawl over him. It nearly cindered Sarah, because her bigness raised her up that much higher. Once more it was the blankets that made the difference that got us through.

We made it to the river. The ditch ran straight down to it. We had to crawl until the water covered us to our necks, the fire was so fierce. Hot blasts one second, wonderful splashing water the next, cooling our bodies with the only stuff in the world the fire couldn't burn, the wind lashing wet relief over our faces. We leaned back and lay there worn out, our heads on the shore, the motion of the water rocking us together, then apart, and nothing mattered any more.

I closed my eyes. If anything, it was worse that way. Mattered and sticky, my eyeballs stung like there was soap in them. My lids weren't thick enough to shut out the yellow-white glare; it was still bright red with my eyes shut. The roar in my ears and the wind racing across my face made it seem like I was pitching dizzy through space with the crash going to come any second. I couldn't stand it and jerked my head up and my eyes open.

The fire we came through flared and billowed, right to the water. We had to get up and move farther out and stand neck deep. The wind tore across the water so fast it didn't make waves at all, just flashes of ripples. Out there deep, the water was ice cold with our heads sticking up into a solid scorching blast. Up the water hundreds of heads bobbed, and ducked when it got too hot. Downstream it was the same. Most of them were people, but a lot were crazy scared horses and cows and pigs swimming round and round with no place to go. A little farther off downstream was the bridge. We were better off where we were. The bridge was on fire with people and rigs on it jammed up from each side thinking the other side was safer. It burned through and settled down easy-like while I watched. There were a lot more heads in the water for a while. Then not so many. Deep water takes swimming and strength, more strength than most had left. The dipped-down parts of the bridge from each side blazed until they fell in too.

Across the river the fire raced as hot as on our side, but it wasn't solid to the water yet. A factory stood between, four stories high and maybe as long as ten boxcars, hardly touched by the fire at all. I knew it would go, and mighty soon too. A big thing like that, and so close just across the river would sizzle our heads off right to the water. I yelled at Sarah. "We've got to get out of here. Once she starts, that whole wall will topple right on us."

"I can't," she gasped. "The baby. I'm tearing."

It tore me too. She shrieked and dug her fingernails into my shoulders. "I can't lie down. I can't stand. My God, Emil, *Emil*!"

I had to spread my legs to brace myself to hold her up. I yelled myself hoarse for somebody to come, but with the roar and dozens of other people shrieking too it was useless.

The fire caught the factory all over all at once. It exploded out, fire sailing in all directions and a sheet of it four stories high coming sailing toward us. I pulled Sarah under and ducked. My chest nearly burst waiting for the

350

wall to crash on us, but nothing happened. Choke bobbed
us up. What once was a factory was a white-hot pillar
mushrooming up into the sky. There wasn't any wall on
the water or anywhere, it had gone that quick. We had to
duck again fast. Burning tubs and buckets and broom
handles sailed by the millions out of the flames and arched
toward us. When we came up again the river was full of
them, bobbing and blazing and skittering across the water
in the wind. Boards and bundles of shingles and barrel
staves burned and blew and sizzled and smoked and
steamed trying to set the river on fire. We were lucky none
of them clunked us when they hit. Once in the water they
were bad enough and kept me busy fighting them off with
one hand while I steadied Sarah with the other. For her
it was awful. White-hot fire on both sides of the river as
far as I could see towering up and meeting solid from both
shores in an arch above us, the river speckled with burning rubbish, the water up to her neck ice-cold, and her
baby ripping her insides trying to be born.

"I've got to keep my hands on your shoulders, Emil.
I'll go down if I don't."

"That's all right," I said, "my feet are down solid and
I'm braced good."

"But, I need my hands . . . somewhere else. My baby!
Down there . . . under water . . . Emil, you've got to!

"Oh, Jesus God, Sarah. Got to what?"

"Under my dress. Rip my underpants open."

"Sarah, I can't. I don't know anything about babies.
I just can't."

Women having babies in bed with doctors around, lots
of times they die. What chance would Sarah have here in
the Peshtigo River under a roof of fire falling in? The
littlest wrong thing I'd do could be murder and I wouldn't
even know what I'd done. It would be worse murder than
when I tried to have her take the Emmenagogue.

"Emil, there's no time."

351

I did what she said. I reached down and, ashamed and scared, I pulled up her dress and tore her underpants open.

"Now hold your hands under me. I'm going to yell like you've never heard anybody yell. Don't pay any attention. Maybe I won't be able to talk, so you listen now. I've spread my legs as wide as I can. I'll hang on to you. Keep your hands there loose, just touching me. You'll feel the baby coming. As soon as it's all there, bring it up, careful. That's all anybody could do now, Emil, even a doctor."

"Sarah, it'll drown. How can it help but drown? Even if somehow it doesn't—Sarah, I won't do it, I just can't."

Her face went wild with pain, but no baby came into my hands. Nothing happened like that. I let my hands drop. Her fingers dug my shoulders hard enough to make me howl. Terror swept across her face, begging terror in her eyes, her open mouth out of shape with pain. She hadn't broken up like that even when I ran away and left her alone after the girl with the prophet blazed up and died. I put my hands back and kept them there. She relaxed a little.

"Emil, babies sometimes don't breathe until they're spanked. It won't drown if it doesn't breathe right away. As soon as you feel its head, hold your hand tight over its mouth and nose until you can bring it up out of the water. Be careful of the cord. Oh, God, let the cord be long enough."

She had a lot of terrible pains. It seemed hours we waited like that, the wind going down, the fire dancing as high as ever, blasts once in a while yet that still made us duck, a bellowing cow swimming around and around, but somehow never raking us with her churning hooves, floating rubbish on fire, sometimes a little piece I could lift a hand and splash aside, sometimes a whole smoldering log that took both hands shoving on the underside to work it around us. Sarah winced every time I had to do it, not on account of the danger to us so much, she was used to that, but what might happen while my hands were gone. A dead man floated by. I thought they sank right away and came up afterward. A lot of what I think has to be changed, I guess.

"Rudolph," Sarah whimpered, but it wasn't him, I could tell by the clothes. He was probably dead someplace else, probably back in that store. It seemed like a year ago.

Heads bobbed like before, but slower and not so many. There were five, maybe within fifty feet. Sarah's screams with pain couldn't bring them to help, nor any of my yelling. It was so useless I quit trying.

Something was changing in my hands. Sarah pressed my shoulders as though she was trying to lift herself out. Her head dropped on my neck. Maybe she yelled, I don't remember, but I'll never forget my hands feeling a head, little shoulders, little arms that *moved* and tiny little hands. I held its mouth shut. Slow and gentle, I brought it up, the poor little thing coming into a world like this.

"Sarah, look," I said. I couldn't say anything else. It hadn't drowned. It cried. A few minutes afterward I could bring up the cord and stuff.

Sarah was so weak she couldn't let go of me to hold her baby and she wanted to awful much. She made me hold it so she could see. "My little baby is a girl," she said. "Wrap her careful in the blanket."

I did as good as I could with the rough wet blanket, wondering how long the poor crying little thing could live that way, and Sarah too with river water freezing her when she should be warm. There wasn't anything else we could do. For hours and hours we stood there waiting while the fire burned itself out and died down. Once in a while somebody waded up the shore, but the ashes were too hot and deep to stand in and they had to come back. We edged in a little to get out of the cold water, but there wasn't any place for Sarah to lie down except in the water touching the shore. I eased her down as careful as I could and covered her with our other blanket. I held the baby and stood there shivering while it got darker and darker as the fire died away. Once a cow came close and worried me thinking it might step on Sarah, and once a pig. Maybe they wouldn't have, but I felt better when I turned them off and they went back into the dark. The poor things, they didn't know what to do or where to go any more than we did.

Rudolph most likely dead and Sarah never married. If the baby lived, somebody would have to adopt it. And when she gets old enough to want to know, will she have to hunt and hunt, and hope and hope for her real relations like that lonely little girl in church in Kilbourn? My own niece. Pa's granddaughter. It was awful.

21

IT WAS a million years to morning. When it did come, the Devil had turned it out and I wished for the dark again rather than look. No birds singing. No roosters crowing. Nobody hollering giddyap in the distance, no milk pails banging, no kitchens clattering. Sharp cindered stink instead of breakfast smells.

Where Peshtigo had been, there was only distance. Gray, sickly distance, here and there a stooped-over somebody walking ever so slow searching the ground, little plumes of gray following his feet like puppies gone to ghosts. Out of the gray at my feet two splashes of white floated against Sarah. Dead fish. I looked around. There were hundreds of them belly-up on the water, hundreds more settling against a shore of thick ashes covering the sand. Ashes and water, that makes lye. Lye strong enough to kill fish. Sarah, ripped open after her baby, soaking in it. She couldn't stay in the water. She couldn't lay on the ground, wet as she was and poison ashes inches thick, that would be worse yet. I climbed out to look for help.

When I moved I must have jiggled the baby too much. It cried. It cried healthy. It cried strength and hope right into me. In the middle of hundreds of people dying, this helpless little thing started to live. In the middle of destruction, creation kept right on. For heaven's sake, I thought, I'm carrying a miracle.

I was carrying two miracles. The baby was one. The blanket was the other. The only reason the baby was alive was the blanket. Maybe the only reason Sarah was alive herself was the other blanket she was covered with. That's the wonderful thing about wool, it can be sopping wet and it will still warm a person. Or a baby. Our blankets had saved us in getting to the river. Rudolph passing out those blankets had saved his own baby, had saved Sarah, had saved me. Maybe twenty or thirty other people too, I don't know how many times he went back for another armful.

The lighter it got, the more people I could see, little groups collecting here and there on our side of the river and more doing the same on the other side. It seemed like a mile to carry my bundle the little distance to the closest group.

"Look," I said unwrapping a little of the blanket, "I need a doctor. The mother needs a doctor."

"A new-born baby. My God, afterbirth, cord and everything in one big mess."

A man with one ear crisped took charge. More and more people came up. He sent four men to go get Sarah. He spotted two more blankets and made the ones who had them give them up. He sent a boy up a little knoll to see if the ashes there might be thinner. The boy said the wind had swept the knoll clean. It was the Peshtigo cemetery. The only safe place to lay Sarah and her baby down was a cemetery.

I laid the baby down. The men brought Sarah and put her on one blanket and another to cover her. Somebody took off a coat and doubled it up for a pillow. A woman who said she was a midwife tended the baby.

356

All up and down the river people showed up until there were hundreds of them milling around, looking for each other, finding neighbors when they wanted wives. Once in a while there'd be a joyful shout, but mostly it was empty hunting. From the knoll I could see all around. A few iron tires marked where a wagon had once been. Across the river some brick charcoal kilns, the wheels and boiler of the private railroad up from the harbor, two or three chimneys that hadn't blown down, everywhere cindered corpses, that was Peshtigo. No streets, not a store or a backhouse or a woodpile was left. Up above the old sun turned out his shiniest brand of Monday-morning glory. White clouds hung low all around the sky in thick little tufts, pinned up close to catch the blue and to make the best of the space like a washerwoman short of clothesline. I always used to feel such days were made special to set off something pretty nice down here, but I know better now.

I asked people about Rudolph, but there had been hundreds of strangers in town. Nobody remembered seeing him. Sarah asked about her mother and father, but nobody had seen them either. She cried a little and then asked for her baby.

A kid came poking up the knoll chewing something. I asked him what he was eating.

"Potato."

"Where'd you get it?"

He pointed over where a couple of men were digging bare handed in the sand. I went over there and scratched around and found a hill. They were half scorched, half raw. You couldn't see it had ever been a garden, but somebody must have remembered where it was. I had a couple potatoes out when I felt a hand on my shoulder. I looked around.

"I thought it was you, Emil."

Rudolph! Alive! I jumped up and hugged him and

357

cried like a baby. I couldn't help it. His beard was gone, and most of his hair. His face was one red blotch, his eyes swollen to slits. He looked at me, and all around, and took a potato. We stood there nibbling.

"Sarah's gone," he said, throwing the potato down so hard it smashed.

"Sarah's alive," I said. "She's had her baby. In the river last night. They're both up on that knoll."

Rudolph ran up the knoll crying, "Sarah, Sarah." I couldn't keep up with him.

When we got there the midwife straightened up from Sarah. "You the husband?"

"Yes," Rudolph lied. "How is she?"

"I can't understand it. She's as clean as any I've ever attended. Look at that baby. Born in the river, wrapped wet, and still wet, no oiling, no nothing, and it's sleeping healthy. I just can't understand it."

Rudolph picked up the baby and knelt down to Sarah. He put a swollen black hand to her cheek. They said soft private things. People around backed off a little, and made out they had other things to tend to. Fire and river and ashes they'd gone through, but lost ones meeting each other was too strong for most of them.

About the only thing anybody had left was talk. Some used it and some didn't. Those that did seemed to get good out of it and hearing it seemed to have a little heal in it for most of the rest of us.

"At the hardware store, I been over there, there's sixty dozen ax heads melted into one clinker. I seen 'em. I know it's sixty dozen because—"

"Those fifty horses in the company stable, I don't think anybody got there to turn them loose."

"What good would it have done if they did? Horses always run right back into a fire, you know that."

"I wished it was only horses. I saw a gang of those

358

workers that just came in yesterday make a beeline for the boardinghouse, maybe fifty, maybe a hundred of them, and she went up with all of them in it.''

"God, what a fire. Took everything. Everything.''

"Did anybody see them bulbs of fire tumbling over each other in the air or did I imagine it?''

"I saw 'em. You weren't imagining.''

"What were them damn fire bulbs?''

"Burning gas.''

"Gas, my ass. How could gas get up there in the air like that?''

"From the marshes on fire all the way south past Fond du Lac, from miles of forests burning. It cooks off gas like a coke oven. With a skyful of it, well, Peshtigo was underneath when it touched off.''

"It was a wall of white-hot fire racing from the southwest, everybody saw it. Solid, hard fire. I didn't see no gas. If it was gas, why wouldn't it have burned right with the same fire that cooked it out instead of sailing in the air until it got here?''

"Boys, I've been in forest fires before and bad ones, but nothing like this. Once, down in Indiana I was in a town when a tornado knocked it flat. Same boiling clouds except for the fire. This was both at once, tornado and forest fire together.''

"I was at Spotsylvania. Last night was worse than the Bloody Angle. At least there weren't any women and kids and grandmothers there.''

"I hear Ogden had a hundred thousand dollars in the woodenware factory. Wouldn't allow a lamp from one end to the other. A lot of good that did.''

"What a fire! This'll make news around the world. You wait and see, they'll be writing about it in all the history books, just like the London fire a couple of centuries ago.''

359

"London's a big place. Biggest in the world. You get a hundred miles away whoever heard of Peshtigo? Or ever will now?"

"Dammit man, that's just the point. The shingles and millwork and kegs and lumber that went out of here never made the news this fire will."

"You can't eat news. News won't bring back my wife."

"Of course not. Nor will anything else. But news will bring back Peshtigo and things have to go on. We've got to rebuild. Bury our dead and rebuild. With the business we had here and can get again, with the North Western coming through, there'll be plenty of Chicago money."

"With the woods gone?"

"There's more behind what's gone, and what's gone will yield a lot of lumber from the down timber. Look out there. It's dead and it's black, but it's still timber. We're not licked yet."

"Hell with the plans. There isn't even a roof for tonight or a slice of bread for the kids, or a bandage for their burns. We need help and bad."

"Couple of foremen set out on foot for Marinette at daylight. Should have made the seven miles and be there by now."

"If there is a Marinette."

Thank God Marinette hadn't burned. It seemed a long time, but before noon a train of wagons piled high came out of the east. They stopped across the river. The drivers and the folks who came along looked strange, they were so clean-skinned compared to us and their clothes were so bright and whole. They unloaded a tent, a few whopping big iron kettles, and somebody had even thought to load on a rowboat. They had food, and clothes, and lumber, and stretchers and all manner of things kind folks figured an emergency would call for. A shudder went through me when I saw them pitch off three bundles of long-handled shovels.

360

In a little they had a stove set up and then people making wider and wider circles, hunting. It looked like they'd lost a piece of it, maybe the lid lifter, but when we hollered over it wasn't that. Nobody had thought to bring stovewood. They had to patrol the river and fish out of the water to find anything around that could still burn.

What a difference the river separated. Over there the tent going up, men hammering the lumber into a long table, women sorting out the boxes that had the pans and kettles, people bandaging each other, carrying the rowboat down to the water, turning everything over to hunt for the oars. It was wonderful good to see work going on again. Mostly we stood silent and waited patient. Once in a while though, somebody over there would go at a thing so senseless our side couldn't stand it and we'd have to holler over. Like the oars they couldn't find. One guy started to take a stretcher apart for something to pole the boat with. Half a dozen roars went up.

"Hey you! Let that stretcher alone."

"You brought rope, use that. Tie a long piece on each end of the boat, we'll pull it back and forth like a ferry."

"That's right, use rope, and put some stretchers in the boat, if you've got so many, we need them on this side too."

"Rope is best anyhow. That way it doesn't take extra boat space for polers or rowers."

We had the ferry working in short order. Four men on the rope on each side whisked that boat over and back three times as fast as rowing. It didn't need four, but everybody that was able wanted something to do.

All the time word kept drifting around about the baby up on the knoll. Some said it had just been born up there, others said, no, it was last night. They couldn't figure out how that could be, with the fire all over so one of them said it must have happened in the river. The talk about the baby made people take sides.

"It shows the glory of God and His careful planning."

361

"Planning? Is it planning to kill off six, seven hundred people, some of them babies too, the same time another one comes? I could plan better than that."

"It's an omen. It shows there is good no matter how bad a thing is. It shows that every end is a beginning too."

"Fires come. Babies come. If they happen together, what does that prove?"

"Who is she?"

"What difference who she is? Let's go get her. They can do more for her over at the tent."

"Let her where she is. If they lay her among those awful others, it'll mark the baby."

"How can it mark a baby that's already born? Use your head. Come on, let's go get her."

"She'll cake her milk or something. You see if she won't."

"Hell, she don't have to stay there. She shouldn't anyhow, somebody can take her to Marinette in one of the wagons going back. Dammit, we should be proud of a woman who's not only saved herself, but birthed an innocent babe from the center of Hell. Get her out of here, I'd say, so she can rest."

The more they talked about it, the more reputation they built up for her. "She's a Mrs. Rohland. They came from Chicago just last week."

"I hear he's Ogden's new saddler, a regular whiz bang with horses."

"Old Charley is still the saddler, this guy Rohland is a harnessman Ogden was dealing with."

"She's not from Chicago, she was born right here in Peshtigo and lived out on McGraw Street. Her folks and us are neighbors, at least we were up until last night. I never knew she was married. Her man is plenty scorched, but he doesn't seem to notice it, he's so happy they're safe.

What a time they must have had of it and to think he brought them both out.''

Let them figure it out the way they want to, I thought, but what worried me is the way people finally boil things down to the truth. People are pretty touchy about who's married and who should be. They're all the worse if they're fooled first. That's one thing they won't ever forgive.

I went along with the procession to get her. I hung back along the edges. Out there if a question is thrown your way, anything will do for an answer. Closer in they aim them at you. The woman who had been sent along with me when I carried the baby to the knoll stood at Sarah's head, aside of Rudolph, taking charge of the explanations. The midwife was still there too, but the other one had seen the baby first and she wasn't letting go the authority that gave her to talk and tell. ''Out of the river he came, carrying that poor little bundle, the brave man,'' she said.

''Who was he?''

''Why, him here, her husband, of course,'' she said, pointing out Rudolph. ''Look at him, all swollen and blistered and half his clothes burned off, but he kept the baby from getting a mark on it. Not a mark.''

The murmurs that went up for Rudolph!

Those people weren't lying. They really thought they had seen Rudolph bring the baby out of the river. A night like that, and all they'd been through, how could anybody remember things straight?

They picked Sarah up, ever so gentle, and put her on the stretcher. Rudolph carried the baby. It cried some, then worked it up to a strength you'd never believe such a little new thing could manage. That did more for everybody than a wagonload of breakfast. The stretcher bearers walked over roughness that would have stumbled them before. Men stood straighter. An old woman that should

363

have been picked up by the stretchers long before smiled a little while she waited. That baby was a comfort to everybody.

Down at the river Sarah and the baby were pretty special passengers. They let Rudolph go right along in the boat. They wanted it that way and insisted on it, and made such a hero out of him, it was a pleasure to see.

It must have been two hours later when the burned ones still alive had all been picked up, and the women and children sent over before I could cross. The boatload I got into had all town men, two who'd worked at the woodenware, a saloonkeeper, the station agent for the private railroad that ran down to the harbor, and two others. One of them asked me who I was.

I told him.

"Rohland? Rohland? Same as the man Sarah Hempstead married? The ones who had the baby all alone in the river? Too bad about her folks, but by God, she's got a man for a husband. You can tell her I said so. Where were you in the fire?"

By that time we were across the river and getting out. A whiff of cooking came drifting down so interesting he forgot what he'd asked.

I found Sarah and Rudolph in the tent. Sarah was on her side nursing the baby.

Rudolph sat there thinking. "Better get some soup, Emil," he said. "Let's join the line."

Soup, I could use that. I looked at my watch. It had stopped at half past ten in the river. It was ruined for good now, that wonderful watch from Pa. I looked at the sun. It was late afternoon.

"Has Sarah had anything?"

"They brought her some of the first of the soup. She ate a little of it too."

"What are you going to do with her?"

"She's got an aunt in Marinette."

"I mean, when are you going to marry her?"

"Well, not around here, that's for sure. And shut up about that, they all think we are married. Overhearing anything else would make a terrible mess of it after what they believe."

The soup smelled wonderful. For a long time the smell was all I got. There were two big iron kettles set up and cooking it, like people cook soap out in the back yard, like farmers with too many potatoes boil them for the hogs. We had to stand in line a long time before we got up to it. When we got within maybe two rods, a fellow handed each of us a double-size tin cup. Mine still had a ring left in it from whoever had it ahead of me. They didn't have near enough cups for everybody, they had to be used over and over. I didn't mind, I would have lapped up soup from a puddle. At the first kettle I dipped my cupful and marveled how far soup can be watered out, but before I got it to my face there was a grab at my arm.

"Soup's in the next kettle, boy. Just rinse your cup here."

Somebody laughed. "First time I ever see dishwater taken for soup. You all right, boy?"

I said I was, but it got me to wondering. I never did a fool thing like that before.

They ladled our cups full and we went back to sit on the ground by Sarah to eat it. I never tasted anything better. I think I could have handled about six of those cups. I'd have gone back for a refill, but I'd have had to go to the end of the line again. It just wasn't worth it.

"Emil," Sarah said weakly, "how would you like to have my little girl named after you?"

It gave me a funny thrill. Then I remembered it wouldn't work. Sarah's baby was a girl. I reminded her of that.

"Wouldn't *Emily* do it?"

Emil. Emily. I kind of liked it. I kissed her and then sat quiet to think it over.

Those little clouds in the forenoon had joined together to make an overcast. It started to rain. A regular soaker of a rain after all those weeks. "If it had only come a day earlier," people said and shook their heads.

There was excitement down by the boat. A man on horseback had ridden up on the other side of the river. They left his horse there and pulled him over. "He's got a proclamation from the Governor," the word came up ahead of him. "With the telegraph burned out, he had to ride all the way up from Green Bay. Probably organizing the whole state for help for us."

We gathered in the rain outside the tent to hear him read it. He looked thunderstruck. He looked at his paper. It trembled. He shook his head and put it back in his pocket.

"People of Peshtigo," he said, "if Governor Fairchild knew of your plight, he would ask that this petition not be read. I will tell you about it, but I cannot, I haven't the soul to read it to you. Last night the city of Chicago was destroyed by fire. More than two hundred lost their lives. A few sections in the outskirts are all that remain. The proclamation," he choked, "the proclamation I was to have delivered is an appeal to the citizens of Wisconsin for food, for clothing, for money for Chicago."

Rudolph put his hand on my shoulder. It rested as heavy as a sack of oats. The Rohland factory, our house on Michigan Avenue, all our brothers wiped out. Maybe Pa dead the same time my watch stopped. I couldn't breathe.

The man with the proclamation had more to say. "God be with you until I race your story back to Green Bay and get it on the telegraph. We'll help Chicago, but all Wisconsin will rush aid to Peshtigo."

Rudolph grabbed his sleeve. "Green Bay, is Green Bay all right?"

366

The man looked at him. "A few houses went, but the city is all right."

I knew what worried Rudolph. Our car of harness in the North Western yards at Green Bay. It was the only Rohland harness left. Pa'd need it to start up the Rohland works again. Pa. If he was alive. I felt so heavy I had trouble standing.

"Emil, we've got to walk to Marinette and take a boat. Get to Green Bay and order our boxcar back to Chicago and get home ourselves the first train."

"What about Sarah and the baby?"

"Her aunt in Marinette."

"You coming back to her? After—after——"

"I don't know, Emil, I don't know. A little girl, think of it. I've got a little girl. Pa never did that."

Pa. Most of Chicago gone. More than two hundred people dead. I choked. Were Pa and Ma and our brothers in those two hundred?

Rudolph and I started walking in the rain and the dark toward Marinette. Pa. Was he alive? I kept wondering and wondering. I took out my watch. I couldn't see it. It didn't matter, what it showed wouldn't be right anyhow. I shook it and held it up to my ear.

It ticked.

Really Good!
April 30, 2002